THE LAST ROSES

D. B. Burns Mysteries

THE COURTSHIP OF HARRY'S WIFE

THE LAST ROSES

THE LAST ROSES

By
Jeanette-Marie Mirich

The Last Roses
Published by Mountain Brook Ink
White Salmon, WA U.S.A.

The website addresses shown in this book are not intended in any way to be or imply an endorsement on the part of Mountain Brook Ink, nor do we vouch for their content.

This story is a work of fiction. All characters and events are the product of the author's imagination. Any resemblance to any person, living or dead, is coincidental.

Scripture quotations are taken from the King James Version of the Bible. Public domain.
ISBN 978-1-943959-80-8

The Team: Miralee Ferrell, Alyssa Roat, Nikki Wright, Cindy Jackson
Cover Design: Lynnette Bonner

Mountain Brook Ink is an inspirational publisher offering fiction you can believe in.
Printed in the United States of America

The steps of a *good* man are
Ordered by the Lord: and he
Delighteth in his way. Though he
fall, he shall not be utterly cast down:
for the LORD upholdeth him *with His* hand.

Psalm 37:23-24

Dedication

For Rod, the man who holds my heart.

We see God's fingerprints in our lives—from Him speaking to you when you first saw me—to our coming to faith. How grateful I am for the years we've shared. The joy of hearing the tread of your footsteps on the stairs and the glint of humor in your eyes is a gift.

Thank you for walking life's road with me.
You have made my life an adventure.

The Sound of Love

It's in your voice and footstep,
Your longing for me.
Thank you
For the warmth of your acceptance,
And the love that graces your words.
God has done
A marvelous thing
In undoing
And redoing
Our hard-wired selfishness
To be tender toward Him
And one another.
Our days are bathed
In forgiveness,
And
Sprinkled occasionally
With the words,
"I was wrong."

Acknowledgments

A symphony of words plays through my head when I write. From prelude to finale, a book is a marvelous combination of talents. The writer, dependent on the editors to tweak the work, to focus the wandering plot and correct grammar infractions, is also in need of a chorus of wise voices who pray and advise as the composition is created, revised, and launched.

Amanda Bird began the editing journey with well-chosen full stops and revisions. Miralee Ferrell skillfully wove her editing magic into chords of understanding. Without them the music of the story becomes a dirge fit for a Victorian funeral march.

Paget Barranco of the FBI and their Investigative Publicity and Public Affairs Unit helped tune my assumptions about the expertise of field agents, jurisdiction, the problems they solve and cooperation with local law enforcement. Thanks to her and Jennifer Adams for guiding my creative ideas.

Nikki Wright of Mountain Brook Ink is a wonderful asset to me and continues to help with marketing my novels. Newest asset to the publishing house is Alyssa Roat, who already is working her publicity magic.

During the writing season of my life, I've been blessed with people who walk with me through the edits, or when I'm wringing my hands with characters not behaving themselves. It is a rare man who accepts the challenge of listening to a half-baked phrase and smiles. My husband Rod hands me the manuscript paper, the ink, the pen, then sprinkles my life with laughter which makes this journey a joy.

My Bon-Voyage-with-Jeanie crew, who reviewed *The Courtship of Harry's Wife,* prayed for this newest novel in the D.B. Burns series. The peace that accompanies my writing days is a result of their faithfulness in prayer. Thanks to all of them for making this journey a delight.

The usual cast of characters have lifted up my compositions to our Lord. They remain faithful during this passage. Sherry Bennett, Babs Caraway, Linda Crabtree, Bev Daugherty, Allison Doty, Sheilda Gates, Nancy Garten, Ronda Harrold, Holly Lightvoet, Sharon Pera, Bev Zahl have all been stalwart in their walk with me. Caroline Spada, Melanie Schemanski, Teresa Ortiz, Glenna Norton have joined the chorus of encouragers. I am grateful for their constancy and love.

I've had a ball creating syncopation with Heidi Wright. Her publicity for *The Courtship of Harry's Wife* still gives me joy, and I anticipate a great collaboration with *The Last Roses*.

I am honored by the constant care and love I have received from family and friends. Your word songs of encouragement resonate in my heart.

Chapter One

"THIS IS AN AMBER ALERT. ELEVEN-year-old Drew Albert is missing from Hendersonville," intoned the announcer from the car radio. I grimaced. "The girl, four-foot-nine, Caucasian, is dressed in jeans, a gray T-shirt and an orange, hooded sweatshirt. A silver van with Tennessee plates was seen where Albert waited for the school bus. Please contact the Hendersonville Police Department or call 911 if you have sighted Drew or the van."

I was on the interstate listening to the local channel before the interruption.

"Lord, bring that girl home to her mama," I whispered, unable to imagine the agony of a child vanishing. It was hard enough when my beloved husband's gaze had fixated on heaven and never looked back.

Tears erupted from my eyes. The littlest things made me weep. They'd predicted that in the grieving information hospice had given me. I fumbled for a Kleenex and wished for the soft, linen handkerchief of my across-the-street neighbor, Lyle Henderson. Over the past couple of months, I'd learned to appreciate his initialed and pressed handkerchiefs. I chewed on my lip.

"Life would be a lot easier if evil didn't jump out and grab you by the throat." I did a lot of mumbling these days. Being alone would probably turn me into a woman chatting to herself and answering back. A shaft of sunlight blazed through the trees, momentarily blinding me. When the asphalt was black again, I forced myself to smile. "Gratitude, Delilah," I quoted my meemaw, "is practiced when you get a sweet cherry or a sour one." Well, of late, I'd had a handful of pucker-up-your-lips' cherries. From my husband's death to the man I'd grown to love disappearing like a jet's vapor, I'd been through a bit of trials.

The problems had culminated when I was delivering a trailer full of furniture to my newlywed daughter, where I'd encountered snarled traffic and hand gestures that made me squint. Now, aiming toward my cousin's home in the mountains, I eased off the interstate onto a two-lane road. Bluish North Carolina hills merged with the sky.

I caught a glimpse of four deer hightailing it from the woods to the road. Three turned back, but the yearling leaped over the grass verge to my left. I straight-line-braked. In three strides he collided with the hood of my van then did a somersault off to my right, disappearing into the valley below. I managed to keep the van with trailer on the tarmac. Shaking so hard my teeth clinked like ice in a glass, I glanced in the rearview mirror. The empty trailer was still attached to my vehicle. Although my van shuddered with death-like spasms, the utility trailer was upright. A staccato sigh escaped from my lips. At least this time no one was shooting in my direction.

My hands gripped the lifeline of the steering wheel as the van began to steam. I wrinkled my nose. Something smelled like inner tubes in August. *Well, Lord, I'm in a pickle. I'm open to any suggestions.* A bee danced its up and down waltz by the side window. *I know You are greater than he who is in the world, so I'll set about business and try to listen as I go.*

Prying my fingers loose from their death grip on the wheel, I wiped my hands on my pants and glanced at the empty road. Route 18 was not a popular bit of highway, just a little squiggle on a North Carolina map that led through the mountains toward the house of my cousin. I was an hour-and-a-half away from her home at Piney Creek and farther from the kids' apartment in Raleigh.

An old GMC truck lumbered past.

Hey, stop for a lady in distress, will you!

The day didn't look promising.

In a few seconds a semi sped in the opposite direction. I stared at the truck's red shield logo until the semi disappeared over a hill. Mental telepathy didn't work worth beans. I picked up my cell phone and called my insurance company, the one my late husband Harry had used after he left the Marines. A sweet Texas voice greeted me.

"I've been in an accident." I wrinkled my nose with disgust. "A deer crossed the road ignoring the walk signal."

"Are *you* all right?"

"Just a little shaken. My car is steaming and . . ." I creaked out of the van to investigate the damage. My body, reluctant to cooperate with my brain, was as stiff as an over-whipped meringue. "It appears I've a pool of iridescent yellows and greens growing on the asphalt." I took a deep breath. "You need my info." Being a numbers person, I could recite my policy because the last few months I'd been dealing with insurance agents up to my eyebrows. "Delilah Burns Morgan, policy number 38756, and this vehicle is the 2010 silver mini-van, not my husband's truck. Do you need my Kentucky address?"

"No, ma'am. I've got you right here." Her voice sounded like she was reading from a teleprompter. There was a pause. "I see that everything has recently been transferred to your name." Her words trailed off as she recognized what the change of name meant. "Oh, I'm so sorry for your loss."

I fought the tears emerging.

"I will contact a tow truck to come out. Stay near the car, but away from the road," she directed. "You need to have a doctor check you out, Mrs. Morgan."

"I didn't hit anything but the deer. Actually, I think it hit me."

First car accident.

Probably ruin my record and the premiums will go

up.

"I'll keep on the line until the tow-truck arrives." The woman on the other end was more than accommodating, but I had a list of things I needed to do.

"I've got some calls to make. I'll get back to you."

"I really think you should see a physician. Whiplash happens in a deer-auto misadventure. You won't know until tomorrow when you can't move your neck."

"Thanks. I'll keep that in mind." I hung up and called my daughter.

"Er, Molly." I licked my lips because admitting I couldn't handle something was difficult. "I've had a little car trouble."

"Where are you, Mom?"

"Near Hendersonville. Someone's coming to haul the car to a repair shop."

"You have a flat tire?"

"No. A venison collision." I chuckled as if it didn't matter.

"What?" Molly's voice cracked.

"A deer decided to cross the road. We met in the middle."

She sucked in air. "Are you okay?"

"I'm fine. The car's life's blood is all over the road. I'll get a rental car, then head to Linda's."

"Mom, there probably isn't a rental car company in a hundred miles. Let me talk with Cam."

I rolled my eyes. Since her marriage my independent daughter consulted her husband on the most trivial things. It was not Molly's nature to become a limpet.

"You're *not* coming to get me. Cam's got classes, and you've got a job interview. Linda can get me."

"I'll speak with Cam," she said firmly as she hung up.

I phoned Linda. No answer. I whacked the pillow on the seat beside me, leaving a fist shaped dent. My life was in a nose dive.

I glanced behind the car and got out. Uneven bits of gravel crunched under my tennis shoes as I walked south to examine the trailer hitch. I looked east where the little two-point buck lay still in the tall grass forty-feet below. Was he kaput or simply stunned? I sighed and turned to my next problem. I'd need something to put behind the tires so the trailer wouldn't join the deer in the netherworld. Maybe a big rock so it wouldn't pull the car into the poison ivy in the gully.

Scouting the area for a hefty bit of granite or anything with weight to it, I sighed. "Not fair, Harry," I said into the humid air. "Just what were you thinking leaving me behind to fix every mess that jumps out at me."

Shouldn't quibble with a dead man, but dad-rat it, Harry knew everything, even how to unhitch the trailer.

I squatted to examine the hitch's underside. Kneeling on the pebbly surface of the shoulder, I winced as small bits of gravel imbedded into my worn jeans. Things appeared fine on the underside of the hitch and trailer tongue. I rose and rubbed the stones from my knees.

Hunched over the ball on the car where the hitch sat, I tested the metal with a finger. Without a by-your-leave a black cloud above quickly wrung itself dry. Water ran down my neck and into my shirt until I was wet to the skin. I looked toward the hills. The horizon cavorted with boiling clouds waiting to empty themselves. I scurried for the van. Before reaching it, my cell phone chirped. While pulling the small phone from my pocket, it slickered out of my hands and tumbled into the soggy grass.

"Erg." I swiped a hand across the hair plastered to my face and began to search the wayside for the phone. From the look of the jungle of weeds and tin cans the grass had grown unabated since August. Because the days now leaned into October, I couldn't see a dark object through the trash and weeds. The thigh-high blades of grass wiped themselves dry on my pants. The phone kept ringing. I located it by sonar and snatched it up, then dashed for the passenger side of the van as I said, "Hello!"

"Bon jour, to you too." The baritone voice of Lyle Henderson made my feet slip on the soggy grass. I caught myself from falling by grabbing the door handle. "My son tells me you're having a challenging day."

I flung myself into the front passenger seat. Chilled, I vibrated against the seat like a half-drowned cat. "You called all the way from Paris to commiserate?" Jealousy crept into my voice. After Harry died, I'd wanted to go to France and hide out in a little apartment, continue to learn French, master the art of sauces, and get so busy I could ignore the painful throb in my heart.

"I'm not in Paris." The calm male voice set my heart racing.

"Last time I heard you were heading toward Provence."

"Keeping track of my comings and goings?"

"The kids mentioned your travel plans when you didn't." I grabbed my pillow from the back seat, disrobed it from its case, and blotted my face with the fabric.

"An oversight."

Turning the car on from the passenger seat seemed a good idea. I pulled my purse out from under my bum and scavenged for my keys in the bottom's black hole. "After I refused your marriage proposal, you up and disappeared." My lips scrunched tight after I finished.

He laughed. "I couldn't escape, after all. Everywhere I looked I saw your face. You were in the Louvre, in Da Vinci's lady's mysterious smile. I caught you nibbling crepes on the Champs Elysees, then you had the audacity to invade my dreams, so I came home."

"Oh." I chewed on words that wanted to exit my lips.

"I'll be there in a half-hour or so."

I blinked with shock. "I thought you were home in Kentucky."

"I'm at my family's farm. Just an hour from you. I began driving as soon as Cam called. Shouldn't take me long to reach you."

"I don't need to be rescued. I'm fine. The car will be fine. My cousin Linda can get me when I'm at the repair shop."

"I'll turn around then." His voice was calm.

My heart skipped a beat.

"Well." I wrinkled my brow. "It would be nice to see you." Should I let him know just hearing his voice made my toes itch? That kind of brazenness was unseemly in a grandmother, but it was the truth.

"Okay."

"Fine." I dabbed the pillowcase over my soggy locks.

"Can you give me directions?"

I did.

Then, just like that, he hung up.

The van's windows steamed from my damp clothes. I rubbed a circle in the windscreen. My small aperture showed trees with mountains in the distance. When I finally unearthed the keys a little voice in my head cautioned, "Shouldn't turn the car on in case of a leak. You might blow yourself to kingdom come, and then where would you be?" With nothing to do but count raindrops I dialed my cousin's phone again.

She answered on the third ring. "Hedow?" she snuffled out.

"Linda? You sound like flannel is stuffed up your nose."

"Got an awful bug. Came on all of a sudden." A paroxysm of sneezes concussed my ear before she said, "and I'm living in the bathroom." She blew her stuffy nose. "Don't come if you value your life."

"I can help."

"Declined. Some things should not be shared. Fred's got the shivers too. Head on home." Being a nurse, Linda had a corner on direct. "We'll catch up when I get my head off the pillow."

"Love you bunches."

"Love you back." She disconnected.

Drat! I couldn't use her as an excuse to avoid Judge Henderson.

Chapter Two

"NOTHING HAS GONE RIGHT SINCE YOU vanished into heaven, Harry. The last time the judge saw me I was wearing my wedding finery at my daughter's wedding. Now, I look like a castaway from a shipwreck."

The van shuddered and my crabby mood was punctuated by a clap of thunder. "I postponed making a decision about marriage to Lyle to give me breathing space." I crossed my arms like a bossy school teacher as I spoke to Harry, then caught my gesture, and flopped them back onto my wet pants. "Without a by-your-leave, he takes off to Europe. My fault entirely, but it *is* vexing." I heard Harry's warm laugh as the wind shook the car. "I've managed to avoid thinking about Lyle Henderson for parts of every day, but that is going to change because I can see the headlights of his car in my rearview mirror."

Harry didn't speak. He hadn't lately. He'd been growing quieter in the four months since his death. I'd have to get back to the cemetery for our private confabs.

Flipping down the visor, I looked in the mirror. My hair was a rat's nest, curls every which-a-way and dripping wet. I slapped on some lipstick. My hands shook as the judge's silver BMW slowed. My Madcap Rose lipstick was smeared. I rubbed off the errant swath of color with an icy finger and squared my shoulders as he pulled in behind the trailer. "Face the music." I lifted my chin as if for combat.

Rain came down so fast that the window glass looked underwater. The judge stepped out of his car then maneuvered around puddles, muddy water splashing onto his black jeans. Lyle opened the back door and plopped in the seat behind me. In the confines of the car his leathery aftershave scent drifted to the front.

I turned my head to greet him and a finger of pain shot across my shoulders and lodged in my neck muscles. I squelched a groan. Whiplash may have descended.

In a black and white insulated holder, Lyle slid a cup of coffee into the receptacle between the seats. He took care not to touch me. Before the proposal he would have given my hand a comforting pat. His eyes spoke loud and clear with a-ready-to-head-for-the-hills-look, like my boys when caught filling tennis balls with gasoline, lighting them, and tossing them onto the driveway. What happened to my take-no-prisoners neighbor? Lyle shook his thick head of graying dark hair.

"Drink up, Di. You must be chilled." His voice was more coaxing than commanding.

I drank, thankful for the familiar hot liquid sliding down my throat. It was an expensive, Ethiopian brand of coffee, from the burnt bean taste and hint of eucalyptus. Even taking a sniff probably cost a couple of dollars. The taste was divine.

"You should retreat to my car. I'll start the engine so you can warm up. Put it on tropical if you wish."

"Good idea."

Lyle flipped up the hood on his green rain-slicker and stepped out of the car. The rain made little splatting noises as it hit the fabric of his coat. Coming around to my side he unfurled the umbrella I'd stored in the backseat and opened my car door.

I glanced at the metastasizing mud puddles, then my eyes flitted over his shoes. Not any old shoes for Judge Lyle Henderson. He wore hand-tooled cowboy boots. The kind you order from a Texas outfit that makes them just for you. He and Harry did like good shoes.

I unfolded myself, careful not to jar my neck, then we stood like conjoined-twins close under my puny umbrella.

"Thank you for the coffee. It was perfect." I smiled.

"You prefer it with a little cream, no sugar, I believe."

"Is Josephine your spy?"

"Molly. She thought I had a need to know."

"My engine is leaking."

"Cam informed me." He spoke as if he'd been sucking desert sand for a month. Why he'd be nervous beat me. We walked toward the van's front. The colorful puddle had spread.

"What is that stuff, oil?"

"Most likely radiator fluid."

"Do you think the trailer will be easy to unhitch?"

"The tow-truck driver and I will manage." He shrugged as if it wouldn't be a problem.

We arrived at his car. He seated me on the passenger side. I settled a little stiffly.

"Are *you* all right?"

"Fine."

"I've heard *that* before."

It wasn't a lie. My nerves were intact. Nothing seemed broken. I was a teeny bit sore, though, especially my neck. I sat down onto the car seat again, careful not to jar anything into spasms.

Lyle dropped the umbrella behind me on the car floor, went to the driver's side, and started the engine before fiddling with the heat knobs. The Amber Alert for the little girl came on again. Lyle lifted an eyebrow and glanced at me. "Happens too often, the disappearance of children."

Rain eased down the windows as a gigantic eggplant and orange-colored machine hurtled toward us, honking loud enough to make cadavers rise. The tow-truck slowed, then maneuvered into position to grab Lyle's car and trot back to a garage.

Lyle jumped out of the car and waved at the driver like a wild man on a bender. The driver halted with a screech of brakes. With rain slanting sideways, Lyle stood on the cab's running board for a chat, then ambled back and drove us down the narrow road to a gravel drive. We turned around and faced the drama.

The driver rearranged his rig as particular as a boy on his first date parking the car to impress. Lyle secured the white trailer with rocks in the front and back of the wheels then added a big lock on the hitch.

Like a mesmerized rabbit, I watched a metal ramp spit out from the underbelly of the truck. Hydraulics squealed as they lifted my van then eased downward as gentle as a mother putting her sleeping baby to bed.

After putting my suitcase in his trunk, Lyle made a squelching sound as he slid into the driver's seat. "They'll send someone back for the trailer. We'll follow the truck and fill out paperwork. I can deliver you to your cousin's afterwards."

"Linda and her husband have the flu. I'll need a rental car."

"Ah." Lyle's lop-sided smile emerged. "Shall we take this adventure one-step-at-a-time? Paperwork first, then a hot meal before we scare up transportation."

I nodded. The little kid who disappeared from the school must feel that life was out of control. I did, and all I'd dealt with was a deer's demise and a former suitor reappearing.

The tow truck sped like greased lightning down the twisty road. Lyle kept up. The road was posted forty-five. Lyle's speedometer read sixty.

Lyle cornered too fast into an off-camber curve. As his tires squealed, I made a tiny squeak, and white-knuckled the door's armrest. He glanced at me. A grim smile moved over his lips.

"I'll slow down, Di." His tone was apologetic.

I stifled saying, 'Well, you should,' and just nodded.

Harry had been a careful driver, but a little too slow for the traffic. Sometimes we'd get horns honking and rude hand gestures. Which Harry ignored.

I looked at my fingernails.

"Not speaking to me?"

"Of course, I'm speaking to you." I looked at him. "I'm sorry I gave a stuck-pig squeal. Drives Daddy crazy when Mama does that."

"Okay." His voice was cool.

I fiddled with my hands, wondering if Lyle was impetuous.

Is that why he'd leaped into an unhappy marriage with Clarisse?

The man at the Hendersonville repair shop shook his head over my crumpled van. "Let me get on the computer and check a couple of things." He returned pleased with himself, judging from his grin. Before he spoke, he beetled his brow. "I estimate about fifty-five hundred dollars, not including the paint job. Got to order parts. Take a week before we send her to the paint shop." He stuck his hands in his pockets and rocked back on his heels. "Should have a nailed-down-estimate by tomorrow. By then I'll know about hidden damage. It will be some time before she's ready, though." The mechanic gave the hood of my car the kind of pat you'd give a favorite hound.

I sighed. The five-day delay before getting to the re-painting meant I'd need to drive from North Carolina to Kentucky and then retrace my steps from Kentucky to North Carolina. *If*, they got the van road worthy.

I didn't want to think about it.

"There was an Amber Alert sent out earlier. When little kids disappear is it usually a parent?" I asked as we drove away.

Lyle tilted his head before he spoke. "Often. Custodial problems, fear, anger, all play into the "divorce poison" atmosphere."

"What is divorce poison?"

"One party maligning the other to the kids. Lies or

half-truths used to manipulate the children into not wanting to be with the other parent."

"With Clarisse gone all those years you didn't have to deal with that."

"No. The boys and I avoided that pain. Of course, there was some with her desertion. Hard for a child to learn to trust when a parent disappears." He shrugged.

Our lunch destination was a blue-shuttered restaurant with pansies in oak barrels guarding the front door. People nodded and waved at Lyle as we entered. A few rose to shake his hand, and greet him with, "Judge nice to have you back home for a bit." The waitress behind the chest-high greeting desk made a beeline his direction and did a little shimmy with her hips. Seemed half the women in the led South wanted to serve him lunch. I took a deep breath and sat in a squishy peacock-blue booth seat.

We conversed about the weather. It was not controversial, which was good, since Lyle Henderson and I could be at loggerheads at the drop of a proverbial pin.

They served me warm tomato bisque. Nice to consume sweet creamy tomatoes with a bite of tabasco on a cold day.

Lyle's reuben sandwich leaked Thousand Island out the side and smelled of sweet sauerkraut. He ate fast then studied his watch. "Mind if I make a few calls?"

"Not a problem."

He wandered away seeking a private spot while I sipped my soup.

In August, he'd bolted as soon as I'd suggested he cooperate with our kids' wedding plans. I chewed a bit of French bread. After I'd refused his proposal at the kid's wedding reception—he'd high-tailed it to Paris.

Leaving me was becoming a habit.

I thought about the day after the wedding—the last time I'd seen Lyle. The rice littering the driveway after the kids' reception had crunched underfoot the next morning when Beau Henderson had trotted over. The judge's youngest son was built like his father, tall, square shouldered, spare.

"I'm heading to the airport and back to the Naval Academy," he said in greeting.

"Don't let them whack off all your hair."

"The Navy pays the barbers extra to humiliate us. I'm not a plebe. They nearly scalp them." His fingers had reached for the plate of sticky buns on the counter. "Er . . . about you and Dad. I just want you to know that it's okay."

I wasn't sure that turning down his father's proposal had been the best decision I'd ever made. Had Beau guessed?

"We both need more time." I poured Beau a glass of milk. "I, for mourning Harry and your dad for dealing with the shock of your mom reappearing."

"Oh, what a tangled web Mom created. After eighteen years it's awful to have her return."

Amen to that. I'd spent weeks cleaning up the messes his mother had created. It would have been a sight easier if she'd stayed in-absentia with her paramour.

"Last summer when they fished the bodies out of the lake, I suspected she was one of them. Which was fine with me. She wasn't the greatest mom." His blue eyes clouded to gray.

I hadn't noticed until that moment that his eyes resembled his father's. The same large, oval shape and deep blue looked at me from across the kitchen island.

"Me too. I thought it explained her disappearance. But not your dad. He knew she was in the land of the living soon after the murder victims' bones were in the state morgue. He just didn't inform me that she was loose and aiming for him. It would have helped. For weeks I thought he might have done her in."

Beau had laughed so hard he spat out crumbs and a couple of pecan bits. Clarisse Henderson, ex-wife of the judge and my new son-in-law's mother, was at present alive and kicking in the slammer. Where she would remain, God willing.

"Don't shoot your ex-husband is all I can say."

Beau raised his eyebrows at my comment and snagged another roll.

"It doesn't sit well with law enforcement to plug a hole in a respected judge. And I'm still cheesed off about it. Maybe more so than Sheriff Bellows, who vows he'll keep her in lock-up until the trial." Fearing I'd confessed too much feeling, I nervously licked my lips. "Mainly because your dad almost bled to death in my library."

My eyes had started to water. Beau handed me a wedding napkin, the fancy kind with the bride and groom's names written in silver, and a date with curlicues around it with an embossed vegetable garden at the bottom. Another reminder of Harry, the consummate gardener.

I swiped my eyes, then placed two caramel dripping buns in a plastic bag and handed them to him. "Something for the road."

"I'll see you at Christmas." Beau squared his broad shoulders and strode out the door.

As the judge's BMW backed out of his drive, I'd forced on a smile and lifted a hand. With a solemn face, Lyle had waved in return. On the passenger side of his swank European car, Beau blew me a kiss.

Lyle returned to the table in a soggy rain jacket, smelling of a peppermint candy he'd swiped from the bowl by the entrance.

Putting his hand across the face of his iPhone he wiped water droplets from it scattering them all over me. "The shelter outside is limited." He smiled in apology.

I smeared butter on a slice of French bread and thought about the little girl from the Amber Alert in Hendersonville. Was she frightened? Hurt?

Returning to his phone conversation Lyle shrugged. "Oh, well, that's that then." He placed the phone in his pocket.

"What's what?" I popped a small bit of bread in my mouth.

"I've been calling rental companies. Nothing available until Saturday except a pickup. Do you want it?"

"I could tow the trailer home."

"I'll see to the trailer. It makes sense to have the van and trailer both brought home and let T&J look at them both. That's the repair shop Harry used, and it's near home."

"I hadn't thought about bringing Waylon home."

"Waylon?"

"My van."

Lyle's eyes twinkled, inviting an explanation.

"I've always named our cars after country-western stars." I hesitated.

He nodded encouragement.

I tilted my head. "We had a loose fan belt and the car made this really obnoxious noise, so Waylon it became."

"Okay." Lyle was trying to corral his laughter. "Harry's truck?"

"Johnny Cash. It took so much money to keep it

going."

A chuckle escaped him. "Your first car?"

I looked sideways as I couldn't look him in the face. "I can't tell."

"Scurrilous?" Lyle lost the battle and laughed out loud.

"Sort of."

He raised his hand to the waiter. "Now to your dilemma." He leaned over the table and fixed his gaze on me. "You are welcome to stay at my family's country home until the estimate on the car repair comes in."

I shook my head. I couldn't stay at a strange house with a man I was in love with but wouldn't marry.

"To make things clear, my sister and her husband live in the main house. I have a cabin some distance away. I'll be staying there."

"Oh." I reconsidered. "That's kind of you to offer."

Our waiter sauntered over and slid the bill toward Lyle.

Lyle yawned. For the first time I noticed the dark circles under his blue eyes. His gray pallor from trying to bleed to death four weeks earlier, remained.

"Say, when did you get back from Paris?"

"Last night."

"You must be exhausted."

"Just seeing you has revived me." Lyle fished his wallet from his pants pocket and slapped a twenty-dollar bill and five ones into the leather bill holder. "Keep the change." The waiter nodded and went to the next table.

Lyle smiled his genuine, light-up-the-eyes, smile.

I smiled back. "I gladly accept your offer of shelter. It will give me time to think about the car."

Glancing out the window at the rain drooling down and the trees whipping in the wind, I shivered. A chill air hit us as we left. Huddled under his gray umbrella we marched left foot, right foot, like Dr. Seuss characters.

When the car revved to life, I shifted in my seat to see his face. "The day after you left, I gave Sheriff Bellows Harry's journal and Clarisse's letter to him. I felt I was lying by not letting them know the diamonds in my safety deposit box were found by Harry. Tucking them away for safekeeping may have been a mistake."

"No way to know the provenance of that cache of gems. My guess is, my ex-wife's lover bought them to hide his illegal activities, and Clarisse got the storage unit key when she shot him and the Frogmeijer girl. I told Madison you'd be bringing in something about the case. You don't tolerate hiding truth."

"The diamonds are another motive for Dr. Timmons' murder. It's not looking good for Clarisse and Neely Patrick at the moment." *If they proved to be Doc Timmons' loot, the millions in gems would be government property and likely disappear into someone's pocket and not be used to fund my dream of a swimming pool for the town's kids.*

"Is your family home far?"

His gaze slid my direction then back to traffic. "No."

"Is Hendersonville named after your family?"

"An uncle of about seven greats back. Any other questions?" He smiled.

I didn't have any.

He smiled. "Tonight, a small gathering of about seventy-five people will be at the house. The party is the annual autumn barbecue."

My eyebrows lifted heavenward.

He glanced at my face. "Di, you may be excused from the festivities. No need to put you under more stress."

I juggled that thought with being apart from Lyle. Then there was the problem of party clothes. The only appropriate thing I had was a pair of embroidered cowboy boots. The rest of my sloppy, move-the-furniture-to-the-kids' clothes were squashed into the small bag.

"It's Lexington-style barbecue with a whole pig roasted, not a white gloves affair. But the ladies will be in skirts because there will be dancing."

"Ah." I rubbed my hands on my gray safari pants—the kind that have zippers and pockets everywhere so you can store wadded Kleenex and bottles of water when you're pushing your shopping cart around Walmart. Maybe I should grab an apron and serve the appetizers.

His eyebrows lifted. "I gather from your expression that your wardrobe may not be appropriate. May I suggest a little stop before we head to the farm?"

The boutique he chose had stylish clothes, and prices that would feed a family for a week. I only bought a couple of things. Thinking about a party I began to sweat. Introverts love privacy and I needed some ASAP. Making small talk made my stomach flutter. The night had disaster written all over it.

Chapter Three

THE ROAD BETWEEN ASHEVILLE AND CHARLOTTE was up hill and down dale. My eyes moved back and forth studying the greenery on the road margins, hoping no other deer would have a death wish. I don't mind feasting on deer sausage. I just don't want to be the one to have to apologize for ending its life.

When we got off the freeway, we were subjected to a roller coaster ride with hair-pin turns. Lyle was in his element. I eased back into my leather seat and studied his profile as we drove alongside pastures filled with cattle. He had a distinguished face with lean, high cheekbones and large, wide-apart eyes. A face that would be nice to see in the morning. I shook my head to scatter the thought to the wind.

When Lyle become a circuit court judge, Harry had shown me a copy of the *Lexington Herald.* "If you closed your eyes and thought of what a magistrate should look like, your friend's image would pop up into your mind," I'd said to Harry.

A soft smile had ignited Harry's eyes. "I am proud to call Lyle, friend."

"I am too," I whispered to my absent husband.

Lyle glanced at me. "What did you say?"

I blushed.

By the time we glided up the drive toward Lyle's old home the sky was clearing and the sun winking through rain drenched trees. An antebellum mansion with wings jutting out left and right from the Doric entrance columns rose before us. Lyle must have grown up sliding down a two-story bannister.

My mouth dropped open. "This is your family abode?"

"It's the main house."

"How old *is* your little ol' farmhouse?" We smiled at

one another.

"The house has a log cabin interior that was fashioned in the mid-seventeen-hundreds. What you see had siding added, and a new porch, as well, but most of the house, was constructed in 1840, with a wing or two added later for flare."

"How did it escape the Yankee torching campaign?"

"The lady of the manor claimed her children had smallpox. The Yankees took one look at the hastily dug graves and skedaddled south. The family dug up the silver hidden in the six-foot holes and celebrated with their last bottle of wine."

"My ancestors were probably part of the skedaddling."

Lyle raised a hand in salute. "Figures our families were on opposite sides of that fight. Promises to be interesting." Lyle stopped the car by a white-railed fence. Stepping out into the fresh air, he stretched skyward.

Lyle opened my door. "Come, Di."

We walked toward a horse pasture. Lyle put a foot on a fence rail—resting his arms along the top rail. His gaze wandered from field to fence. His eyebrows met in the middle, drawing a shadow between brow and nose.

"Are you worried about something?"

"Fence needs painting. I'm in charge of the outdoor maintenance. What with one disaster after another I've been too busy to get down here. Work needs to be done before winter sets in." He thumped the fence with his right hand as if he'd made up his mind about something.

"I've managed a paint sprayer or two."

"No, thank you." He shook his head. "If you went home with work-worn hands, I'd have to do some fancy talking to your friend Josephine, let alone our neighbor George, who treats you like a princess. How would I explain I offered you bed and board with strings attached?"

Lyle lifted his arms and spread them wide, encompassing the horse pasture, the sky, and the tree-lined hills beyond. In that one gesture Lyle seemed to shed the weight of the world as if a too-snug coat was flung aside and he could breathe.

Harry once said a man could breathe deep only when he was home. This North Carolina land didn't smell like the bluegrass. The air was overwhelmed by pine with a bite of acrid mud tossed in.

Three horses posed in the pasture, waiting to be photographed. The trio had ears up and heads turned our direction. A black, a roan, and a horse of a curious shade of merlot were quarter horses.

"I want you to meet someone." Lyle whistled a cheery four-note-tune. A horse nickered in reply. Lyle reached his hand out to me. I didn't hesitate to allow his fingers to wrap around mine, which surprised me, because I'd determined not to encourage his courting. He gave me a small squeeze with his fingers then again put his hands on the fence.

The strawberry roan mare trotted toward Lyle. She stopped, then lifted her head as if waiting for accolades. Lyle whistled again. She began to gallop.

Soon a long nose protruded over the railing and bumped Lyle's outstretched hand. He rubbed the mare's muzzle with his knuckles. Raindrops glistened on her coat and her breath hinted of the sharpness of fresh grass.

"Her name is Lily. Gloriosa Lily to be exact."

"What type of lily is that?"

"Grows in Africa and blooms after the first rains when the dry season ends. Saw one in Kenya's Masai Mara as the morning sun eased over the acacia trees. The flower was a brilliant color, as if all the sunrise reds had exploded in it." Lyle smiled at the memory.

Lyle was a straight-up-serious guy, lawyer turned judge, not some nineteenth century English romantic. My female antenna went on alert.

The black stallion pushed his side into Lily, who

eased right. Thrusting his nose forward, he aimed one brown eye at Lyle.

"All right, Diablo." Lyle laughed and scratched behind the horse's left ear. "Let's take a ride tomorrow. Lily is the perfect horse for you, Di, gentle, obedient, an easy ride. And Diablo will keep me busy." Lyle moved down the line-up of horses to pat the shoulder of another mare. "Meet fastidious Francine." The roan tossed her head as if agreeing with his assessment.

"I'd love to go for a ride."

He nodded once then said abruptly, "We have to go." As he turned to leave, a breeze stole through the trees sheltering the house, stirring my loose hair. Lyle's hand reached up to keep the hair from my eyes, but his fingers ran through my curls. I leaned toward him, like I had when he'd returned from the hospital after Clarisse had done her darnedest to make him a corpse. Feeling the warmth of his breath on my cheek made me quivery.

"Well, Lyle, it's about time you two showed up. You haven't been here in forever." Lyle's sister, Cissy's voice carried beyond the drive. I lifted my eyes her direction. She stood on the verandah with a smile so broad you'd think she'd won the lottery. We walked toward her, not holding hands but close enough to touch. Wafting around her was a collision of scents. Spices of cinnamon and nutmeg comingled with mustard and the tang of vinegar.

Cissy untied a rhinestone-studded apron from her waist and started down the wide verandah steps. She was *Southern Living* magazine's version of a lady of the manor. Her floral skirt, frilly blouse and sparkly earrings would suit a night out in Charlotte. Even her hair glittered. "Delilah, I can't be more pleased to have you here!"

I swallowed. Hard. I'd forgotten Cissy had proven to be more drill-sergeant than lady of the manor. After Lyle was shot, she had pushed her way to his hospital bed and demanded to speak with his surgeon.

"I've asked Lyle more times than I can count to bring you and Harry. Lyle claimed his cabin wasn't finished. Wasn't *perfect,* if you ask me. Lyle wanted things ship-shape before you and Harry came last summer."

There hadn't been an invitation last summer, because Harry was aiming toward glory after November's diagnosis.

I felt tears prickling my eyelids, so I stared beyond Cissy to the chandelier lit entry. "By then it was too late, with Harry's passing."

Lyle reached for a handkerchief.

Cissy didn't notice my distress. She shook her head at her brother. "Park the car, Lyle. We don't have much time." As Lyle returned to his car, Cissy cozied up to me and kissed me near both cheeks, like you see in European movies where they kiss the air near your ear. "Delilah, you'd better get inside now and get settled. I've got a few people arriving to celebrate the coming of winter. Not a time for celebration if you ask me, but nobody did."

I let out the breath I'd imprisoned. Even at the kids' wedding Cissy had flummoxed me.

Cissy's husband, Conrad, emerged from the house, nodded my direction, and loped toward Lyle's now parked BMW. Conrad Davidson, all limbs, moved fast. Lyle opened the car trunk and eased out my small shopping bag and worn suitcase.

"Conrad will handle the luggage," Cissy called to her brother.

Lyle mouthed, 'No,' and began to walk our direction.

Conrad blocked his path. They did a feint and parry until Lyle, eyes squinting with frustration, released my suitcase and shopping items. With a satisfied smile, Conrad hoisted the bags and marched our direction.

"I know Lyle still isn't supposed to lift anything after getting plugged." Cissy summed up Lyle's nearly dying on us with a cavalier remark. "I'll show you where to freshen up." She moved toward the front door not waiting for my response. At the sound of tires crunching on gravel Cissy spun around and clapped her hands. A Dodge pickup was parking by the pasture fence while a line of vehicles snaked along the tree-sheltered drive.

Cissy waved. "Oh, drat! Everyone's here early."

Amid a chorus of hello-ing and horn honking, Lyle joined us. "Before we are inundated with visitors let me explain something. This part of the country is ripe with Hendersons. They will descend on us with hearty appetites and not just for food. Hendersons are skilled at worming out information, whether by innocuous chit chat around the kitchen table or prying information out that's bottled up as tight as Fort Knox, they'll find golden nuggets for gossips."

"Are they all judges, then?"

"Wait and see." Lyle wrangled my suitcase from his brother-in-law.

"No, Brother. Let Conrad carry the bags up, we've guests arriving who haven't seen you in forever."

Lyle nodded.

Conrad dutifully traipsed up the stairs, bags in hand.

I trotted after him.

Chapter Four

WHEN I RETURNED, LYLE WAS ON the verandah meeting and greeting. His lopsided smile appeared as he moved to my side. Lyle eyed my new blueberry-hued skirt, matching blouse, and comfortable cowboy boots. "You look gorgeous."

Inhaling deeply, the heady scent of juniper and pine nearly flattened me. Lyle took my hand and pulled me toward the newest arrivals. I wriggled with discomfort at meeting strangers. Lyle removed his hand as if he'd been slapped.

"I think I can handle a family gathering if they don't quiz me about propelling that deer into eternity."

His eyes softened, but his smile no longer extended to the corners of his lips.

I small talked in a pseudo-reception line until a leggy blonde stepped onto the verandah. Jangling an arm full of tinkly metal bracelets, the blonde waved with her fingers at Lyle so her bracelets sent off a shiver of sound. Putting her hands onto the exact spot on his chest where Lyle had red stitch marks from a surgeon's scalpel, she asked, "Is this where that nasty ol' bullet tore into you?" She rubbed her index finger over his clavicle.

Lyle smiled. No wonder half the women in our county went gooey-eyed around him, Lyle put up with their flirting.

My face was hot.

"Lynette, I don't believe you've met my friend, Delilah Morgan."

Gently Lyle put his hands on my shoulders. He guided me closer to the touchy-feely woman and himself further from her batting eyelids. I held my breath.

"Charmed to meet you." The voice of the

statuesque blonde was light and airy. She smiled sweetly at me and patted her curls, then turned from me to watch Lyle as he stepped away.

I fanned my face with a napkin.

Lynette's lips flickered into a pout. Her male escort leaned over and whispered into her ear. She shook her head, then turned toward Cissy's quiet husband. Conrad slipped a friendly hand around her arm and kept it there as he escorted her to the buffet. She seemed unaware of the men ogling as she bent to take a napkin from the table.

Someone poked me with an elbow, igniting a bonfire along my spine. I turned and faced a petite woman who eyed me like a starving person does a tasty appetizer. "I heard tell, you and Lyle are . . ." She was cut off by Cissy beating a triangle with a metal rod. The clatter could make a herd of cattle stampede.

"The Pig and Poke Barbecue is officially ready to serve!" Cissy brandished the rod like a branding iron. "Now fill up your plates and scatter around. And don't y'all bore Delilah here with Henderson myths."

"Myths?" a man shouted. "No tall tales here, just the gospel truth."

Laughter rattled the fancy chandeliers. As soon as she could flounce to his side, Lynette stuck to Lyle like warm taffy on unbuttered fingers. Cissy lifted her head, widened her eyes, and marched toward the pair. Our hostess linked her arm in Lynette's with such force I thought they'd both tumble to the floor. Then she pried the blonde from Lyle's side and vectored toward the bar.

Musicians with fiddle, guitar, drums, and sax set up in the foyer. They played country-western music which fit the theme of southern hospitality with a western flare. Couples ate or began to dance in the parlor or on the verandah. Trying to be invisible, I sidled into the living room.

"Did they ever identify that body found near here?"

I craned my head around to locate the speaker. She was standing by the fireplace with a glass of cider in her hand.

A woman in a green floral dress shook her head. "The girl found last month?"

"Yes. Paper hasn't said anything. Not even a coroner's report. Kind of odd, don't you think?"

I pretended to study the walnut sofa table, brushing my finger across the smooth finish as I eavesdropped.

"Not even cause of death?" The first woman drew her brows together until they formed one straight line.

"Young girl's all I know. A suicide most likely. Maybe she was bullied or suffered a heartache."

"Not too far from here, though. Couple of miles downriver. They certain it isn't the McElfish girl that disappeared last March?"

"Calling it a Jane Doe." The woman speaking swallowed more cider, and they linked their arms and wandered off.

I shivered.

"That Lyle sure knows how to pick 'em," a male barked in my ear.

A stocky man in pants the color of a dirty mushroom stood inches from me.

"Take Clarisse for instance," the stranger hurtled on as I looked for an escape hatch. "Drop-dead gorgeous with her big blue eyes, and then, well, here *you* are!" He expanded his arms to encompass the room.

"I'm an old friend of the family."

"Ain't nothing old about you, honey."

"Mr. Henderson is my neighbor and plays with my grandson." I hoped mentioning I was a grandmother would stop his chatter.

He waggled his eyebrows. "That Lyle, I could tell you stories." His breath was the oaky scent of bourbon.

I wasn't sure where this conversation was going

and didn't want to find out.

"Better not. You might scare her off," rasped a female voice. "I'm with this poor, besotted male." Facing me was a woman with a figure reminiscent of a bowling pin. "Call me Lil." She stuck out a hand with a ring on every finger, and shook mine with the strength of someone who milks her own cows. "Roy here," Lil jerked a thumb toward the man, "is Lyle's second cousin, and a Henderson too. I'm Roy's wife. Your head's probably spinning with all the names and faces. You'll sort us out, given time."

"We Hendersons are the nobility of the South." Roy slid his thumbs under his belt and rocked on his heels. "We're clean living, God-fearing folk who love our horses, whiskey, and wives in that order."

"Wives as in more than one?" the man who brought Lynette yelled as he wandered our way.

Lyle moved beside me, blocking infatuated Roy from continuing his conversation. Lyle bowed formally. "I know this is an imposition, Mrs. Morgan, but may I ask a favor of you? Cissy wants a concert. My boys bragged about your piano playing." Lyle shrugged his shoulders as if to say, 'I've nothing to do with this.'

I slowly exhaled. "For *you*, I'll play." I smiled into his blue eyes. "Do you have a request?"

"Something classical. I want them to know that a girl from Appalachia doesn't just play bluegrass."

"Ah, Mozart and bluegrass, an interesting combination." The flashy blonde's companion lifted an eyebrow as if judging me. "Since this gentleman refuses to introduce us, I'll do the honors."

The man bowed and reached for my hand to kiss. I kept it at my side.

"You are more beautiful in person than in the picture on Lyle's desk."

My mouth flew open as wide as a baby bird gobbling a worm.

"I'm called Randall."

He winked.

I blinked.

"Randall Maximilian Longworth, meet my neighbor, Delilah Morgan." Lyle spoke distinctly, as if nailing something into place. An old rivalry perhaps?

"Rumor has it that you and my old friend Lyle, are very *good* friends, Mrs. Morgan." His intense expression reminded me of a python waiting for a hog. Any little slip and he'd have gossip to slather as thick as good barbecue sauce. Did he like information so he could have power over people?

"Judge Henderson is my *husband's* best friend."

Maybe Jesus becomes your best friend in heaven, but I couldn't for the life of me use a past-tense-verb to talk about Harry. I wasn't about to inform that rascal, Randall Longworth that I was a widow.

Longworth licked his full lips. "My family are friends of your mayor, and Charlene's family of course. My daddy has done business with the Higgenbottoms and Frogmiejers for years." He lifted his chin and stared at me—a power move I'd heard about from a psychologist.

Enlightening the stranger about local politics and Harry's aversion to our wheeler-dealer mayor wasn't on my agenda.

"I'm often at the mayor's parties. Haven't seen you there, though."

"The mayor and my husband were not the best of friends."

"Were?"

Turning toward Lyle I said, "shall we see if your piano is in tune?"

Sitting at the piano, my stomach was tight, like a clamp on a bleeding artery. I sucked in a breath and searched for Lyle's face in the crowd. He stood at the back of the room, arms crossed, smiling. I chose Chopin. Hard to sell Chopin when images of a flattened deer merged with Lyle's pushy boyhood friend. My mind zizzed around like a squirrel with its tail on fire.

The arpeggios in Waltz Opus 64 were rough. After spending the last few weeks sewing a wedding dress and ducking bullets, I was rusty.

When the mini concert was over, I stood, bent over the piano, and stoic as the librarian Lyle accused me of impersonating, launched into Jerry Lee Lewis's "Great Balls of Fire." Lyle grabbed his sister and danced through the crowd warbling, "You shake my nerves and you rattle my brain." He had a nice baritone, but Lyle swing dancing Cissy around the room brought the house down. Others joined in until the room was jiving.

"Ladies and gentlemen," Lyle shouted into the melee. Most revelers were alert enough to stop their chatter, but liberal consumption of alcohol had two men holding onto the foyer's pillars and singing out of tune. Lyle waited until eyes, focused and unfocused, were on him. "I use the latter term loosely, of course, since most of you are Hendersons."

His comment drew a sputter of laughter.

"It is time that y'all headed home. Our guest needs to recover in the peacefulness of country life, sans roaming woodland residents. That cannot happen with stomping in the foyer."

Lyle's intimidating judicial eyebrow raised. "My sister and Conrad wish to bid you good-night and say a blessing." That shut everyone up.

In a tweed jacket and brown jeans, Conrad replaced Lyle. The scholar, in a blue oxford buttoned up to his Adam's apple, was under-dressed, in sharp contrast to his flashy guests. Nothing ostentatious about Conrad, except his polished, mahogany-hued cowboy boots.

Conrad cleared his throat. "It is closing in on All Hallows' Eve. Which means to the illiterate, All Saints Eve. A time to celebrate God's bounty. The harvest is about in. But if you want to linger, we could always use a few more hands, 'cause work's never done around here."

As the laughter tapered off, Conrad bowed his head.

I did too but kept my eyes open. Mothers learned to do that, just in case.

"May each of us, with gratitude, enter into this time of Thanksgiving for God's provision, with joy. He has brought the rains, the sun, and the time to create the food we harvest. Thank you, Lord for your care." Finishing with a hearty amen, Conrad smiled peaceably at his guests.

Watching the last car lights stream down the drive, Lyle paced the veranda while I aimed for the kitchen. Better to tackle the piles of dishes before the food congealed on the plates. The pungent scent of smoky barbecue sauce lingered on the empty platters in the sink. The tables had been cleared, glasses were stacked neatly on the counters, and the meat was in bags ready to freeze. There was no sign of Clint and Bessie, Cissy's staff, but they must have been running around like headless chickens to get things in order.

Conrad and Cissy were standing over the dishwasher. He glanced my way and shook his head. "Oh, no you don't. We've a mind to soak the rest of the things and get to it in the morning." Conrad waved his lean hand toward the big country sink on the west wall and a smaller prep sink.

I inched out of the kitchen as he said, "Cissy and I are headed upstairs. You should go too." Switching off the lights, Conrad gently picked up his wife's right hand. "By the by, my love. I made sure that Buddy Smith sat in the passenger seat and his missus drove."

"Good. He was snockered." Cissy kissed him on the cheek, letting her lips linger.

"You need to head up to bed, Delilah, and Lyle needs to get on home to his bunk." Conrad's voice was soft, but his expression not. "Don't want you collapsing on us."

"Shoo!" Cissy wafted her hands my direction. "Clint and Bessie will be back in the morning to clean up. You aren't to lift a finger."

"I'll get bored." I muttered aloud as I aimed toward the stairs.

"Not if Lyle has anything to do with it." Conrad snaked his arm around his wife's hips and drew her toward his side.

The glow of the moon shone through the curtains. I thumped the pillow, trying to make it civilized. Strange house, hard bed, and an owl's cries penetrating though the windows made sleep evaporate. Cissy's party haunted me like a Halloween apparition: booze, the remarks about Lyle's past, and the guests' minds gyrating with sexual innuendo was unsettling. Harry and I didn't serve liquor at our parties. Made me wonder about my across-the-street neighbor. He'd not had much to drink during the evening. Was he a light drinker or maybe only if he felt pressed at a party? I dozed, fell into deep sleep, and dreamed of Harry.

He stood on a tree-lined hill with his back to me. With hammer in one hand, nails in a pouch at his waist, Harry mended a fence. The thump of hammer on nail repeated like a drummer setting the beat. The sun radiated around him with the little golden spokes you see in pictures of the Lord. It was hard to look straight into his face because of the bright light and the movement of the air that danced to an unsung tune.

Trying to climb the hill to reach Harry, I moved as if swimming through mud. Harry turned and looked straight at me. He waved his friendly wave, fingers bunched as if tied together. Wanting to grab him and hold on, I beckoned for him to come near. He shook his head, then wandered over the top of the hill. In two long steps he disappeared down the other side.

I must have cried out, because I woke to Lyle flinging open the bedroom door and rushing to the bed.

"Oh. You're here? Did I wake you?"

He thrust a hand through his tousled locks. "No, no. It's fine. I slept next door, in my brother's old room." His dimples flashed.

I tried to sit up. My neck muscles protested so loudly that I bit my lip to keep from groaning.

"I heard you crying and didn't know what to do."

I would have nodded, but nothing moved right. A fierce cramp dug into my shoulder muscles.

"I had a dream . . . about Harry."

Lyle stood at the foot of my bed, feet apart as if ready to flee. "Never be sorry for missing Harry. I miss him every day." A catch in Lyle's rumbly voice testified to the truth in his statement.

I closed my eyes and took a little breath. I lay supine as a two-by-four.

"You mustn't expect your grief to vaporize because of passing time, Di. You will miss Harry all of your life." He spoke softly. "He was your great love. I understand."

Harry's tender current flowed through my days. He'd opened the world for me. My love for Lyle was as consuming. This funny, handsome man with a red scar on his chest that should have been on mine, filled me with joy. In taking the bullet for me, Lyle had opened my eyes to his sacrificial love.

It simply wasn't right to act on my *feelings*. Let alone say it out loud. What kind of a woman would up and remarry right after she'd buried her first husband? Safest thing for me to do was change the subject. "I've found out what whiplash amounts to. I . . . can't seem to move my neck." Tears leaked out my eyes and into my ears.

Lyle stepped closer to the head of the bed and put his right hand on my rigid neck muscles. He moved his warm fingers to my shoulders. I tried to rise to show I was mobile. Getting an inch off my pillow was taxing. A muffled groan issued from my lips.

"Well, you're not driving home today." He pretended to frown, however, his eyes were dancing. "It's not that I didn't want to manipulate you into staying a few days. When you can move your neck, we'll see about getting transportation." Lyle held up his hands as if to say, "not my fault," as he retreated to the foot of the bed and crossed his arms, waiting for my usual protest.

I didn't have one.

"May I suggest breakfast in bed? I'll send Bessie in to take your order." Lyle's fake frown exploded into a grin.

I didn't have time to lay about. The sculptress doing a bronze of Harry was to be in our small town in five days. I would have thumped the pillow with my hand, except my head was glued to it.

An hour after Lyle whistled his way out, Cissy's housekeeper, Bessie, poked her head around the doorjamb.

"I 'spects you don't remember me from the wedding, you being busy and all." The woman's feet didn't make a dent on the carpet as she tiptoed toward the bed. The word lean applied to her in triplicate.

"No need for tiptoeing. I don't have a headache, only a spasm in my entire body." My usual smile felt like the curves were missing. "As I recall, you had a handsome man as your escort."

"That'd be my Clint. Best man in the mountains. And I'm not the only one saying it." She rubbed her hands down the canvas apron she wore. "That doesn't include Mr. Lyle because he resides elsewhere now."

Her eyebrows came together, hard.

"Oh. Of course not." My voice went whispery like an octogenarian. Talking loudly took effort.

"Mr. Lyle's a keeper too." Her eyes dared me to argue.

I blinked.

"And I've known him since he was skinny-dipping in the river with his kid brother Hal."

"Ah." My eyes avoided hers as I caught where she was going. "How many people around here know Lyle asked me to marry him?"

"A handful." Bessie crossed her arms tight. "We 'uns ain't talking about his proposal, since your saying no to Mr. Lyle ain't exactly something we want spread around."

"Good. I don't want him embarrassed."

"Shoulda thought o' that before you up and humiliated him."

"She didn't humiliate me, Bessie." Lyle came into the room and smiled at us both. "Miss Delilah is mourning her husband and I jumped the gun. In due time we'll talk about it again. Am I right, Di?"

"Yes. And thank you."

"Nothing to thank me for."

After breakfast a doctor made a house call. His spasm pills made me loopy. I managed to get out of bed, but I couldn't put one foot in front of the other. Even my using the bathroom required assistance.

When evening shadows crept into my room, someone tapped gently on the door.

"Enter." My word was slurred because my lips felt tingly.

Lyle poked his head in the doorway. "I've retrieved

your trailer and parked it near the stables."

"You've been away all day?" The meds had knocked me for a tizz, and the day had disappeared.

Dressed in tan chinos and a navy plaid shirt, he tiptoed into the room with his hands behind his back.

"You needn't be cautious. I'm not an invalid." My lips curved into a half smile.

"Oh, perhaps I should give these to Cissy." More than a dozen roses emerged from behind him.

"No, don't." I creaked upright.

He shook his head in empathy and gently put the bouquet in my arms. The light-pink petals were edged with ruffles of mauve, like a little girl's petticoat. The gift was a loose bouquet not uptight and scentless hot house flowers, but spicy-perfumed floribundas.

"They're lovely, thank you."

"Couldn't resist pink roses. About the same hue as the nail polish you wore at the kids' wedding." A smile flitted across his lips. "By-the-by, the doctor said any loud sounds can tense your muscles into cord wood. So, I'll tiptoe, thank you very much."

He waited for my response. I didn't have words for his kindness.

After a bit he said, "I've also a little surprise. My cousin Susalee is a masseuse. She can come if you would enjoy a massage."

"I've never had a massage."

Lyle's face registered shock as he put a hand to his cheek and shook his head. "I hadn't thought of that. Maybe it wasn't such a grand idea."

"It's very thoughtful. I think I'll try one."

An hour or so after I was pummeled, I said to Molly on the phone, "They want you stark naked!"

"Yep." Her laughter rippled over the distance. "Did you take it all off?"

"Not quite. I figured my undies wouldn't affect her

wailing the tar out of my neck."

"Feeling better?"

"More like a beaten biscuit, all lumpy in places."

"You treating my father-in-law kindly?"

"I've only seen Lyle once today. And it's the other way around. He has been . . . er, more than solicitous."

"Ha, Mom. You're using your novelist's vocabulary because you can't say how you feel."

I'd always squeezed my emotions into a box and closed the lid tight, until Harry had learned to prime the pump. With Harry I was safe. Trying to express myself sometimes came out sideways. As they had in most of my dealings with Judge Lyle Henderson.

Chapter Five

A ROOSTER CROWED WHEN IT WAS so dark, you'd think the world had been swallowed into a sink hole. Not just a little gurgle either, but a full-throated, repetitive, swagger of a crow. Struggling to roll over I squinted at the alarm.

"Three a.m. is too early to wake up," I muttered with disgust.

Because I'd been snoozing for almost twelve hours I couldn't go back to sleep. Instead I recited Harry's *"Ode To: The Roistering Rooster."* Harry's poems always set me in a happy mood. Awake, with my mind skittering around to a non-starter story, I prayed for the lost girl from Hendersonville and recalled the conversation I'd overhead at Cissy's party. Was this a local girl whose body was found by the river? Lately the news carried more and more stories about kids vanishing. Living in a small town probably had advantages. You always know your neighbors and keep an eye out for one another.

After breakfast, Susalee, the masseuse lady, came to flatten me again. Before she put on soft music and dimmed the lights, I brought up the missing child. "Have they found the child taken from Hendersonville?"

"Off to Gatlinburg with her father. Seems the mother agreed to the trip and conveniently forgot. Quite a to-do for the sheriff and school district. Payback after a nasty divorce, is my guess."

"I'm so glad she's safe. Interesting name for a girl."

"Lots of parents get creative with kids' names these days. I stuck to Emma and Abigail. Nothing fancy." We laughed. When done with her torture, she slipped out of the room.

I fell asleep on the massage table.

Blame it on the drugs.

I woke to Lyle's footsteps in the hallway. Funny how you recognize someone by their steps. Harry's had been purposeful, a Marine's stride. Lyle's was light-footed, with a confident athlete's easy tread. I smiled at the thought.

I overheard voices in the hallway—Lyle's and his sister's.

"A little gathering for board games might be fun." Cissy's robust voice penetrated through the walls.

"I don't think Delilah's up for that." The door creaked open.

My meager covering tried to waterfall off the narrow massage table and pool onto the floor.

"Oh, dear!" I struggled with the thin sheet.

"Ah, you're awake?" Lyle peeked in the doorway.

"What are you doing in here?" I squirmed to keep the covering, well, covering.

He turned his back to me. "Inviting you to lunch."

"I'm not ready."

"How about in ten minutes?"

"Only if you leave."

Lyle never turned around as he whistled down the stairs. The inviting citrus of his aftershave lingered. The man must have a collection of scents lining his bathroom counter. I breathed deeply and climbed down from my perch.

"Lyle is back to pushing his luck." I stuffed one foot in my jeans leg. A spasm went up my just loosened back. Bending over was a trial. I stuck the other foot in the left leg and hopped around to zip up the pants. "Next thing you know, he'll be bringing the four o'clock tea on a tray and sitting right down in this bedroom." Tightening my jaw from the discomfort of movement, I flung on my comfy flannel shirt and let the tails hang out. I stared at my boots standing by the tall maple chest. I couldn't wiggle a toe without pain erupting, massage or no. "Nope. I'd rather be barefoot." I thrust a hairbrush through my tangle of curls and stared at my reflection in the mirror. "And, no. I don't know why I talk to myself." My heart was lighter as I navigated all seventeen uneven steps of the staircase in my zebra-striped flip-flops as I thought of Lyle's consideration.

Cissy met me at the bottom of the stairs. "Heard the thump-thump of your shoes and thought I'd grab a moment. Did King Kong wake you this morning?"

"Your rooster set to yodeling about three, I believe."

"He's from Texas and has an attitude." Cissy pushed open the swinging doors to the dining room. "I realize Lyle's proposal was a little premature after your husband's death."

Surprised that she'd open that tender subject, my mouth screwed into a tight bow.

"Con and I wanted you to know we understand your reluctance." Cissy patted my hand like I would a dementia patient. "Lyle does have a few problems to settle first, his ex-wife Clarisse being a major one."

I raised my eyebrows, hoping that would suffice as a head bob. I wasn't certain what would come out if I opened my mouth. Probably nothing edifying.

My hostess sat down at the foot of the table and waited for the rest of the household to join her for a fancy brunch. I drank half the water in my glass to avoid conversing about Lyle's and my relationship. Slathering on a smile, I chatted through savory crepes, trying to ignore the echo of pain moving from neck to shoulders to my bum.

After two days of slothful living I had gained the flexibility of the Tin Man. With my stiff mobility a distinct improvement, Lyle invited me to tour his cabin in the woods. We settled into his sturdy pickup and clicked on our seat belts. His vehicle choice, a four-wheel drive, Ford dualie should have told me something. After less than a mile we left the asphalt road and crunched onto gravel.

"You seemed uncomfortable at Cissy's party. I concluded it was some of the guests and their conversation. I do apologize. We live in a time when coarse jesting has gone from supper clubs to dinner tables."

"I was a bit unsettled, that's all, what with the car accident and wanting to hide instead of meeting your guests."

"Still, I'd better explain Randall Longworth who can demand center stage." Lyle's voice was courtroom serious. "We've been friends since first grade. We were on the football team together, competed for girls, partied hard in our youth. We've had our moments, but he's proven to be a friend."

I lifted my eyebrows.

"You're right. His ego is the size of the state of North Carolina. I also wouldn't trust him within four feet of you." Lyle laughed.

After twenty-minutes of cement-mixer agitation, the lane smoothed to a pot-holed drive. Lyle dodged the gravel-filled caverns with the skill of an auto-cross participant. Encompassed by evergreens and stands of rough-barked hardwoods, the road seemed invaded by shadows. We topped a hill and Lyle braked, pointing the car east. In a clearing, cut trees were stacked with Lincoln Log tidiness. The meadow below shimmered in autumn's golden sunlight. Lyle climbed from the truck and offered me his hand. I maneuvered out of the vehicle with the pace of an octogenarian. Pushing my rhinestone-studded sunglasses onto my nose, I studied the landscape.

Sprinkled on the foothills of the North Carolina mountains, the tree canopy shivered as a tumult of wind scattered crimson and gold leaves high into the air. *Like a bride tossing a bouquet.* I bit my lip. Thinking about weddings wasn't the brightest idea. There was Lyle, waiting, while I was at full stop with brakes stomped to the floorboard.

A silver ribbon of water swept through forest and meadow. The murmuring of the trees and rustle of dried leaves scratching the forest floor enveloped us. To my left and perched on the brow of a rocky outcropping, a building of sharp planes and windows reached toward the sky. My eyes grew wide. Was this Lyle's cabin? I expected an aged, log structure, resuscitated with new chinking. The house soared above the meadow and rippling water below. The peaked roof resembled an off-center, angular cathedral.

"I thought. Well, expected . . . some sort of old building."

"Originally the house *was* two falling down tobacco barns. I took the walls apart to use the wood and designed as I went. In the summer the boys and I do a project or two."

"That's an understatement. Come on." I grinned. "You shouldn't keep a lady waiting."

He shook his head. "Good fake, Di. You're in pain. I shouldn't have taken you on this adventure so soon."

"I wanted to come."

He eased me back into the seat, a soft smile playing on his lips. We drove down the meandering road, emerging from the play of light and shadow onto a gravel drive. Under a stone-columned portico, the home's entrance faced away from the river. There were no plants to soften the cement, stone, and wood entry, which fit with the sleek style of the building.

Lyle hopped out of the cab like a gazelle, sure footed and sleek. He opened my door and stood with a twinkle in his eyes as if he were holding a present. Descending from the cab, I grabbed Lyle's hand and tugged.

He stood still as if he was rooted to the ground. "Whoa! What's the rush?"

"Curiosity."

"Which killed the cat."

"Race you." I sprinted. My neck seized up. I continued anyway. Call it stubbornness which I came by honestly, because making do on the hard-scrabble land of Eastern Kentucky isn't for the faint of heart.

I halted in front of a nine-foot door. My sprint had unleashed a conflagration. Rubbing the back of my neck I squinted at the door and the Carolina limestone surround. Brass studs gleamed in the dark wood.

Harry was a straight-forward type of man. You buy an old house, you furnish it with antiques. Across the street from our Victorian, Lyle had filled his 1830 Georgian with his own creations of modern furniture and a handful of antiques. Lyle's discombobulated tobacco barn must be full of surprises.

Lyle placed the wicker hamper holding our lunch beside the door and fiddled with the key and lock.

I tapped my left foot. "You're moving like molasses on an icy morning."

"Di, your need to snoop through my house is amusing." Putting his left hand on the wooden door, he teased it open. I sprang forward. There was a spark in his eyes.

I took a step back.

"You're staring, Lyle Henderson!"

"One has permission to gaze at the woman he...uhm...is attracted to," he retorted as he bowed.

I stifled a grin, so he wouldn't get any ideas, and walked into a wide foyer. Black and white photographs hung on the walls of the entry. Pictures of old doors from ancient buildings, cottages, and cathedrals were framed in matte black. The floor was laid with wide wood planks found in buildings made a century or two ago. Judge Lyle Henderson's cabin wasn't what I had expected. Take off his black robe, hand him a drawing board and, voilà, he's a magician conjuring up a modern masterpiece out of withered timbers. Immediately I felt surrounded by warmth. Perhaps it was the art gallery walls housing places I'd like to see, or may be the warmth of the wood, but the front hall gave a promise–a promise of peace.

We stood in the entrance, which expanded into a titanic room where the peaked ceiling must have been twenty-feet high. The curved sofa was cushy enough to drown in. A floor-to-ceiling limestone fireplace filled an entire wall. Thick, rough beams held up the tongue and groove ceiling.

With hands full of the hamper, Lyle kicked the door shut, then followed me through the foyer into the great room.

As I suspected, the living space was a meld of modern and traditional furnishings. Lyle's Kentucky home had similar pieces. We wandered toward the water side of the house.

I slid my hand along the silk-smooth top of the coffee table. "Did you make these furnishings too?"

"The end table," he lifted his chin to a small chest with three drawers standing beside the sofa, "Cam put together." Lyle placed the hamper on the couch and opened the top drawer. He pulled it from the cabinet. "Dove-tails." He pointed to the sides of the drawer. "Cam fashioned the piece from an old bit of cherry."

"If Cam doesn't like medicine, he can open a cabinet maker's shop."

Lyle laughed. "Probably pay more than an eighty-hour-work-week and little gratitude. Guess you can tell I'm proud of what the boys did here? Generally, we made a mess and loved doing it."

I paused at the wall of windows overlooking the river. "Some view, Judge Henderson."

"I find it pleasant. Come, I want you to see a special room." He bent and reclaimed the hamper.

Did he have a library here? I froze. I'm certain I turned red as a boiled beet as my thoughts veered back to Cissy's house party. Too many innuendos and roving eyes for my taste. Although Lyle had been a perfect gentleman, I was having second thoughts about coming.

Lyle looked at the shock on my face and laughed. "No, Di, not the bedroom."

Lyle moseyed toward the kitchen as slow as a beachcomber savoring the texture of the sand. I followed, but paused in the dining area and ran a finger over the grain on the oval table. Hadn't seen zebra patterned wood before. It was gorgeous. Tapered legs rested on a handtied rug.

The kitchen shone with stainless steel appliances, and gleaming granite countertops rubbed shoulders with a marble tile backsplash and ancient wood beams. Lyle settled the hamper on the counter, then leaned on the center island. I performed a slow pirouette to take in the design. The floor was light, clear-coated cabin-grade hickory. I wanted to get down on my knees to feel the knots, mars, and discolorations.

"Delilah, I've a treat for you."

"I'll *bet* you have."

"Delilah! I'm referring to gelato. I've got some in the freezer." He put his hand over his heart. "I'll have you know that you shock me, dear, with your suspicions."

I laughed at his phony act.

"Ha! You may laugh, but I am stunned. I believed I had proposed to a lady dressed in tidy librarian clothes. I now find I'm wooing a woman who wonders where the bedrooms are. And you think *I'm* a reprobate?"

I smiled. I was still the same person he'd been courting since July, a housewife dressed in jeans and untucked shirts. He knew I was not a ravishing forty-year-old eager for a romp.

Lyle's sarcasm lightened the day's atmosphere, removing the awkwardness I felt being alone with him in his cabin.

Lyle shrugged like a ham actor and opened the freezer portion of his refrigerator. He slid out a long drawer, examined two plastic containers, then stuck his head past the drawer and peered inside.

"Someone has been eating my gelato. Did the kids mention coming here recently?"

"No."

"It doesn't matter. I've got another container."

"Do you always have dessert before your meals?"

"If possible."

Once Lyle had provided us both with cones overflowing with creamy, dark chocolate, the kind that makes you dream of tiny European chocolates, we wandered to the windows framing the river and rolling hills.

When we returned to the kitchen to wash our sticky fingers, Lyle opened the door beneath the sink, then palpated the towel hung on the inside of the door.

His tidiness wasn't a surprise. I'd already discovered my neighbor was a perfectionist when I'd been forced to re-order his household items after a break-in. Obsessive, orderly, everything in its place was his style.

Lyle rose to his feet. "Next on our tour are the guest quarters."

We wandered through the foyer and entered a hallway. The hall ceiling was nine feet high and the space broad enough for two to walk abreast. Lyle opened the first door on our right. A four-poster bed stood in the center of the room. The eighteenth-century bed was cherry and dressed in a hand-made Ohio Star quilt. I glided to it, each step carefully placed, so I wouldn't jar any part of my body and cause another spasm.

I wanted to put my nose inches from the perfect stitching but was reluctant to bend over. "May I touch?"

"Anything in the room." He lined up beside the quilt and looked hopeful.

I examined the quilt pattern before easing my gaze toward him.

Worry lines marked his brow. I bit my lip. What was going on? I put my hand on his injured chest and gave a hesitant smile. His eyes focused right above my head.

"Shall we adjourn for lunch? While you plate up the meal, I need to see something."

Feeling dismissed, I wandered back the way we'd come while Lyle remained in the bedroom. My heart hurt.

Something scraped across the floor of the room I'd left, then Lyle marched along the hallway, opening and shutting doors one after the other. His steps were direct, as if he was on a mission *Something had disturbed him. Was it something I said?*

Plating Bessie's chicken salad sandwiches, I watched Lyle emerge from his wandering and stride out to the deck that faced the green-blue river. He unfolded two Adirondack chairs and sat with his hand on his chin, lost in thought. When I joined him, he stirred and gave me a hesitant smile. We dined at a small table, under the shade of a white canvas umbrella. He was mute about his explorations. The light breeze disappeared. A cooler, stiffer wind began to spurt around the corners of the cabin.

I reached across the table and put my hand on top of his. "You are a world away."

"I get contemplative when I'm here."

"Seems to me you're usually too busy slapping tile on walls to meditate."

Lyle lifted an eyebrow. "Delilah, I've a mind to sit here all day and relax." His voice said otherwise, it was tense, his eyes alert.

"Enough is enough. You need to finish your sweet tea and get on with the tour."

"I see."

"Do I get the rest of the tour or do I traipse through the house by myself?"

"Of course, I will accompany you." The words were strangled. What happened to the joy bubbling in his voice from the beginning of our outing?

Lyle stood, then put a hand down to lever me from

my chair. "Up and at 'em my dear." His fingers were warm and wrapped mine like a package. A smile moved across his lips and his eyes sparkled as he kept my hand in his as we headed inside. He started to walk me down the wooden staircase. I stopped on the second step.

"What about the rest of the rooms in the hall?" I pointed wistfully past the door where I'd coveted the quilt.

"You may peek inside but not enter the rooms. I'll explain later."

Four doors were fitted into the hallway. One was a linen closet, another an office, the third a bedroom, much like the one I'd explored.

"No bathroom?"

"En-suite bathrooms." His voice was distant.

The air had been sucked out of our day, and I didn't know why.

Chapter Six

Nary a word crossed our lips as we descended the curved wooden staircase to the first floor. A family room stretched to picture windows. They revealed a grassy hillside with the river a hundred yards away. To our right, French doors led to a stone patio. With the sun obscured by gray clouds the river gleamed grayish-green. *The colors must change continually.* Lyle took my arm, guiding me past rattan chairs and a matching love seat. He hesitated before opening the last door. When he eased the parson's door open, the room echoed the house design: masculine, linear, and sharp.

I had taken one step into the room when he cried, "Stop! Don't move. Something is wrong."

Right foot dangling in mid-air, I froze, took a deep breath and tiptoed backwards.

"That clinches it. There has been more than one person using my cabin." Lyle stared at the floor in front of us, an uncharacteristic wrinkle in his brow. He squatted to examine a footprint on the beige carpet.

The heeled print appeared much smaller than mine. Not Molly's shoe size, either. Molly wore the same size nine shoes as I.

"Di, ease out of the doorway while I examine the bathroom." He walked next to the wall on the edge of the thick carpet and was gone a couple of minutes. "Just as I thought, someone has been eating my gelato and sleeping in my bed."

"Is that why you've been distracted? You were worrying about a Goldilocks invasion?" I laughed.

"Have I?" He looked surprised at my assessment. "My apologies. I need to make a phone call. May I escort you upstairs, Mrs. Morgan?"

Lyle retired to the front portico, closing the

gigantic front door for privacy. I walked around to the back deck. The song of the river tumbling over rocks was muted by the distance, but still cushioned the air. Above the hardwoods, a series of yellow and green hills rose to touch the graying sky. Another rainstorm was on the horizon.

"We'll need to stay a while."

I jumped at the sound of Lyle's voice.

"Didn't mean to startle you, Di."

I turned. "Want to tell me what's bothering you?"

He ground his back teeth. "All the bedrooms have been used and the bed linens changed." He frowned. "I put on the plain white ones when I stayed here. No sign of anyone using them three weeks ago."

"Who do you allow to use your home?" My thoughts scurried to Randall Longworth, who I wouldn't trust hog-tied to a tree.

"A handful of people have keys. There's a set at the main house. Cam and Beau, certainly. If I have guests who wish to use the cabin, they check with me."

"Is something else bothering you?"

"I've called the Lexington field office of the FBI. Special Agent Madison arranged for an FBI team from Charlotte to arrive here by mid-afternoon. I don't want locals. Word gets around here fast."

"Nice you now have Madison as a friend, instead of an adversary."

He nodded.

Was Lyle telling me everything? Why the FBI? Did this have something to do with Clarisse? Had she been here before she shot him? Was somebody else gunning for the judge? Were judges targets these days? My mind rabbited around so fast I aimed toward motion sickness. Anxiety wouldn't help Lyle's dilemma of house intruders. 'Get a grip, Delilah,' I heard Meemaw order in my head.

Lyle reached over and lifted my hand into his and squeezed it. "Let's take a breather until the team arrives. I've a few books in my office you might enjoy.

I'm going to psychoanalyze trout."

After visiting the office, we left the house and wandered toward lower elevation where the torrent of water rushed furiously by. Lyle, dressed in a fishing vest and waders, had a fly-rod in his hand. I carried a book of 20th century poems. Reading usually gave me focus and poetry took me to places of the heart. Did Lyle find solitary activity soothing? I sighed, because I didn't know.

I fingered the tattered book cover. A comforting feeling. The wild grass was long, and we threaded through the field crushing the stems under our boots. The air held moisture waiting to be released and smelled of pine resin, the scent that perfumes a house at Christmas. Sitting on a pair of rain slickers, I opened a page from the small red-covered book and read Rupert Brooke's familiar lines from his WWI poem. "If I should die, think only this of me: That there's some corner of a foreign field that is forever England." Brooke's idealism had always bothered me because of Harry. Harry had faced war's ravages with realism and not made it elegant.

I shook my head to scatter thoughts of Harry into the autumn sunlight. Lyle played catch-and-release with the brown trout. His casts unspooled from an expert's hand, his line arching gracefully above the tumbling river. Drawing his rod back and forth like a conductor before a waiting orchestra, Lyle kept his eyes on the clench-fisted boulders protruding from the flood. Lyle continued casting until a beige sedan trundled up the gravel drive and disgorged three people.

Lyle hoisted his rod over his shoulder. *"FBI."* He mouthed as he passed me.

I remained seated, listening to the river bubble over worn boulders. I couldn't concentrate on iambic pentameter when Lyle was worried. An hour later he returned, his face grim. The FBI remained in the house.

"We need to head back. I can tell by the way your shoulders slump you're tired."

"If you want me out of the way while they work and you oversee, I can stay here," I offered.

He lifted one eyebrow. "Never do I want you out of the way," he said as he took my hand.

As we mounted the plantation house steps, we overheard Cissy snap, "I can't believe you asked her to dinner!"

My eyes widened. I didn't want to eavesdrop, but the window stood open to the verandah and her loud voice carried to the pasture.

"You were eyeballing her the whole night of the party, and now I have to play hostess to Randall Longworth's mistress."

"Uh-oh." I looked to Lyle.

"She's his office manager, *not* his mistress." Conrad's voice was as forceful as Cissy's.

"Shows what you know about things."

"Lynette is Freddy's little sister. He's my best friend." Conrad's voice was steady. "The least we can do is have her over."

"Freddy's useless. All he's done is sell you a couple of horses. And not cheap, either."

I took a teeny step backwards and would have slunk down the steps if Lyle hadn't blocked my retreat.

"She and Rand are invited for Friday." Conrad was firm. "With Lyle and Delilah, it will be a nice gathering."

"Nice, my foot. I won't have you inviting people over without talking to me. It is a bit presumptuous."

"I thought I lived here too." Strident footsteps retreated toward the kitchen as we entered.

As twilight shadows fingered the foyer and climbed up the stairs, Lyle flipped on the entrance chandelier. Its Hungarian crystals shot the walls with diamond glitter. I hastily climbed the stairs, not wanting to interfere with a domestic dispute.

We gathered before supper for small talk and drinks. I fiddled with my hands while Lyle poured water for me, wine for his sister, a mixed drink for himself and his brother-in-law. Tension riffled the living room's air. I glanced at the Davidsons. Conrad stewed in a sturdy wing chair, stiffness in every move.

"Sit here, Delilah." Cissy's eyes darted everywhere except at her husband. "What did you think of Lyle's little mountain cabin?"

"Spectacular."

"I was just telling Cissy that you'd like it." Conrad spoke into the tension with a voice as smooth as a radio announcer.

"Yes, you did." Cissy's words snapped back like a rubber band. "Everyone does. That's why you go there so often."

"I love the fishing." Finishing his drink, Conrad stood to pour another. Lyle refused a refill.

Hoping to smooth over the ripples, I smiled and looked at the fireplace so they couldn't see the worry in my eyes. "I enjoyed your party."

"We like to celebrate the end of summer with a bash. Hendersons have been doing it since the mid-thirties."

"She means the 1830s," her husband interjected. "Hendersons, one way or another, have been the major land owners and socialites for millennia."

"It's only natural," Cissy shot back. "Cream always rises."

"So, it does," Conrad muttered.

Lyle leaned on the fireplace mantle as if he hadn't a care, while the knots in my neck transferred to my stomach.

"Think Di and I will be off in the morning. She's in need of a clipboard to get her commitments in order, and I've some things to get done."

Despite the tension, Lyle's reference to my

compulsive method of keeping myself organized prompted an internal smile.

Cissy fixed her snapping brown eyes on me. "Oh, Delilah, it has been too short. How I've loved having you . . ."

"Dinner," Bessie interrupted in a rolling drawl.

As we left the room, Lyle lingered at the small bar. I glanced back as he put his handkerchief around Conrad's glass and placed the wrapped object on a shelf under the counter.

The next morning, as rain cascaded down the gutters, we headed toward Asheville. Dull clouds smothered the hills, reflecting my feelings. Lyle arranged for a truck driver from Longworth's company to transport my trailer to McKeansville. The van, however, was still in the car morgue awaiting autopsy. I expected a call anytime. Anytime, in the South, meant from here until Christmas, which was two months away.

I did not say a word about Lyle's suspicions of his brother-in-law, however, I'd wager infidelity glided through his cerebral cortex. Maybe there was an indiscretion in Conrad's past, but tension in marriage could result from something as simple as squeezing the toothpaste tube from the middle. The night of the party, the Davidsons had been playful with each other.

"Um, I enjoyed your sister and her husband. It was nice to see them in another context. Weddings aren't conducive to conversation."

"I apologize for Cissy's remarks as we were leaving. 'We're holding our breath as we wait to hear about your engagement,' isn't something I wanted to hear either. She and Con are a little disappointed that they couldn't rope us into the domestic bliss corral."

"Sisters can be opinionated."

"Are you referring to your sister Susanne, who wrote me a note of commiseration?"

"She didn't!"

"Three pages, on hand-crafted paper, telling me how you'd spend an hour deciding which hairbow to use. She kindly ended with, 'give her time, Lyle.'"

"Oh." I felt the lines on my forehead deepen.

Next, I'd have Meemaw putting her oar in and really messing things up.

I sunk into the curvy seat of the BMW and rested my head as we drove from the wooded foothills into the bluish Appalachian range. Nerve pain still fired along my neck.

We talked of safe things—what he did in Paris, the country houses tucked in among the hardwoods on our journey, and the coming of the holidays. Neither of us returned to my refusal of his proposal, nor did we bring up the FBI traipsing through the cabin. I had a million questions, especially what had happened to the glass Lyle had hidden. It was gone when I'd checked. Lyle had run an errand before breakfast returning as Cissy sat at her accustomed place at the table. Had he taken it for the FBI to do a print match?

Lyle drove as skillfully as he had when we'd been rammed by the Hummer in Paducah. But he drove fast. I kept squinting at the speedometer.

"Just say it."

I looked out the window after spying 80 on his dial. "Well . . ." I stammered, biting back the words, speeding like a demon on steroids. "You drive like an expert."

"Right." His word was starchy. "Anything else?"

"The posted limit seems a little less than 80."

"It is."

"Do you get many tickets?"

"Not recently."

He slowed. A 2019 Stingray whizzed past. I expected him to take up the chase, but he remained at a steady 73 in a 65 zone.

"We'll stop for lunch in Asheville. I thought we would dine al fresco at the Grove Park Inn. Will that be acceptable?"

"I've heard it is wonderful."

His hesitancy in asking if I'd like something or other wasn't like the man I'd grown to love. Had I offended him with my implied criticism of his driving? I missed the decisive Lyle. If I nodded my head like a bobble ornament, however, I was afraid he might start bossing me around again.

We ate on the terrace. Bluish hills jutted north and west in the distance. A haze filled the river valley below. A damp breeze circled our table.

"You're chilled." Lyle stood and removed his jacket then placed it over my shoulders.

The collar of Lyle's windbreaker smelled of aftershave, his verdant forest scent. Harry hadn't worn aftershave. He'd smelled of good country dirt and sweet grass. Lyle smelled like a TV ad come to life. He looked it too, with his runner's taut muscles and clean-shaven face. Not that he had to shave. Being part Cherokee, he had smooth cheeks. *Wish I hadn't thought of the touch of his skin.* I focused on the stone terrace wall and the spa entrance below it. Comparing one man to the other was indecent.

The mist gave way to a hazy blue sky. However, the air remained damp, as if waiting for rain clouds to congregate and begin another deluge. We finished our coffee and separated to attend to nature.

While washing my hands in the little girl's room, I heard a familiar voice from one of the stalls.

"So, I said to her, 'Olive Lorraine, you are plumb crazy to make friends with Delilah Morgan. Next thing you know she'll have you visitin' her black church and doing cartwheels.'"

I sucked in air. What an unwelcome act of Providence that McKeansville's first lady had ended up in the Grove Park Inn's fancy bathroom while I was there.

"Olive Lorraine Patrick's a Catholic, Charlene." The voice in the next stall bit into the quiet. "Anyway, what did you expect after Olive's husband got arrested on an attempted murder charge? Olive Lorraine went over to the dark side when it came out that Neely had been Clarisse Henderson's lover. With all the trauma her reprobate husband put her through, Olive's a little flighty. Give her time. She'll come around." Lydia Hamilton's voice was California-cool as she spoke.

My mind ricocheted from my shock at encountering Charlene and Lydia in the lady's room, to Olive Lorraine's gestures of friendship. I'd better be on my toes when it came to her.

"And the nonsense about Delilah Morgan's mother being some big shot in the DAR." There was a sneer in Charlene Higgenbottom's tone. "Pure fantasy. The whole family hasn't enough brains in their heads to make a sentence, let alone a paragraph."

Lydia, in the stall nearest the door, started cackling.

I raced out of the bathroom drying my hands on my pants. Last thing I wanted to do was see Charlene Higgenbottom and her friend, Lydia Hamilton, especially when I was traveling with Lyle.

Lyle stood in front of a giant stone fireplace in the lobby as if he belonged, like a major domo in a palace. A thoughtful smile curved his lips.

I leaned close to him. "We've got to get out of here. Charlene Higgenbottom is in the bathroom."

He laughed. "You think we need to hide from Charlene?"

I grabbed his hand and pulled him toward the front door. "Not hide, exactly, just not be seen. Can you imagine the tongues working overtime in McKeansville?

He stopped at the massive entrance doors, blocking my hasty exit. I wanted to squirt around him and hightail it to the car.

"Mrs. Morgan." He smiled like a pickpocket at work. I backed up a step. "I'm escorting you home after a car accident. I know you're grateful to my sister for her hospitality and wonderful nursing care while you recovered, so you needn't go on about it."

He spoke loud enough for the desk clerk to lift his head and look our way. "Moreover, I intend to see that your car and trailer are returned to McKeansville within the week. It is the least I can do for Harry's wife."

"But, we . . ."

He cut me off with his forefinger tapping my lips. "I know that you are still in pain, Mrs. Morgan. Perhaps resting a little longer would be in accord with the doctor's orders."

"What in the world is . . ."

"Well, Judge Henderson! What a delightful surprise!" Charlene's rasp disrupted my critique of Lyle's odd behavior.

"And who might your friend be?"

I eased around with the speed of a slug. Charlene had a new hair color, dark burgundy with blonde highlights. To set it off she wore a hot pink pants suit. I blinked.

"Delilah." Her voice went up an octave with her shock. "Are you and Lyle . . . *together*?" Her nostrils were pinched so tight that air couldn't escape.

"Mrs. Morgan was in an accident on her way home from visiting Cam and Molly. My sister lives nearby and extended her hospitality." Lyle's voice was as crisp as burnt pizza.

Before Lyle could embellish his tale, Lydia Hamilton sidled up to Charlene. They exchanged the scrunched-eyed kind of look that bodes ill will.

"Oh, Charlene. We must be off. We've *so* much to do this afternoon." Lydia Hamilton ignored me. Not a look, not a smile, just a lift of her tan chin. Her husband was a professor in Harry's department at the college, but they avoided us socially as if we had a contagious disease.

"Lydia." Charlene Higgenbottom sounded tense. "I believe you know Lyle's *close* neighbor, Delilah

Morgan."

Lydia Hamilton didn't know what to do. Shake my hand? Nod? Or say some inanity that would soon be forgotten. I was a pariah in Charlene Higgenbottom's circle, and Lydia Hamilton was the newest member of the posse.

"I imagine you are in a hurry to return home for the unveiling?" Lyle deliberately threw salt on a festering wound of the Higgenbottoms-Morgans rivalry.

Even though Harry had passed on to glory, his likeness, in bronze, was to be erected in our small town. The press was coming for the dead poet's immortalization. If Harry had had a pen and legal pad up in the wild-blue-yonder, he would be scribing a poem protesting his lionization. The event would have offended Harry's sensibilities. Harry believed you didn't glorify anyone but the Lord.

Charlene's face puckered up as if she'd bit into a vinegary pickle, and the color on her cheeks matched that of her hair.

"Well, no. Er." She looked furtively away. "Lydia and I have some business here in Asheville with the Botanical Garden. We will not have the pleasure of attending. Cyril also will be out of town."

Lydia nodded up and down like a puppet on a string.

"Pity. National news organizations are coming from New York, Washington D.C., and Lexington." Lyle paused a moment. "I should think it would enhance your husband's next campaign to be seen shaking hands with People Broadcasting's anchor or STN's star, Evan Collins." He smiled, then tilted his head toward them, waiting for a response.

Charlene's eyes went round as a frog's eyes. You could almost see the synapses rampaging in her brain. "We don't have time." Lydia shook her head. "We've meetings to attend, as well as a trip to Charlotte to assess their Botanical Garden's natural soil amendments."

I imagined sprinklers and a large pile of compost as their focus. I kept my face straight but, it was a struggle. The judge's lips twitched.

"We mustn't keep you ladies, then." Lyle lowered his gaze with a dip of his chin. "We realize how important the Garden Club is to the welfare of our community. Good afternoon."

Charlene and Lydia bustled out the lobby doors with their heads fused together, muttering unintelligibly.

"Well, that was interesting." I couldn't stifle a smile.

"In what respect? The liver-and-onions type of interesting, or a scenic drive?"

I smiled broadly. "The former."

Back in the car we wound through the forested neighborhood toward the freeway, grins on our faces. The whole town would need ace wraps from their tongue sprain before they were through dissecting us.

"I keep thinking of manure in relationship to their intelligence gathering." Lyle kept his eyes on the road.

"They might have fainted right in front of the lobby desk had either of us uttered that word."

"But their conversation was full of . . ."

"Don't!" I held onto my ribs.

"It." His dimples flashed as he laughed.

Chapter Seven

Since we were coming back in the late afternoon, Lyle and I would be alone in my house. My gardener, Sidney, was off to his country house near the railroad tracks. Josephine finished her household work by four, then headed home.

Lyle turned his head to look at me when I sighed. I'd meant to keep my relief in but seeing the 1890s house I called home made a smile inch across my face. Lyle nodded as if in agreement with my sense of peace.

Two days remained before the unveiling of the sketches of Harry's statue. There was barely time to prepare for the sculptor's visit. A clipboard would be handy. My thoughts had been scattered of late and I needed to pin them with words.

With arms filled with purse, pillow, and assorted papers, I had to juggle my keys, then thrust them into the lock of the backdoor with more force than necessary. Standing at the stove was Josephine, housekeeper and best friend. She had a youthful grin on her beautiful dark face and the cant of her head looked sassy.

"Yikes!" I was so startled I whammed my hip against the door.

"I should say." Josephine's eyebrows nearly crossed. "You think I'm letting that pushy judge drive you home and then take up residence, you've got another think coming." She huffed air out of her nose to emphasize her displeasure. Josephine seemed formidable with her tall stature and crossed arms.

"You're the one who has been conniving to get me married to the man."

"So, I have. But since you're re-luc-tant, I need to chaperone. No sense letting Miss Busy Body next door get on her cell-thingy and make hay."

"He's going home, *immediately.*"

"No, he ain't. I've dinner in the oven. Three places are set. I'll invite Mr. Judge myself."

The metallic clip-thunk of Lyle rolling my bag up the terrace steps penetrated the door.

"You trying to kill the judge?" Josephine flung open the door. "Man nearly died on us."

Lyle laughed. "I insisted. Delilah is a little sore from the deer-meets-headlights encounter."

And from whacking her ribs in Paducah.

Josephine stepped back from the door. "A man recovering from blood loss and near death shouldn't be trucking anything, anywhere." Josephine wrestled my bag from his grasp.

"Got any lemonade, Josephine?" Lyle asked her as politely as a British lord inquiring of the queen.

"Usual spot, Mr. Judge. I knew you were coming."

Stepping in front of her, I crossed my arms. "Shouldn't you be tending to your mama and daughter?"

"They're off to the Reverend's for a special dinner. They'll pick me up in my car when I'm done here. Meantime, I'm keeping an *eye* on you two."

Lyle doubled over with laughter. "Thank you," he managed to sputter, "for keeping an eye on Miss Delilah."

"It's *you* I'm keeping an eye on, Mr. Judge. So, keep your hands at your sides, like a gentleman."

"Cam had a few things to say about you being a crabby chaperone, Josephine." Lyle dropped ice cubes into a glass.

"Huh," she snorted. "I told him about-to-marry people need to look beyond the moment. Cain't happen if they're fixated on the heaving bosom in front of them."

Lyle wiped his tearing eyes with a paper towel. "You do have a way with words, Josephine." He poured fresh lemonade into his glass. "Care for some, ladies?"

"When I get back from trotting this bag to the

laundry room." Josephine called over her shoulder. She emptied my dirty clothes into the hamper in the laundry, then settled beside Lyle on a counter stool.

After hoofing my nearly empty bag up my backstairs to the bedroom, I returned to see them hunched over a hunk of blue cheese and crackers.

"You don't say!" Josephine slapped the granite slab with amusement. "I'd like to have seen that. Man must have been crazy to flirt with Miss Delilah. She'd deck him, sure."

"Unlikely they'll meet again. They live in very different worlds." Lyle turned as he heard my footsteps on the floorboards. "Delivering your four-poster to Cam and Molly's condo make you feel better?"

"My bedroom needed rearranging."

He gave me his steady look, the one that made my heart beat faster. "And your ability to sleep, has that improved?"

Sleeping in a huge bed, alone, had been impossible. Missing Harry was like a toothache, one minute I was fine, the next a throb.

"The Jenny Lind bed will be exactly the right size."

"That little antique?" Josephine shook her head. "It's a three-quarters bed, Judge. Miss Delilah had to make sheets for that bed or pay a fortune having fitted sheets shipped in. The bed is dwarfed by the high ceilings and larger furniture. Hmm, hmm. Nothing seems right, just now."

Lyle lifted an eyebrow. "I'll be attending the soiree for your sculptor. The college reception hall is an elegant setting. Are you adding a touch of Harry to the chandeliered opulence?"

"I haven't planned anything."

"I've a few ideas. Would you allow me to have a hand in the décor?"

"That would be nice." I was surprised and sounded it.

"Leave it to me. I'll rope in George. I'm sure he's bored with our sedate little town after our summer adventures."

"Things are a little tepid." I sounded bored.

Josephine went toward the stove.

Lyle whipped his head around to look me in the eye, a grin plastered on his face. "In a manner of speaking, things have become routine. Perhaps pedestrian is a better word choice."

"Don't go lawyerly on me, Lyle."

"Wouldn't think of it, Di."

Josephine opened the oven door and let the garlic and onion scents of her casserole invade the kitchen. "Looks like it's done."

Before Josephine would leave, Lyle had to back his car out of the drive. He laughed at her obdurate stance in the driveway, then waved out of his car window and aimed toward his home. We all knew it would be dead easy for him to traipse across the street for a rendezvous.

After her daughter Savannah arrived Josephine slid into her car seat and buckled up. "Getting dark this early is a nuisance." She waved goodbye as I aimed for the house.

I was tired and it was late enough to grab a glass of water and head for bed. I climbed the stairs and tried the new bed. The mattress didn't have my body curves. I kept awake trying to reshape the new foam into a body-hugging space. The tossing and turning made me think of Clarisse in her tiny cell at the jail house. Lyle's ex-wife was a flight risk, the D.A. stated. No bail allowed. I'd deep-sixed her from my thoughts until now. I'd felt the Lord nudging me in regard to the woman one time before, but I had conveniently ignored it.

"I will not do anything so rash as to visit her!" I huffed aloud to the Lord. "That woman almost killed Lyle." That said, I started counting sheep in French. I was up to the five hundreds when I sat up straight.

"If you want me to saunter over to the jail, I'll do it. But I don't know what to say." That was a prevarication. I knew what I wanted to say. But it wasn't Christian to tell her she was a lousy mother, a lousier shot, and deserved to be incarcerated for the rest of her miserable, greedy life for plugging a hole in her ex-husband and probably one in her lover all those years ago.

"I'll do so first thing in the morning." I thumped my head onto the pillow. *A mistake when you're recovering from whiplash.* I got up to take an aspirin, then returned to bed.

I woke to Josephine's easing my bedroom door open. "If that don't beat all. You lying around like a potentate while I'm dusting the furniture. Rise and shine, Miss Dee Dee."

While pulling on my workout clothes, I prayed about my half-hearted promise to the Lord. On the treadmill, I began negotiating. The Lord's silence was loud and clear. I fixed my heart on obedience.

"I expect you'll have broken through Clarisse's hard heart." At least I hoped He had as I dressed for the jail house in white cotton shirt, black pants, and then struggled while putting on my comfortable cowboy boots. No stripes in sight.

With my prune-face, Josephine would put things together as quick as butter melting on a hot griddle. I'd have to ease out or Josephine would alert Lyle. I descended the staircase like a sneaky cat.

"Where you off to?" Josephine called from the library.

Grabbing a rain coat from the coat rack by the front door I didn't stop. "I have some business with the sheriff." Visiting the judge's ex would take a heap of words to explain. I wasn't up to the task without caffeine on board.

The police station was an experience. I signed in with Sarah McEntire, the newest recruit. I got a pat down, then was ordered to take off my boots. Who knew you could put a knife or something sharp in your boots?

Clarisse entered the visitor's room like she was the Queen of Sheba. She flung herself into a metal chair and thumped her model-thin arms on the fake wood table. She glared. A cheetah eyeing its prey came to mind. A sure sign she was not happy to see me. I lowered into the chair opposite her. Her eyes locked on my face.

I scraped for words. "Er... Are they treating you well?"

"What do *you* care?" Her entire face snarled. "Does my false arrest keep you up nights?"

I wasn't going to give her jab any credence. After all, her arrest was justified. I kept my face still as a frozen pond.

"I wanted to tell you that it took some time, but I forgive you for shooting Lyle."

"I wasn't aiming at *him,* you know." Her anger would have stopped a charging hippo. "I don't need your sympathy or forgiveness. My lawyer is petitioning the court. I'll be out of here by the end of the week. Count on my being around town until my hearing."

Her lips curved up on one side like a sneer.

I chewed on my lower lip.

"Rumor has it that Lyle actually got down on his knee in front of hundreds of people and proposed to you. Must have been some sight, Lyle groveling."

Lyle hadn't groveled. His proposal was so tender it still made me teary.

"He can't marry until we're divorced, so don't get your hopes up."

My stomach tightened. Maybe I'd better check on that to see if it was legal and all. I squirmed in my seat across the table from Clarisse. I put my hands on the table in a peaceable gesture. She grabbed my wrist.

The guard rose. I waved him off.

"I'll fight the divorce, you know. It will help to have a noted judge in my pocket when I appear in court."

Using Lyle to wiggle out of charges of attempted murder, assault, robbery, and fleecing the town with her missionary scheme, made me see red. Ferdinand-the-bull, white-lightening red to be exact. I leaped to my feet, pushing myself so forcefully away from the table that it shoved toward her.

Clarisse smirked.

My heart pumped with the precision of a pneumatic hammer. Oh, help! I wanted to smack her. If I did, maybe I'd be in the slammer beside her. I backed away with my fists clenched. Keeping words stuffed down my throat was the hardest thing I'd done in a heap of Sundays. I signaled to the deputy guarding the door, then walked out without another word.

The door clanged behind me. "Erg!" exploded from my mouth.

"That was an interesting exercise in restraint," said a familiar baritone voice.

"What in tarnation are you doing here?" I whipped around to face an amused Lyle, and an unsmiling sheriff.

"Had business here." Lyle cocked his head. "And you?"

"The good Lord kept telling me to come. We had a falling out—the Lord and I. So here I am, but it didn't do any good."

"Eye has not seen, nor ear heard." Sheriff Bellows stared at me.

"Look. I didn't expect repentance ... *exactly.* A little softening would have been nice, however."

Lyle retrieved my raincoat from the desk sergeant and gently put it over my shoulders. "Sweetheart, let me walk you home so we can talk about it."

We had to ease around two deputies who were hovering like eels in a bed of coral. I shook hands with the sheriff, then walked out into the sunshine and free air.

As we descended the cement staircase to the sidewalk, Lyle lowered his chin and gave me his serious look. "I imagine that you want to consult a lawyer regarding my ability to propose and legally marry you."

"Her statement is tumbling around in my mind." I slapped my hands up to my lips. "Why do I always tell you the truth?"

"It is your nature to be forthright. I wouldn't have it any other way. As to the divorce, I'll stay out of your investigation into its reality."

At that moment my stomach grumbled.

"Couldn't eat before you came?" We turned the corner by the college president's house, then aimed up our street. I shook my head. He looked at his watch. "Brunch is in order. Would you accompany me to The Coop for a slight repast?"

I nodded. We retraced our steps, walked past the courthouse, then down the street, side by side. A few faces turned our direction. I stumbled on a sidewalk crack. He grabbed my arm to steady me and more people stopped to stare. I slipped my arm out of his as quick as a lizard downs a fly.

"Might as well give in. Lips have been flapping since Charlene called her sister, Maylene. Within minutes her beauty parlor clients sent a missive about town regarding the Asheville encounter."

"Oh, dear."

"The whole town is in on the tale of the judge, his ex-wife, and the neighbor lady he's courting."

"Lyle, what are you going to do? This could ruin you."

"Unlikely. This storm I can weather. How about you?"

"McKeansville has macerated me since Harry and I married and we settled on his family's farm." I shrugged.

"So, being mincemeat for the gossips is acceptable to you?"

"Not exactly."

"Thought not. One step at a time, Di. The first step is dining at The Coop."

Chapter Eight

THE MORNING TURNED BRISK WHILE LYLE walked me home from breakfast. I flung my coat on a hanger and marched upstairs. Through my bedroom windows, I saw clouds building in the west. I shivered at winter aiming our way.

Now that I'd changed the bedroom around, it was high time to do a little housekeeping. I descended, then reclimbed the stairs burdened with plastic garbage bags. With a magic marker I wrote, "give" on one, "recycle" on another, and "keepsakes" on a third.

For a man who spoke at national meetings, Harry lacked sartorial splendor. Mostly, he wore gardening clothes with plaid work shirts and didn't have many fancy clothes. He did love a good pair of Italian shoes, though. Harry said, 'walking or standing on feet that throbbed, made your face screw up so tight babies cried out in fear.'

When Harry died, I'd taken one of his plaid shirts and put it on my pillow, just for the scent of him. Now, surrounded by Harry, his plain work clothes that still had a smudge of garden dirt at the hems, I sank to the floor amid the pile of clothes. I grabbed his soft white sweater and embedded my face in it. My mama handknit the sweater and had given it to him this past Christmas. Harry hadn't had time to wear a hole or put more than one drip of coffee on its front. I let myself get lost in my tears for a while, then squared my shoulders and set to work.

I loaded Harry's truck and drove the bags of clothes containing so many memories down the side street near the railroad tracks to the mission. His ties I kept. One could always make something with silk. I'd half a mind to fashion quilt squares. And the plaid shirts would make stuffed animals for Christmas. I'd make one for each of my kids and one for me. I selected red plaids for the festive colors.

When I returned, Josephine cornered me by the back door.

"Your eyes are all red from crying. Time you fessed up. Something bothering you since you snuck off to the jail house to tell that Clarisse a thing or two?"

"I didn't do anything but tell her she was forgiven. It's letting go of Harry inch-by-inch that's troubling."

"Well, it *should* set your heart to hurting. You and that Mr. Harry had a marriage that was the envy of the whole town. You sure you're not sobbing about waving goodbye to the judge?"

I gave her my squint eye. The one I used when the kids made rude noises at the table.

"Well, I thought not, but it doesn't hurt to ask. I bet he came home from his Paree vacation, 'cause he missed you something fierce." She flipped her dusting cloth hard against a cobweb that had appeared overnight. "Yo' blushing, Miss Dee Dee." She squinted back at me.

"I need to haul the vacuum into the closet." It was a feeble attempt to stop her scrutiny. I marched up the backstairs and didn't look back when she said, "Bingo."

"'There's one good thing about having household help,'" I muttered as I attacked the closet dust balls. "They clean up your messes. But it's another thing to make them your closest friend and let them see your heart. Josephine is going to push the judge at me as ferociously as Harry did."

By early afternoon, Josephine left to take her mama to the doctor. The house was quiet. I finished rehanging my closet and was sweating like a sumo wrestler in a sauna. Lugging two large bags of my trash down to the kitchen, I decided to cheer myself up by practicing arpeggios on the piano. Settling on the mahogany bench, I closed my eyes. All I saw was Harry's face smiling as he scribbled poetry while I played.

I tried a rendition of "Ode to Joy." With my face screwed into a pucker, I stumbled through the masterpiece then rubbed the ache out of my hands.

"You've earned a cup of tea, old thing." I rose from the bench as the front doorbell chimed. Peering through the glass section of my door, I spied my next-door neighbors, George and Mamie, standing by the mail slot. George's eyes roved left then right as if searching for miscreants. He seemed different than the bored man who had retired in March, when Harry was failing. It was the way George held his head and the fact that his jaw line was more distinct, like the people who'd had plastic surgery and gotten everything tightened. Last week I'd seen him jogging in step in his driveway dressed in running pants and a tee shirt. Next, George would be entering in old people competitions as a weightlifter.

I spied Lyle behind them. My eyes rested on the white bakery box in his hands. Dessert wouldn't sit well with my diet, which I'd been able to maintain until I'd gotten whiplash and laid around like a slug.

I opened the door to my guests. Lyle's white and black Shih Tzu puppy, Bartles, wormed his way between George and Mamie's legs and squirreled toward me. He edged past me and began to reshape the hall rug into a more comfortable spot.

I waved them in. "I'm about to start a kettle for tea. Do come into the parlor and join me."

The puppy cocked his ears, then led the way to the kitchen as if he owned the house. In a way he did, because Lyle had been beating a path to our door since Harry's diagnosis.

When I returned after putting the kettle on, Mamie swiveled her head, searching for something. "Where is your stereo system?"

"In the back, near the kitchen."

"I don't see the speakers." Mamie's eyes studied the room. Since the Salases moved to town, Mamie had been part of the Higgenbottom entourage. Mamie's defection from her social set had left her oddly adrift.

I smiled. "We don't have any in here."

"I'm confused. I often hear piano music coming from your parlor."

Lyle nodded toward me. "That would be Delilah. She's an accomplished pianist."

Mamie blushed. "I didn't know. I've been told you were a girl from the mountains that trapped Harry."

I looked at my hands. "I think Harry trapped me."

Mamie hadn't visited much. Our friendship dance was new for both of us.

"I suppose everything I've been told about you is a lie."

I smiled. "Probably not everything, Mamie." I rescued the tea kettle from boiling over and served slices of cake and tea. Mine was so thin you could see through it.

After tea and cake so moist I almost licked my lips, Mamie gave me a parting hug. "I can't thank you enough."

"For what?"

"For opening a door and letting me walk in." She gave me a shaky smile.

"I was just being neighborly." Something I'd wanted her to accept since they had moved in next door sixteen years ago.

George looked at Lyle. "Take care of our girl, here."

A smile flitted over Lyle's lips. "Always."

After they left, Lyle picked up the empty plates to ferry them to the kitchen. "Did you call your car repair company?"

"Yes. J&R said they'd put Waylon on the schedule. You don't need to worry."

He placed the remainder of the dessert in the bakery box. "I wasn't worried. I wanted to help."

He toted the box into my kitchen and put it in the refrigerator. The cake would have been fine if it were a plain chocolate cake. I could resist chocolate. But it was coconut with a buttercream frosting and a raspberry jam layer. *I'll palm it off on Josephine tomorrow. Her mama loves coconut.*

By the time we'd finished cleaning up, a stiff breeze was blowing from the north, bending the backyard chestnut tree.

I walked him toward the foyer. "Thank you for the cake. Tell Miss Phyllis she outdid herself."

"I will." He clipped Bartles' leash to the dog's collar. "When does your sculptress arrive?"

"Tomorrow afternoon. She'll spend the night. She wants to see Harry's college office. Said if she could see where he worked and lived it would give some sense of him." I shook my head. "I cleaned out his office so the new head of department could come in. I did ask for a postponement on emptying his space, what with one thing and another, but they gave me only a week. Hope we can get access."

Lyle and I stood together, easy and light, then tried to say goodbye as Bartles scraped at the door, leaving little marks in the dark wood. I squinted at his perfidy, then reached out my hand toward Lyle for a proper handshake. Lyle took my right hand and used it to swing me into his arms. The goodbye was more of a very nice hello. The kind you say in airports when greeting your long, lost love. My heart was tearing around all creation when he finally shut the door and walked resolutely down my front steps.

Bundling up, I headed for the cemetery. I hadn't visited Harry since my deer adventure. I thought I'd fill him in on life.

"Well," I began, while walking down the hill on Franklin, "you were right about Lyle. However, it's too soon to let go of you. You're still haunting my dreams."

I huffed up the incline toward the iron gates as the maples lining the streets waggled their rusty leaves in the wind. In front of me a scurry of chestnut-brown tree droppings flew across the sidewalk. Their dry frames ticked like a herd of mice. Autumn smelled musty as it danced all the way to the arch proclaiming, "National Cemetery." Behind the arch rested most of the town's dead, the Civil War soldiers fallen in the battle of Perryville, and Harry's assorted ancestors.

"You loved this season, Harry." I picked my way among the piles of fall colors thickening the ground. "But I've always found it a time of mourning. The kids went back to classes, leaving the house empty of laughter, you'd head for the college, while I was left to sort summer's outgrown clothes and wrestle with plot twists and odd character traits for my latest novel."

I plodded toward the prominent Morgan enclosure. My eyes squinted as they spied the Morgan graves. "Oh, oh."

Someone hovered over Harry's grassy rectangle. By the time I'd raced through the iron gate to his family's plot the lavender blur was playing dodge ball among the dogwoods, heading for the exit. "Drat!" I looked at the newest offering the town nut had placed on Harry's grave.

I'd put up with Star Wars figures, stuffed animals, and garish plastic flowers. But I was shocked by what was before me. Reclining on Harry's earth hump was a nude figure. One of those half-sized mannequins used for display cases. The plastic bag in my pocket wasn't a match for the seductive maiden lounging on Harry.

"Really, Harry! What in the world did you say that caused your besotted devotee to pull this stunt?"

I heard tires on asphalt. A car pulled into the parking area behind me. Envisioning some little kids coming to say hello to grandpa and getting a gander at the naked lady, I slipped off my fleece jacket and flung it over the offending nude. But it wasn't a family with preschoolers. It was Sheriff Bellows.

"Afternoon, Miss Delilah." He doffed his police hat in a gracious salute.

"Good afternoon, Sheriff."

"I heard you were heading this way so thought of

having a little chat."

"Oh?"

"Mrs. Henderson isn't someone I'd recommend you see again." Bellows crunched through the leaves until he loomed beside me. "She's a contrary woman used to getting her way. Must have given Lyle fits over the years."

Bellows moved his head slowly to and fro, but kept trying to look past me to the lump under my pink jacket. I moved closer to him, blocking his view.

"Women with egos the size of Clarisse Henderson's don't like getting crossed. You breathing on this planet sets her off."

"I've done nothing except forgive her."

"Well, that's the problem. In her twisted mind forgiveness is intolerable. Narcissists don't see that they've done anything wrong. It's everyone else that's the problem." Bellows looked me square in the eye and lifted his eyebrows. "What you hiding, Miss Delilah?"

"Well ... Harry has an obsessed fan."

The sheriff stepped around me, removed my jacket from the recumbent figure, and sighed.

"This happen often?"

"Often enough."

"I'll see what I can do about it." He picked up the figure and put her under his arm.

"Thank you. I thought I'd have to cart her home in front of God and everybody."

"Actually," Bellows said with a chuckle, "maybe I should let you. That news would probably make tomorrow's front page."

I'd spoken with the sculptress, Louisa Campbell, right before Harry's passing. Something in the tenderness of her mother and child statue I'd seen in Lexington had made my heart quiet. When I'd called her, she'd been thoughtful and sympathetic. An artistic, quiet soul, I'd reckoned.

You'd think a sculptress would have been an Amazon, but Mrs. Campbell was about five-foot nothing, and so animated her feet did the Cha-Cha around her suitcase before Sidney lugged it upstairs. She gestured around her. "I itch to see where the *Great* Harry Morgan *really* lived."

I was bowled over by a muscled tornado. "Do you have the drawings for me to examine?" I asked as she fidgeted in the foyer. How did I explain I liked to be prepared so I could control my emotions in public?

"They're ready. But it will ruin tomorrow's surprise if I show them to you. Trust me. You're going to love the idea." Her words came in gallops.

Surprises were for other people. I liked things orderly. Spell things out and we'll get along fine. I began to have doubts about her.

Mrs. Louisa Campbell had been in the house all of three minutes, enough time to hang up her coat, when she barged into Harry's study and plunked down at his desk. Not that his desk was sacrosanct, but really. He was only four months dead and having someone take over his space was unnerving.

I tried to blink the thoughts away as I observed the sculptress in Harry's sanctuary. Louisa Campbell had her elbows on Harry's leather-edged blotter and looked as if she wanted to move in. I took a deep breath so I wouldn't throw her out on the sidewalk.

The light from the room's bank of windows sparkled on the gray of Louisa's head as it had when Harry had occupied his chair. Beside Louisa was a stack of paper Harry had used. Harry was a snob about what he took notes on. He was persnickety about his pens too.

"Mont Blanc pens." Louisa picked one up. "The only ones he used, I suppose."

Harry had carried them in his breast pocket. I swallowed hard. The pens had been a gift from one of our exchange students. "I borrowed my father's fountain pens for years. Can't write a decent poem without a fountain pen," Harry had declared after opening the package. "These are perfect, thank you, Michael." The boy had blushed with pleasure. True to his word, Harry only used them.

Louisa put her lips together and let out a low whistle. "Remarkable. All this light, the books, this aged desk." Her fingers rubbed a half-round scar on the cherry desktop. "He lived in a different world, not a modern one. A man close to the earth. Living creation." She tapped Harry's pen thoughtfully against her cheek. "He was a man who had a way with words, you know." Her voice trailed off momentarily, then she shook her head. "The simplicity of the language he used made me think, hard. When I read about the farmer, in your husband's trilogy of the hardscrabble farms, who eyed the winds growing into Stygian-hued thoroughbreds bent on assaulting the land, I cried." Louisa placed Harry's pen carefully back in its holder. "In the beginning was the Word," she whispered as she rose.

Talking about Harry's poem, "The Gathering Storm," caught me off guard. I shut my mouth, watched her wander the room, finger his Scrabble box tidily resting on a table between two chairs where he and Lyle had played. I gazed out the window at Sidney dismantling Harry's vegetable boxes so I could redesign the garden, and thought about yelling, *Stop! No more change. Leave everything as it is. Put the pen in its proper place, dust the maroon Scrabble box, but don't move it.* I sent the thoughts flying.

"Don't let them make this a shrine, like poor Faulkner." Her words were abrupt, like slamming on the brakes without an obstacle in sight. "Harry Morgan would hate it."

Harry lived *carpe diem.* But hadn't I pulled in the reins and ordered my world to stop? I shook myself. Louisa echoed Harry's sentiments. *Get on with life, Delilah, and stop wallowing in the past.*

"From all I know of him he was a modest man."

I kept nodding my head like a puppet.

"He hated adulation, didn't he?" Not waiting for an answer, Louisa whizzed out of the room and entered the parlor. "Ah, the room where he lived with family." She sighed. Her eyes probed the soft colors, the stained-glass window where a shaft of muted light pulsed through the gold and pink glass and pooled by the piano. Louisa touched Harry's worn wing chair. Patting the leather footstool in front of it, she sat down. "Have you been able to sit in his chair since he passed?"

How in the world does Louisa Campbell know that was Harry's favorite seat?

"No," I choked, caught by her passion and sensitivity. I lowered myself to the love seat and picked up a velvet pillow to finger.

"Thought not. Heard about you two from writer Ewan Stirling. He said it was a love match from beginning to end. Must be hard saying goodbye to a man like Harry Morgan." She let out a teeny- weeny sigh. "I've read him for years, of course. Fell in love with him, just a smidgen."

She looked at her fingernails, which were very short. I hadn't noticed the broadness of her hands while she fingered Harry's library, but now I realized they were working hands, not unlike Meemaw's.

I offered a tentative smile. "Many people did. He has quite a following in the northeast. Women liked his straight-forward narrative style—men, his truth telling." My smile grew until my lips began to curl up a little. Harry found city people enjoying his country romps amusing.

"Got to admit, that's what hooked me. Harry Morgan didn't parse words. More prophet than politician."

"Harry didn't aspire to be a diplomat." I smiled broader, remembering his encounter with an Ivy League college president who had pretensions for political greatness.

Harry received an award from a university that had rejected him some twenty years earlier. At a reception, glittering with wealthy alumni and benefactors, the president wormed his way to Harry and spoke loudly. "Honoring you, Professor Morgan, is the proudest moment of my career."

Harry lifted a bushy eyebrow, reached out a hand, and pumped the president's with vigor.

"That's mighty nice of you to admit that honoring a man of a different persuasion politically and religiously made you proud. I'd hoped it would have made you think."

I had put my hand on his arm. Stopping Harry right there seemed a good idea.

Harry gave me a wink. "Are you not stirred by the amazing ingenuity of your students, their creativity, the wonder of a sunrise over Boston harbor, the mewing of a new baby?" Harry smiled softly.

I sucked in a breath, knowing that a killer jab was next.

"This university sends forth graduates that alter the world we live in. My question will always be, are they doing it in love and service, or for power?"

That quote had ended up front page, center, in the New York Times. So, had a picture someone had snapped of the university president stalking off and ordering a double scotch.

"Something smells mighty fine." My guest gazed toward the kitchen.

"Would you care to settle in, then join me for dinner?"

"No. I've a mind to eat quickly and get to your

husband's college office. Want to see if it matches what I'm picking up here."

"Harry's office was cleared out so the new man could come in. I've his writings in boxes in the basement."

"Has the new man changed things around?"

"I don't know. In fact, I forgot to turn in the keys. We could go there, and I could turn them in."

"Time's a wasting. Let's go have a look. I can still get a sense of things even if Harry's books and papers are gone."

Chapter Nine

WE FLEW THROUGH JOSEPHINE'S *BOEUF BOURGUIGNON,* barely tasting the earthy flavor of the mushrooms and Caesar salad before heading to the campus. As we strolled through the mild night, I got on my cell phone and asked security for entrance to the English Department's building.

Fresh-faced Dewey Wilson met us at the door, his shiny new badge gleamed in the entrance light. When I introduced him to Louisa Campbell, Dewey's ten-pound ring of keys jingled as he half-genuflected.

I only had a key to Harry's office, which I relinquished to Dewey, but Dewey had the master for the entire building. *"Someday," Harry once intoned in his pretend god voice, "we will open all these old doors with a little plastic card. No sound or charm. Maybe they'll tear down these old bricks to keep pace with the times." He slapped a hand on the brick façade. "Stick up metal and recycled plastic cubes." Harry didn't cotton to the Internet, either. Said it made him want to throw something across the room.*

Harry preferred a second-floor office. "This way I can keep up with you in the aerobics department." He'd crossed his arms and made his declaration while watching me peddle my fake bike in the sunroom.

Our footsteps barely sounded on the worn wooden stairs.

"There's a light on in the English office." Dewey sounded puzzled. "I'll open the door to check things out."

As Dewey sauntered into the waiting area, Louisa Campbell and I stepped behind him. Even though it was after hours, the room was flooded with the kind of lights that make your face blue-white and your veins stand out.

A girl's giggle echoed from the office on our left—Harry's old office, currently occupied by a rail-thin academic with a goatee. I straightened up tall and squared my shoulders, not knowing if I was ready for the changes I was about to see, or the skinny professor holding after hours coaching sessions.

Dewey Wilson put a finger to his lips and tiptoed closer. We tiptoed behind him. I handed him the keys, careful not to jiggle them together. Dewey twisted them in the lock, then flung the door open. The wood thudded against the soft plaster.

"Great Scott!" Dewey Wilson jerked like he'd been shot.

I gasped, took a step back, and collided with Louisa.

Professor Hamilton lounged against the new professor's Danish modern desk like a model in a magazine ad. In his arms was a young girl who looked more than eager as she wrapped herself around him and caressed her lips with his. They were not fully clothed.

Hamilton's office was across the hall.

I took that all in before I shut my eyes. No use getting an ugly picture that would not easily be erased.

"You're under arrest for trespassing," Dewey Wilson stuttered as he unearthed his radio from its holder and spit out, "Got a B&E at the English Department. Get here ASAP."

"Now, wait a minute." Hamilton held up his hands in protest.

I opened up my eyes to see him hastily thrust the girl aside.

"I work in this department, so I am not trespassing."

"Explain that to the law." Wilson snapped his phone back into its case. "I've witnesses that say you're in Professor Morgan's old office at 7:30 in the evening, having a lip-fest with a minor. Right, ladies?"

We nodded like choreographed Motown singers.

"We were doing research." Hamilton stepped into his pants and glared our direction, then he waved a sheaf of papers he'd picked up from the desk.

"Hey, Dewey," said a voice behind me.

I scuttled out of the way to make room for his boss.

"Hey, Ozzie. Got us a situation."

"Looks like it." Ozzie scratched his gray hair then whipped out his cell phone and began snapping pictures.

"You can't do that!" Hamilton's voice was shrill and obnoxious.

"Get dressed, young woman." Ozzie didn't respond to Hamilton. "Sheriff's on his way."

"No need for the sheriff." Hamilton's sputtering caused spit droplets to scatter like rain. "All a misunderstanding. Like I said, we were doing some research here. Illustrations of Harry's poems on fertility."

"Harry didn't have any poems on sex. He didn't write them," I snapped.

Ozzie turned to look at me. "Now, Mrs. Morgan, I suggest you and your friend sit in the waiting room until we get this sorted out." He was as polite as a maître d' at a fancy restaurant.

"Not in your life, Ozzie Mackenzie." I stomped my right foot. "We stay as witnesses."

I looked at the girl as she buttoned her shirt. Dewey watched her closely.

"Keep your eyes from popping out of your head, Dewey." Ozzie put his hands on his hips as he stared at his assistant. "Look at the professor if you must." Dewey swiveled his head left, however his eyes stayed on the girl.

I didn't recognize the girl until she swung her head to get the long hair out of her face. The hair-flinging exposed a satisfied smile, and I saw her mother's image. I didn't know which of the Higgenbottom twins I was looking at, but she was a Higgenbottom, and all of fifteen. We were in for a bumpy ride. At that point, Sheriff Bellows ran into the room or I might have said something—the campus security guards didn't know they were up to their necks in political trouble.

"Oh, he . . . llo, Miss Delilah." The sheriff barely caught himself. His face turned ashen when he recognized the mayor's daughter. "Get your coat on, Kaylene. And you," pointing a finger at Hamilton, "put your arms behind your back." Bellows jerked his head toward a deputy behind him.

"I'll finish dressing as I explain this little mix up." Professor Hamilton gave a dismissive wave of his hand, then attempted to tuck his shirt into his pants.

Bellows thumped his arms on his chest as he crossed them. "Cuff him, Roddy."

"We were looking over some of Harry Morgan's papers Delilah left behind." Hamilton wriggled his arms as they were pulled behind him and handcuffs slapped on. "Morgan's got a batch of poetry that should be published. I'm collecting the erotic poems to send them off." His voice faded as he began to realize the impact of his words was like marshmallows hitting a steel wall.

Louisa Campbell broke into a tight smile, took a step toward the reception room, and shrugged.

Papers were scattered across the top of the dark cherry desk. I scrunched up my eyes.

Bellows held up his hands when he heard me snort. "Now, Miss Delilah. Easy does it. We'll sort through the papers after I book the professor. You need to sit down."

He was right. I did. My knees were shaking. Ozzie took photos as Kaylene Higgenbottom and her lover were escorted from the room and marched down the staircase to a squad car.

The police snapped on clear latex gloves like surgeons

wore in medical movies. After fingering papers and stacking them in boxes to cart away, the police made a drawing of Dewey's analysis of the "crime scene." That's what they labeled Harry's old office, *a crime scene.* Watching the hands of the clock move as slowly as a snail on sleeping pills, I began to fidget as I sat near the reception desk.

Louisa brought me a cup of water from the office fountain. "You need to calm down. Although, I must admit, this scene is enough to make a nun take up swearing."

The campus police and local deputy looked at me and Ozzie. "Er, we need to look over Harry's things and see what might be missing."

I nodded. I'd stored Harry's papers in the basement. Time had vanished with break-ins, a wedding, and the judge being wounded, so I'd not examined them. I hadn't a clue if something was missing.

Harry had never done anything in this room but encourage students and laugh. He had a great laugh, one that lit up a room. I bowed my head. Louisa prowled around, her footsteps thumping on the hardwood floor.

The new head of department had a rug front and center by his modern desk. Harry hadn't liked carpet. Said he wanted to know who was sneaking up on him. I was so mad, I thought I'd spit nails, then felt an angry tear streak down my face. A linen handkerchief tickled my cheek.

"Thought you might need this." Lyle Henderson stood by my feet, dressed in his running clothes, which didn't make sense. It was dark out.

When I had collected myself, I wadded up Lyle's now-damp handkerchief. "Harry said there was something odd about Stephen Hamilton's getting the position at the school. Hamilton hadn't written anything of significance and couldn't write a cogent sentence." I sniffed. "Harry said Hamilton got his appointment for political reasons because he was a returning local."

Louisa stood in the doorway and looked at the crowded bookshelves along one wall. "There was a pile of papers on the desk. What was he doing in this office?"

Lyle's lips twitched. "Don't think he was researching iambic pentameter."

Louisa rolled her eyes.

"Or limericks," George added from the doorway. "Hello, Miss Delilah." George ambled over and patted my shoulder.

I gave them a half-smile. "Bellows call you two?"

"We were in the vicinity when a little bird chirped." George was dressed in work-out clothes that were ringed with sweat. "And who might you be?" George turned to shake hands with Louisa.

I wafted Lyle's handkerchief in Louisa's direction. "Louisa Campbell meet Lyle Henderson and George Salas. Both good friends of Harry's."

Extending her hand to George, Louisa pumped his hand up and down like priming for water. "Nice to see you again, Lyle. Been a couple of years since the party in Lexington."

Louisa knows Lyle?

Lyle lifted his head. "Quite a shindig, as I recall."

Louisa turned to me. "My guess is that your sexy professor was in here more than once."

I frowned. "What makes you say that?"

"Opportunity. He looks the type that would keep his house clean and dirty others." Louisa's nose was pinched with displeasure.

Lyle crossed his arms. "Better check out Hamilton's office to see if he's stolen anything."

Dewey looked up. "I'll check with my supervisor and see if we need a warrant. Maybe I should check with the sheriff instead." Dewey scratched his head in confusion.

As the clock aimed toward eleven, Lyle got a judge

out of bed to sign the warrant papers. We stood by the door of Hamilton's office as the police began their search.

"First things first." The deputy accompanying us ushered us to one side of the room. "We're looking for evidence that Hamilton had other . . . er . . . encounters." He peered in the top drawer of Hamilton's desk. Lyle stepped behind him and stared over his shoulder.

After searching the middle drawer Lyle frowned. "Don't look, Di!"

The deputy read aloud a letter from a New York publisher congratulating Hamilton on his series of poems. I recognized the titles. Harry had written kindly, thought-filled observations of students, more character sketches than serious poetry. A couple of his limericks were pokes at a stuffy faculty member trying to claw her way to the top and land in a prestigious eastern university.

Lyle studied the poem Dewey held. "Add stealing and plagiarism to the list of his offenses. These are written in Harry's hand."

Deputy Fisk pulled notebooks from a desk drawer and flopped them onto Hamilton's desk.

By two a.m. we'd trooped to the police department, and I'd signed my John Hancock on the police report. As the four of us lined up to say goodnight to the sheriff, McKeansville's mayor barged into the entryway, nearly knocking over a deputy as he shouldered past. The mayor had a gun. Not a little pop gun either, but a shotgun. One that would plug a gigantic hole in the side of a barn.

I backed up.

"I'll have your badge if you try to stop me from killing him." Higgenbottom waggled his gun at the sheriff.

Lyle stepped smartly in front of me.

Louisa Campbell shook her head in unbelief.

"No use standing in front of Delilah Morgan,

Judge. I know she's behind all this. Trying to humiliate my family is just her style."

Higgenbottom moved close to Bellows, but wisely pointed the gun ceilingward. As the mayor stared down Bellows, Stephen Hamilton stepped out of the interrogation room. Policemen on either side of the shady professor couldn't hide the pedophile from his audience.

When Higgenbottom spotted the professor, he spread his legs in a gunfighter stance. "Get ready to meet your maker, you varmint."

Louisa's mouth pinched with disgust. "Timing is everything, they say."

Attempting to become invisible, Hamilton ducked behind the slight figure of the town's white haired detective. Bellows reached out and wrestled the gun from the mayor. Weaponless, Higgenbottom lunged, his hands tightening around Hamilton's neck like a boa constrictor around a squirrel. Hamilton collapsed on the floor, the rotund mayor with him.

I didn't want to think about the words that spewed about the room, but the air was blue by the time three deputies managed to tear the enraged mayor off Hamilton.

I was mighty surprised that pear-shaped Cyril Higginbottom had the where-with-all to attack anyone. Higgenbottom was winded, though, when he stood up and dusted off his navy wool pants.

"Cyril." The sheriff's tone was kindly, but his eyes could have penetrated steel. "I think it best that you get to the hospital and see to your daughter."

Higginbottom jerked his head in the direction of Hamilton. "I'll see him hang for this. And as for you, Mrs. Morgan, using your husband's office for nefarious purposes will get you tarred and feathered around here."

I recoiled, hitting my hip on the oak reception desk. "That pervert broke into that office. And it hasn't been Harry's since he died. Hamilton abused his authority.”

Lyle reached out to pat my hand.

“Cyril.” The sheriff’s tone made my hair stand up. “Mrs. Morgan is justifiably horrified at the events that have taken place in Harry’s old office. If you so much as breath a word of it publicly, you will have a lawsuit on your hands, as well as the entire state finding out that your daughter had been meeting with the professor for some time.”

That shut the mayor’s mouth into a straight line, but his gaze skittered my way, smoldering like coals of fire.

We escaped the sheriff’s office and took a collective deep breath. The sky was strung with stars as all four of us headed to Lyle’s car.

“I don’t think Hamilton will be heading up the mayor’s exploratory committee for the senate.” George tried to keep a straight face, but his lips couldn’t help rising to a smirk.

“Nor will Hamilton be appointed chair of the department.” Lyle couldn’t keep his voice flat.

A snort escaped my lips. I shouldn’t have laughed. The whole thing was a disaster. Louisa and I stood in front of Lyle’s BMW and laughed till we cried.

“Exploratory committee isn’t a euphemism, Lyle,” George managed to sputter.

Chapter Ten

"NICE LITTLE TOWN YOU'VE GOT HERE, Delilah," Louisa said as we climbed the steps on my porch. "Remind me to get out of Dodge before the gunfight."

I turned toward Louisa. "With all the hoo-ha, I don't think I'll sleep a wink."

I was out moments after my head hit the pillow. I woke at 5:32, regretting my body clock's internal chime for devotions and exercise.

Forbidding gray clouds crowded the sky. The front yard was a muddy, brown mess. Sidney had pulverized the soil so we could transform Harry's prize vegetable garden into something more aesthetically pleasing. The yard looked like the bottom of a swamp. When the doorbell rang at 8:12, I figured it was George with another *bon mot*. I trotted to the door, leaving Louisa to pour herself a cup of coffee, while the police were in the basement clearing out Harry's boxes so they could compare his papers with those found in Hamilton's office.

When I opened the door, instead of my witty neighbor, three reporters thrust microphones in my face. I pushed a microphone away from my nose. "Mrs. Campbell will speak to the press after the unveiling."

"We're here about the robbery in your husband's former office." Jim Bouchard, a local man, stood his ground.

"It's a police investigation, so I shouldn't comment." I tried to wave them off.

"We heard *you* caught them in the act." A sallow woman in a rain slicker leaned toward me.

"Ask Sheriff Bellows any questions you want. I've company and mustn't tarry." I narrowed my eyes at movement near my hedge. A man in a Tennessee-orange rainslicker was setting up a camera on my lawn. Beside him was the judge, investigating the overlarge tripod. Lyle proceeded to circle the apparatus as if fascinated. The camera man and Lyle exchanged a few words, then the judge moved my direction, and the cameraman slunk off toward the sidewalk.

"Morning, Mrs. Morgan, Mr. Bouchard, and company." Lyle eased past them. "Mrs. Morgan is not receiving visitors at this hour. Perhaps another time."

"Who are you?" blurted out the woman in dreary rain gear.

"Local judge." Jim Bouchard's stage whisper made me smile. "We'd best be off."

Once inside, I sipped my morning coffee while staring out the turret windows. The press encamped near the large holly close to the road. Sidney arrived in his ancient Land Cruiser as the camera man commandeered the sidewalk. My gardener took one look at the press and sauntered over to the tractor I'd rented. He took his time climbing into his seat, but when the camera was aimed his way, he revved up the motor like a teenager on a first date. Sidney rototilled the front as if nobody was watching, however, he lined up his rows for good camera angles.

Sidney edged close to the shrubs guarding the drive.

"Hope he misses the plantings by the house." I was talking to myself again.

Sidney had fragile nerves and wouldn't take kindly to me squawking. Best not to rile him or he'd stomp off to the garden shed and sulk. I wandered into the kitchen to avoid snooping out the front windows.

Josephine entered the kitchen and unfurled her dripping umbrella by the Aga stove where things dried in minutes. "A gaggle of cameras are aimed at your front porch."

"I've been told by an officer of the court that they can linger on the sidewalk, but not accost me on my front steps."

"Huh!" snorted Josephine. "You gotta watch out

for the fellow from the *Chronicle*. He'll get a story pieced together with half-facts and half-fiction and nobody can tell the difference."

"He's always been fair to us."

"That's 'cause Mr. Harry was *somebody*. Us *nobodies* find ourselves skewered like chicken on a spit."

I escaped to the parlor where Lyle and Louisa sat with their coffee and chatted. They seemed fine without me. I headed for my hidey hole next to Harry's office. I hadn't spent much time in there since Lyle had been target practice for his ex-wife. The scent of gunpowder and blood lingered in my mind. I stared at the blank computer screen. I reread chapter five of my newest novel. I wrote two pages worth of words before Josephine's steps pounded across the hall flooring.

"Luncheon is served," she announced in a voice loud enough to be heard in the next county. "And since I've set a place for you, Mr. Judge, you might as well stay."

Half-way through the chicken salad, Josephine turned to Louisa. "You look a little tired, Mrs. Campbell? Y'all up late last night?"

"A little." I interrupted so Louisa wouldn't have to serpentine around Josephine's word barrage.

"Uh-huh." Josephine lifted her chin. "You, Mr. George, your houseguest, and his highness, the judge spent time at the police station last night. Anything I missed?"

I winced. "We didn't breathe a word to you about our nocturnal activities because the whole thing is embarrassing."

"First time you've left me out of the adventures, Miss Dee Dee. Don't think I like being sidelined."

Lyle looked her straight in the eye. "Until the sheriff gives a press conference, we're not going to discuss last night's events."

The judge's word was law with Josephine, so she gave up prodding. Knowing her, however, she'd try her divide-and-conquer techniques.

Lyle was monosyllabic during lunch. When his phone interrupted Josephine's cookie presentation, he glanced at it. "That was my timer. The item you asked me to deliver, Louisa, arrived this morning. I'll take the papers now." They scuttled off to a case Louisa had placed in the foyer. Then he dashed out of the house. *What is he up to?*

Louisa and I had planned to walk to the conference center. Currently, with two television trucks parked on the street in front of my house, and a platoon of reporters congregating on the sidewalk, the press gauntlet looked forbidding. Reconsidering our stroll, Louisa and I headed for her truck. When the reporters saw us backing out of my driveway, they jumped in their cars and followed us down the street toward Liberty Hall.

I'd made lists and put them on purple clipboards for the catering company. The unveiling was to be a simple affair. Magically, Liberty Hall had been turned from boring vanilla to vibrant peachy orange. Vegetables and mums were scattered across the serving tables, heaped on round tables, and lying, as if freshly harvested, in front of the dais. Among the glory were calligraphic copies of Harry's vegetable poems. The ones he wrote after the chickens had come home to roost with the Pulitzer Prize.

The caterers were smoothing crisp white tablecloths when I walked in. The entire shebang was to honor Harry, and I wanted him there so badly my heart was on fire.

Louisa grabbed a deep breath. "You smell the cinnamon breezing through the room?"

My face softened at the scent of pumpkin pie and the sight of tables filled with Thanksgiving abundance.

Lyle whizzed past me. "That's more like it. Nice to see your face not all scrunched up with tension."

"I haven't been wringing my hands, I'll have you know." Under stress I usually wadded up tissue or fiddled with my hands. Being an introvert was a minus in large gatherings. I smiled at Louisa. "For the judge to organize this display of autumn splendor amazes me."

As if he heard, Lyle turned from sliding a cake onto a glass stand and winked at me.

Josephine's daughter, Savannah, stood by the raised platform with her school newspaper badge. The seventeen-year-old's olive-green dress was calf length and modest. As a wee thing we'd all paraded Savannah around town in the stroller. Harry had taught her to fly fish as he had our children. Toward the end of Harry's earthly sojourn, Savannah had been at his side for hours, holding his hand, and turning her head so he couldn't see her tears.

I crossed the room and put my arm around her shoulders.

She leaned her head against mine. "Look at all the *real* reporters."

"Don't be intimidated, dear. They probably can't win art contests like you."

She smiled and bent her neck like a swan investigating a lily pad. Her dark curls tangled with my reddish blonde ones. The girl, two inches above my five-foot-seven, took after her mother's side, who were tall enough to play basketball. Her father may have been tall too. I don't know. He was the invisible man. A white man, for certain, because Savannah's coloring was fairer than her mother or grandparents, and her eyes were green.

"Could Ryan get a picture of you after the speeches?" Savannah pointed to a classmate.

"It would be my pleasure." I kissed her cheek, then backed up to look at her.

The room filled. I continued my scrutiny. She was an open and shut girl, every emotion filled her face and bounced in her eyes. In that we were alike, much to the amusement of Harry. As death was closing in, he said, "Keeping you two from hijacking all the emotions in the room is a daily challenge."

He'd laughed, we'd laughed, then when he was asleep, we hung onto one another and had a sob.

I tore my focus away from Savannah and glanced around.

Half the college and many of the town citizenry stood kneecap to kneecap nibbling appetizers and filling the room with a staccato hum. I jumped like a frog on hot asphalt when Louisa grabbed my hand to trot me up the steps to the small stage. When introduced we plastered on smiles.

Louisa squared her shoulders and looked out over the gathering. "I want to wax eloquent about Harry Morgan, how he sculpted phrases until they were lean. Harry Morgan struck the reader with the stark truth about a subject. Few have the lethal skill with words Harry Morgan employed. I admire the man, to put it tidily. His words bring life to ordinary things and shine a new light on familiar subjects."

Finished, Louisa tugged at a black cloth covering an easel. She flipped back the cloth. Before us was a five-by-eight-foot sketch of Harry sitting on a park bench, chickens at his feet. It was perfect. Even the little bits of corn in Harry's hand looked real.

"I want a series of chicken statues throughout the town, drawing people toward Harry." Louisa spoke so softly I bent toward her to hear.

"What did you say?" asked the college president.

"I envision life-size sculptures of chickens placed through town, leading visitors to Harry's statue. Perhaps a poem or two on plaques as well. My model is a small town in Eastern Oregon called Joseph, where sculptures are an integral part of the landscape. I've created an on-line album where you can see the effect that art has on the community."

Thinking my bit finished, I was set to sprint off the platform when Louisa nodded her head. With my feet aimed toward the stairs for a quick exit, I jerked to a stop. Someone wheeled out a large table. A lump hunched under a cloth. The commission hadn't been finalized until June. Could she have created a facsimile?

"Mrs. Morgan, would you please remove the cover?" Louisa stepped back.

Wasn't certain I wanted to see Harry in miniature. To me he was bigger than life, with his eyes filled with love and his contagious laughter still in my heart.

Unsteady, I pinched the corner of the fabric. Beneath the linen shroud, Louisa had captured Harry's smile, his eyes crinkling up at the corners. I ran my fingers over the minuscule hand resting on a Silky. The lifeless hand wasn't familiar. I brushed away a tear.

Louisa spoke into the silence. "I need to add more to the scene after spying out Harry's old office and library. There should be books, with a pen at hand, and a journal. Capturing Harry Morgan creating might be interesting."

Indeed, it would.

A barrage of questions hurtled toward her. When the locals' questions petered out, reporters began their inquisition. I wanted to sample the expensive roast beef on toast points rather than stand with Louisa and squint under bright lights.

"Mrs. Morgan." Evan Collins of a cable network waved his hand. "Can you describe your feelings on seeing this rendition of your husband?"

I looked straight at Collins and took a shallow breath. "Exquisite and life-like. Louisa captured Harry's kindness along with a hint of his sardonic smile."

As we stepped from the microphone someone shouted, "Any comments on the robbery in your husband's former office, Mrs. Morgan?"

I jerked my head toward the voice of Jim Bouchard. He raised his eyebrows with expectation.

"We are carefully analyzing Harry's papers to see what is missing." It was my don't-mess-with-me voice.

"Heard that they caught the man in the act."

Louisa started to laugh. I poked her in the ribs with my elbow. The one Harry called 'a lethal weapon.'

"There was an arrest, yes."

"I looked over the arrest sheet." Bouchard had a smirk from his eyes to his lips. "Seems the only ones brought into the police station last night were a drunk and Stephen Hamilton of the English Department."

That remark set tongues on fire. The decibel level would have been illegal in some places.

"I believe Sheriff Bellows can answer your questions better than Miss Delilah, Jim." Lyle stepped beside me. His voice, which carried to the farthest reaches of the room, was firm as granite. Jim Bouchard nodded, capitulating.

When the afternoon shadows began to merge, Louisa drove home to her farm east of Lexington, and I aimed for my quiet, orderly home, glad to be walking the familiar streets so I could clear my head. The reporters were still nibbling on free food when I passed the Salases craftsman-style home. Lyle pulled into his drive as George waved from his front porch. I waggled my fingers in return.

In the shadow of the door, a coldness crept over my neck like stealthy fingers. Coming from farmland, I knew a storm was in the offing. Sure enough, an hour or two later, the deluge hit. I heard the sump pump turn on and settled back into my pillow with a new mystery.

Rain was beating against the window when I woke at 5:30. The newly spread topsoil had transformed the front yard into a cesspool. Harry's raised vegetable beds usually kept the water from making a lake between my front door and the street. Since we'd flattened the dirt, our transformation resembled chocolate pudding.

The T.V. weather girl promised rain for the remainder of the week. I began to edit a piece I'd created while Harry was incarcerated in a hospital bed. The writing was a sharp deviation from my Revolutionary War novels. Harry had encouraged me to branch out and see what happened. Somehow, World War II had burst into a barrage of words.

"Miss Mamie's on the phone," sang out Josephine as my hero in the western desert slithered behind enemy lines.

"Good afternoon, Mamie." I put my phone on speaker so I could be hands free. "Enjoying our inclement weather?"

"I'm thinking of buying a row boat." Straight as a die, Mamie's cracking a joke made me laugh. "I got a call from Charlene Higgenbottom. She wanted to know if the rumors about Stephen Hamilton and her daughter were circulating."

Mamie sounded puzzled. George, a closed lip sort of man, wouldn't have shared that information.

"Er..." I fumbled for words. "Your call is the first I've heard of any rumors."

"Well, you're not known for gossip, Delilah. Was the girl you saw at Harry's office one of the Higgenbottom twins?"

"Why don't you call Bellows?"

"You'd think you were one of George's operatives," she said in a tart voice.

"I'm not at liberty to say. The girl is a student. Her name is probably best kept out of circulation."

"Especially if she's still in high school." Mamie sounded shocked. "I've been told Lydia Hamilton and Charlene aren't speaking to one another."

"I wouldn't know about that."

"I'm asking you to pray for me. No one in our circle believes Stephen would take liberties with a young student."

I kept silent. Liberties weren't what he was taking. Kaylene might be the first Frogmiejer relative in four generations to lose the Miss Wilderness Road competition.

"I'll certainly ask the Lord's wisdom for you,

Mamie."

She disconnected.

At eleven, on day three of Noah's flood, the power fizzled out. I went on the hunt for matches and lit all the candles in the house. The sweet scent of vanilla mingled with pine in the parlor, however the illumination was restricted to small ovals near the candles themselves. The scent reminded me of Lyle's tree-surrounded cabin. We'd stepped on pine needles as we'd headed to fish. I drank in the scent, then thought of the light's limitation. It was as sparse as the information about Lyle's cabin and who was using it. Was the dead girl found floating on the river somehow connected to whoever had used Lyle's cabin? Shouldn't the FBI keep Lyle informed? He would tell me when they knew something. After all we were in this together, sort of.

I spied the judge trudging through my front swamp to see if we had survived. He carried his dog until they were in the foyer. Water dripped down his little Shih Tzu's back and ran over his furry face. Lyle resembled a boat guide at Niagara Falls. I confiscated his raincoat, opened the front door, and shook it like a dusty rag. I hung up the sopping coat on a coat rack beside my door, then looked critically at the wet patches on his shoulders.

"It's warmer by the stove." I steered him toward the kitchen.

Josephine was chopping onions and wiping tears from the sharp assault on her senses. She was going to add Walla Walla sweets to the large kettle of soup boiling on a burner. "No use fighting the elements to eat at home. I'm setting a place for you and your little rat dog." She eyed Bartles with suspicion. When the puppy first appeared, Josephine had announced that dog training wasn't something she wanted to deal with.

After circling his tail for a few minutes, Bartles settled on the rug in front of the four-oven monstrosity. Lyle warmed his hands and smiled at Harry's folly.

Josephine stepped over the puppy. "Remember when Mr. Harry bought this fancy stove? Mr. Harry said it was a necessity, what with all the neighborhood kids running in and out. He said it was what famous cooks in Europe use for large gatherings in castles. This shiny metallic thing took us months to figure out. Had only two burners, a warming tray and four ovens. Not just any burners, mind, they were ginormous, with one set at 750 degrees, the other 350 degrees."

After lunch Lyle wandered to the library and settled into Harry's leather chair, dog in his lap, eyes on the pages of a book. My neighbor's presence was a comfort. As I walked toward the hidden office attached to the library, I fingered the bullet hole left from Clarisse shooting him. The slug must have slowed after passing through Lyle, because it hadn't penetrated the thick sliding door and landed in my office. Gathering my computer and a handful of research papers, I commandeered Harry's desk, plunking my computer and papers from the D Day museum onto its well-loved surface. Lyle seemed engrossed in his reading, *First Democracy*.

Even though he'd been Harry's best friend, had I ever really studied Lyle? Until fourteen weeks ago when he'd sat across the table from me at The Chicken Coop and announced he was courting me, I couldn't have said the color of his eyes.

Rain assaulted the windows. I worked until forty-two-percent power was left. Not knowing how long the electrical outage would last, I powered down and grabbed a clipboard to scribble to-do lists. Lyle remained in Harry's chair, dog slopping over his pant legs, Lyle's eyes occasionally glanced my direction.

It seemed wrong.

Too soon.

I looked at my hands, then the tidy list. First item—practice the piano for twenty minutes every day. I walked to the parlor and sat on the Steinway's bench. Limp sunlight dripped across the ivory keys. I mechanically performed scales. My fingers felt like thumbs.

A tear left an oval dot on middle C. Harry should be here, laughing and playing games with his best friend. Even with Lyle filling Harry's library it felt cold and empty. I shook my head.

The power flickered on at 2:30. I glanced at my guest, who lifted his eyebrows but didn't move. Times when he and Harry would spend a convivial evening playing Scrabble seemed a distant memory. Eventually, Lyle rose and lit a fire, then he and the puppy resettled. Lyle stretched his feet onto the leather ottoman.

In a few minutes Josephine stood in front of the door, hands on hips, shoulders straight. "You taking up residence in Mr. Harry's chair?"

I lifted my head from the hymnal in my hand.

"'Cause if you are, I'm thinking of charging rent."

"Obviously, I've overstayed my welcome." His tone was light, his grin contagious.

"I don't know about that. S' far as I'm concerned, you can be here permanent. But the lady of the house, she's got another opinion altogether."

"That's an understatement, Josephine. The lady of the house is a little set in her ways."

I rose from my bench to let them know I still breathed.

"Ain't that the truth. You can always finish the dusting while I run the vacuum," she offered with a laugh.

He left at half-past three with Bartles tugging at his leash. It had been a trying afternoon. Not because of Lyle, but because Harry should have been part of our day. Harry with his laughter and sharp insight. I missed Harry so much I wrapped my arms around my chest and held on tight.

Josephine marched down the hall to gather up the tea things.

"You hear that, Miss Dee Dee?"

"What?"

"Your sump pump is making gurgling noises. And that's not all, your downstairs sink isn't draining."

"I'll check things out." I made a run for the basement stairs, grabbed the handrail and almost catapulted down the crooked wooden steps. Josephine tromped behind me with no hurry in her steps.

The hole around the sump pump was full and beginning to lap over the rim.

"Grab some towels, Josephine! I need to suck out water, pronto." I galloped to the tool area to find the shop vac.

After Josephine hurled towels at the mess, she started the sucking job while I squatted by the pump and dialed my cell phone.

"Toby, this is Delilah Morgan." I struggled to keep my voice calm, considering the odor assailing my nose was sewage. "I've a problem with the sump pump. It can't keep up, and I think there might be more to it than too much water. Are you available?"

Toby mumbled something I hoped was a "yes."

"Great. Come right in. You know where the pump is. We're a little occupied at the moment." I turned to Josephine and pointed at the water burbling up toward my basement floor.

With Josephine manning the drowning sump pump I went to the outer wall and looked at the sewer pipe going through it to the sewer line. It dripped. And the water wasn't just muddy.

"That is sewer water backing up into my basement." I gritted my teeth.

"Doesn't smell like a health spa."

"Toby will be here before you know it," I reassured myself as well as Josephine. "He was a sprinter on the track team." The water was lapping the hole. I piled towels on top of towels.

"Uh-huh." Josephine aimed the nozzle of the shop vac like a Jedi-knight with a light saber. In five-minutes flat, Toby came pell-mell down the stairs, his big rubber boots flapping. First, he looked at the pump, second, he examined the water pooling in the pump's hole, and then Toby sucked air between his teeth.

"Reckon that's not a sight you like to see, ma'am." Toby scratched the thatch of red hair on his head. "We've got a sewage problem. When did you have the sewer-line installed?"

My eyes went from the water trying to escape its pen, to the expectant face of Toby Meadows.

"Can't recall ever messing with the sewer line."

"Not on the shop's records, either. I've got them on my phone." He held up his smart phone and showed me the Morgan page. "You've a sewer line failure. Saw Sidney churning your soil earlier. Could be, he cracked the line with his compacting. I'm turning off the water. And I noticed your downspout was damaged. Probably why your sump pump can't keep up."

I heard the house phone ringing upstairs. I didn't trot up to answer it. Josephine went, but not at a trot, because she lugged a laundry basket full of soaking towels with her. After a minute or so she shouted downstairs. "It's Mr. George. He's wondering if you are all right, seeing he spied the plumber's truck taking the driveway curve like there was no tomorrow."

"Tell him a little sump pump problem," I hollered back. "We'll be right as rain in a jiffy."

"I ain't commenting about the rain, Miss Dee Dee."

"We've daylight enough to snake out the sewer line. If that doesn't do the trick, I'll get the backhoe in place. We need to see where we are." Toby dashed up the stairs as he talked.

My eagle-eyed stare was glued to the pump. The

muck bubbled, splashing the towels yellow brown. Last thing I needed was that offal mess slopping all over my basement. Fumigators would have to wash down the walls if I let things get out of hand.

The rain on the basement windows turned soft rather than hard ticking. Rain was letting up. Must have been a half-hour before I heard the disjointed rumble of Toby's machine starting. So, the snaking out the line hadn't done the job. I chewed on my lip. Through the tiny basement window, I saw Toby and his dad—the father in Meadows and Son plumbing— by the dogwood. Beside my leafless tree, the line for the sewer went through the house wall and joined the hundred-and-fifty-foot run toward the avenue.

The water in the sump pump hole subsided. I patted a pillar in approval and walked up the stairs to change into shoes that didn't ooze water and smell of a barnyard. Thought for certain the arrival of Meadows's large truck and trailer would have brought the judge over. Nary a sign of him.

I caught a glimpse of the Meadows' operation when I went to dump the garbage. A twenty-year-old camellia had been removed to a dirt pile by the corner of the house. In the steady rain, the Meadows were digging a huge hole by the north wall, near the downstairs hall bathroom. When they were satisfied that the pit was by the sewer line, they went at it with shovels. The light faded into silver.

After she snooped on the plumbers' antics, Josephine said, "Miss Dee Dee, what else you need for the night, aside from your makeup and a nighty?"

That turned me around mighty quick.

"What?" I scrambled into the warm kitchen.

"No 'what' about it. You coming home with me, 'cause you ain't staying in a house with no water."

I would have retorted that I'd make do, but I could see by the line between her eyebrows that she'd have none of my can-do attitude.

"Why don't you go on home. When the Meadows

finish, I'll check into the motel near the bypass."

Josephine huffed. "You not wanting my hospitality, Miss Dee Dee? You hoping the judge might come visiting?"

"Of course not. Who said anything about me staying with you?"

"You think I'm going to let you tear around town and neglect my Christian duty to be neighborly? You're staying with me until the Meadows can figure this thing out. By the by," she added, walking up the stairs to finish packing for me, "the judge is at a meeting with that FBI's agent Madison. Something to do with the Miss Clarisse, I reckon." Josephine said Madison's name with respect wrapped around it. He'd earned it by clapping Clarisse in jail and keeping her there.

When Josephine left, she had my suitcase in hand, so I couldn't sneak off by myself.

It was Mammoth-Cave dark when I heard a knock on my back door. Toby and Jason Meadows stood on the stoop, drenched and up to their armpits in gooey mud.

"We've got us a problem, Mrs. Morgan." Jason Meadows spoke as if he was attending a funeral.

"Well, come in out of the rain and tell me about it."

"No, ma'am. You don't want in your house what we've got on our boots. You see, your sewer line done collapsed. Couldn't go more than twenty-five feet with my snake. It's pooling by the foundations of your house." Father looked at son and lifted his shaggy eyebrows into his hairline.

"How could a sewer collapse?"

"Well, ma'am, it's the original line. Back in the 1890's, when this house was built, lines were made out of rolled tar paper and sealed with more tar. For the last hundred-and-twenty years no roots penetrated that barrier." Jason Meadows rocked back on his heels as he explained.

"You mean flimsy paper has been connected to the city line all these years?"

"Well, yes. The weight of the land begins to compress that paper over time. Must have been all the one-eighties Sidney did on the lawn that caused the final demise."

Toby Meadows looked apologetic.

"What about the water line? What is that made out of, a log?"

"No, ma'am." Toby stood on one booted foot as if afraid to deposit more dirt on the cement stoop. "We did some digging and came upon the water lines. It appears that there is more than one of them."

His father gave a curt nod. "Three, actually."

My mouth flew open. "Three!"

"Sometimes they get clogged with sediment, so the owner puts in another one. On a house this old seems that's happened once or twice." Jason Meadows smiled.

"What is the diameter of the pipes?" I felt in a fog and my voice sounded it.

"Two are three-quarters, one a half inch." Jason Meadows looked somber. "I'd recommend replacing the water and sewer lines."

"I'll need an estimate."

"Long way to the street from here. I'm thinking somewhere between seven-to-ten thousand, give or take."

I give, they take. I got the picture. They didn't look all that happy about it, though, which was a comfort. If you're going to fork over money the recipients ought to look sorrowful.

"We're mighty sorry about your inconvenience, Mrs. Morgan. Especially at this time, you being a widow and all."

I believed Jason Meadows would have put his hat in his hands and twisted it round if the rain hadn't changed from steady to deluge.

"I'll be fine, Mr. Meadows. Don't you worry about me. I'm staying with a friend until I can flush the toilets."

They nodded, then were off for a late dinner. I hadn't thought about eating until then. Automatically, I went over to the sink to fill the tea kettle with water. All that came out was a wet air burp. It was a tick past eight and too late for Josephine's mama to have me arrive for dinner. It would throw off her schedule. I drove Harry's old truck to a fast-food burger drive thru and ate in the dark as the rain drizzled down my windows.

Chapter Eleven

Josephine's cottage was orderly. Everything had its place and better be there, or else. With her mama suffering from the Alzheimer's, moving something got her confused. I was spending the night in Savannah's purple and green room. I plopped my purse on the spare bed and carefully put my water glass on the little table between the twin beds.

Above Savannah's bed hung a painting of a maple tree in autumn's riot of color. A stack of her paintings butted up against the outside wall. She was a realist. No orange-red cubes for Savannah, she liked sketching faces and creating shadows on summer porches.

Savannah was giving her grandmama a shower. From the bathroom I heard Savannah singing with Miss Vickie. The girl took the tenor part while Miss Vickie sang soprano about Moses going down to Egypt.

A few verses later Josephine led her mother from the bathroom. "Sometimes it takes two people to help Mama shower. But tonight's a good night. Right, Mama? You let Savannah scrub you from top to bottom and then rub nice lotion on you."

"Feels mighty fine, that cherry-smelling lotion." Miss Vickie sniffed her hands and smiled.

Savannah came into the bedroom wringing wet from the wrestling match in the shower.

"You get a drenching every night?"

She shrugged. "It's to be expected."

I looked up at the girl who'd hopped down the road to our house since she was tiny. "You look like your granddaddy. He had a giant wing span when he played center in high school. Those long arms must be as handy playing volleyball as they are corralling your grandmother."

"I would call playing volleyball simply practice for life with my grandmother. You need quick responses, whether on the court or in the shower." Savannah patted her hair with a towel and rubbed cream into the curls to keep them soft. You couldn't rub her hair dry; rubbing would break off her curls.

"Your mama feeding you enough?" I squinted at her thin arms.

"Oh, law. Not you too. I'm not trying to be skinny. I just don't want hamburgers. I serve them all the time, and the smell of frying burger makes me want pizza. Of course, I don't eat that either."

"I reckon I'm a snoopy godmother."

Savannah laughed. Then her face turned serious as her green-brown eyes squinted. "When you and Mr. Harry got married, did you like it?"

Keep a straight face and talk plain. "Well, to tell you the truth, Savannah, having Mr. Harry kiss me made me all shaky inside. Marriage is about revealing love, sometimes being best friends, other times cherishing one another through the hard things. As for having sex, when you're married to a good man, a tender man, for us it was great."

"You see, I've got some friends that are talking about it." Savannah's face looked troubled.

"Most kids do."

"I mean . . . they think it's silly to wait until you get married to have...you know." Her dark eyes skittered away from my face.

"Sex?"

She nodded and grabbed a fuzzy purple pillow to hug.

Okay, Lord. Here goes. "I'm a follower of Jesus, so that means I try to obey the Scriptures. Some people say our culture has changed and what God said two-thousand years ago isn't relevant. I figure, negotiating with God isn't a smart thing to do. I've tried it a time or two and it never works out."

I could tell I'd lost her. Her hands had a strangle

hold on the corner of her pillow.

She scooched under her bed covers. "Night, Miss Delilah."

"Good night, dear."

I turned out the bedside light and snuggled into a squishy twin bed under a heavy, purple duvet. The rain cascaded down the roof and gurgled through the gutters. *What wasn't Savannah saying?* She hadn't grown up in a family with a mother and father, only Josephine, her grandmother, and her granddaddy, until he passed. Was she afraid to talk to her mother about the things that troubled her?

Morning crept in dreary and cold. Hustling to get to the disaster at my house, I was startled when Josephine's mama sidled into the bedroom. In Miss Vickie's hands was a wicker basket of sewing things.

"What do you think, Miss Dee Dee?" She held up a quilt square for me to admire, and her eyes began to shine.

She knew my name! A grin shot across my lips before I moved to get a closer look at the appliqued wreath of roses. Among the fabrics comprising the wreath I recognized remnants from my summer cotton dresses. I stared at a dusty pink rose bud fashioned from a dress I'd made five years ago. Ever since Harry had died, my cotton summer dresses had become a negotiating point with Josephine. She'd notice a zipper not working properly or a rip in the hem. Josephine was right about the dresses being rags. But they were comfortable, fit perfectly—or had, until I had sat around eating too much while Harry wasted away.

"Very nice, Miss Vickie. Have you been working on it?"

"Me and Josephine been workin' steady, 'cause it's got to get done."

"Josephine!" I hollered in a voice that would raise the dead. "You've got some explainin' to do."

Josephine came running. Her eyes glommed onto the ten-and-a-half by ten-and-a-half cotton square.

"Uh, oh."

"I thought my dresses were ready for the rag bin." I sounded huffy.

Josephine sniffed. "I decided to repurpose them."

She eased the basket and quilt square from her mother's hands, giving me her twinkly eyed look. As if looking sweet would slather over the matter.

"I took them." Miss Vickie fingered a rose-pink flower. "The pinks were perfect. We decided to make you a quilt for your wedding."

"My wedding?"

"Everbody in town is talking about it. Even though I saw you refuse Judge Henderson when he got down on his knee and all. That was a nice party you were giving in your backyard. Molly looked so pretty all dressed up." Miss Vickie scratched her curly gray hair and furrowed her brow. "It wasn't your usual party, now, was it? What with the band and all." Miss Vickie nodded her head, trying to recollect the wedding reception. "Josephine says give you time about Judge Henderson. Mr. Harry wanted it, so's must be right."

Miss Vickie gazed at me for approval. Last night she hadn't recognized me, today, hallelujah, she knew my name even if she was a little muddled.

"Oh, Miss Vickie." I took her hands in mine. "Your quilting is such a sweet thing."

"I'm not the only one. The whole quilting circle at church has passed out the squares and bits of your fabric. Your Baltimore Album quilt is going to be a sight to behold. Nothing but the best for you, Miss Dee Dee. I know what you done for us. Why, the very food on this table comes from your hand."

Harry and I hadn't done anything but share, and Josephine worked hard for her salary.

"So romantic, you and the judge." Miss Vickie careened another direction. "I'm planning on wearing my yellow hat . . . unless you get married at Christmas." Her voice grew thoughtful. "Then I'll need a red one, won't I, girl?" She turned to her daughter.

"That's a good idea. We can plan a Christmas wedding, Miss Dee Dee, so Mama can have a new hat."

From Josephine's tone she wasn't happy that I was postponing saying yes to Lyle or maybe she was teasing. Sometimes with Josephine I couldn't tell.

We watched the weather report as we sipped coffee. The meteorologists predicted the rain would continue. Moist air from the gulf was to blow our way for five more days. Usually all you had to do was check out Kansas, and you'd be close to certain that their weather would be ours in a couple of days.

Savannah hoisted her backpack and dashed out the door at 7:30. Alice Mercer, Miss Vickie's caregiver, blew in at eight, a newspaper tucked under her arm. She put the newspaper in front of Miss Vickie and disappeared into the laundry room, giving us a brief nod as she strode by. There was a scowl on her face, unusual for her cheery countenance.

"Well, looky here," Miss Vickie cried out while I gobbled up the pancakes that Miss Vickie had made for me.

"What is it, Mama?"

"Why that nice Hamilton boy has his picture in the paper. Remember how he used to come to the store to talk with you?"

I sipped my coffee with sloth-like leisure.

"That was a long time ago, Mama." Josephine's voice was taut.

"About the time your daddy ran into trouble with the bank loan."

Josephine put down her mug. "I guess it was. You'll be heading home soon, Miss Dee Dee?"

"Nope." I watched Miss Vickie's attendant take off her coat and grab a mug for coffee. "Tell me about Stephen Hamilton, Miss Vickie. I don't recall him being around much."

"He was in college back then. One summer he come back to help his daddy on the farm. That was when he'd come around." She nodded her head emphatically. "Yep. Mighty handsome man was that Hamilton boy. Took after his daddy in his looks. Whatever happened to that nice boy?"

Alice Mercer shot a look at Miss Vickie that would have flattened a dirigible. My eyes scanned from Josephine to Alice who had been classmates in high school. Both of their mouths were tightened up like desiccated prunes.

I looked at the headline. The college president, Jeremiah Benson, sent an e-mail to the alumni, and students stating, *Earlier this week Professor Stephen Hamilton was arrested in the office of the Liberal Arts Department. Professor Hamilton will remain on our staff with full pay and benefits until this is cleared up.*

"You know that the Hamilton boy is a professor, girl?"

"Yes, Mama, I know."

I said my goodbyes and headed back into the rain. No use quizzing Josephine about what her mama was saying. My fingers itched from wanting to drag it out of her, though.

Multi-colored little flags dotted my yard and could be seen two blocks away as I drove down Sycamore Avenue. Meadows Plumbing Company was creating a trench from my house to the street. They were not alone. Up to their necks in mud, Lyle and George were digging out my plants and moving them to a big dirt pile by the basketball hoop.

I walked back from garaging Harry's truck and stood beside the ditch in my yard. "Having fun?"

Lyle was soaking wet with water puddling around his feet. He grinned. "Nothing matches a machine you can drive."

I pointed to the large backhoe in my yard. "You been digging with that?"

George's eyes were lit with glee. "Lyle bribed them.

He promised to buy lunch if they'd let him have a turn."

I looked at the gulch and noticed a little squiggle to the right in what should have been a straight line. "Hum. What did you promise, George?"

He laughed. "Not to arrest them in the foreseeable future. By the way, the garden club sent out an e-mail about your yard renovation. They were a little rude about it, so Mamie shot one back. She said she'd gotten a peek at your plans and that you're putting in a moat to keep out the riff raff."

"From the size of the canal, Mamie's not far off. I'd envisioned a small divot, maybe four-foot-deep, a couple of feet wide, not the Grand Canyon. How big is the pipe they have to put in?"

Lyle held up his arms making a circle.

"Why the archeological excavation, then?"

"Exploratory holes. They don't want to tangle with the water or the underground electric lines." Lyle lifted his eyebrows as he spoke.

"Well, ask them when I can get the water turned back on."

"A few days, Di."

I scrunched up my nose with displeasure.

The excavator's earthworks went through my shade border. My garden plants perched uncomfortably in the dirt mound. The azaleas were askew and straggly, the way plants look when autumn breezes strip them bare.

"Thank you for rescuing the plants."

"My pleasure." A smile spread to Lyle's eyes. "Now, off to the trenches before the enemy takes the high ground." He put his shovel over his shoulder and marched toward the end of the channel.

In the backyard my bourbon roses drooped on their stems as if depleted of energy. Yellow and pink petals scattered across the bark and curled on the drowned grass.

At one o'clock the owner of The Coop, Carter

MacDougal himself, delivered lunch in his beat- up '95 pickup. He took one look at the motley assortment of men in my yard and shook his head.

"Don't think I'd recommend this particular crew," he said, eyeing Lyle. "Looks like a bunch of amateurs to me, Miss Delilah. Iffen I was you, I'd fork out a little extra cash and get some professionals."

When Carter finished pouring hot coffee and making snide remarks, he squelched back to his truck, whistling with satisfaction. Undoubtedly, MacDougal had collected the lowdown on the canal digging operation. The info would be slathered all over town by 1:30. Presently it was a quarter after the hour.

As the sun shifted toward two, the men went back to slopping through the lawn, Josephine polished Harry's desk, and I sorted paperwork—a job I found satisfying because I could put papers in tidy files or in the round bin by my desk. The peace was interrupted by Josephine's phone ringing. She answered with a crisp, "Hello?" Josephine doesn't chat on phones.

"What you say?" Her alto voice rose to a high soprano.

Her anxiety got my attention. I glanced at the desk clock. 2:48.

"You call the police?"

Her question rocketed me from my chair.

Josephine waited for an answer before saying, "Okay, good. I'll go there *now*."

She threw her phone into her pocket then broke into a sprint. I dashed after her.

"What's the matter?"

"Miz Perkins at the corner of the old road and War Admiral Lane says Savannah got into a car with some girl. She's called the police."

I grabbed my purse from the kitchen counter. After school Savannah helped with Miss Vickie before she headed to her job at a burger joint.

We ran out the back door toward the cars. "Miz Perkins said Savannah opened the door and tried to get out. A big man came from the front seat and shoved her back in. Then they took off real fast."

I grabbed her arm. "You're not driving. George will take you to the sheriff."

In case Josephine decided to take off anyway, I grabbed the car keys from her hand. Raising my arms above my head and waving as if demented, I jumped over the little squirrel statue by the rhododendron and bolted to Lyle.

"Lyle! Savannah's been kidnapped!"

Lyle took a millisecond to grasp my statement. He grabbed my arm and signaled George, then we ran back to Josephine.

"George!" Lyle yelled above the din of the diesel motor. "Get Josephine to the sheriff's office, pronto. We'll meet you there."

I dialed the phone as he talked.

"Mamie? I need you to go to Josephine's. Stay with her mama. I'll explain later." Mamie Salas didn't ask any questions, which was a relief, because I didn't have any answers. As we ran across the street to Lyle's car, Josephine and George peeled out of his driveway and sped toward the center of town.

Lyle eyes squinted as we climbed into his car. "I wanted to speak with you privately, without Josephine. Thought George could handle her while I ask a few questions. Are there any boyfriends in her life?"

"No."

"Then we don't need to think about an elopement."

Slow-motion children from the elementary school trooped across the street. We got to the police station in a long seven minutes. I opened the car door before Lyle put the car in park.

Bellows stood in the entry of the gray-stone police building. "Find a dark-blue or black sedan with a Kentucky license." He patted Josephine's hand, as he spoke to his staff. Spying Lyle, the lines around the sheriff's eyes diminished.

"We've also sent an Amber alert. Josephine, do you have a current picture of Savannah? I'll need to get it to the networks and on the Internet."

She didn't. I produced one from my bulging wallet, then wrapped a supportive arm about Josephine. Josephine trembled so hard I could barely keep her upright. George scooped her up in his arms and carried her to a wooden seat beside the front desk.

Bellows swiveled our direction. "My office. Y'all congregate there."

His office was the first door after the entrance. We wandered in, dazed. The room consisted of tidy bookshelves and a wall of windows, with the only vibrant color a painting above Bellows' metal and wood desk. Four chairs lined up along one wall. George guided Josephine to one. She nearly collapsed on the seat. I put my hand on top of hers, then sat beside her. Josephine's fingers were icy.

"Whoever grabbed Savannah must have been desperate. The snatch happened in broad daylight." Bellows spoke so loudly I jumped. He rubbed the back of his neck. "Stupid move. Small towns have snoopy neighbors. We'll soon have a cell phone picture and license plate number."

Josephine and I had bolted out of the house without coats. With a pool of water growing under her feet, Josephine shivered. "Josephine's cold," I said.

"I'll go find something," George said. Bellows left with him.

Lyle kneeled in front of me and took Josephine's hands in his and began to pray. And not some old, mealy-mouthed "Help me, Lord" prayer, either because he began in a loud voice that must have penetrated the door. "Lord, You are good. You love Savannah more than we can ever know. You know what is happening. You know where she is. In the Name of

Your Son, protect our girl. Surround her with Your hedge of protection. Let no one move a hair on her head. You thwart the evil doers that have kidnapped this child of Yours. May these evil people fall into their own traps. The traps they have dug for others. Praise You Lord for Your care. Minister to Josephine's heart. Give her strength. By Your name we ask that You direct our steps and right now reveal Your love to Savannah."

When he finished he rose, still holding Josephine's hand.

George opened the door, armed with two blankets. He wrapped them around both of us with a look that said, "Sit." I parked in a chair beside Josephine, who'd collapsed into herself.

"How similar is this to the others?" Bellows asked one of his detectives.

Lyle raised his head and sauntered into the hall, closing the door behind him.

George studied our sorry selves. "Well now, ladies. I think dry clothes are in order. I'll give Mamie a call." He sidled out into the hall.

While the door was briefly opened, I heard Lyle exclaim, "Three girls from around here?"

"They didn't . . ." Whatever the sheriff was saying was cut off when George slammed the door. Clutching my blanket, I rose and stumbled to within an inch of the door. Couldn't hear a peep. Josephine remained hunched as if she'd been struck in the solar plexus. I walked back to her and put my arms around her shoulders.

"You know what they do to fatherless girls like my Savannah?" Her voice was a whisper.

"Yes." I would not play games with a mother's deepest fear.

Josephine buried her head in my chest and

sobbed, a racking bark of a sob, all low and chopped up. I stared at the clock above Bellows' desk: 3:45 stared back at me. They could have disappeared in Lexington by now.

"That lamb's all I've got, Miss Dee Dee." Josephine's body convulsed with her pain.

"No, dear. You have me and your mama. You have the judge, George, Reverend Daniel, and the whole congregation."

My words didn't help the ache in her heart. Her child was missing. You can't toss out words to comfort that kind of pain.

Chapter Twelve

IT HIT ME THAT HARRY WOULD say exactly the right thing, then Josephine would smile through her weeping. Missing Harry brought me to tears. We sobbed together, making a wet mess of the blankets. They were not very absorbent, being fleece.

The door opened. George took one look at us and sucked in a breath. "You'd better handle it, Lyle."

I put my head on top of Josephine's bowed one and closed my eyes. Next thing I knew, Lyle was squatting before me. He was out of his sloppy, yellow rain jacket, but his face was still muddy.

He placed his big hand on Josephine's. "We've some news." His words made Josephine sit up and straighten her shoulders. "The sedan was spotted near Nicholasville. A credible witness was in the opposite lane and stopped at a light when she saw the car pull into the Feed and Seed store's parking area."

The sheriff walked into his office, his jaw stiff with tension. "Our witness observed the driver and a man in the back seat getting out of the car. Then a blonde girl climbed out of the right side. The two men bent into the car and pulled out a second girl." Bellows scratched his upper lip, seeming to hesitate. "Our witness thought the second girl looked unconscious. Turning around, our witness, a doctor, headed back toward the feed store. She went into the store to see if they were shopping. No one had seen them. The doctor saw the Amber Alert on her phone and immediately called the police. Nicholasville police have the car and are dusting for fingerprints."

"How long ago?" My voice was old-woman quivery.

"They have a twenty-minute head start. We don't yet know what they're driving. The local L.E.O.S. are checking the store's surveillance videos. That will tell us what was in the parking lot when the sedan arrived. They might have switched cars with one they parked earlier. We may even get the faces of the people in the car."

Loud voices and a lot of feet raised a ruckus in the police lobby. Sticking her head in the door, Deputy McEntire waved at Bellows. "Boss, we've got the press and the mayor demanding answers to the Amber Alert." Lyle rose and went into the hallway.

Sheriff Bellows ran his fingers through his thick black hair. "You sit tight, Josephine. I'll face the lions." He stepped out of his office into a firestorm. Shouts of "Sheriff!" echoed before the door closed.

In a few minutes Lyle returned, walking in backwards to fill the doorway with his body, and protect us from the throng. Lyle pointed to the door in the side wall. "That door leads to the alley between the police building and a bike repair shop." Lyle studied Josephine's defeated posture. "Seems the best way. Ladies, before this becomes a three-ringed circus, I invite you to my home. We'll have Josephine's mama join us there. Reverend Daniel's heading to George's. As soon as Savannah is identified, the press will be camped out on Josephine's lawn, Di. Maybe we can confuse them."

Disasters, big and minuscule, thrust the press into a person's face as if they were a plaintiff getting grilled instead of a victim of some outrage. Lyle wanting to protect Josephine from the onslaught brought a smile to my lips for the first time since the awful phone call had sent us scrambling.

The judge made a run to get his car and drive it down the alley. George dashed off to get his. Josephine and I slunk out the back door, glancing left then right. We ran to Lyle's car as icy rain stung our faces. Josephine didn't speak the whole way to Lyle's house. For her to go mute wasn't good. Josephine processed by talking.

The judge's tidy, two-story Georgian stood directly

across the street from my fluffy, three-story Victorian. His home was a little boring but could accommodate a crowd. He parked in the back by the garage, and we hot-footed it to the kitchen door through a new spasm of rain. No one saw us from the street.

Lupita was scrubbing a single potato when we entered the judge's white-and-stainless-steel kitchen. The kitchen normally shone like mercury-glass Christmas balls, nary a crumb in sight. In the somber gray sky and mood, the kitchen appeared tarnished. Lupita looked first at the judge, then at each of us, her eyebrows nearly meeting. Not a word escaped her lips, but I could see her putting two and two together and coming up without four.

Bartles loped into the room and jumped onto his master's legs.

"Hey, fella." Lyle picked up his puppy and held him close.

The front door squeaked. The voices of George and the reverend carried into the far reaches of the house, then their footsteps thudded our way until the men entered the kitchen.

"Didn't think standing on ceremony was important. We didn't knock." George plopped down on a center-island stool and propped his elbow on top of the granite.

Face taut with stress, Reverend Daniel went to Josephine. He didn't speak, just rested a hand lightly on her shoulder. Lifting her tear-stained face toward him, Josephine let out a tiny sob. A child's sob, full of despair.

The sound was all Daniel needed to enfold her in his arms.

Lyle placed the puppy onto the floor. His hand reached for mine. I took it and squeezed ever so gently. In the suffocating pain of Savannah's disappearance, the tenderness in front of me was overwhelming.

Lyle eased me into the dining room. Lupita and George followed.

"I don't know what to do for her." My voice was clogged with unshed tears.

"None of us do." George shook his head. "We're charting a new course."

"What's going on, if you don't mind my asking?" Lupita looked from Lyle to me, to George, then back to her boss.

"Savannah has been kidnapped. We're forting up here. We'll keep the ladies in my home until further notice." Lyle's tone proclaimed no arguments allowed.

My lips made a grim line. The kind you see in pictures of Scrooge.

"We will have a full house, Lupita. Josephine will be here with her mama. I believe you know that Miss Vickie has a few problems."

"Josephine told me."

"I'll make a list of things we'll need until Miss Delilah's water is back on." Lyle's eyes looked past me to the walnut sideboard holding a vase of mums and greenery.

I opened my mouth to protest but shut it when George nodded agreement. An argument wouldn't help the situation.

Lupita nodded her head. "The Spice Girls were supposed to go out to lunch tomorrow to see what we could do to help with Miss Vickie."

"What?" George's voice rose in confusion.

Lupita shrugged. "Oh. Our nickname, courtesy of Charlene Higgenbottom. Miss Delilah, Josephine, the judge's secretary Janice, and I eat lunch together twice a month. We're friends. I'll call my husband and tell him I'll be late." She hurried into the judge's office to talk in private.

Lyle parked himself at his dining table to scribble a list. Lupita wasn't gone more than two minutes before she walked back. "I'll put Josephine and her mama in Beau's old bedroom while you, Delilah, can sleep in the first-floor bedroom." She smiled at her solution to the bedroom shuffle.

Well, at least we'd have a floor between us, which would be a relief.

"Steaks," Lupita said as she looked at the list. "I'll plan for seven people. That includes Pastor Daniel, you two, Mr. Salas and your wife. That way Miss Mamie doesn't have to fix a meal with all this business going on."

Lupita untied her black apron and grabbed her coat, the judge's list, and her purse before walking into the rain.

When the news hit at five o'clock my cell phone went into hyper mode. I'd already called my kids, but everyone who had my number began to ring me. By six I turned off my ringer and then headlights shone through the windows. Lupita parked her Accord in the alley behind the judge's house as Mamie drove in. Mamie and Miss Vickie got out of their car. Miss Vickie took two steps then stood stock still in the judge's drive and waggled her head back and forth. Lupita scurried past them, her arms full of bags of groceries.

Mamie attempted to take Miss Vickie by the arm, but the older woman evaded her grasp. "Come on, Miss Vickie. Let's get out of the rain."

Miss Vickie flapped her hands and rubbed them down the front of her coat. She didn't move.

"Oh, Mama." Josephine's voice dropped to a whisper. Josephine moved cautiously down the steps, waiting to see what mood her mama was in. I followed with an umbrella.

"Let's get you out of the rain, honey." Josephine took her mother's arm as I put the judge's big black umbrella over their heads. "We're having a party at the judge's tonight."

Miss Vickie's eyes lit up. She made a step toward the back door then stopped, looked at me and smiled.

We walked up the stairs arm in arm. Seeing the judge coming out the door to trundle the luggage in, she went over and kissed Lyle's cheek. "You having a party for me?" she asked, wide-eyed.

"Yes, ma'am. An un-birthday party."

"Suits me." Miss Vickie stepped into the house and took off her bright red raincoat. Suddenly she turned to Josephine. "Where is that little girl that helps me with my hair?"

None of us had words to answer.

Chapter Thirteen

No news came during the night. My mind roamed in dark places, imagining my grandchildren disappearing, and remembering my little boys, so fragile at six months gestation that they went to be with Jesus. Together. Savannah was alone.

I didn't undress when I closed the bedroom door, I fell to my knees and prayed. Then I read the songs of David. Psalms weren't always a comfort, but David recognized the evil in the old world. Snatching Savannah was an evil thing. I tried not to think about what could be happening to her, but images invaded my mind. Heading to the kitchen to make a cup of tea, I heard voices in Lyle's study. I paused outside the open door. Bartles lay curled up on a chair, his tiny chest moving rhythmically, while Lyle and Pastor Daniel stood with arms about one another.

"This is your lamb, Lord. This little one. Yours to care for, Yours to shepherd. Put Your arms around her. Bring her home." Pastor Daniel's words challenged the Lord. "Use us, Lord, however, You will. We are in your hands, as is this sweet child."

I tiptoed away and searched through the cupboards for tea bags. While the pot heated, I wondered about the two men in the study. Lyle, I knew a little about. Pastor Daniel, however, was a mysterious man. The pastor didn't talk much about his past. "You can see the pain of suffering in his eyes, little girl," Harry said after meeting him. Harry had admired him for being a man who "shouldered his load."

Breakfast was a dismal affair. We gulped coffee, nibbled on toast, and listened as the diesel machines in my yard concussed the air. Lyle made phone calls while I hid in his living room eyeing the throng of press that had grown like mushrooms in spring. Their congregating gave me an idea.

I needed to scamper home. Lifting an umbrella from its holder by the front door I spied Madison of the FBI and Sheriff Bellows marching up the walk. It was déjà vu. They stood awkwardly side by side, exactly like they had in July when they had accused the judge of bumping off his wife, Clarisse.

The law men's eyes were straight ahead, jaw lines tight. I prepared my heart for bad news.

After an awkward greeting we gathered in Lyle's living room. Josephine sat on Lyle's sleek leather couch while the law dripped rain water on the marble in front of the fireplace.

Madison was the first to speak. "Some fingerprints in the sedan match ones we found on Savannah's Bible. No other fingerprints. Video shows them leaving in a white van, Tennessee license. We found it abandoned off Interstate 75 near Corbin. Have a good head shot of the driver. We've an APB out, otherwise, nothing new." Madison's voice was devoid of emotion.

Savannah could be anywhere. Girls disappeared every day. Did notices in rest areas do any good, or would we just keep busy jabbing at the wind?

"I had a little chat with President Benson before I wandered your way." Bellows didn't smile. "He's getting a lot of pressure to reconsider his support of Hamilton. Hamilton's family, though, recently gave millions to the English Department for a new building. Going to be difficult for the college."

Lyle tilted his head and rose from his seat. "Is there anything in Hamilton's past that might influence Benson?"

Josephine made a dive for the Kleenex on the side table.

"A felony was expunged from his record. Seems the former sheriff made a deal with the family."

Bellows shrugged. "Hamilton paid a fine and got off with public service. Cleaning trash along the 127 for a few hours."

"What was the charge?" Lyle's eyes resembled a calculator, adding up one thing and another until he got the right answer.

"When he was seventeen, he hit a bicyclist and took off. Most likely alcohol involved but couldn't be proven because we didn't find Hamilton until the next day."

I cleared my throat. "This has been a dry county until recently."

"Twenty-minute drive and you could fill up your car with beer in those days. Kids did it all the time. Heck, Bourbon County still *is* dry, while Christian County is wet."

That wasn't news. Every drinker in a dry town headed for the next county to stock their larder. The mention of Hamilton made my thoughts zig over to straightening up a few things. "I'd like to get Harry's papers back from your office to sort and file." I crossed my arms for emphasis because I was still miffed that all Harry's boxes had been carted away.

"They're evidence, Miss Delilah. And Hamilton is going to use them in his defense." Sheriff Bellows mouth was tight like saying the words was odious to him.

"What?" My one word exploded out of my mouth like a cannon ball.

"He says they're poems Harry wanted published under a nom de plume." Bellows looked at his hands holding his wet police hat. He was blushing.

"What the sheriff is saying, Miss Delilah," Madison stumbled in, "is they are a bit different than Harry's usual poems so, uhm, we need to keep them out of circulation for a while."

Lyle strode over to them. "What are you saying?"

"Erotica. Plain and simple." Madison spit out the words like arrows. "Didn't think Harry knew the word."

I thumped down beside Josephine. "Are they in Harry's writing?" My voice squeaked like Mickey Mouse.

Bellows looked at me then skittered his gaze to Lyle. "We'll need an expert to determine that."

Lyle's eyes were hard. "I'll recommend one to the prosecutor."

Bellows nodded his head. "The D.A. will appreciate your help. Not often a small-town prosecutor gets a case that's become national news."

"What I mean is"—I sputtered like a leaky hose I was so flustered—"Harry didn't write things about sex. He said it was a private matter, between a man, his wife, and God."

"I can't say who wrote the poems." Bellows wouldn't give me eye contact. "Hamilton claims they were Harry's poems and has issued a press release accordingly."

"Untangling truth from lies is difficult, Delilah," Meemaw once claimed. "That's why if you always tell the truth you can remember what you said." That was before the Internet, where lies get spread like manure over all heck and gone.

"What does a man have after all is said and done but his reputation?" I asked. "This lie could ruin Harry."

"We know, Miss Delilah. We're treading carefully." Bellows used the voice he reserved for frightened children.

If Harry had written poems about our love life what would the children think? Would Lyle get scared off because I liked to surprise Harry? Did Harry write about sneaking off to the car so we wouldn't disturb the kids? I shook my head. Harry would never have written erotica, would he?

The room was too quiet. Everyone gazed anywhere but at me, even Lyle, whose back was toward me. I lifted my chin. The crisis at the moment was Savannah, not Hamilton's tangled mess of a life.

After Bellows and company left, I grabbed an umbrella and walked down the alley behind Lyle's house and onto the familiar cracked sidewalks leading to the cemetery. I wanted to have a chat with Harry.

Poking into Harry's grave were psychedelic plastic butterflies bouncing impolitely on the end of wire poles. Wind and rain washed my umbrella with tree leaves.

"Oh, Harry!" I stood and cried for a bit until it got tiresome. "You'd fix this mess in a slick minute. I don't know how to help Josephine. Same lost look in her eyes as when she told us she was pregnant. And Savannah. That little sweetheart always had us tied up in a pretty knot." The wind sighed with me.

"I need to get a bench so I can sit and commiserate." I leaned against Harry's tree, the one guarding the Morgan's graves, and let the constant drip of rain merge with my breathing. "You know about Hamilton, Harry. But I can't protect your reputation from lies. You always said, "Truth takes time. It's easier for people to believe lies!'"

"Like the ones they believed about My son," came from the still small voice I recognized.

"Yes, Lord, they did, and still do."

Pushing away from the towering maple, I started to direct my steps home, then turned back. "Oh, Harry. The sewer line broke and belched sewage into the basement. They dug up your rhododendrons! The ones you planted to surprise me when I came home from losing the twins." I smiled at the headstone beside Harry's grave. "I remember their faces, Harry and how the boys fit in the palm of your hand." I closed my eyes and envisioned two Harry replicas playing catch with Harry. They were tow-haired like Harry's baby pictures and had his bright shining eyes as they ran through thigh high grass, their child's laughter bubbling up until it spilled over into my heart. Imagining Harry romping with our boys in heaven's grasslands gave me comfort. Walking back, my steps slow against the driving wind, I didn't feel the cold on my hands as peace warmed me.

It took me ten additional minutes tromping along side streets, to avoid the assault by the press. Reaching the street behind my house, I cut through Sophie Brixton's tidy backyard, ending up at the gate Sidney had installed in my fence. Once secluded I made phone calls. First to the kids who'd threatened to descend upon us. I told them they couldn't be spared from their parenting, school work, or putting food on the table.

I dialed numbers from my church directory.

Ten calls.

The last one was to organizer extraordinaire, Mamie. Afraid of her saying no, I took a deep breath. "Would you be willing to serve coffee to the press loitering in front of our houses?"

"Why?"

"Two things, really. To let them know we're a friendly little town concerned for their welfare, and to keep Miss Vickie busy." I tapped a pencil eraser on the counter.

"This will be interesting."

"We're charging for the coffee. The breakfast fund at the school needs some cash. It will help with buying eggs and juice."

"I didn't know that was a problem."

"Been one for a long time." My lips tightened at the thought of hungry kids.

"I'll get a coffee can and put a note on it. Seems appropriate."

"I've coffee and big coffee urns." As I hung up, I wondered if Lyle would approve of my maneuvers. And then, why had I thought of him instead of Harry?

Within five minutes, Mamie bustled into my kitchen with Olive Lorraine at her heels. I grabbed a corner of the center-island for support. I wasn't used to Olive Lorraine Patrick trying to be a friend. I'd have to watch which way the wind blew. Never pays to let your enemy take up residence in your home until you're certain she has changed her ways.

Olive Lorraine was pale, the kind of sickly pale you get if you never see daylight. Her eyes looked into mine instead of glancing around at my house and counting my *objects d'arte*. Olive Lorraine was also thinner. Having her husband in the slammer couldn't be easy. *I wonder if she's sleeping much at night?*

"Delilah, I need to tell you something." Mamie ran a finger over my black granite counter as she spoke. The tone in her voice told me what was coming might not be palatable. "Charlene and Lydia came over yesterday linked arm-in-arm and saying they were still best of friends. They said Stephen Hamilton had nothing to do with what went on in Harry's office and his arrest was your fault. That you were spying on Stephen as he was helping a student with a paper. They accused me of betraying them by becoming friends with you."

Olive jumped in. "Stephen Hamilton has had a bad reputation since he was fifteen, Mamie. As for Delilah's catching him in the act of seduction, the man had his shirt off and, the girl was half-naked, according to a little bird in the police department."

Mamie's mouth flew open. Small towns tend to relay info faster than the Internet. "What should I say to Charlene and Lydia?"

"Ignore them." Olive Lorraine lifted her chin much as a pugilist set for a bout. "That's what I'm doing. I'm learning that true repentance isn't just not doing something, it's changing the way I think." Olive avoided my eyes, but her voice remained steady. "The way I've thought about Delilah was sin, Mamie. Don't let them poison your mind with their lies."

You could have knocked me down with a puff of wind I was so shocked at Olive's defense.

Mamie eyes had a glimmer of determination, as if she'd decided something. She turned to me. "Tell Olive about the school kids."

I tapped a fingernail in the counter. "Some children come to school hungry. A group has been supplying the schools with extra cash to feed them breakfast before class. The plan is to get the press to donate to the cause."

Olive Lorraine gave a sad sort of smile. "I'd like having something worthwhile to do, especially if it involves kids."

The wistfulness in Olive Lorraine's voice surprised me. I'd never questioned whether she was childless by choice. Maybe Charlene and company weren't the only ones making assumptions in this town.

The clanging of machinery in the front changed in volume as I entered the library. Glancing out the turret window I observed Meadows the elder, Toby's grandfather, finessing the metal scoop toward the front sidewalk. The press oozed nearer to the Salas' yard, distancing themselves from the digging crew. With luck, Meadows would be able to finish the sewer line by evening and turn on the water so I could move home. The happy thought of being home by nightfall lingered until I saw a city vehicle pull into my drive.

A trench-coated woman with a scowl imprinted across her face, marched up to the Meadows patriarch and held up her hand. He put the backhoe on idle, climbed down, and bent his head to look at the paper she waggled at him. He said something. She jerked her head forward like a mad goose. He grabbed a clipboard from her flaying hands. She started yelling.

The press snapped pictures. Old Mr. Meadows—he was at least eighty and maybe nearer eighty-five— marched over to the reporters and waved the clipboard in their faces. I think he shouted, because I noticed his animated gesticulating. The city official snuck up behind him and tried to snatch her clipboard. He whipped around so fast you'd have thought he was on a tilt-a-whirl.

The patriarch of the clan held the clipboard out of her reach, while the rain turned the clipped papers into mush. Meadows thrust the clipboard at reporter Jim Bouchard and turned back to face his adversary.

More yelling attracted the camera crew from Lexington. I ignored the fuss and finished one page of editing before the doorbell rang. The beveled glass in the front door panel gave Mr. Meadows three heads.

I opened the heavy front door. "Come in." I smiled at him.

He was elbowed aside by the clipboard woman, shedding mud as she stormed into my foyer.With slow-motion deliberation Mr. Meadows removed his boots before entering.

"Thank you. How very considerate of you to remove your muddy boots." I acknowledged his thoughtfulness before the red-faced woman could open her mouth.

She looked at me with hard, brown eyes, then spit out, "The city will not allow you to damage the sidewalk with your sewer repairs. I have it in writing and signed by the mayor."

"Oh." The mayor's involvement did not surprise me. A Harry-ism zinged into my brain. "Shall we let the manure pool over the walk to the streets, then?"

Her jaw dropped open.

"Good suggestion." Mr. Meadows' drawl was smooth as silk. "We'll grade your landscape to make it easier to let it flow to the street. I think I can get that special nozzle over at the hardware store, you know the one I mean? Sort of jet propels the matter so it can reach the runoff drain."

"You can't do that! It's a violation." The woman stamped a foot on my yellow pine floors in front of the library doors. Mud splattered onto my walls.

"Of what?" I fixed my stare at the mud easing down the wallpaper. "Seems to me my next-door neighbor, the mayor's sister, connected to the sewer line last spring. Do I have the proper permits?" Mr. Meadows nodded yes. "Do you think there's a lawsuit in the offing, Mr. Meadows?"

"Most likely. I'd check with Judge Henderson. He'll give you the up-and-up."

"Do you have anything else to say, Miss . . . what is your name?"

The woman's navy trench-coat had covered up her identification tag—if she had one.

"You haven't heard the last of this," she threatened, shaking her fist in Mr. Meadows's face.

"I think it is time for you to leave." My unfriendly words made her back away.

She stomped out of the doorway, leaving a trail of gunky droppings behind her. Ms. Trench Coat tried to slam the door, but it proved too heavy to allow her the finale she wanted.

I had to hang onto my sides I laughed so hard. What a relief to laugh when life was catawampus.

Mr. Meadows grabbed at the wall to steady himself. "Must admit, Missus, that was some performance you gave."

"I liked the visual of a jet-propelled gun aiming the remains of the day into the drain."

We shook hands.

He walked out in his argyle socks, humming.

Chapter Fourteen

Sitting at my desk, I frowned. Nobody wanted me to interfere. Lyle's eyes said, *I'll take care of things,* and Bellows' glower was like a warning shot across my determination.

Idleness was a bore. The fifth chapter of my new book was undeniably pedantic and escaping to the attic to quilt was not on my clipboard. I paged back and stared morosely at the beginning chapter's opening sentences. "In 1935, Addis Ababa was a ghetto, not unlike the dock areas of London. Twisting pathways wandering among the narrow houses, competed with muddy ruts and sewage."

A knock on my front door provided a welcome interruption. The prisms revealed Lyle.

I opened the door. "Hey."

"Miss Vickie has rustled up lunch at the Salases. I'm ordered to bring you back or she is going to give me a piece of her mind."

"That would prove interesting."

"She's keeping up well today. However, no one has told her about Savannah."

I studied the profile of my escort. Something about the set of Lyle's jaw gave me comfort. "Any news from the FBI?"

"No. Madison hasn't called."

I slipped into my raincoat. "I meant the team that came to your cabin. I'm using the word 'cabin' loosely because it's a mansion."

"I have been informed there was a significant amount of blood on the carpet in the downstairs bedroom."

I shuddered. "Do you think someone was killed there?"

"Perhaps." He sounded sad. I couldn't imagine

living in a house where there had been a murder.

"At least six sets of fingerprints were found that didn't match mine."

We stepped onto the verandah and surveyed the yard. It was a muddy mess. "Cam's and Molly's?"

"Apparently not. Conrad's and Bessie's were found. They and Cissy would be the only people with access."

My mind was in overdrive. "That leads to a few questions."

Lyle opened the Salases screen door.

"How often is it cleaned? Who would use your cabin without permission? Why? When and how did they find out about its remote location?" We tabled our conversation as we walked inside so Miss Vickie wouldn't overhear.

We were finishing up our tuna sandwiches when Bellows tromped in. Mamie kept Miss Vickie clearing dishes so they both remained in the kitchen out of earshot. Looking at Josephine, the sheriff's mouth formed a soft smile. "The whole town is up in arms about this, Miss Hudson. You don't steal children from McKeansville, Kentucky and get away with it."

I looked Bellows in the eye. "There have been others, I believe."

Bellows nodded. "From the three counties touching ours. One near Bracken Grove, another off east toward the freeway, and last year a girl from Gravel Switch. We've had the FBI in on all the girls disappearing. Found one with her boyfriend in Tennessee getting a marriage license. The other two haven't been heard from."

Lyle put his palms on the table and leaned forward. "What do the girls have in common?"

"All high school juniors or seniors, and they were thin and attractive. The two we haven't found were involved in church youth groups. Savannah was as well." I bobbed my head in agreement. "None of them had boyfriends or dated much."

"Were they targeting virgins?" Josephine's voice was moist.

"That would be my guess."

A cell phone rang, and I heard Mamie say, "Hello."

Lyle pushed himself away from the table. "I believe someone Savannah knew was in the car. She wouldn't climb in with a stranger."

Bellows rubbed his dark hands together. "We think it was a new girl at the school. The girl hasn't returned to classes and her number has been disconnected."

We walked the sheriff toward the front door. He retrieved his rain-soaked hat from the entry table then left.

Mamie joined us at the door. "Louella phoned from the church. A meeting has been organized." Mamie looked pleased at the prospect. "We need to get there by five thirty."

I took a quick breath and waded in, trying not to offend. "Since all of you are new to our congregation, I'd better explain a few things. Feelings run deep when it comes to our children. There might be some emotions y'all are unfamiliar with."

"I can imagine." George pursed his lips. From his sour expression, George would rather let an alligator nibble his arm than head for a meeting with shouting.

Miss Vickie shuffled in as we reentered the dining room. Her feet no longer stepped forth with authority but slid across the floors as if afraid not to have contact with something solid. She patted her hands dry on one of Mamie's floral aprons.

"That's some kitchen back there." She pointed behind her. "I made the counter so shiny you could put on your makeup." She eased down into a dining chair and put her elbows on the table. "Almost as shiny as your daddy's counter at the shop. He'd polish it ever' night so it was clean and fresh."

"Since Josephine worked for me, then how did she get time to work at the butcher shop?"

"Friday night and Saturday Josephine would help out her daddy. Had to during high school too, after her brother went off to the army." Miss Vickie reached for her empty glass. "More sweet tea, Josephine, would be a fine thing." With a full glass of tea swirling with ice, Miss Vickie smiled, sipped, then half-closed her eyes. "On Saturday's that Hamilton boy would come, all slicked up with his big smile. Just like in the picture."

Josephine's face was expressionless, like a civil war picture where you have to pose and not move even an eyelash.

"Got himself a first-rate education, I'll bet. He seemed a smart one, that boy." Miss Vickie drank from her glass as Lyle settled into a seat beside her. "Didn't the newspaper say he's here at the college? Well, don't that beat all. Coming back home to be a professor."

Something told me that Hamilton's shenanigans weren't new.

About five, we skirted the press by tromping through backyards and crossing a street near the elementary school to get back to the judge's. As soon as we entered, Miss Vickie commenced to looking in cupboards to find Savannah. "Why, I do believe that little girl is playing hide and seek." *Dementia isn't for the timid.*

Josephine and her mama didn't come to the church. When George asked Reverend Daniel if anyone had questioned the kids from school, things got testy. I reckoned Lois Cox was going to hit him with her big white purse when she swung it his direction, but her sister-in-law grabbed the handle and made Lois sit down to cool off.

Reverend Daniel licked his lips. "Good suggestion, George. Kids notice things. I believe the FBI has been asking questions at the school. George, we're compiling a list of kids that knew Savannah. Have Madison set up a time to speak with them and see if someone from church can be included. Make certain, though, that their parents or grandparents are there.

That way, there'll be no trouble."

Reverend Daniel handed a piece of paper to the church secretary. She thrust it toward the front pew, asking if anyone could add student's names.

Our preacher cleared his throat. "Have each of you sent out the picture of Savannah and the alert on your mobile phones?" Heads all around us nodded. "Good. I want you to do one thing more. Start calling your out-of-state family members and tell them as well. I've a feeling Savannah might be heading south."

There was an audible groan. The fear of Savannah disappearing forever made me tremble like a lost puppy. I gripped my knees with my hands to stop them from shaking.

Mamie knitted her eyebrows together, bewildered.

My mouth was dry as I whispered, "It's an expression from slavery days, Mamie. The people sold south, simply disappeared."

Mamie's eyes teared.

Reverend Daniel cleared his throat. "Josephine and her mama need us right now. I expect you to do your Christian duty to see to their needs. And no mac n' cheese. Josephine said she's still dreaming of it after Mr. Harry's funeral." That brought a chuckle.

The reverend hesitated before continuing. "I have an announcement to make. As of this minute I'm taking a sabbatical. There's a little one lost to us. As the shepherd of this flock it is my duty to go in search of her."

"Amen, brother," throbbed a deep bass voice. It was echoed in the room.

George fidgeted.

"Would the elders of the church plan Sunday's service, the prayer meeting, Sunday schools, and whatever else Mrs. Abbott can suggest?"

Mamie leaned toward me. "Can he do that?"

I nodded. It was the right thing. But how was he going to get more information than the authorities?

"I've contacted churches from here to Tallahassee

and west to Abilene. They are having someone check out truck stops. We all know what happens at rest areas and truck stops, don't we, now?"

I raised my hand. Lyle wrapped his hand around mine and put it back in my lap. He nodded to the reverend.

"What happens at truck stops?" I mouthed to Lyle.

"Trafficking."

I jerked back so hard in the pew that it sounded like the thump of a coffin lid. I'd only imagined someone playing a trick or at the worst, raping Savannah then letting her go. But, grooming her to be a hooker? I couldn't even think about that for more than a millisecond.

Lyle picked up my shaking right hand and held it in his two big ones. He felt for my pulse. I could see him counting the beats. He didn't look happy.

I can handle it, I wanted to say, but I wasn't sure I could. I didn't know anything about trafficking, or prostitution for that matter. I must have had my head in a sand dune. Everyone else in the congregation murmured and exchanged uneasy glances as if they knew exactly what the reverend was talking about.

I was thankful Josephine wasn't there to see and hear all of this.

George rose to his feet. "Where are you going to start, Reverend?"

Reverend Daniel looked first at the floor, then into George's curious eyes. "In the beginning, I'm going to fast and pray. I'd ask those of you who feel led by the Spirit to do the same. Then, and only then, will I move. I've sent a message to my old military buddies too. I want it to be so hot for whoever took our girl that hell is going to look like a temperate zone."

"Amen!" shouted a woman behind me.

Omer Reading, the attendant at the country club, nodded toward the reverend. "What we need here is a marching song, so we's ready to get up and fight. Fight for our kids that are being swept up by the drugs, and sex, and things of this world."

And the music came. A low, reverent murmur merged into, "The Battle Hymn of the Republic." The words swelled to the rafters, throbbed in our hearts, and lifted our spirits. Because, we had seen His glory. Over and over we had seen Him work. I lifted my hands and let my voice join the chorus.

We left the building encouraged and hopeful.

George took Mamie's hand and said, "We'll meet you at home. Meeting with Madison and Bellows may become a long night."

Lyle handed me his car keys, then headed toward George's car. Mamie and I moved down the cracked sidewalk toward the BMW. Reporters with cameras lounged on the little lawn that fringed our parking lot. I was preparing to run the gauntlet of microphones when Reverend Daniel walked up, stiff as a guard at the Unknown Soldiers' Tomb in Arlington, and stood in front of us, and with the elders, formed a human corridor for us to dash to Lyle's car.

As Mamie and I stepped into Lyle's house Josephine tackled us. "Well, this mess done drug you out of the church meeting mighty early. Those things can wander along for hours." She was a grayish color, the same color she'd turned when the judge's ex-wife had plugged a hole in her in Paducah. I rushed into her arms. She gave a big sniff. Eventually Josephine stood back. "I suppose you want a report on my mama? I'll share over a cup of decaf coffee."

"Good. I've missed your sass since you've turned mute. Mamie here," I jerked my thumb her direction, "needs to get acquainted with it, because you are going to be temporary neighbors."

As I spoke Miss Vickie strolled down the stairs in her fuzzy Christmas slippers. Even with dementia she still looked like a formidable hospital matron not taking any nonsense from staff or patients. "Where's my yellow hat? The one I wore to Mr. Cam's and Miss Molly's wedding? I feel a need for a hat."

Shaking her head, Josephine sighed. "Nice and safe in the hat box in your closet, Mama."

I looked around. The only hat in sight was the judge's running cap. "I could make this fit your head until we find your yellow hat."

"Jest the thing."

Miss Vickie made a beeline for the hat tree by the front door and plopped the blue U.K. hat on her curly gray hair. We oohed and awed, because she was statuesque, and looked magnificent in her floral house dress with baseball cap. She made for the stairs, humming a happy melody.

Chapter Fifteen

By 10:00 THAT EVENING, THERE WAS still no sign of Lyle or George. Josephine wandered into the kitchen and sat down on a stool housed under the center island. "What are you serving for breakfast?"

"Josephine, it's late. I'm not deciding on breakfast until tomorrow morning."

She raised her eyebrows.

"Go to bed, Josephine."

Josephine slid off the stool and huffed her way to the dining room. She closed the door with a bang, reminding me of my kids when they were thirteen and having a snit fit.

About midnight I began pacing in my small bedroom. "Why pray when you can fret," Meemaw said more than once. Putting my fears on hold, I got down to the business of praying, starting with praise, because running right to God with my demand list was more than cheeky.

"Holy God, Your righteousness overwhelms me." I dropped to my knees beside a blue chair, waiting. He often spoke to me in the silence. After only a few minutes I heard pebbles hitting the bedroom window. Not God's usual way of communicating.

Lyle and George stood with arms wrapped around one another's shoulders like two tipsy sailors pausing in the midst of their bender. I pursed my lips tight. Lifting his head skyward, Lyle burst into song. Not any old one either, but a jazzy version of "Blue Moon." George attempted harmony, but he wasn't a tenor, so ended up singing the melody along with Lyle. Lights turned on in the houses down the block. In a couple of minutes, the pug dog next door began to howl. Bartles scurried under the bed skirt.

No one had serenaded me before, especially when

inebriated. I threw on my bathrobe and dashed for Lyle's kitchen door barefooted.

"Ah, George." Lyle pointed to my feet when he spied me. "She's got pink toenail polish on. Come on, darlin'." He stepped onto the veranda and wrapped his arms around me. "Say goodnight to George and point your tired friend toward his bedroom."

"Have you two been drinkin'?"

George grinned. "Nary a drop. Our minds are befuddled by the law. Just spent hours, untangling jurisdiction with Bellows, Lyle, and Madison pointing fingers at one another and lifting the roof off the police headquarters with their yelling. Cut us some slack, Delilah. We're a couple of sorry men that need succor." He looked hopefully in the direction of his house.

Lyle waved his hand above his head to say goodnight. He shut the back door and stood in front of me. He would have attempted a kiss if Josephine hadn't appeared. She shook her head and stepped right up to Lyle.

"Nothing yet, dear lady." He clasped her hand, his brow furrowed as deep as a spring field. "Savannah's friends parted with her as she turned the corner of the Wilderness Trace road. They said Savannah wasn't acting any different than usual."

Josephine's eyes were so sad I started to cry. Lyle reached into his pocket and produced one of his initialed handkerchiefs.

"To bed, ladies. Tomorrow comes in a few hours. We're having a conference call at ten to rethink our approach. A few of George's old friends volunteered to help. Sleep while you can." He looked sternly at Josephine. "Hop to it, Josephine. You're no good to us brain dead."

I arrived in the dining room at 8:45, showered, but still groggy. On Lyle's dining table was a Tropicana rose in a bud vase. I dropped into a cushioned chair and stared at a leaf-green placemat.

"Ah," Lyle said, emerging from the kitchen. "Thought I heard someone. Breakfast will be with you in a moment."

I closed my eyes until the aroma of coffee tickled my nose. When I opened one eye, a mug of coffee, orange juice, and a plate of eggs benedict was before me.

"Oh, Lyle, you've mastered sauces."

He cleared his throat. "Not exactly. I've a friend who helped. I merely arranged the food."

"And thought of me." I pointed to the rose. He must have gone into the garden early to clip the flower. I took a tiny breath, shaken by the thought of his kindness. In the midst of my preoccupation and sadness he created beauty.

He bent to kiss the top of my head.

"I'm required at the kitchen sink." Without another word he left the room.

From the hollandaise perfection slathering my one egg, I knew Carter MacDougal of The Chicken Coop had invaded Lyle's kitchen. It was the amount of lemon that made Carter's sauce special.

Lupita arrived as I brought my plate to the sink. She studied the judge washing the egg poacher and sniffed.

"Five minutes late and I'm out of a job. I suppose you're going to start the laundry next?" Lupita hustled the dry cleaning toward the stairs.

"Can't live without you," Lyle crooned, winking at Lupita. She smiled, shook her head, but kept moving, not even removing her coat in her haste.

Lyle's phone rang. He dried his soapy hands and plucked his phone off the counter. "Hello?" He listened for a moment, then grabbed my hand. "I'm putting this on speaker so Miss Delilah can hear too."

"I'm asking for some advice," said my new son-in-law, Cam.

"Shoot." Lyle kept the speaker on as we walked toward his office.

"I'm finding myself in a difficult situation. Molly has to quit her job for health reasons."

"What?" Lyle winked at me as we arrived in his office.

I shook my head. Molly hadn't said anything about being sick.

"I'm calling to ask you if I should take out a loan? Get a part-time job? Join the military so we can pay for my schooling?" Cam sounded worried.

"Have you gotten Molly's advice?" Lyle plastered a grin on his face. Which was odd.

"She's a little occupied at the moment."

"Stomach problems, Cam?"

I leaned toward Lyle's desk to let it support me.

"You could say that."

"Son, are you calling to congratulate us for becoming grandparents?"

"Yes, Dad. I am. It is totally out of the blue. We didn't expect. I mean, it's nuts, Dad. We haven't been married six weeks."

"Hallelujah!" Lyle hit the top of his desk with the palm of his hand. "Finally, something good. We'll sell the fatted calf to help if we must. And, as to the little dividend, not surprising considering what you two have been up to."

"Dad! After the doctor told us we wouldn't have children, this is a surprise."

I shook my head with wonder. "Doctors have been known to be wrong. Harry always said it is called the practice of medicine for a reason. Physicians are still working on it."

Lyle's lips slashed into a smile. "My suggestion is, we have a family powwow and decide what to do with the trust fund your grandparents set up for you boys."

After he'd hung up, Lyle danced a little jig step around his desk, grabbed me about the waist, and cut a rug repeating, "We're going to be grandparents!"

three times.

Molly and Cam's baby would be my sixth grandchild, Lyle's first. With his face lit up like he was on fire, he resembled Harry's goofy expression when we'd first become grandparents.

I smiled, then thought of all Harry was missing.

He spun me about until I was breathless. "This is great news."

"Molly's sick. Maybe she needs me?" I said in my worried voice.

"She needs her new husband, Di." Lyle was right. Leave and cleave. But I wanted to help. My mind stuttered to a halt. Right now, my radar needed to be aimed on Savannah and helping Josephine carry on. I took a deep breath, hugged Lyle, and went to change my clothes.

The conference call found George sitting at Lyle's shiny, mid-century desk, looking like the CEO of a big corporation, lined paper in front of him and colored pens in a mint julep holder.

Lyle lounged by the fireplace, his feet on an ottoman, a legal sized notebook in one hand and a pencil in the other. I hunkered down on the love seat opposite the fireplace. The phone rang.

George picked it up. "Hello." I could hear breathing through the speaker Lyle had placed on his desk.

"Hello, George. Good to hear your voice. Been a while."

George cleared his throat. "How are they transported? Seems everyone at church knew about truck stops but where is the hub?" George didn't waste any time but doodled a line of question marks across his paper as if lost in thought.

"Used to be Toledo, Ohio." A woman's voice came out of the speaker. "But trafficking has become more coastal, borders, major cities. Places where kids can be lost in the jungle."

Savannah wasn't lost. God knew where she was. He just needed to let us know. So, I asked Him while Lyle sat writing notes and George questioned his colleagues.

Josephine materialized at 10:30 with a pitcher of my kind of sweet tea, half sweet. Her eyes were black pin dots under a brow of divots. I'd never seen her complexion purplish, but it was. I jumped up and gave her my seat, then served ice tea while she collapsed into the settee.

I leaned over her. "Your mama okay?"

"Sidney's playing dominoes with her in the kitchen. You know how she loves dominoes."

Sidney would let Miss Vickie win, in spite of his competition with Josephine.

Josephine grabbed my arm. "I'm so worried my brain is stumbling around. What is happening to her is all I can think about." Josephine sunk her head onto my shoulder. I patted her back.

The conference call took an hour and a half. Lots of questions from agents, FBI, CIA, and one person, a special agent no less, from Naval Intelligence. We still didn't know which agency George had worked for.

This was Lupita's day to do the laundry. We planned to meet at 'The Chicken Coop' in appreciation to Carter for his breakfast magic. We shoehorned into Lyle's BMW, with Miss Vickie in the front seat patting Lyle's knee and chatting as if she was going to a Sunday School picnic. Come to think on it, the outing probably was an event for her. Lyle drove the opposite way from town to fool the gaggle of reporters who were in front of his house.

I glanced to my left as we aimed toward the bypass and saw Candace Abernathy sitting on her porch with a satisfied smile. Should have known Mayor Higgenbottom's sister would be keeping an eye on things. Candace had been a pain in the backside since we moved in twenty-three years ago. Rain, sleet, or tornado warnings hadn't kept her from peering our way and setting the town's ears on fire with our doin's. Harry's witty revenge had been a characterization of her, a snoopy chicken sitting on the hen house porch swing, pumping and gossiping while spying through binoculars at the activity in the hen house next door. It had been composed in iambic pentameter. Harry wanted an old world feel to the poem, as if the neighborhood gossip was an eternal problem.

I chewed on the edge of my lips, then caught Lyle gazing at me in the rearview mirror.

"Expect the news that we're leaving to be flashed about town." His words were so quiet you could hear a bug's lethal splat on the window. "Maybe Candace will report we're heading toward Harrodsburg. By the time we circle back, the gaggle of reporters flocking onto my lawn will have headed there."

When we got to The Coop, Lyle parked in the alley behind the restaurant. "No reason to let the beauty parlor ladies get on their cell phones." Lyle's mouth was turned down with disgust as he nodded toward Maylene Frogmeijer's establishment across the street. I followed Lyle and Josephine's mama through the back door, ready for the eyes of the community to swivel our direction.

Head waitress, BethAnn Tate, spied us entering and slid open a door to the meeting room. A place where we could conspire in private.

George dashed in, all motion, hands waving like pennants in a stiff wind. "Mamie will be here shortly." He ground a chair across the tiles to sit beside Lyle. He and Lyle got right to it, Lyle with his legal pad, George with his expertise in spying. They were plotting something that generals might use in a military campaign from the way they talked and scratched arrows and question marks on a list.

Miss Vickie unrolled cutlery from her red paper napkin and played with the knife. *Tink, thump,* went the knife, first on the table, then on her water glass, then back to the table. She peeled down the end of the paper on the straw, real careful, so she could blow it. I reached out too late, as she shot the wrapper past Lyle's ear.

Miss Vickie studied the lunch offerings. "I cain't have lunch before breakfast," she protested to BethAnn. "It ain't right. Be like having dessert before dinner."

"Carter has finished with the breakfast service, ma'am," BethAnn protested.

"I'll see to it, Miss Vickie." I rose and marched across the black and white tiles like a soldier heading to combat. I aimed for Carter MacDougal's inner sanctum, a place I'd never been allowed entry because the chef/owner kept an eagle eye out for intruders.

I pushed open the door to a space twice as big as my kitchen, with three grills, two ovens, ditto for the microwaves and three fryers, on account of this being the South. Carter's kitchen was so clean you could see your reflection in the stainless steel. As soon as Carter felt the draft on his nearly bald head, he spun around, his cleaver raised.

I jerked my hands up in a surrender posture. "I come in peace!"

"You come to steal my sauce recipes, Miss Delilah," he accused with a chuckle.

I shook my head.

Breaking into a grin, Carter bowed from the waist, almost frying his bum on the burner behind him.

"Miss Vickie is a little turned around this afternoon, Carter. She thinks it is early morning and wants breakfast. Moving her to the judge's has been a little confusing."

"If Miss Vickie wants breakfast, Miss Vickie gets breakfast. I'll write the order myself. Hey, Shorty!" Carter shouted to his assistant. "Take over the grill and get Polly to man the fryer. I've business in the front."

Shorty Ferguson hopped over to the grill. And I

mean hopped. The man had lost his left leg in Iraq. His prothesis was so springy, Shorty could pounce like a snake spotting dinner.

Harry had opined that the Presbyterians won the softball tournaments because Shorty played third base. Shorty could hit and run so fast that the catcher didn't get the ball out of his glove before Shorty made it to first. Until Shorty had returned from rehab, the Baptists and our church had won the league championship.

Carter thrust the swinging kitchen door open with such force that it slammed into the gray wall stopper and shivered against the wall. The man was always in a hurry, had been since he'd opened the place when he'd returned from his stint in the Navy.

"Any news about Savannah?" he whispered when we were out of earshot of the customers crowding the counter.

I shook my head.

"Pity." His jaw balled with tension.

Carter sauntered into the room like a boxer into the ring, shoulders forward, his eyes narrowed—ready for anything.

"Miss Vickie." His politeness was at odds with his stance. He bent over her, resting a hand on the table so he could look in her face. "What would you like for your meal?" Carter's mama had taught him good manners. He never talked down to a soul, whatever their hue, or if they were ragged and could only afford a cup of coffee.

"I always say your grits make my mouth water." Miss Vickie patted his hand like she would comfort a post op patient. "Cain't go wrong with a heap of grits on this fine a morning."

"Anything else?"

"Why of course, Carter. I'll take two fried eggs over easy and a piece of your wheat toast. You got any of your mama's raspberry jam? Her jam was the State Fair winner back in '68."

"I'll see that you get some, ma'am. Coffee also, Miss Vickie? I believe you enjoy it black."

"If a man remembers what you put in your mouth, he's a keeper, Josephine, and don't you forget it." Miss Vickie batted her long eyelashes.

Carter backed out right fast, and our meals arrived soon after.

When Lyle finished, he put his napkin carefully on the table. "We're heading out to do more interviews. I'll be home about six for dinner, Delilah." His voice was decisive.

"Okay." The one word was a little curt, because I was irked about taking orders. After all, I was not his secretary.

"Might try a little sugar, Mr. Judge," Miss Vickie shouted. "I's can see Miss Dee Dee, here, is needing a little more than an announcement of your intentions. Iffen you's want to get her to the altar, you's got to apply more sugar."

"Right." The judge bobbed his head. "Miss Delilah, my apologies for not getting your opinion about my afternoon schedule. After you finish lunch would you accompany me to the car so we can clear the air?"

"You don't have to tell me your schedule. I simply don't care for taking orders." All I wanted was for him to communicate. It didn't have to be a memo in triplicate.

"I've noticed." His voice was apologetic.

We cleared the air in the alley with a laugh and my blessing for him to continue his questioning. He glanced to see if any eyeballs were directed our way, then pursed his lips with disgust.

I turned slowly around to see Earl Inman strolling into the alley.

"Earl." The judge greeted the reprobate shop owner with a cold voice.

"Well, if it ain't just my luck to see Mrs. Morgan." Earl licked his thick lips, then moved to my side quicker than a cat hunting a vole. "I heard about your car accident from Joey at T&J's auto. I've a loaner vehicle if you've a need." He took a step closer, hovering by my left elbow. "No cost to you, of course, since you're a close friend and all."

"That's more than kind." Lyle held up his hand. "Mrs. Morgan has the use of *my* car." He spoke too loud for politeness. "I'll give you a call if we run into a conflict." Stepping in front of me he shook Inman's hand so firmly Inman bounced up and down a little.

"Allow me to escort you to my car." Lyle waited until Inman headed back the way he'd come.

"I feel I've got my personal protection agent when you're around." I smiled up at him.

"Good! Let's see how the debt adds up over forty years or so."

Our luncheon party straggled out of the restaurant as we laughed.

Lyle dropped us off at Mamie's house, then headed out to do more sleuthing. With work to do at home, I pushed through the gate between our houses so I could get to my back door, then jumped when a voice behind me said, "Hide and seek. This sure is fun."

Miss Vickie had outflanked Josephine and followed me home. I sighed and took her arm so she wouldn't trip on the flagstones. The last thing we needed was Miss Vickie sneaking out of the house to hold court with the press. She didn't know about Savannah and if they asked questions, it might twist Miss Vickie around so tight she'd be spinning like a top.

"This is fun, Merna," she shouted toward me. "But we have to be quiet or Mr. Lawrence will find us sure. Quick!" She grabbed my hand. "Let's head for the basement. You still got the oranges we swiped?"

I nodded, held onto her hand, and guided her straight to the downstairs bedroom. "A little rest before the sun gets hotter might be a good idea." If she had to visit the bathroom we'd be in trouble. Water was a long way in the future.

Chapter Sixteen

THE DAY TURNED WARM. BY MID-AFTERNOON, a rested Miss Vickie ambled over to the side yard where my vegetable garden still was intact. While harvesting broccoli for dinner, I smiled at her as the cell phone on my hip buzzed. Juggling the phone, a broccoli head, and tomatoes had me agitated.

"Hello!" I shouted into the phone when I finally got it to my lips.

"Well, hello to you too." Lyle sounded cautious. "You mad at me?"

"No. I'm picking green worms off the broccoli heads while fighting the phone holster. I'm sorry I was brusque."

I handed my tomatoes to Miss Vickie and started toward the house.

"You're forgiven." Lyle voice was tender.

His forgiving cheesed me off a little, because I had a good excuse for being testy. Forgiveness had nothing to do with it. It wasn't as if I'd asked to be forgiven. I swallowed hard and realigned my thinking.

"Thank you." I was embarrassed at my pique.

"I need to talk to you about what we've found, Di. Savannah had been asking about her father. Nobody could tell her who he was."

"She asked me too, while Harry was getting feeble."

With Josephine as closed-mouthed on the subject as a rusted pickle-jar lid, we were unlikely to find out who he was. Could he be involved in her disappearance? Maybe trying to make up for lost time? Getting the name of Savannah's father out of Josephine would take an adept interrogator. Should we anoint George as chief detective?

Lyle was still talking. "I'll be going home to pack a

bag."

He disconnected as quick as a thumb on the end button. I frowned. With my mental gymnastics, I'd missed what he'd said. I had a feeling he wasn't going to Paris. In my head I packed a suitcase too. I'd pack light. Harry had liked my suitcase to have empty places.

Miss Vickie settled on my verandah, a glass of sweet tea in her hand, but her eyes stared off into the vivid-blue-skies. To keep an eye on her mama, Josephine wacked the verandah bannister with a dust rag so hard the thumps could be heard inside the house, her soul was far away, however. You could tell by the shadow in her eyes. I half-listened to Miss Vickie's conversation about making proper Kentucky Burgoo wondering about where Lyle was taking me in our search for answers.

"And so, when you put the carrots in is most important." Miss Vickie lifted her gaze as Lyle drove his car past the kids selling lemonade and the reporters chatting on his lawn. My neighbor inched his car into his driveway before disappearing around the back of the house.

Miss Vickie scrunched up her eyes. "That man didn't listen to a word I said. Miss Dee Dee, you rest yourself. I've a mind to tell him exactly what he needs to do to make you say yes." With this pronouncement Miss Vickie bounced out of her seat and headed across my front yard.

I started to go after her. Josephine blocked my way with her body. "Leave her be, Miss Dee Dee. Ain't every day she connects things, and Mr. Judge can handle my mama."

Miss Vickie marched across the street with her head high and her feet stomping. She could have caught up with the judge before he parked his car in the garage if she hadn't stopped to sample the lemonade and nibble on a sandwich.

I held my breath. If Miss Vickie took a mind to it,

she would regale the cameras with the story of Sadie Cummins who'd chopped her husband into little bits and buried him in her marigold beds. That was in the 40s and had been on Miss Vickie's mind of late.

Lights blazed from Lyle's upstairs window. It couldn't have been more than five minutes before I saw Miss Vickie leaning on the judge's doorbell. Now I mean, her finger was practically attached to it. I winced. It just wasn't done. He got to the door so fast, he must have catapulted down the stairs.

Josephine's mama wagged her finger in Lyle's face. He cocked his head to listen. He nodded a couple of times, then turned to wave at me before glancing to my left-side neighbor. Candace Abernathy sat in her porch chair, taking it all in. He saluted her and offered Miss Vickie his arm. They entered his home and he closed the door upon the google-eyed press and neighbors.

In a few minutes Lyle and Miss Vickie reappeared. His right arm steadied the old woman striding beside him, his left carried a bag. Miss Vickie walked across the street as if she hadn't a care in the world. She stopped to exclaim over the mud mess in the yard, then she vectored toward Meadows' plastic fencing. Lyle looked puzzled. I wasn't going to rescue him. Miss Vickie was a part of our lives and we all had to adjust moment by moment. Eventually the pair made it to the verandah, encumbered with three juicy tomatoes Miss Vickie gleaned from a planter by the side yard. Miss Vickie grinned so broad her gums were showing.

Lyle's forehead was rumpled up as if he was worried. He dropped a shabby duffle bag onto the porch. From the scars and deposits of dirt on the outside, his boys must have used the bag as a football. I handed him a tall glass of ice tea. He raised it, then downed half before speaking.

"I have been informed," he said in a courtroom voice, "that a fiancée expects her intended to frequent her doorstep, not pull into his drive across the street and merely wave."

"S'pect so, Mr. Judge." Josephine nodded agreement.

"I have also been informed, that to ignore said fiancée, is a catastrophe in the making." He looked into my eyes with a glint of humor.

"You got that right, son." Miss Vickie unburdened her vegetables into Josephine's hands and plopped down into the wicker love seat.

Lyle glanced longingly at my front door. "I've a need to speak with you, Di. Will you accompany me to the library?" We got as far as closing the front door before he put his hands on my shoulders and turned me toward him. "I do not mean to offend you, dear." The sparkle in his eyes told me that he took Miss Vickie's advice with a grain of salt.

"I wondered what I needed to pack and am a little anxious because you seem in a hurry."

Lyle hesitated as if restructuring his words. "Let me explain. Sheriff Bellows gave us the names of the other girls who have vanished from the area. George doesn't believe in coincidence. Neither do I. George has his bloodhounds on the scent via electronics. I've chosen to approach this a different way."

Then I could too. All I needed was the sheriff to cooperate. "I need the names of the families so I can speak with them. Perhaps there was a common friend among the girls. Then we leave, right?"

"Don't go haring off on me, Di. I've more to tell. Reverend Daniel has gotten an answer to his prayers. Not an answer I think wise, and George is adamantly opposed to the good reverend's harebrained idea. However." Lyle held up a finger when I opened my mouth to speak. "I will be accompanying the reverend on a little journey. Without you, dear." His lips tightened. He didn't look pleased.

"Where?" I stammered.

"We're heading south in Samuel Peabody's semi. At a suggestion from Bellows we're heading toward Atlanta to visit Daniel's mother. He said he'd speak to

Madison, so the Feds keep their noses out of Daniel's 'home' visit. The reverend believes Savannah was taken to Atlanta and is set on searching for her in truck stops. Not a safe venture for a man of the cloth."

Safe? Reverend Daniel at least had some street savvy, being from the inner city. Lyle had zilch. What was he thinking? Was he going to give a lawyerly oration to thugs, hoping to mesmerize them with his eloquence? I must have looked skeptical because he burst out laughing.

"I can box, Di."

I crossed my arms tight. "That will certainly stop bullets."

"Ah, my beloved friend. Trust your almost fiancé."

Surprised, I blinked at his acknowledgment of our growing relationship.

He kissed me on the top of my head, a nice brotherly kiss.

"Nope, no siree. That was the lamest excuse for a kiss I've ever . . ."

He interrupted my rant by a long, slow, go to bed now, kiss. I couldn't breathe. "I, er ... uhm."

"Say you'll miss me, Di."

"Miss you?" I sounded pitiful, as if stranded on a sinking ship with the only lifeboat leaving.

"I'll call."

"Call?" I echoed. "You'd better do more than call, mister."

He drew me into his arms. "I need to go, Di. She's my girl too." I nodded against his chest.

"Is Daniel going to talk to Josephine about what he's doing?"

"I don't think so. She's too fragile. Letting him get close was an aberration prompted by grief. He'll find Savannah if it kills him. I'm going to see it doesn't."

I nodded and clutched the handkerchief tighter. "You take care of yourself, Judge."

"Mrs. Morgan." Lyle tilted my chin up and looked me in the eyes. "Keep a light in the window."

He strode to the verandah while I stood rooted to the yellow pine planks in the foyer. The veranda shadows surrounded Lyle as he bent low to speak to Josephine. He held her hand, then straightened and walked down the sidewalk without looking back. A shaft of light struck his graying hair.

Night came as slowly as getting maple syrup out of a cold jar. Bluish shadows appeared on the lawn and in the empty spaces where Harry's raised vegetable beds had been. Reporters headed for their cars. Street lights flickered on with geriatric leisure, casting jaundiced oblongs onto the sidewalk. I turned on Harry's prized lighthouse, the one with the twelve-day battery, and carried it across the street to the judge's house. The window with the candle would be at his house, since no movement had occurred in the hole-digging department. If he'd meant a real candle, I'd have to search through the Christmas decorations.

Thinking the word Christmas made me teary. Christmas without Harry was a non-starter. He had been my best gift since the day we'd met. Without a doubt, Harry had the Christmas spirit slathered on like a child overdoing French perfume. It wasn't just for us, mind. It was for the whole town. Nobody knew that Harry was the town's secret Santa, making certain the Salvation Army had enough gifts for the kids on its list and food aplenty.

Don't some people escape the Christmas madness by going on a cruise or sitting on a beach with an umbrella drink? I should think about that some. This was the year for my kids to be with the in-laws, it being an uneven year.

The first night Lyle was gone I wandered through the downstairs, admiring his handmade furniture. Touching the smooth beveled edge of a cherry sofa table I set to wondering how to get the sheriff to hand over the names of the people who'd lost their daughters. Josephine needed some answers. People tend to clam up when it comes to law enforcement, but moms sobbing over lost children loosened lips.

By eleven I had gotten info on the Internet and formulated a plan. While in the bathroom scrubbing my face, I heard my cell phone ring. Toweling off the soap I mumbled, "Hello," into the minute mouthpiece.

"Thought you might still be awake," Lyle rumbled through the ether. The sound of his voice made me smile, despite the sharp taste of soap on my lips.

"I tucked the ladies in about an hour ago. Where are you?"

"Near Chattanooga in a rest area. The good pastor asked questions that earned some hostility. I sat him down and gave him the what-for. The truckers thought he was soliciting, rather than searching. His questions were ambiguous, but their response was a surprise. Seems there is an organization that trains truckers how to spot traffickers. The drivers thought your minister was up to no good." Lyle laughed.

I didn't think it was funny. What they were up to was dangerous. If the kidnappers caught wind of their search, who knew what they might do. "Where will you be tomorrow?"

"Atlanta."

"Are you going to swing back to your farm?" Would a visit to his sister's land him in the midst of continued marital conflict?

"Might. What is the prognosis of your garden dig?"

I began to chuckle. "Well … it's like this. Mr. Meadows has to use his equipment on another project. Tonight, he and his grandson are going to slip the pipe into place and early tomorrow morning cover up the trench before they move the machine. By the time the-powers-that-be show up, they will be near the Knobs Region way out at a farm."

"You'd better keep your head down. I've an old combat helmet in my office. I'll let you borrow it for the verbal barrage."

"I'll need earplugs, instead, for the limited vocabulary I'm likely to hear." I waited for him to speak, but he was silent. "Josephine says it's odd not having you in the house."

"Does she now?"

"Her mama misses you too."

"Ah."

"So . . . er . . . I'm letting your dog stay in my room. It's a little lonely here."

"I see. Anything else I need to know?"

"Everything's under control."

"I imagine so." His reply was dry. "Goodnight, Di." He hung up before I could tell him about the list I'd compiled of missing girls.

The abrupt end to our conversation left me stewing. *Does he think I don't miss him? Did he hang up because I didn't mention that the house was empty without his presence? I didn't even wish him goodnight!*

The bedside clock had a green illuminated dial that flickered like a hot ember. I finally tucked it into the drawer of the bed side table at 2 a.m., so I wouldn't keep staring at it and counting the minutes.

It was still dark when I heard Josephine rumbling around in the kitchen. I put my head under the pillow and managed another hour or so before she intruded and plopped a cup of coffee by the bedside lamp.

"Time you get up and give some advice. You're good with telling people what to do, so I'm sitting here listening." She sunk onto the taupe and cream duvet, just missing my feet with her rear end.

I lifted my head out from under the pillow. "Umm." Opening one eye I gazed at her slumped shoulders. Inching upright, I fumbled around until my fingers connected with the mug.

I managed, "Thanks," before a large slurp. "We've plans for the morning. Your mama and Miss Mamie will be busy with the coffee service, so I thought we'd go for a drive."

No response. Josephine's fingers twisted around each other as if she were playing with fringe.

"I've acquired the phone numbers of the other parents whose daughters vanished." I'd spent a while checking out the old newspaper articles on my computer until I had a list of missing girls and their parents' names. The phone numbers had popped up through the online snooping programs. "We can visit and ask questions. They might lead us somewhere."

"They're not going to lead us anywhere because they are still missing." She was about to cry.

I lifted my chin and glared her direction. "I'm not coaxing you, Josephine. You can sit here all day, watching Lupita dust, head to my house and dust yourself, or come. It's up to you."

After pouring a third cup of the judge's special coffee and getting myself dressed, I dialed the phone and connected to a woman named Weldon. She agreed to talk to us. We headed for the Weldon farm, twenty miles east and a county road north. The land was off by itself, with a creek running at the bottom of its lowest pasture. The corn fields surrounding the place were harvested, their stalks laying like dead soldiers on muddy ground. It drizzled, but from the west a patch of blue was rolling our direction.

"You gonna do the talking, right?" Josephine's voice was as tense as a guy wire.

"Most of it." I slowed her car over a deep pot hole.

"I've got nothing to say." Josephine crossed her arms in her, don't-you-push-me-none pose.

"I thought the Weldons might say a sentence or two."

"Huh!"

I pulled up in front of a stumpy barn with peeling red paint. A man slammed out of the back door of the farm house and strode our way. He toted a shotgun.

I opened the car door and instructed Josephine. "You stay put." Stepping onto the soggy drive I heard the car locks click. Josephine received my squinty-eyed scowl, then I turned to the gun-carrying male.

"Hey." My greeting to the scowling man didn't change his expression.

"Don't need no reporters. You two skedaddle out of here." He eased the gun toward me but pointed it low.

"I'm not in the news business. Your wife invited me to come talk. I'm a friend of the girl who disappeared in McKeansville."

"Well, now." He puffed out his chest reminding me of one of Harry's Road Island Reds. "I wouldn't mind talking to a pretty lady like you. We can do it out here. My wife's feeling poorly."

I eyed the dangerous position of his finger on the trigger. "Fine by me. I'll have my friend stay in the car, if you don't mind. She's a little nervous with your gun aimed our direction."

His belly began to move a little, then a laugh rumbled up from deep inside. He put the gun over his shoulder and grinned at me.

I put my hands on my hips. "I grew up in hard-scrabble farm country. No man intimidates me with his guns or macho attitude."

Mr. Weldon pushed back his Carhartt cap but didn't speak.

The drizzle diminished to a mist. My hair transformed into a rat's nest. I wrinkled my nose with disgust at my hair forming corkscrews.

Before Mister Weldon could move a step toward me, I heard from inside the house, "Now, you bring those ladies in here, Jim, or I'll be coming out to fetch them."

Jim Weldon shuffled his right foot, then jerked his head toward the back door. "I guess Evalina has improved." He drew up a chunk of stuff from his throat and aimed the spittle toward the barn. "Come in and set." He put his left thumb through his overall straps but kept his right hand firmly on his gun.

Josephine stared at me through the windshield. I waved at her to join me. She moved her head left then right and didn't unlock the car. I shrugged at her and marched into the house with the gun wielding vigilante behind me. We entered a clean, white kitchen. The imitation brick linoleum floors were cushiony, the glasses in the pass-through to the dining area, sparkly.

Evaline Weldon studied me as I walked toward her. I thrust out my hand. She shook it firmly. There were callouses on her fingers and permanent wrinkles in her brow. From the look of her youthful hands, Mrs. Weldon couldn't be more than forty-five, but she looked sixty. Sun, wind, and farm life aged a woman. So did sorrow. Looking into her soft blue eyes I could feel her grief.

"Thank you for allowing me to come." I fiddled with my hands, twisting them around and around. "My friend is a little skittish about guns. Don't think I'll coax her out of the car. It is her daughter Savannah that was taken this week from McKeansville."

"Jim, go hang up your Winchester. I'll see if she will come in. I've hot coffee and an apple crisp crying to be eaten."

My hostess was gone in a flurry of pale legs, floral apron, and determination. Evalina Weldon's husband grunted, then secured his rifle on the rack hung along a kitchen wall.

Feeling his dutiful protection should be complimented, I said, "My daddy has a Winchester about the same vintage. Your wife must appreciate your vigilance. I know my mama does."

He grunted one more time before searching for a coffee mug. As Weldon poured himself a drink, his wife opened the kitchen door. Her left arm was around Josephine's shoulders. They both had tears coursing down their cheeks.

"Didn't want this all to be raked up again," mumbled Jim Weldon. The farmer's face contorted with emotions he wouldn't release. The couple exchanged a look of anguish that nearly ripped a piece from my heart.

Evelina put her hand on her husband's arm. "Jim, we've got hurt that only Jesus can bear."

While we talked, Jim Weldon sat at their worn kitchen table, his head lowered in grief, his eyes occasionally seeking those of his wife, giving what strength he could in the overwhelming tragedy of their daughter's disappearance.

Evalina swallowed hard. "She was on her way home from her youth group. It was a Wednesday night in late October." I had to lean in close because Evalina's voice kept trailing off. "The Dobbins dropped her off at the foot of our drive. It's about a quarter mile from the house."

I nodded.

"It was a wet night. Dark before seven. That was the last she was seen. When she didn't get in the door by nine, I called Meriwether Dobbins. She said Elise had been dropped off at 8:30. Jim called the sheriff. They came right away but couldn't really see much. We searched in the ditches beside the drive, went into the pastures, then called neighbors and the church. Had twenty people scouring the hills and valleys that night. It was as if she'd been swallowed up by the dark."

"The police found tire tracks and made a cast of them," interjected her husband. "Tracks weren't from the Dobbins' car nor mine. Camaro, late model. Freddie Dobbins said car lights had been in their rearview mirror most of the way from the church. They didn't see what make or model. After dropping her off, the Dobbins went on home to put their little ones to bed."

Jim Weldon sat up and lifted his chin. "Elise was on the yearbook staff and worked on stories for the school paper. She wanted to be a writer." There was pride in his voice. He handed me her photo. I studied the picture of Elise Weldon. She is a blue-eyed blonde with dimples and a shy smile. I'd almost put it in past tense and internally shook myself for the thought. *How long would it take for me to think of Savannah as truly gone, never to return?* I still couldn't do it with Harry. And I refused to do it with Josephine's sweet daughter. Was it a coincidence that they both worked on the yearbook staff at their high schools?

"May I have a picture of Elise?"

Jim Weldon handed me a photo of a group of girls in softball jerseys.

"Elise was a pitcher on the school team."

After teary goodbyes we drove back to McKeansville in silence.

"Before lunch I need to stop by your house." I turned the corner onto Wilderness Road. When Josephine opened the front door, I made a beeline for Savannah's room. On her perfectly made bed was the fuzzy pillow she cuddled. I grabbed it and headed to the front door.

"What you doing?"

"When we find Savannah, she will need a lovey."

Josephine dissolved into tears. We stood on the front porch and cried, the same as we had when Josephine announced she was expecting. Out of nowhere a jerk photographer arrived and snapped our picture as we clung together and sobbed.

Chapter Seventeen

Ten minutes after we pulled into Lyle's drive his doorbell rang. Lupita came into the kitchen, her eyes troubled. "A man wants to speak with you, Miss Delilah."

"Who?"

"A friend of the judge's. I think Judge Henderson forgot to tell you he was to stay overnight." This might be difficult if Miss Vickie started parading around in her underwear when she felt like it. One never knew what might occur.

A black suitcase stood in the entry hall beside a fine leather briefcase. Bartles inspected each bag with a sniff. How long was the judge's friend planning to stay?

A man was in the judge's office fingering Lyle's silver letter opener when I strode in.

"Mr. Longworth. What a surprise." I stammered my greeting like a kid told to make a speech without preparation.

"I feel the same way, *Mrs.* Morgan." Bartles circled Longworth and made sputtering little barks in the back of his throat.

"Lyle is out of town. I'm sure you understand that under the circumstance it will be impossible for you to stay."

"Oh, I always stay with Lyle when I'm here on business." Longworth walked up to me with a condescending smile.

The puppy jumped up to Randall Longworth's knees and sank his teeth into Longworth's pants. "Hey!" Longworth swiped at the dog with the back of his hand.

Bartles gripped tighter.

"Come on, boy." I put my arms around the pup.

His muscles were tense. The puppy released his grip on the pantleg with a snap of his jaw and made a weeny little growl in the back of his throat. Keeping my arms firmly around Bartles, I stepped away from the unwanted visitor.

"The house is full," I said firmly. "Lyle has a number of guests."

"He explained." Randall Longworth smoothed down his wet pant leg while glaring at the dog. "Lyle said you might be reluctant to allow me entrance, but he didn't tell me his dog would object as well." Longworth grinned, not a nice sort of grin either, one that made me aware he thought I was an ignorant hillbilly. "You can reach him on your phone." He leaned toward me as if he wanted to point his finger in my face to make his point.

I lifted my nose a little. "I'll do that." Placing Bartles in the entry hall I closed the door then fumbled with the phone on my belt. I searched my contact list for Lyle's number. Mr. Randall Longworth flipped up his phone and went to speed dial.

"I've got him." As he handed me his phone, his eyes gleamed with pleasure.

"Rand," I heard Lyle say. "She kick you out?"

"Not yet!" I replied. "What in tarnation are you up to Lyle? Thrusting your friend in the midst of grieving women isn't exactly a grand idea."

"Whoa there, Di. He's come to help."

I put my hand over the cell phone. "Lyle says you're here to help. How do you intend to help the Feds, local police, and George's spy friends?"

Longworth slanted his eyes my direction. "I know the Feds don't like civilians poking their noses into their cases, so as an owner of a prestigious trucking company with a fleet that travels in every state of this fine union, I'm simply asking my drivers to flash her picture around and to keep their eyes open. Any objections to my arrangements?"

His irritating, know-it-all voice grated on me. I

scrunched up my lips. "You were saying," I said through the phone to Lyle.

"Rand's fleet of trucks will be watching where we can't. He's in town to help with logistics. George's friends are setting up a command center at his house. Rand will assist."

"Can't he stay at George's?"

"I've been told George has a full house."

"When did this all get put together?" I was a little nettled about not being in on the planning.

"Last night. I had to cut off our conversation because the good reverend needed a hand escaping from a pugilistic trucker. I would have told you otherwise."

"Oh." I mentally backed up. "What do you want me to do?"

"Give him my bedroom and help feed the hoard that will descend on Mamie and George."

"Okay. Have you found anything else about your cabin?" I'd intentionally mentioned the cabin to see Longworth's reaction.

Randall Longworth's eyebrows went skyward, then he looked away fast, as if to hide his expression. I'd need to keep a close eye on him.

"Not exactly focused on it at present."

I wanted to tell Lyle that I missed him, but not with Longworth inches away from my face. "Is Reverend Daniel all right?"

"He has a shiner that matches his preaching robe." I could hear Lyle smiling over the phone. "Don't tell Josephine."

"Fine."

"You're a bit monosyllabic. Call me later and we can talk. Let me speak with Rand."

I handed Longworth his phone. Leaving the room, I overheard Longworth say, "Your cabin keys? Thought I put them under the front planter last year."

Had Longworth kept Lyle's keys and used the cabin as a pied-a-terre? And the blood? What about the blood?

I kept moving. Lupita needed to get Lyle's room prepped for the newest houseguest, and I wanted to inform Josephine of Randall Longworth's unwelcome presence. *I will pack my overnighter and vamoose to my house.* The water was most certainly on now. My mind tumbled about. *My only problem with changing residences is Miss Vickie. I don't want her to go into a tizz.*

The rain picked up, until the drops all merged into streaks of cold. I slinked around the block to the house behind mine with nary a reporter the wiser. Stepping briskly through Miss Sophie Brixton's back yard, I ran into trouble.

"That you, Delilah Morgan?" she hollered from her back porch.

"Yes, ma'am." I turned, reluctance in every move.

"You get yourself up here, girl, afore you catch your death."

I ran through the pelting rain toward her back stairs.

"Land-sakes." She shook her head at the sight of me. "You are one heap of wet. Inside, while I pour some coffee. Haven't seen you since the wedding. How have you been?"

"Beside myself with worry about Savannah."

Miss Sophie poured two steaming cups of liquid ambrosia and handed me one.

"We've all been praying. Miss Vickie doing all right?"

"A little confused. She and Josephine are staying at the judge's to avoid the press."

I stirred in a teaspoon of sugar then sipped. It was dark, rich, and exactly what a cold, miserable day needed.

"I heard that you were too. Word gets around here mighty fast on account of Ms. Abernathy can't keep her eyes off her neighbor's doin's." We both chuckled.

"I've given her a few things to go googly-eyed over."

I offered a half-smile.

"Don't we all!" Miss Sophie ought to know. She'd made the entire town googly-eyed over the years. Sophie Brixton had been the first woman on the city council. In the early 1960s when she'd been asked to move at the city council table, she stood flat-footed in front of the mayor and informed him that she, 'sure as shooting' wasn't going to take a back seat to a white man.' The mayor had backed up a step and pulled out a chair for her. Out of respect, everyone in town pulled out a chair for Miss Sophie, except our current mayor.

She eyed my nearly empty mug. "You need a refill?"

I shook my head.

"I heard Meadows senior was down at the jailhouse, because the mayor's sister called the sheriff and had him arrested for disturbing the peace when he was moving his equipment!"

"What?" It sounded like I squawked. "She didn't!"

"Sure did."

I reared back in my seat. I'd have to do something about Mr. Meadows's incarceration. He was an old man! "I'm going over to check to see if I've water. Then I'll go to the police station and give Bellows what for." I stood up, unwilling to expose to her that I connived with Meadows Plumbing to get things finished, paperwork or not.

"Settle down, Miss Delilah, and listen to a little advice." Miss Sophie spoke in her teacher's voice. I remained standing. "You know my granddaughter does cleaning for the Higgenbottoms? She says that they are up to no good when it comes to you and Mr. Morgan, may he rest in peace." Miss Sophie took her time sipping her coffee. She looked up to catch my eye. "Ever since Miss Charlene arrived back in town, she's been spitting mad. And the mayor is spewing about you finding his daughter playing footsie and then some in Mr. Morgan's old office. My Delores says he paces around, talks to the city attorney, and scratches ugly messages on his desk notepads." She straightened her shoulders before rising. "Stay as far away from the mayor and Miss Charlene as you can."

"I intend to."

"Those two have run this town into a mess." Miss Sophie huffed air between her lips. "Ambition does that to a person. That, and being hungry for money. That's the root of many evils, says the Good Book. Love of money and love for power are wrecking this town. And we keep re-electing the stinkers."

"That's because they keep buying people's votes." I crossed my jeans-covered knees. "Other people's money. Time was, when thinking people could smell a rat and call it a rat. Now they wait for their little bit of payback to grease their palms."

"Love thy neighbor, my Aunt Mable!" Miss Sophie crossed her arms and thumped them down on the table top. "More like, love myself, and to heck with everybody else."

She made me think there was hope on the horizon for changes in our town.

"You've got to hurry off, so scoot. Since everybody and their Aunt Fanny are telling you to say yes to the judge, I'm thinking it might be best if you two take your time. Tell the judge he'd better keep on pursuing you, but maybe in slow motion. You need to sort things out. If he doesn't, Miss Sophie will give him a piece of her mind."

I laughed. My oldest daughter Mindy had also said to take things one-step-at-a-time.

"But then again, if you think I won't go over to his house to tell him to stop the delay and marry you quick, well, you don't know Miss Sophie!"

"Miss Sophie, I'm not..."

"Pooh! Not ready my foot! Harry wanted you two to

get on with it. I don't see why anyone else should object."

"I do." My words were as soft as a rose petal. Was everyone as double minded about Lyle's courting as I was?

"Do your mourning, girl." She patted my hand. "But don't let a good man escape."

I saw the flash of Candace Abernathy's binoculars as I snuck up my back stairs. I gritted my teeth. *Don't let me turn into a snoopy old woman, Lord. Nothing sadder than living vicariously through your neighbor.*

Straightening up, I turned and smiled broadly and waved in Candace's direction. The sunlight reflecting off her snooping binoculars went out. Maybe I should wave every time I saw her glaring at me from her porch. Would she think it neighborly or cheeky?

The faucet gurgled and produced only air. So much for avoiding Lyle's irritating houseguest. Needing to get a couple of things done before I was stuck at the sheriff's office for the rest of the day, I dialed Lyle's phone number. "Hey," I said when he answered. "Do you know a lawyer in town that can help out a friend of mine?"

"I know a couple. Josephine take on the press?" The deep throb of a diesel engine rumbled in my ear.

"Clyde Meadows got hauled in for disturbing the peace early this morning. I'm probably next. It was in my yard."

"Colluding, were you?"

My mental thesaurus went to work. "Sort of." I sounded sheepish.

"I detect remorse." He laughed.

"A friend got in trouble trying to help me."

"And something else. Hmm. Must be trying to stand on your own two feet without manly interference. Am I close?"

"Bullseye. There is one other little item you missed. Bartles doesn't care for your houseguest. Your childhood friend gives me the willies too."

"Good!"

I hesitated, unsure what to say to that. Worrying my lip for a moment, I sucked in a breath. "Is there something about your friend Longworth you need to tell me about, aside from his inflated ego?"

"He has been known to enjoy the company of women." Lyle's voice trailed off.

What was he saying? After a few seconds of silence, I blurted out in a rush, "I miss you."

I heard an intake of his breath. "Well, that's a start."

"Lyle. I'm an idiot when I talk to you because you mean something to me, and it's not right. You shouldn't."

"I see." His baritone was a pool of quiet.

"What I meant to say is, I don't know you well enough. And decent people don't fling aside their mourning and jump into bed with a virtual stranger."

"Is that what you think of me?"

"Not quite. I do know you love hash browns and will swipe them when you can. But do you like cream in your coffee? Are you really divorced from Clarisse? Do you want to live in your house not mine?" I babbled.

"About the jumping into bed, Di," I could hear the laughter in his voice. "I've got this on speaker phone. The man of the cloth is raising his eyebrows."

"Sheesh. You know what I mean, Lyle."

"That I do, dearest Delilah." He was silent for a couple of heartbeats. "Cream in my coffee with dessert.

Yes, I'm really divorced. I'll show you the paperwork. I think your house more fitting, with all the kids and assorted grandkids that come attached. I've never been audited by the IRS, only one traffic ticket this decade, and if I could kiss away your fears, I'd do so." The sound of another voice came through the speaker, interrupting us. "I need to go, dear. I'll call soon." And Lyle was gone.

How did he know I was afraid? It wasn't of marriage or what the town might say. I was afraid of losing Harry again. Forgetting how he looked when he was sad, a downward smile that tore at my heart.

Chapter Eighteen

I grabbed my pink clipboard, thinking I should start a list of the pushy friends eager to see me abandon Harry to take up with Lyle. The sky's dark clouds fled east, leaving their damp residue leaking from the shrubs and trees. Even Harry's old turquoise truck had showered because I'd parked it outside. Opening the back door, I found Sidney standing on the porch, gazing toward the rose garden.

"Afternoon, Miss Delilah. How is Josephine holding up?"

"Not well. She has dark circles around her dark circles. I hear her feet pacing all night long."

Sidney scowled. "I could come over and let Miss Vickie beat me at checkers again."

"That would be kind, Sidney. Did you need something?"

"When they hauled Mr. Meadows off to jail, I took it upon myself to finish his job. The water line is now covered. A little of the sewer line is left, but he attached it to the city drain late last night. I was over holding the Coleman lantern so he and Toby could see. But you can't use the water, yet. The city turned it off."

"Drat!" I glanced at Sidney.

"You going to do something about Clyde Meadows?"

"I'm on my way."

"Finished mulching the roses. There's a frost a comin'."

I wasn't ready for the roses to curl up and die on me. I stared at the rose-wreathed trellis. The stems were spindly, and petals of pink, yellow, and white lay on the ground like discarded party favors.

"How about settling the side yard vegetable garden in for the winter."

"You keepin' it?"

"Certainly. This house needs herbs and vegetables. A small plot will suit me fine."

Sidney marched off to his tasks.

With a passel of cars in his driveway, George had been parking his car in mine. He'd given me the keys insisting that I drive it, because he thought Harry's old truck wasn't reliable. It was half-past noon when I pulled into the police station's parking lot in George's new fifty-thousand-dollar Mercedes that couldn't haul dirt. I parked the shiny blue car well away from all the others. As soon as a new car leaves the lot it becomes a ding magnet, and within the week there's a dent in the fender. Harry called it, "putting our snootiness in its rightful place." As I was extracting myself, Madison backed in beside me. He was a little too close. The FBI special agent shoved his door open, contacting George's passenger door. I sucked in my breath.

Madison scrutinized the car. "Not a scratch. But I'd park away from others if I were you. You've got a new model there."

I bit my lip to keep from saying something I'd have to apologize for, then apologized to the Lord for thinking it.

Madison fell into step beside me as we headed across the parking lot. "We haven't anything new to report about the case."

"I'm actually here about a friend of mine that ran afoul of the law."

"Well, well, well, Miss Delilah." Madison clicked his tongue as he walked me up the police building's stairs. "Didn't think you had felons as bosom pals."

"You'd be surprised. I've tons of acquaintances that have seen the inside of a jail cell." I didn't enlighten him about some in my family being in the policing business from Eastern Kentucky through the mountains to Tennessee.

When we stepped into the building, Deputy McEntire took one look at me and frowned. "Mrs. Morgan, I'm guessing you're here about Clyde Meadows."

"You'd be guessing right."

"He's in the sheriff's office with his lawyer. The sheriff got a call from the governor."

I lifted my chin. "I'm glad he's getting pressure for slapping a misdemeanor on that sweet old man." My voice wobbled with anger at the notion.

"The sheriff didn't have much choice. Mr. Meadows was breaking the law by disturbing the peace."

"With a shovel? He and Toby were filling the ditch by hand. According to Sidney the motor on the backhoe was cold as a January morning."

Madison strode over to the sheriff's door and rapped smartly. "I love small town life. Never a dull moment." He smiled the kind of smile that was waiting for the other shoe to drop.

"Yes?" Bellows hollered so loudly Deputy McEntire jerked backwards.

Madison let me go in first, which was a smart idea, because I might have elbowed past him, I was so worried about Mr. Meadows. I shouldn't have been. Clyde Meadows lazed in a chair drinking coffee as comfortably as he would sitting in his own kitchen.

The men rose when I came into the room, including the sharpest lawyer in town. The one every person considering divorce tried to hire.

"Miss Delilah." Lawyer Vance Taylor bowed his head my direction. "Lyle said you would be heading this way."

"I'll pay the fine, Sheriff. Mr. Meadows was employed by me to finish his excavation. He's not at fault, I am."

"That won't be necessary, ma'am." Clyde Meadows settled back in his seat. "I'm taking Candace Abernathy to court for defamation of character, false arrest, and something else … er what was it you suggested?"

Bellows pursed his lips. "I think I made reference to trespassing, assault, and disturbing the peace."

"Ah, yes. Toby made a video with his cell phone of her harassing me as she hit me with her umbrella." Clyde fiddled with the John Deere cap in his hands.

"She hit you?" I was shocked. Candace Abernathy spent her life on the porch eating cookies. With her girth it was difficult to imagine her having the strength to flail away with an umbrella.

"I fended her off. I was a Marine in Korea." His eyes were lit with amusement.

"We're heading to the ER for a medical exam," Vance Taylor announced. "She took a couple of whacks at his arm. There's a cut and bruising. The pictures and doctor's notes will look good in court."

Bellows raised his eyebrows. "I'll pretend I didn't hear that."

"I guess I'm not needed." I turned toward the door.

Bellows shook his head. "I want you to stay, Miss Delilah. Mr. Meadows and his attorney are about to leave."

When the room held only Madison, the sheriff, and me, the sheriff closed the door. "Got a call from Jim Weldon about an hour ago. It would be a waste of my breath to tell you to stay out of the investigation, Miss Delilah. I am, however, going to ask you to be careful. The Weldons are decent folk. Jim said you brought comfort to them both. Other parents around here might not take so kindly to your interference."

The other parents the sheriff referred to were a couple south of town. I intended to arrive unannounced so they couldn't call Bellows. "Okay." Easier to agree with the sheriff than tell him what I was up to.

"I've had a request from Clarisse Henderson to speak with you again. Not that I recommend it. My advice is stay clear of the woman." Sheriff Bellows' dark eyes glowered. "One other item," he said in a different tone. "Some of us in law enforcement went to a seminar and have been trained to spot trafficking victims. The speaker was an obstetrician living in North Carolina. The doctor heads a private foundation that rescues the girls. The group gives them a home, brings in counselors, whatever is needed to help them heal." He fiddled with a stack of papers on his desk until he found a business card. "You might want to give Dr. McLeod a call."

My breathing was too rapid. What was happening to Savannah would take years, maybe a lifetime to undo. This must be what had frozen Josephine into an automaton. I held the card to my chest as if given a precious jewel. Answers were needed, but I didn't yet know the right questions. By mid-afternoon the rain had cleared. Icy drops, however, slavered down my neck from the trees as I headed to George's car. The past days of heavy rain had left a soggy residue. Dropping off the Salas's car in my drive, I meandered around the neighborhood to avoid the press. I arrived unhindered at the judge's back door.

Josephine waylaid me as I went to change to drier clothes. "Where you been all afternoon, Miss Dee Dee?"

"Errands. I still don't have water, which means I'll be here again tonight."

Josephine huffed out a puff of air. "Good thing! You ain't leaving me with that man. He's got things on his mind that's best not spoken of."

"I'm going to take some protection to bed with me. The man's ego is so inflated I'm not certain what he might pull."

"Not your gun! I thought Mr. Judge confiscated it."

"He didn't. But I've something else in mind than my peashooters."

Josephine looked at me like I'd lost my marbles.

"Is it true that Miss Mamie's taking cooking lessons?"

"Tonight, Mama is teaching about red-eyed gravy, fried chicken, and properly mashing potatoes. By the time she's finished, Miss Mamie will beat all the ladies in the church at the competition next summer."

I almost smiled at the thought. "Care to go car shopping with me? We've a couple of hours before sunset."

"You heading to Lexington to get one of them little play cars?"

"No. Your Camry has too many miles on it. We're going to look for a replacement."

"Mr. Harry said when he gave me that car that two-hundred thousand miles would just break it in."

"He exaggerated a little."

Josephine crossed her arms, unmoved.

"A couple south of us had their daughter vanish nearly two years ago. Thought we'd show up and ask some questions."

"No, ma'am. I'm not facing a shotgun again."

"He's a car dealer. I doubt if he is going to greet his customers armed. Maybe after we snoop around, he might think about it, though."

Josephine went with the enthusiasm of a scared recruit facing the drill instructor.

It took twenty minutes to drive south to Buck Mays' Used Cars. It was on the side of the 127 heading toward Limestone Bluffs. Newly mown grass shone in front of cars lined up facing the road, their rears pointed toward a little blue shack. As soon as we pulled in, a man emerged from the one-story building. His tanned face, red plaid cowboy shirt, and black Stetson matched the man on the oversized billboard between Tatler Corner and McKeansville. Tall-heeled, tooled-leather boots peeked out from his black jeans. He greeted us with a friendly wave. The fringe on his leather jacket waved too.

"I sure ain't talking to that man!" Josephine huffed.

I stepped out of the car ready to keep him at

arms-length. Mays ambled over, moving as if his cowboy boots pinched.

"Howdy! What can I do for you ladies?" The dealer took off his hat and swept it low. Josephine slid from the car then hiked over to a silver Mazda and bent down to check the price sticker. Getting him alone might be a better idea than dealing with Josephine harrumphing and crossing her arms.

I gestured toward Josephine. "My friend is in need of a replacement car."

"I'm certain we'll have something here for your friend, but what about you? I've a racy sports car around back. Last year's model with only a few thousand miles on it."

"I might be interested in a smaller car."

"Why don't we take a look around back and see if anything catches your eye?"

He offered me his arm. I refused, negotiating the rough asphalt and puddles by myself. Buck Mays chattered as we walked, his voice rising and falling with the rhythm of waves at the seashore. He could put one to sleep.

"Well, here we are. Isn't she a beauty?" He ran his hand over the orange-red hood of a late-model Corvette. "As you can see, a custom paint job." I must have looked interested because, after a glance at my face, Mays said, "I need to see to your friend since she's the one interested in a new car, then perhaps we could talk about this car." His smile was confident, albeit a little bit too slick.

"We're really here to give my friend a little something to do. You see, she lost her daughter and I wanted to cheer her up."

"Sorry to hear that." He shook his head nice and slow, an empathy shake. "Must be hard losing a child."

"Yes," I agreed, thinking of my two little boys planted within touching distance of Harry's grave.

"Well, now," he said, reaching out and patting my

hand. "You're a good friend and all to try to comfort her."

"Wasn't there a family around here who lost a daughter a couple of years ago?" I kept my voice casual, but my eyes were alert.

"Yes, ma'am. My wife and I. Our daughter never came home from school. She disappeared one day. Figured she'd run away, what with the trouble she was having with her grades."

"I'm so sorry."

His face contorted into a sad, troubled expression. With a quick turn of his head he stared into the fields beyond the car lot. Eventually he turned back to face me. "It still troubles us." He swallowed hard. "About that car ride..." He moved closer. "I bought it from a man who loved the smooth ride and the feeling of freedom a small car can give. Not a lot of miles on it. No accidents, but I'd like to move it off the lot, so I could cut a deal that might make both of us happy." I was going to have to remove sports cars from my wish list because flying about the countryside in a sports car that couldn't haul dry wall wasn't practical.

"Miss Delilah?" I heard Josephine holler from the front. "You finding anything?"

"I'd better check on my friend. Excuse me." I turned away from Buck Mays. He reached out and put his hand on my arm. Harry had dubbed it the salesman grab. They either pump your hand or make you linger by the thing you're coveting.

"You look mighty interested in this automobile, Miss Delilah."

"Nope." I tried to shake off his hand.

Josephine and a woman in a nurse's uniform emerged from the right side of the blue building and glared our direction.

"Buck Mays, you know the lady came to look at a car for her friend. Not the fancy sports car you can't get rid of." The woman's voice snapped with anger. "Don't sell her something she doesn't want."

He dropped his hands to his side as if he'd been scorched.

I blushed, thinking I really needed to decide about a new car and not be attracted to a kid's toy car that could go seventy in ten seconds.

The woman marched up to us. Josephine trotted behind her. The thunderous look in her eyes said she knew his number, a con man with his slick voice and salesman friendly smile.

"She's fine, Melissa." Buck puffed out his chest as broad as a peacock. "She wanted to sit in the sports car. I was helping her."

My face tightened.

"I apologize for my husband. He can be overeager in selling his cars."

Mr. Mays licked his upper lip with the tip of his tongue then slid his tongue into his mouth and lodged it against his cheek.

Josephine's eyes roved over a Mercedes, Lexus, and Corvette. "Miss Dee Dee, I thought you were going to look at sedans with me. Doesn't look like there's a sedan in the back lot. Expensive cars, though."

"Mrs. Morgan, would you and your friend care to join me for coffee?" Melissa Mays gave a hesitant smile.

"Certainly. Josephine, do you have time?"

"As long as my mama is happy, I'll take time for coffee."

We left Buck prowling the cracked asphalt in front of his car lot and followed his wife to a coffee shop in their one-street town.

The waitress working the coffee shop greeted Melissa with the kind of tone you'd use on a skittish child. She finished scrubbing the counter with a washcloth and soap while we found a rough wooden table with mismatched chairs stuffed under it.

On closer inspection, Melissa's shoulders sagged, and her eyes had permanent circles under them. Worn down with cares, I'd guess. Melissa Mays lifted her head when she had settled in her chair. "You're here about my daughter."

"Yes, ma'am." Josephine's voice had lost the oomph she'd displayed trying to deliver me from the woman's husband.

Our new acquaintance looked toward the waitress. "Coffee all around and throw in three pieces of your Derby pie."

I didn't volunteer I'd been on a diet. Derby pie, all seven-hundred or so calories, would sweeten the conversation. And, I *had* missed lunch.

"I'm Josephine. My friend is Delilah."

"I know." Buck Mays' wife extended a hand that looked as overworked as the rest of her. "Saw your picture on the news. You doin' okay, honey?"

When Josephine's hand met Melissa's, their touch unleashed a flood. Josephine went through four napkins, Melissa a couple.

I was dry as the Mojave.

"I don't have words," Josephine finally said.

"Of course not. Neither do I. Carly left twenty-two months ago. They think she ran away because of home troubles."

I sat up straight as a rabbit's ears on alert. "Did your daughter have any problems at school?"

"No. Straight A student, top of the class. Her daddy was in the army when he died, so she was to get a scholarship from a veteran's organizations. Going to U.K. to be a veterinarian." Melissa dabbed at her eyes. Thankfully, the coffee and desserts arrived, and we could breathe for a few moments.

"You didn't come to buy a car, did you?"

I swallowed the teeny bite I'd taken. "No, ma'am. We came to ask questions. It didn't seem right to let the police do all the work. I think there might be something to so many girls in our area disappearing."

Josephine played with her napkin, not willing to enter the inquisition.

"The police think that Carly ran away."

"Do you?"

"No. She was a good, kind girl. Carly would never leave without telling me. She might not tell Buck, though. They didn't get on too well." Melissa stirred sweetener from a little pink packet into her coffee. "They'd had a fight the night before she disappeared. I was at work. I do the 3 a.m. to 3 p.m. shift at the nursing home. My son Jason said there was yelling and slamming of doors."

"What was it about?"

"Don't know. Most likely something with the business. Carly balanced the dealership's receipts. Buck could be casual about bookkeeping, but Carly turned into a bulldog when a penny or two was off." Melissa Mays tried to hide a yawn behind her right hand.

Josephine put her wad of soggy napkins on the table top. "Mrs. Mays."

"Call me Melissa."

Glancing at her watch, Josephine frowned. "You must be tired after a long shift at work. We won't keep you." Josephine's slow Kentucky accent cushioned the air.

"It has been my pleasure." Melissa Mays granted us a tender smile.

I picked up the check that sat on the scarred dark wooden table.

"I insist." Melissa wormed the bill out of my fingers. "I'd have brought you back to my house, but Buck might have made an appearance." She sounded displeased by the prospect.

I wasn't going to arm wrestle her for the bill. Judging from the frayed collar on her uniform it was a sacrifice for her to feed us. I asked for a box for my dessert. One bite wouldn't push me out of my skinny jeans, but two in a row might.

I picked up my purse. "Melissa, do you have a picture of your daughter?" Mrs. Mays nodded, opened her wallet, and plucked out a photo. Three girls posed in front of a 1940s style car, attempting to look cool. "Which one is your daughter?" Melissa pointed to the one in tortoise shell glasses. "Why don't I meet you at the car, Josephine? I've a need for the little girl's room."

Josephine nodded and stepped outside with Melissa Mays while I washed my hands. When they were out of earshot I sidled up to the waitress and put two twenties in her hands.

"When Melissa Mays comes in, see that she gets what she needs, then tell her it's on the house. Give me a call when she's used up that amount." I slipped the waitress Harry's business card with my number scribbled on the back.

We were half-way back to McKeansville, when the first three measures of Chopin's "Minute Waltz" played. I looked at my phone mounted near my steering wheel and pushed the red dot on my phone.

"Hello."

"Delilah, it's Linda. We've news." My cousin Linda sounded her old self, not the stuffed, congested fluey voice of last week. "I'm working the E.R. shift over at Blowing Rock."

"You sound better."

"Listen!" The urgency in her voice made me rear back. "We spotted your girl. That sweet bridesmaid at Molly's wedding. She was here about an hour ago but was hustled out before I could call security."

"What!" I pulled to the side of the road and parked Josephine's car on the gravel. Josephine leaned over so far her ear was almost touching the speaker.

"We've got it on video. She was with a girl who has a ripe appendix. Your Savannah filled out some paperwork before a red-haired woman grabbed her arm and hauled her out to a car. The nurse didn't look at the form until the sick girl had been put in a room. The words, HELP ME! SAVANNAH, were scribbled across the page."

"Oh, mercy." Josephine had her hands clasped in

front of her and she rocked back and forth in her seat.

"The nurse is getting grief from the police lieutenant. We've been trained in spotting girls who are trafficked. No excuses. Good news is, the police have a picture of the car she was thrown into and have sent it out. Bad news is, roads lead from here to every point on the compass."

My hands went clammy. "Her mama's with me, Linda. What can you tell us about the other girl?"

"She's still in surgery. All we got from her was a name. She said, 'Call me Mara.'"

I gasped. In Hebrew it meant bitter. Naomi had said in scripture, 'Call me Mara,' after her husband and sons died. It came from a heart of despair.

"She's a kid." Linda spoke in a voice marked with sorrow. "Maybe eighteen. She's got needle marks up and down her arms, Delilah. That and a laundry list of STDs."

The card Sheriff Bellows had put into my hand popped into my head. "Ever hear of a doctor named McLeod?"

"He's sitting in front of me."

"We're on our way."

I quickly calculated the time, logistics of Miss Vickie's attendants, and dragging Josephine up into the mountains when her mama might need her. I wanted to text the info to Mamie.

"Hold it! The FBI has a man flying in from Lexington. Name of Madison. We've a small airport. Get a plane."

"Right." George's cadre of friends had flown in from Washington D.C. Maybe one of them had a private plane nearby.

I punched in George's number. "Listen George, I need to get to Blowing Rock ASAP."

"Madison called me. It's arranged. Head to the McKeansville airport."

I turned the car onto the road. "I'm bringing Josephine."

Josephine began to sputter in the seat next to me. Words weren't intelligible.

"I'm coming too." George's voice was firm.

"We don't need a chaperone, George."

"I'm a field agent, not some desk jockey."

I noticed my speed was seventy-five in a fifty-five zone. I slowed incrementally. "We need to find a nurse's aide for Miss Vickie."

"Mamie's going to sleep over at the judge's tonight. They're as tight as bedbugs."

Thank the Good Lord. With Miss Vickie's care settled, I aimed for the airport. Josephine cried beside me.

"There's a tissue package in my purse."

"She's alive," Josephine choked out as she blew her nose.

When we climbed out of the car Josephine's eyes grew saucer sized.

"I ain't going up on that flimsy little thing." She pointed at a plane the size of a gnat parked among several others.

Fortunately, George was standing beside a Gulfstream V.

Josephine shook her head.

I'd never been on anything smaller than a feeder airplane from Chicago to Lexington. This gorgeous plane reminded me of a kid's toy when it comes out of its box-shiny and all the details perfect. "If I can, you can." I spoke with more bravado than I felt.

"Let's go, ladies." George waved at us.

My only luggage was my dessert box and purse. Good thing there wasn't any security, or some airport guard would be eating my Derby pie for their snack.

"Savannah will want to see you first when we find her." I patted Josephine's shoulder.

She marched up the plane's little staircase like a victim heading to a firing squad.

We hit a few updrafts that made Josephine grab my arm and pray so loudly George ducked his head.

We skirted a storm system and came in fast. I braked with both feet jammed onto the floor.

Even though the curvy road to the hospital was nothing compared to our landing, George's careening along the two-lane road made Josephine's fingers burrow into my arm.

At the hospital's entrance Linda's familiar face caused the tension in my shoulders to relax. My cousin took one look at Josephine and hugged her so hard Josephine staggered backwards. "Mara's in the ICU because of a ruptured appendix and infection."

Josephine glanced from one of us to the other. "Thought you'd look alike. You and Miss Delilah sure are different."

That set Linda to laughing. "I should hope. I'm from the North Carolina branch of the family. "This,"— she gestured to her dark hair and cute figure –"is from a Cherokee ancestor."

I peeked in the ICU's window. The girl's frail white skin reminded me of a scrawny, discarded doll.

Linda slid in beside me. "All she could say when she woke up was, 'Thank the Lord.' We asked her what happened, and she clammed up. Doctor McLeod was with her for a time. She cried and cried, then held on tight to his hand."

Staring through the ICU's window, Josephine stood so still birds could land on her. "You know who that is?"

"No, I didn't see her face."

"The Weldons' daughter, Elise." Josephine's voice was tight with tears. "You need to call them, Miss Dee Dee."

"I'm told she doesn't want to see them." Our attention was so fixed on the girl that we hadn't heard Madison's approach. "We've found it a common response. Trafficked victims are ashamed and believe they are at fault. I've heard too many, 'If I hadn't . . . It's my fault because I ...'" Madison's face was ashen. "It takes time for the mind to begin to heal." It was the first time I'd heard raw passion in Madison's voice.

I saw a spark in Josephine's eyes. "These little lambs ain't done nothin' but get caught up in an evil thing."

George stepped beside us. "You and Josephine should speak with her, Delilah. Most hurt children will open up to a woman, because it's men that have been violent with them."

I squared my shoulders and handed Linda my white dessert box and purse. "Come on." I reached for Josephine's hand.

I didn't need to coax her. We slipped on the gowns and gloves Linda pointed to and entered. Josephine walked in front of me and over to the hospital bed. Elise was skin and bones. Clear tubes snaked around her arms, pumping life into her.

Josephine put her hand gently on the girl's arm. "Well, Miss Elise. I spoke with your mama and daddy recently." The girl's pale-blue eyes looked up at Josephine. "You see, my little girl was kidnapped two days ago, and I thought your parents could help me."

A tear slid down the girl's face. Josephine rubbed her thumb over the girl's hand.

Elise began to sob. "You don't know what I've done."

"An' you don't know what I have." Josephine brushed a hair from the girl's cheek. "But our Jesus, He forgives it all, ever last thing."

"Not this." Elise turned her face into her pillow as she choked out the words. "They made me do things."

"I knows, lamb, and so does Jesus."

Elise buried her head on Josephine's chest, her body relaxing against Josephine like a spent child. Minutes ticked by. Josephine didn't need me. I was turning to leave the room when Elise cried out.

"You!" The girl's arms wrapped around Josephine's neck in a strangle-hold.

"What?" My heart pumped so fast it made my head swim.

"I saw you," came the muffled reply.

"That's Miss Delilah," Josephine whispered into Elise's matted blond hair. "She's my friend."

Elise shuddered. "Please don't let her take me back to the house."

"Ain' nobody taking you anywhere, child." Josephine sat on the bed and began to rock the girl. "Nobody's going to hurt the Lord's lamb." All kinds of lights on machines began to blink, buzzers went off, and nurses dashed into the room.

"Out!" ordered a gray-haired woman in scrubs.

The girl clung to Josephine, thin arms turning even whiter from the exertion. "No." Elise grabbed onto Josephine's arm as she sank back onto the bed.

The nurse stared.

Josephine stayed.

I ran out of the room. For that sick little one to be frightened of me was too much. I buried my face in my hands and cried.

"Know what that was about, Miss Delilah?" Madison's voice was edged with suspicion.

"Back off, Madison." George's bark made me jump. "Miss Delilah reminds her of someone. We'll get to the bottom of this. Where is that scoundrel, Lyle?" George muttered, as he patted my arm and harrumphed in my ear.

Madison paced like a nervous ocelot. The staff, who finally emerged from the ICU, directed scowls my way.

Madison stopped a passing nurse. "What did the girl say?"

"She claims that woman was part of the gang that kidnapped her."

"Impossible." Madison frowned. "Miss Delilah wouldn't hurt a fly. Well, that doesn't include Neely Patrick, of course, but that was an aberration." Madison rubbed a forefinger over his bony nose. "The Weldon girl said something about a house. Did she say anything more?"

The no-nonsense voice of the scrub-clad nurse broke in. "She is hallucinating. It was time for her morphine."

The soft caress of a lullaby came from the ICU. Josephine had sung that melody when Savannah was fractious. I cried harder. George sniffed and kept patting my arm with two fingers.

"Someone who'd hurt that sweet child looks like me." I spoke into George's ear.

"I'm not so sure. She's doped up and isn't thinking clearly."

I shook my head. "Her response was visceral. I really frightened her. Has someone been impersonating me?"

Madison cleared his throat. "George, do you think the Weldons could get a flight from McKeansville too?"

George tossed Madison a half-smile. "Consider it arranged."

Linda guided us to a cell phone area.

"Mr. Weldon. This is Delilah Morgan. I want to thank you again for your hospitality and let you know that I'm at a hospital in Blowing Rock, North Carolina." I took a breath and counted to two before saying, "Your little girl is here, Mr. Weldon."

Jim Weldon gasped and began to choke.

When he stopped coughing, I said, "She's had surgery for a ruptured appendix and is quite sick."

"We'll be there in a few hours." His voice bounced with hope.

"There is a plane waiting at the McKeansville airport for you both. Pack a bag for a few days. Housing will be arranged."

Ordering people about seemed natural, but I didn't like the tone in my voice. I hung up the phone and walked back to my cousin.

"Delilah, you need some things." Linda looked me up and down like a fair judge does a sheep. "Let's head for the gift shop first. They might have overnight supplies."

My stomach rumbled as I made a list of all we needed for the night. Linda smiled her serene smile. "Dinner is on me. And I'm not opting for the yellow gravy they serve in hospital cafeterias."

The others joined us in a cozy diner, but I couldn't coax Josephine to desert her post. Our salads had arrived when Dr. McLeod joined us. His face was lined with worry. "You are aware of the trauma our young patient has endured."

George and Madison nodded grimly.

Linda took a deep breath. "Yes. The physical wounds will heal. It is always the memories that break them."

"Some girls recover in time. Others remain as vulnerable as children, unable to process their emotions. Decision making can paralyze them."

I would have been in better shape if, over dinner, Doctor McLeod hadn't illuminated us about trafficking. Imagining what Elise had been through kept me awake, praying. How can anyone heal who has been so wounded?

Chapter Nineteen

I WOKE TO MY RING TONE. The bed beside me was empty. A note in Josephine's hand perched on the pillow.

"Hello?" I managed.

"Sorry to wake you." Lyle's warm voice rumbled into the still room. "George told me all, and that you were sleeping in this morning." The clock dial read 8:00 a.m.

"Good to hear your voice. Where are you?"

"Downstairs in the coffee shop. Shake a leg, Mrs. Morgan, they've English muffins with peanut butter waiting for you."

It took me five minutes to throw on my clothes, put my hair in a ponytail, and wash my face. I read Josephine's message as I dashed toward the stairs.

I came in after the Weldon's arrived. You needed your beauty sleep. I'm off to the hospital.

Seeing Lyle across the room made my heart beat faster. He had a reddish bruise along his right cheekbone, as well as a raccoon's circle around the left eye. When I crossed the room, I put a hand to his cheek. Before I could back up and see where else he was bruised, he clasped me to his chest. His kiss made me vibrate from head to toe. I closed my eyes and when I opened them, the woman in the booth behind him hid most of her red face behind the menu. One eye, however remained fixed on us, not on the man across from her.

Lyle turned and bowed to them. "First thing in the morning greet the woman you love with at least a thirty-second kiss. Starts things off right."

The man stirred the cream in his coffee and glanced at the woman opposite before his focus darted to the menu. Her stare would freeze a steam bath.

Lyle and I sat on the same side of the booth. When

I started to speak, Lyle tapped a long finger on my lips and said, "Drink your coffee, Di, while I catch you up."

"Tell me about your black eye."

"You ought to see the other guy."

"Uh, huh." I leaned closer to capture his news.

"The Weldon girl woke about two. She explained it was a picture of you she'd spied. I'll bet it was the one on my desk in the cabin."

"Oh, Lyle!"

He rubbed his right hand across his face. His eyes were so troubled, I teared.

"They've taken Elise's fingerprints and will compare them with the FBI's collection. If they are a match, I'll tear the house down with my own hands." Lyle's voice had broken places in it. I pulled his hand from his face. His eyes were grayed with despair.

"No, dear." I rubbed a finger on his cheek. "We don't need to destroy your beautiful work. That's what the enemy does. He takes what is good and lovely and refashions it so it becomes repugnant." I felt tears welling and let them trickle down my cheeks. "We will pray through the rooms, one by one. God alone can cleanse a house." Lyle's eyebrows shot up as he studied me. "But, if you can't bear it," I stumbled on, "I'll help you dismantle it, one board at a time. We can use them for something good."

Lyle's other hand cupped my face. "Delilah Belle Morgan, you are a gift to me."

We headed to the hospital after breakfast. Outside Elise Weldon's room, the reverend stood with his arm encircling Josephine's shoulders. My feet skittered to a halt, not wanting to disturb whatever he was saying to her. Lyle walked right up to them and put a hand on the Reverend's arm. Startled, Pastor Daniel jerked back, then gave a sheepish grin.

Daniel and Lyle were black-eyed bookends. The right eye of my pastor was swelled shut, while Lyle's left one looked as if someone had run amok with black and purple eye makeup.

"As soon as they get the fingerprint analysis I want to head to my cabin. The FBI might be able to uncover more than fingerprints." Chin thrust forward, Lyle stood like my daddy's coon dog ready to hunt.

I smiled. An investigation would give us something tangible to wrap our minds around. We'd include George with his super-sleuth expertise. Josephine and Daniel could work together while Lyle and I paired up.

Madison emerged from Elise Weldon's room. "A word, Lyle."

After a minute of listening, Lyle looked so sorrowful I wanted to fling my arms around him. He gave me a swift glance, then took my hand. Madison was on my other side.

"We need to speak with you in private," Madison said into my ear.

Do they think I had something to do with Elise's kidnapping? Am I going to be in the hoosegow with Clarisse?

Madison directed us to a doctor's lounge where a coffee urn, donuts, and water sat on a plain oak table. Special Agent Madison locked the door and stood in front of it like a Marine guard at an embassy.

"I, ah, ahem . . ." He faltered, then looked beyond my face. "Elise's fingerprints were found in the upstairs bedroom at Lyle's cabin. She also reported they were taking Savannah to Norfolk. They had a client there."

"Oh, no." My hands bracketed my cheeks.

"I'm heading to Virginia in a few minutes. Lyle is meeting a forensics team at his home."

I nodded. "I'm ready."

Madison and Lyle moved to either side of me, hemming me in.

"Not you, Delilah." Madison's hands balled into fists. "You're going back to McKeansville on a mission. It's going to be rough. I've come up with a plan and want you and Lyle to cooperate."

"Of course. It will be good to do something other

than sit around and worry. Okay, pray and worry." *I'll not tell Meemaw I have a hard time differentiating.*

"Lyle?" Madison's voice sounded as if he were coaxing a reluctant witness.

"It's imperative that Madison and I find Savannah *and* the kidnappers. The only clues we have are at my cabin. If they believe the cabin is empty again, they may use it."

"That's a good idea."

"Not really." Lyle's voice was scratchy. "We decided it has to appear as if I've dumped you and I'm leaving for a while. Madison thinks our break-up would be the catalyst that would cause me to flee and cause the traffickers to return."

"That's ridiculous." I shook my head. "Why would that bring out the traffickers?"

Madison put his hands behind his back. "We have a theory. Elise mentioned a woman's voice directing the men who took her. We need to catch that person to find Savannah. Seems likely she's a local. That cabin is well hidden."

"What does that have to do with us?" I turned toward Lyle.

"It's guesswork, Delilah. You will play your part better if you don't know. You have to appear a jilted fiancée."

"You want me to lie?"

"Yes." Madison was firm. "Tell the town Lyle's a rat for making you promises he won't keep."

"I won't do that." I'd lied to the used car salesman and Miss Vickie. That was enough fibbing for my entire life.

"I'll do the lying." Madison began to walk around, his feet softly thumping on the carpet. "Just don't undo it. Get everyone's sympathy."

"Even our kids?"

"Especially your kids."

I reached out my hand to Lyle. "Where are you going to be?"

"The world's going to think I'm heading to Europe."

"That's not answering the question."

He thrust his fingers through his hair. "In the woods, covered in bug spray, waiting for someone to enter the cabin. They can't let me loose in the area for everyone knows me, so I'm hidden away, letting them do the work while I twiddle my thumbs."

Madison licked his lips. "We can't promise a thing except trouble, Miss Delilah."

"I know." My voice went quivery like a person on a vibrating machine.

Madison patted Lyle's shoulder and swung out of the doorway.

A knot of pain welled up in my chest and nearly strangled me.

"I want our girl back, sweetheart," Lyle said into my hair. All I could do was nod. "We can't think of another way." I looked into his somber eyes. "I want Josephine, her mama and you to remain in my home. Her house is too vulnerable to interlopers and yours still doesn't have water."

"Uh—huh."

"Don't make this any harder, Di."

"What do you expect me to say, Lyle Henderson?"

"That you'll pray."

"I will. But you know I'm a lousy liar."

"One of the things I love about you."

I grabbed his sweater front and pulled him to me, planting a thirty-second kiss on his lips.

"I love you," I said into his gnarled, blue sweater. "And I don't want to say a mean thing about you." He cupped my face with his hands and kissed me so gently that we both gasped.

We were crying when we left the doctor's lounge. *At least it makes our supposed break-up more authentic.*

Lyle took George by the arm and led him down the corridor. When Lyle leaned forward and spoke a few sentences, George reared back as if struck and waggled a finger in Lyle's face. Lyle shrugged and walked toward Josephine.

I didn't overhear that conversation either, but from Josephine's shocked expression and eyes growing larger than golf-balls, the judge was in for it. He was red in the face by the time Josephine was through with her tongue lashing. She stomped off to speak with Reverend Daniel. At least Lyle didn't have to. Lying to Pastor Daniel would be sacrilegious.

All the way to the airport, Josephine was speechless, which is saying a lot since she'd become uncorked at the hospital. The flight home was miserable. Lyle was headed toward excitement and danger, while I went home to make coffee.

During dinner at Lyle's, Randall Longworth smirked at me across the dinner table. I ducked my head, studying the whirls on Lyle's cherry table top, because Longworth might read on my face that I'd planned a little surprise if he dared to put a toe over the threshold of my room.

Miss Vickie ate a nibble of chicken leg, took off her shoes and waggled her toes. Bartles brushed past my legs, seeking the amusement of her moving digits. Miss Vickie waved her chicken leg my direction. "That was a good idea, Miss Dee Dee."

"What was?"

"Why feeding those people protesting on the sidewalk. I didn't know that there was trouble over at the school. Should let those little children learn together. No need to separate the black children from the white children. That's what they used to do."

Randall's eyebrows met his hairline.

I shook my head at him so he wouldn't disturb her.

Josephine wiped her lips with her napkin. "That isn't the problem, Mama. You're helping raise money for the school by *feeding* the people on the sidewalk. It's a very good thing for you to do."

Miss Vickie blinked and jerked back from one of

her time-travel places. "That's what the real estate lady said. That we were feeding little children who didn't have food. Where are their mamas? Every mama makes sure her children get fed before they go to school."

"Some people are a little short of money, Mama."

The puzzled look on Miss Vickie's face deepened. Josephine squinted at Randall Longworth as he opened his mouth, daring him to speak. "I think you and I should tidy up the kitchen while Miss Dee Dee makes phone calls."

"You want some privacy, Miss Dee Dee?" Miss Vickie looked at me with childlike curiosity.

"I have a few things I need to get done."

I went to Lyle's office in search of a notepad. Bartles trotted behind me. Longworth fell into step behind Bartles. The man couldn't take a hint if it came with a bazooka. I turned and glared at him. From under his hairy brow, Bartles did too. The rain drummed on the windows like fingernails tapping on glass.

Longworth, ignoring my four-footed guard, put his hands behind his back. "Cold night ahead. Heard there might be a frost."

"Yes."

"You warm enough by the kitchen?"

"Toasty." I eased toward Lyle's desk, then looked in the top drawer. Lyle's desk was swept clean, not even a speck of lint on the top.

"I see." Randall shook his head.

I unearthed a notepad with a fancy Atlanta hotel name emblazoned across the top.

"Let me know if I can be of assistance." His patronizing gaze moved over me like a cold wind.

"I'll send up smoke signals."

He chuckled. "Lyle seems to like feisty women, as I recall."

I wanted to plug my ears with my fingers. "Good *night,* Mr. Longworth." I walked out the door and didn't look back. Bartles followed me, a tiny growl percolating in the back of his throat.

I emptied the drawers in a seven-drawer chest in my bedroom to lighten it for moving, then shoved the wooden tallboy in front of the door. Randall Longworth would have to catapult over it to reach me. If he managed that, I had plan B by my pillow.

I fell asleep to Bartles making slurping noises. I couldn't have been out long when I was jerked awake by the sound of footsteps on the kitchen floor. I suspected Miss Vickie was up for a midnight snack until I heard a rap on my door.

"Delilah?" Longworth's deep male voice sounded through the door. Bartles sat up in his bed and growled.

"Don't even think about it! You step a foot in here, Randall Longworth, and you'll be rearranging your face for the rest of your life." I fingered the handle of my favorite cast iron skillet.

"I've had an idea."

"I'll bet you have."

"Listen. I spoke with Lyle earlier. I know you must be hurting since he's decided to call off the wedding."

Lyle had called his friend but was too busy to dial me?

My lips formed a sliver. "I hadn't said yes … yet."

"Thought you'd appreciate a cup of tea and company."

"No, thank you."

"Well, I'm available to help if you've a need."

I hadn't one. Especially from Randall Maximillian Longworth. I didn't sleep much for the worry, until I put the puppy in bed with me.

Waking at 8:23 to pans clanking, I dragged myself into the kitchen. Lupita was the only human visible.

"Sorry to wake you," Lupita apologized. "Our house guest is at the Salases. Josephine was up with her mama most of the night and is sleeping in."

"Where is Miss Vickie?"

"Getting the coffee ready for her 'company.'" Lupita jerked her finger toward the reporter congregation that were now at the Salases. "She is brimming with energy this morning."

I groaned. "Where's the paper?"

"Er . . . hasn't come yet." Lupita avoided my eyes. Which was puzzling. We'd been friends since she began working for the judge.

I ate a piece of buttered toast, sipped coffee from a mug, then headed out the door in rain gear. Rain dribbled across my shoulders. Hallelujah! Since it had rained, frost hadn't ruined my roses.

I walked undisturbed toward my house. The rose garden flowers drooped under the weight of the water. Harry always said, "it was a poor man who didn't carry a knife." I'd taken that as gospel and had the habit of attaching a Swiss Army knife to a holder on my belt. I whipped it from the leather holder and cut off some flowers. Ten minutes later, an armful of roses accompanied me into the kitchen. Dead leaves, curled and bug chewed, all hit the wastebasket. I put the roses in my green vase, using holly leaves for filler. I would add water when I got to the Salases. Giving Mamie flowers to brighten up her kitchen was the least I could do to thank her for caring for Miss Vickie and the TV crews. I wandered to my neighbor's, offering in hand. Olive Lorraine Patrick's fancy car was front and center in the drive. Eight other cars sat bumper to bumper around hers.

George's office was crammed. The small contingent I had observed coming and going had morphed into twelve. My neighbor Hank Abernathy was busy at a computer and beside him, Ed Mays, the police sergeant, was lending his expertise. As soon as I stood in the doorway, eyes swiveled my direction, then all and sundry refocused on the job at hand. A newspaper on George's desk was open. Olive Lorraine slid over and plopped a legal pad on top of it.

A thin man stood within touching distance of Olive

Lorraine. Hadn't seen him before. Olive Lorraine leaned over to him and whispered in his ear. He winked at her. They seemed to be mighty friendly. Lyle's secretary, Janice, typed on a computer. Out of the corner of her eye she shifted her gaze to my face, then smiled.

An intense group was fused in place around Randall Longworth. The cocky smile on Longworth's face suggested he was delighted to have everyone focused on him. "Janice, make sure you contact my office manager and get the schedule for my fleet."

Janice lifted a hand in acknowledgement and went back to her task.

Longworth seemed a natural for politics, his ego was the size of the state of Kentucky.

"My boys will keep an eye out for Savannah and any other girls needing help. I've contacted five other large trucking firms. They are alerting their drivers as I speak." Randall Longworth's voice was precise and loud. He studied a paper in his hand and squinted. "I've assigned George and Reverend Daniel to head further south. My bet is, the traffickers are heading toward Miami. Lots of ways to get out of the country through that port." Longworth's eyebrows lifted to my face. "Lyle is on his way to Europe. A little something about a broken engagement." An audible gasp came from Janice, who clutched her hands together so tight she might cut off their blood supply.

I stood in the doorway with the flowers clutched in front of me like a bridal bouquet. I tried to put them behind my back so I wouldn't look pathetic. Olive Lorraine was the first to reach me.

"Oh, I am so sorry."

Why Olive Lorraine Patrick should care a hoot for me was a mystery. But she was sincere, so I accepted the commiseration from Harry's old girlfriend.

Mamie's face had turned chalk white. "What happened?"

"Lyle got tired of waiting." Randall Longworth

made his announcement with a lazy smile that didn't quite reach his eyes. "Seems your Miss Delilah here is great about saying no, but her getting to yes was never going to happen."

I would have dabbed at my eyes to appear pathetic, but Mamie didn't give me the chance. She clasped me to her bosom. I held the vase high to keep the flowers from spilling onto the floor.

"You poor dear. Jilted." She commiserated in funeral tones. "I don't know what's the matter with the man! I'll have George talk to him." She released me from her strangle hold, then tromped into the kitchen with the vase of flowers bobbing as she moved.

Janice was the next to enter the empathy squad. "Lyle's not getting enough sleep. He never would have done that if he were rested."

"Yes, yes. All of you need to give Mrs. Morgan your love." Randall's sticky sweet voice was irritating. "To my mind, she's gotten out of a difficult relationship. Lyle can be somewhat picayune."

"I won't hear a word against him." I narrowed my eyes. "I've been the difficult one. Harry was my life. Lyle's attentions have been. . .challenging."

Longworth's sardonic smile wasn't lost on me. When Longworth grabbed a breath, the stranger beside Olive Lorraine lifted a suspicious eyebrow and took over the questioning. "Morning, ma'am. George told us about your private investigations. Seems mighty dangerous for civilian women to be cruising around the countryside asking questions."

I shrugged. "Pooh. No one is interested in my questions. I've only got speculations, no real facts."

"Let's hear them." He took a step toward a flip chart mounted on a stand. "Give us the wild, the wise, and the lamebrained. I've been on enough missions to know that if you throw up plenty of information things might sort themselves out."

I frowned. Who was this character to ask for my input? "And you are?"

The lanky stranger dipped his head and tossed me a sideways grin as if he'd been caught with his hand in the cookie jar. "I'm sorry we haven't been formally introduced." He stuck out his hand. "I'm an old business colleague of George's. He can attest to my reliability. The name is Hunter, William. Most folks call me Will." His hand was firm in mine—all muscle, no flab or moisture.

I licked my lips. "Buck Mays lied to us about his step-daughter. He said she was having trouble at school. The only trouble she had was with him. She might have run away, but she fits the profile of the other girls. Smart, attractive, modest, and hardworking." I took the two photos out of my pocket and placed them in his hands. "None of the girls had steady boyfriends. All three girls were involved with church groups." My voice got softer as I spoke. "Elise Weldon is a very astute girl. She will be able to identify her kidnappers if they are in the FBI files. I'm focusing on Mays. He had no reason to lie to me." It was all I had to report. Madison wanted the connection between Elise and Lyle's cabin kept secret.

I went into the kitchen to retrim the roses and add water and found Miss Vickie and Mamie measuring coffee into a thirty-six-cup pot.

"Why your eyes all puffy and red, Miss Dee Dee?" Miss Vickie put her hands on her hips and cocked her head sideways. "You having trouble with my friend, the judge?"

"You might say so," muttered Mamie as she thumped a plump donut onto a serving plate.

"That man's a good 'un, but he been alone too long to know how to treat a lady like you. Say, where is that little girl that helps me in the bathroom before she goes to school?"

Olive Lorraine's spy friend strode into the room his eyes darting from one to the other of us. "Mamie, we've got some questions about Savannah's kidnapping."

When the words emerged from his lips Miss

Vickie's eyes grew large. I clasped Miss Vickie's hands in mine and turned her to look at me. "Lyle and Reverend Daniel have been looking for her. They will find her, dear."

"Why'd y'all not say something?" Miss Vickie dropped my hands and stared at all of us. "You think this old lady's mind's so feeble she cain't pray?" Miss Vickie thundered so loudly the man beside me went into a soldier's chin-tucked pose. "You think 'cause my mind's slipping, I cain't plead with heaven? Well." Miss Vickie rolled up her sleeves. "Lord, I may be losing my marbles, but I knows you got an eye on that lamb." Miss Vickie marched around the kitchen, her face set like thunder. Olive Lorraine's friend backed toward the hallway. "Now, send your Spirit to comfort Josephine like you said you would when your children have troubles." Miss Vickie's face broke into a smile. "And you get Savannah home to her mama, 'cause a girl needs her mama when somebody harms her." Miss Vickie's eyes began to leak.

I handed her a Kleenex.

"And another thing, Lord. Miss Dee Dee here needs her man to get back down on his knees and ask her again. This time she'll say yes, 'cause Mr. Harry wanted her to say yes."

I let out a puff of air so loud that Mamie jumped.

Miss Vickie clapped her hands and hustled over to the coffee urn. "Well, the good Lord is attentive to the needs of His children. Now, we'd better get to fixing up the coffee, Miss Mamie, or your guests on the sidewalk will get cold."

We'd had her with us for the moment. I looked about the kitchen and squeezed Miss Vickie's hand, but I wanted to speak with Lyle. To tell him about what his little conniving with Madison had wrought in my life. Thinking about the congregation of eyes in George's office, I dashed out of Mamie's back door and did the roundabout through her flower garden and into mine.

Josephine stood watering the plants in the sun room when I whizzed by. I froze in mid-stride.

She wasn't as curled into herself as she had been since Savannah's kidnapping. And a soft smile curved her lips. If we could keep her busy, if the reverend remained interested, when Savannah comes home ... well ... Josephine would be herself again.

That was a lot of ifs. By the time I'd reached the sanctuary of my office, my mind refocused. Somebody local must be getting paid for information on the girls. Getting info on anyone looking like they'd just struck gold without evidence of effort was my first priority. That person surely was up to their neck in no good. I sat as still as a Civil War statue before I dialed Lyle.

"Just hearing your voice is a relief." Lyle's rumbly voice made me smile.

"I've been fending off unwelcome sympathy hugs because some rogue has abandoned me."

"Not from ol' Rand, I hope."

"He tried." I put Lyle on speaker phone and settled back into my chair, my hands twiddling with a pen.

"And?"

"He's doomed to fail. I think it's mighty convenient for your friend Longworth to show up. With George gone, and Mamie up to her eyeballs in feeding and housing George's spy friends, he's taken over the investigation. I need some insight into your new boarder."

Lyle spoke into my ire. "Let me summarize. Randall Longworth's father set up his company's repair garage here back in the '60s. Longworth, Senior began making money hand-over-fist in a few years."

I thudded a glass paperweight on papers riffling in the breeze from my open door. "Something is niggling at me. Do you think Longworth is involved with Savannah's kidnapping?"

"Whoa. Where'd that come from? I'd say not. Rand never has skirted the law. He loves money, has expensive taste, and takes extravagant vacations, but he works hard and earns his keep. Can't see him involved in trafficking. He wouldn't like the inconvenience of jail. Crimp his style. His arrival is a little curious, though. He was here two weeks ago. Usually Rand is in town every other month."

"A call from the head of my repair shop brought me to town." I whipped my head around to see Longworth lounging in the doorway. "Good of you, Lyle to think me incapable of financial wizardry, even if your reason is I'd be uncomfortable residing in the local slammer."

Randall Longworth's ears were a Merlo-color, so were his cheeks. He should be embarrassed. He'd invaded my house and office without an invitation.

"Think nothing of it." Lyle's voice betrayed humor. "There's trouble with your business?"

"I asked a few questions about billing last time I visited. My man here seemed to think someone's been cooking the books and making a tidy profit. A little padding here, a slight of hand there, pretty soon someone's got a bank account in the Bahamas."

"Find out who?" Lyle's tone said he was interested.

"Not yet. The disappearance of this schoolgirl is more urgent."

Feeling ashamed of my suspicions I smiled at him. A genuine, non-manufactured smile.

"Well, at least I've gotten to see your eyes light up, Mrs. Morgan." Longworth bowed slightly.

"Excuse me?" Lyle said.

"Not to worry, Lyle. It was the kind of smile that says, 'Maybe I misjudged you.' Which you have. Apparently, you two are not broken-hearted lovers and you're not escaping to Europe."

"Keep it quiet, Rand. We're cooperating with the FBI on an undercover operation. What brought you to Delilah's?"

"I needed to apologize to your girlfriend for telling the assembly about your desertion."

"That all?"

"Well ... no. I thought *if* you were out of the picture, I might offer moral support."

"You mean make a move on her. Delilah isn't Clarisse, Rand."

The edge in Lyle's voice made me look sharply at Randall Longworth.

"It was a mistake, Lyle."

"It was forgiven." But the do-not-try-it-again warning in Lyle's tone was clear.

Randall Longworth bobbed his head as if Lyle could see him. "I'm leaving, Lyle." Longworth edged out of my office. I looked quickly at my desktop to see if any of my books were evident. A stack cluttered the space. Had he seen them? Longworth's footsteps on the wood floor receded. When I heard the front door open and shut, I puffed out a sigh.

"I have my fry pan *du jour* in the bedroom," I told him.

"Good," said Lyle. "Keep it within reach."

Chapter Twenty

Problems I had galore, all jumping out and taking up residence in my mind. I needed to work with something other than words. I headed to the attic sewing room. Sewing was therapeutic. Maybe I wouldn't think about Savannah or Josephine for five minutes. I rubbed between my eyebrows where a headache centered.

The stack of Harry's silk ties rested on my cutting table. I grabbed one, sat in the rocker by the small window and began to rip out the stitches. If I did ten ties per day, I'd have the pile done in three days and off to the dry cleaners for cleaning and pressing the silk. My neck started hurting on the fifth tie. It was maroon, one of Harry's favorite colors. I kept at it, laying the ties one on top of the other, their points tidily aligned until tie eight. Lyle had given Harry the tie a couple of years ago. It had chickens parading around and a few eggs here and there. Harry wore it at Easter and when he felt saucy.

What if Lyle is trying to break things off with me and a fake break-up was his gentlemanly way of preparing me? I skewed my lips right. Not possible. Lyle was a straight-up guy and never lied to me. Tease, yes. Out and out fib, no. I felt better. *Why can't I use my fertile imagination for writing?* I did neck rolls to ease the pain.

Josephine thumped the vacuum nozzle up the stairs in a cleaning frenzy. I finished tie ten, stood up and stretched, then reached for my cell phone to call Lyle. It rang before I had a chance to dial.

"Hello." My voice sounded tight from the pain of my throbbing head.

"Mom." Molly was so loud I put the phone away from my ear. "Any news yet about Savannah?"

"They think she's been taken to South Carolina."

"Do they know where?"

"Not exactly."

"How's Josephine?" The vacuum turned off. Most likely, Josephine was switching it to a different plug.

"Better since the Weldon girl has been found. She's almost her old self."

"We're praying, Mom. I feel so helpless stuck here." Molly got all the info about Savannah on a blog George had set up. I knew something else was on her mind. "Did you feel this lousy when you were pregnant?"

"The first three months were a little difficult." She didn't need to know I'd bonded with the toilet and making chicken soup caused dry heaves.

"This stinks. I'm eating peanut butter on toast 24/7. When do I get to eat ice cream?"

"Give it a couple more months. I'll deliver the dill pickles. I've a couple of jars left from canning last year."

"Hey, I, er . . . got a phone call from a friend. She said there's a rumor going around that you and Judge Henderson have called off your dating."

"You will have to ask your father-in-law, sweetheart."

"Mom, you two are perfect for one another. Did you have a fight?"

"No, dear. He's off on a trip just now. Maybe that's why people are talking."

"Well, Cam and I worry about you, living all alone in your big old house."

"As long as there aren't any deer wandering around, I should be fine."

"Your water back on?"

"They're working on it." At least my lawyer was haranguing everyone down at the courthouse. Apparently, someone at city hall contacted the water board and everything was on hold.

My head ached. Josephine's vacuum was halfway up the attic stairs and was making an unfamiliar wheezing sound, which didn't help a whit.

"Uh-oh . . . got to go, Mom." In her haste to disconnect, Molly's phone sounded as if it hit the floor.

Mine made that chirp noise that signals a text coming in. My heart beat faster. Maybe it was a secret message from Lyle.

I've found something of Carly's that might help with your investigation. Meet me at the car dealership at four. Melissa Mays.

I glanced at my cell phone. It read 3:31. I'd have to get moving.

"You done making excuses to Miss Molly for your no good, almost fiancé?" Josephine asked as I squirreled around her vacuum hose trying to get down the stairs.

"Lyle," I said in a high-minded voice, "is taking a breather from courting. He has chosen to keep looking for Savannah, just not letting the town gossips in on his mission."

"Huh. I didn't suspect him as a fickle man. You want to move out of his house and back to mine?"

"I've thought about it."

"You say the word and I'll have Mama packed in a slick minute."

"Thank you." I kissed her on the cheek.

"Really, Miss Dee Dee. Show some respect." She laughed. It was the first time I'd heard her laugh since the awful phone call.

"I'm taking the truck on an errand. Be back by dinner."

Stick shifts didn't intimidate me, but the play on Harry's steering wheel was enough to make me seasick. Sitting behind the wheel and having to keep correcting its trajectory made my neck hurt even more.

"Sheesh! I probably resemble an old drunk weaving my way through traffic," I muttered as I shot toward the bypass.

The day was warm. Harry's side window proved a little contrary. I managed to roll the window down, but I was still sweating. I took a deep breath, hoping the wind in my hair would cure a headache. If Harry had been driving, I'd have closed my eyes and thought of my mountains, the ones around Horsetail Falls where Mama and Daddy had their farm. Instead, I sang "Country Roads," and tapped my cowboy boots to the tune while changing the words "West Virginia" to East Kentucky. I felt a smidge better, but my head still pounded.

The problem with old things is they've got no get-up-and-go. Harry's truck wheezed and rattled up a long hill. *Wonder where I'll be in twenty years?*

A silver car drew up behind me. It sped up and cruised past like I was standing still. After pulling into Buck Mays' neon-lit car lot, I parked near the road and looked at my cell phone. Five minutes to spare. It was a good feeling, being early. Keeping people waiting was rude, my mama always said. I stepped out of the car and saw the silver speedster hurtling back toward McKeansville. Must have forgotten to turn off the iron. Whoever was driving turned into Mays' car lot and parked beside Harry's turquoise truck. I couldn't see into the dark windows of the cloud-colored car with a cat statue on the hood, but I smiled my friendly smile. The sleek door opened.

"Hello, Mrs. Morgan." Randall Longworth levered himself from the driver's seat, his condescending smile intact. Somehow Longworth made the company of Buck Mays seem inviting. "Tsk, tsk. Lyle letting you drive this old thing is a sad commentary on his negligence. What that antique needs is a junk yard." He actually kicked the rear tire and slapped on a wiseacre grin. It broadened when he looked at my face, which felt tight with anger.

"Lyle didn't let me drive this, I *chose* to drive Harry's truck." I was too loud for politeness.

He held up his hands in protest. "I recognized you when I passed, so I stopped to make my apologies."

He extended his right hand. Automatically, I did the same, then jerked my hand back.

"I was wrong to insult you in front of your friends. If you can't say yes to Lyle, maybe he's the wrong man for you." His mouth curled into a sly smile.

"Did you come to apologize or dig yourself into a deeper pit?"

Longworth began to laugh. "Well, I'll hand it to you Miss Delilah, you put a man in his place."

I crossed my arms.

"Apologies aren't my specialty." He shrugged as if excusing his bad manners. "You are right. I'll keep my nose out of your business. If you want to wait till kingdom come to marry Lyle and he's fine with that, it's no matter to me."

"Is that an apology?" I gave him my squint eye, thinking of how politicians seem unfamiliar with the word apology.

"The best I can do." The office door flew open. Buck Mays and two other cowboy-pretenders emerged.

"Hey, boys." Longworth waved as he greeted them. "The lady and I are old friends." He stretched the truth so far it was going to snap back and sting him. When Randall turned to grin at me, the largest buckaroo drew back his fist and laid a haymaker on the side of Longworth's chin. Randall Longworth went down with a thud onto the asphalt. He didn't even twitch, but lay prone, eyes shut, hands crumpled up beside him. Wanting to take off like a jack rabbit, I leaped toward my truck as someone grabbed the back of my jacket. I fell to the tarmac.

"Not so much as a peep," an Elvis look-a-like hissed. He stared down at me while his moussed hair bounced on his forehead as if it were rubber. I twisted to my side and kicked him in a place Harry advised would incapacitate a male assailant. He buckled over. I jumped to my feet and sprinted toward the highway, eyes front, heartbeat staccato. I dialed 911 as I ran. Boots pounded behind me. I got as far as the flashing neon entrance sign when Buck Mays wheezed up and pulled a gun.

"Get moving to the back lot, Mrs. Morgan."

"What do you think you're doing?"

"Teaching you to keep your nose out of other people's business."

With Mays pointing a gun at my chest, I inched my feet back the way I'd run. I held my phone close to my side, concealing it. The other outlaws hustled an unconscious Longworth into the rickety office.

There wasn't another person in sight, just Mays' cars lined up ready for inspection. As we rounded the corner of the building aiming toward the back, the 911 operator drawled, "McKeansville Emergency Services." Mays grabbed the phone from my hand and tossed it into a wooden tub filled with dying shrubbery and cigarette butts. The rear door of the office opened and crashed against the building's wall. The fake cowboys exited with the unconscious body of Longworth. They hauled him between the used cars and onto a dirt trail. Longworth's feet plowed through the dirt making two narrow lines pointing toward fields beyond. We shuffled behind. A copse of trees obscured us from the road.

Mays was a local.

We'd seen the others' faces. That didn't give us much prospect of surviving. About fifty yards behind Mays' used car lot was a tobacco barn. We tramped that way. The ground, adorned with rusty car parts, an engine block here, a radiator there, had seen better days. Behind the rickety barn were unharvested corn fields.

At the hands of the largest man, the barn doors squealed open. The tobacco barn was weathered. If they locked us in, we could get out of the rickety sides.

I was marched in. Longworth dragged. Three vehicles were stuffed into the barn, a paneled truck, a riding lawn mower, and a small car covered in canvas. The place smelled of burnt tobacco, acrid and irritating.

Mays pointed to us. "Tie them up and throw them in the panel truck. You'll find what you need over there." He jerked his head toward a work bench cluttered with buckles, ropes, and tools. Mays handed his gun to the larger of the duo. The man fingered the hand gun with expertise, which eroded my nugget of confidence. "I'll call the boss and find out what to do with them." Mays slipped out of the wooden door and disappeared.

His thugs threw us onto the filthy barn floor and attempted to tie us up. I wasn't a help because I used my elbows to jab them in the solar plexus. The Elvis impersonator smacked the back of my head, hard, then clamped onto my hands and bound them behind my back in an unmovable knot. When they were through trussing me up like a sacrificial goat, they applied their expertise to Longworth, but left his legs free. While the side-burned one hung onto a limp Longworth, the other opened the truck's back door. They shoved me in and hefted Longworth beside me. When his head hit the floor, it made the hollow thumping sound of a ripe watermelon.

The smaller man bent close to me. "Not through with you yet." He hog-tied us together, back to back, before slamming the door shut. Longworth moaned loud and long.

I felt around the knots with my fingers. They weren't as secure as Fort Knox. The villains hadn't patted me down to check for weapons. My knife rested under my jean's jacket. Longworth writhed like a wounded rattler. I sat upright, jerking him sideways.

"What the . . ." Every breath Longworth took shuddered my body.

"Watch your language, Mr. Longworth." I whispered because I feared that the goons were close.

"You?" Longworth was mumbling and hard to

hear.

"Yes, me. Now hop to it and help ease my knife from its holder at my waist."

Longworth got a little personal as he fiddled around with his fingers. I'd probably put him off his game if I mentioned it, but it was galling having him touch me at all. I wanted Lyle, who'd at least apologize.

"If you can cut the ropes, we can surprise them." My words were more breath than a whisper.

"Lady," he said nastily, "do you know what this is all about?"

"They think we're butting into something they want hidden."

He wiggled around so much I had trouble staying upright. "Let me know if I nick you."

"Don't worry, you'll know." He sawed for a bit. The rope was as tight as before.

"Hey, I think I've cut a couple of them."

I listened to heavy footsteps on the cement floor, the screech of the door, then, nothing. Randall worked vigorously, his shoulders moving up and down. Mine did too. My head began to throb again.

"Almost there." He sounded relieved. He jolted us backwards with a sharp tug. The ropes connecting us fell away. My hands and feet were still bound but I could move.

I scooched over and found the door unlatched.

Using a foot to pry the lever up, Longworth lifted the truck's door until a crack of light was visible. It was silent as a morgue at three a.m. We stuck our faces into the aperture. Daylight streaked through the wooden boards of the barn walls.

"Hey, Buddy, you should set it inside the barn. That way it'd look natural."

The muffled voice from outside made my head prickle. Whatever Buddy was going to set, I wanted no part of. I wriggled past Longworth and pushed the door open with my shoulder.

"What are you doing?" Longworth whispered.

"Vamoosing." I dropped onto the floor and landed in a roll since my legs were still trussed. I spit out the dirt that invaded my mouth.

Longworth joined me on the floor. The truck was parked between the mower and canvas-covered car. The angle of the sun's rays slanting through the windows told me it was about five, give or take a few minutes. Lying on my back, I used my feet to quietly close the open doors.

"Smell that?" Longworth's voice was agitated.

I nodded.

That, was gasoline, ripe and pungent. I peeked around the back of the vehicle toward the half-open barn doors. Buddy held a gas can and was sprinkling a trail of liquid across the front of the building. We knee-waddled toward a low hay crib. Puny as it was, we used it for shelter, laying almost flat in the dust, dirt, and bits of hay. Randall at least hadn't forgotten his task. He whittled away at the ropes on my wrists. I closed my mouth tight as he made a few unfortunate pricks along my arm.

Buddy slid one of the barn doors open wide, then flung the gasoline can in an arc toward the three vehicles. Gas splattered from one side of the barn to the other. A few drops landed on us.

"You lock the van door, Vic?"

"I think so. It's too late now, any who. They're going to be fricasseed in no time." He laughed. "Hurry up, Buddy."

As Buddy flicked his Bic, Randall's sawing hit pay dirt. My hands were free. I grabbed the knife from him as smoke began to fill the flimsy-sided tobacco barn. My eyes teared as I finally cut Randall Longworth free. He rubbed his wrists then high-tailed it to the back of the barn. I worked on my ankles until I was mobile.

A work bench, with small windows close above it, sat under the sloped roof. I headed toward the only opening I saw. The smoke crawled along the floor, then rose, seeking to escape. Longworth emerged from a cloud of gray, coughing and wiping his eyes.

I sputtered, "Get closer to the floor."

The fire was a wall of flames, moving fast toward the van and its gas tank. On the bench a pile of rags stood beside canning jars. I tossed Longworth a rag and took another to tie against my nose.

"Help me onto the bench."

He swung me up. I landed on the flat wooden surface. Rusty tools hung from nails above my head. Smoke wrapped its tentacles around us. Lying on my back, I kicked out the windows with my boots.

So we wouldn't get cut from the glass fragments, I placed rags on the window frame, then slithered through the opening and onto the uneven ground.

"Come on!" I urged through my tears.

"It's too tight," Longworth coughed back. A dark cloud of acrid smoke roiled over him.

"Kick out the frame!"

"I'm working on it."

It wasn't the frame that went first. It was the boards around it. Climbing through the opening, Longworth got his leg caught between the sill and the wall's siding. Dark ringlets of smoke formed around him as he swung like a pendulum an inch from a vole hill. Kicking free, Longworth fell flat on his face. His left leg crumpled under him. I had visions of another five minutes of un-consciousness, but he staggered to his feet before sinking to the ground again.

Longworth moaned like a woman in labor. "I've cut my leg."

The barn began to crackle. We were inches away when flames shot out the barn's sides.

I pulled him to his feet, put his arm around my neck, and hauled him away from the burning barn. We aimed for the unharvested corn field. I didn't look back.

Longworth had enough adrenalin to move smartly, but he groaned as we did an awkward sprint into the waving corn plants.

To our right a truck's engine sprang to life. There was enough daylight for them to spot us. Plunging among the tassels, we moved diagonally across the field toward a line of oak trees. Sirens wailed in the distance.

"Hey, Buddy! You see movement over in the corn field?"

I stopped right quick. The shouter was only a few yards away.

"Nah, Victor. You're getting spooked. Nothing's moving out here except rabbits looking for their holes."

Longworth swore in my ear. I clapped a hand over his mouth. He began to snuffle through his nose. The sirens drew closer.

"Mays says he saw something. Go have a look see."

"Right," came the sarcastic reply. "It's probably a deer. Hand over the shotgun and I'll fetch us some dinner."

Flames turned the sky orange as they fanned out of the barn's roof.

Longworth bent to examine his wound, leaning so hard on me that I fell against a desiccated corn stalk. Its bony leaves rattled.

"You hear that, Buddy?"

"Yup!"

"What you make it out to be?"

"Racoon, maybe a squirrel stocking up. Don't be so nervous, Vic. They's almost done in the barn. Only thing we didn't do was baste them." Overcome by his wit, Buddy began to snicker.

"Can the truck lights afore the firemen sees them." The other man was curt.

The truck lights went out as the barn's side wall exploded. Fragments of hot wood showered the bare ground. Sirens oscillated closer. The noise gave us cover.

I lurched with Longworth toward the woods. Deep footprints revealed our path in the wet mud of the rows. We'd be easy to follow.

In the dimming light, I could see Longworth's skin torn to the bone, a deep, jagged tear about two inches long. Clutching his leg, Longworth tried to staunch the bleeding as we moved.

I stopped him, took off my rag nose cover and tied it tight around his injury. "This will have to do until I can get you to safety."

Longworth dragged his leg through the dry corn sounding like a snare drum band.

"See." We could hear Victor yelling above the noise of the arriving firetrucks and the explosive fire. "Something's out there."

"Yeah. I heard it too. They didn't get away, Vic. They were locked in."

"I think you forgot about the lock." Vic's voice tapered off. "If they ain't fried like bacon in there, Mays will have our hide."

Chapter Twenty-One

WE HAD TO KEEP MOVING AND find a hidey hole in the woods. Randall Longworth helped by pushing off with his good leg and giving stability to our three-legged race. Corn stalks made their skeleton sounds behind us. I panted from lugging Longworth's athlete-gone-soft body.

"They're closing in." Longworth huffed beside me.

"We're not dog meat yet, Mr. Longworth."

We reached the end of the corn row and stared at ten feet of plowed ground, a split-rail fence and thick woods. I riveted my left arm around Longworth's waist and said, "On the count of three we'll make a run for it. Go under the fence. I'll go over and help you on the other side."

He hesitated, which I'd suspected he'd do, so I put my fingers on his belt loops and heaved him beside me. An Olympic sprinter had nothing on the gallop I commenced. At the fence I deposited Longworth by a post and vaulted over the top rail. He wasn't a help at all. He clung to the ground and crabbed sideways, more grovel than scurry. As soon as his right arm cleared the lowest rail, I grabbed his hand and hauled him to his feet. Spasms twisted around my neck seeking a place to set up residence.

Vic and Buddy thrashed through the field. I watched the corn stalks disappear in their path. They were two minutes behind us.

Following a deer trail in between the trees, I sought deep cover. A creek sputtered nearby, noisy enough to muffle our huffing, puffing rampage through the woods. I unholstered my knife and cut off a little bit of my shirt bottom and put it on a low hickory branch close to the stream, hoping to steer them west while we hiked northeast.

"In." I ordered Longworth.

He didn't object.

I elbowed my way through the hard cane until knee deep in the shadowed and dark water under the tree overhang, I guided him over slippery rocks and up the other bank, leaving a clear trail among the oak trees. I ripped off another bit of cloth and put it on a fragment of cane. Helping him hobble through the shrubs leading west, I put up with his mumbled objections. Around a bend we reentered the stream and headed north. I made Longworth squelch an eighth of a mile before we climbed out of the water and fought the cane to get up a bank. It was nearly dark by the time we aimed toward the road. No noise from the fire, none from our pursuers.

Randall flopped down by a fallen log and began to remove his rag bandage.

I shook my head. "Better keep it on until we get to an ER."

"Something's crawling up my leg." He pulled a small black leach from his wrap and began searching for others. "This is disgusting." He tossed another leach into the underbrush.

I checked my legs for the nasty invertebrates, then helped him remove two more from his pants hem. The little vampires seemed intrigued with his blood. "Let's get some distance from here, circle around and head toward the firetrucks." Wary, we moved until rustling in the underbrush on the trail above us stopped us flat.

I pulled Longworth into a crouch. "Quick. Find a fallen log."

We jumped off the semi-path and stumbled over a stump. Tumbling down the slope toward the water, we stopped short of a drenching by colliding with a lichen-covered oak. Scuttling behind it, I yanked Longworth into the darker shadows and lay flat. We'd made enough noise to scare up the locals. A young buck crashed through the woods to our left, aiming for higher ground.

"There!" One of the men's voices made me catch my breath and hold it. "What'd I tell you? They's circled back and are heading to the road." We put our heads above the curve of the trunk and watched as a flashlight's glow bobbed above us. Their voices faded and the light disappeared into the gloom of night, following the deer.

"Thank you for dragging me to safety."

"You're welcome." I slapped a mosquito nibbling my ear.

"Although, I guess you should thank me. I *am* the one who cut us free so we didn't burn to death." Randall snaked an arm around my shoulders and drew me close.

Shaking free of his overfriendly grip, I scooched over a foot or so. "You, me, and the Good Lord. And He'll have something to say about you being too prideful, Mr. Longworth." We were whispering but I'd heard that a whisper carries as far as speaking normally and I wanted him to be still.

"I don't know about what He'd say, Mrs. Morgan. We haven't been on speaking terms of late."

"*That* I can imagine." I rolled my neck to ease the tension, miffed with the Lord that I was in danger alongside a reprobate.

"Can get mighty cold outdoors on an October night." The man played a one-note tune.

"Watch out for that clump of poison ivy you're sitting beside, Mr. Longworth."

That got his attention. He raised his hands overhead in an effort to avoid the offending weed.

A shotgun blast shattered the night.

"What the devil?" Buck Mays' voice reverberated from the path above and to our left. "What you fool crackers up to?" I heard boots moving fast toward the sound.

"I tripped," called out Buddy.

"Sheriff has arrived from McKeansville and he's

asking questions. Starting with that old turquoise truck in my parking lot."

"I swear that I heard Mrs. Morgan and her friend in the woods."

"You two might as well hightail it to the road 'cause they ain't comin' out of that inferno." Mays voice sank to a low growl. "The boss's toady will pick you up there."

"I tell you," Vic's voice dropped to a sniveling whine, "they made it into the woods, tromped the stream, and headed back this way."

"If you're such a great hunter, why'd you discharge the gun within earshot of the law?" Mays spit out his question. "You boys are tracking your tails. I saw a big buck go trotting by right before I got here. Git to it. Cain't chance any of us getting caught up in this."

Longworth shifted, ever so slightly. It sent a piece of the fallen log careening down the slope toward the stream. When it hit a rock, it sounded like fireworks.

"See? What'd I tell you." Vic sounded cocky. They began moving our direction.

Longworth's muscles were so tense I thought he was ready to bolt. I grabbed his arm to restrain him. We kept our heads glued to the ground, not caring if we were sniffing poison ivy leaves.

A ground squirrel skittered up the hillside beside us and dashed toward the trail. Wet leaves flew under his feet.

"Look-a-there!" Buddy sent a blast of pellets toward the squirrel. The shot splintered the log above us, showering our backs with wood shrapnel.

"Give me that!" demanded Buck. "Now git, afore you cause any more consternation."

Scuffling sounded from the trail. I popped up my head. Not six feet away Buck Mays fought Buddy for the gun. More figures emerged from the gloom.

"Well, hello, Buck," drawled Tom Bellows. "I can see by your shotgun y'all are hunting a little early this year."

"Actually, found these two wandering around on my land and were giving them the what for."

"No law against discharging your gun on your own land, Buck. No hunting, though, especially without a license."

Take them all away in handcuffs, Sheriff.

"Oh, we ain't hunting, Sheriff." Buddy's words were spoken so fast they barely registered.

"Not anymore, because I'm confiscating your weapon."

The slap of wood on a palm caused Longworth to lift his head.

After a long pause Bellows said, "Well, now, I've been following a blood trail from the edge of the corn field to right about here. Care to illuminate me as to how that came to be?"

"Vic here cut his hand," Buck improvised.

"McEntire, shed some light over here so I can see what your injury looks like, Vic. You might need medical attention." The sheriff spoke softly, which was dangerous.

"No matter. Stopped bleeding and it's fine now." Vic fumbled around for words.

"Let's let the paramedics take a look-see," Bellows continued in a slow drawl. Was he laying a trap? "Now, Buck. I spied Harry Morgan's truck in your lot." The sheriff paused. "Miss Delilah thinking of selling?"

Something niggled at me to lay low and not stand up and holler for help. I decided not to argue with the Lord and let out the mating call of a male cardinal. About the only bird call I'd mastered. Bellows would know that they court in March, being a country man. As soon as my lips stopped moving Longworth hissed, "Hush!" in my ear.

"Yep. Cut her a deal she couldn't refuse." Buck's voice was moving left.

"That surprises me some. Thought she'd keep it in the family for sentimental reasons. The car next to it looks pretty fancy. You taking up selling more foreign cars these days?"

Ignoring Longworth, I gave a second call, ducking my head when he tried to clap his dirty fingers over my mouth.

"I take whatever deals I can get, Sheriff." Mays laugh was phony.

"I'll bet you do. My deputy will see that y'all head back to the barn. Seems the fire marshal wants to ask a few questions. Something about the fire's origins. He's thinking it looks mighty suspicious."

"Ain't nothing valuable in that tobacco barn," Mays stuttered. "Worthless junk tossed there when Melissa's dad cluttered up the place."

"It'd help if you'd mosey along with my deputies here." Bellows' voice faded. "I'll be following right behind." Their footsteps disappeared. The call of a female cardinal sounded off left.

I responded.

"That you, Miss Delilah?" Bellows whispered in the dark.

"Yes. And Randall Longworth. He's injured his leg."

"They chasing you?"

"Yes. Tried to make us barbecue."

"Miss Delilah, I reckon this has to do with your little investigation." I heard the dismay in his voice. "Keep your heads down and follow about ten feet behind me." His voice was firm. "And stay out of sight. McEntire," Bellows said, his voice muffled as he probably spoke into his radio. "Get the SUV and drive to the edge of the woods. I've wrenched my ankle and need assistance, then I'll take the SUV and you remain with the fire investigator until Fisk relieves you." I didn't hear Sarah's reply to her boss but shook my head. The man lied as easily as Lyle. Must be something about the law that made them prevaricate. Bellows turned to glance at us. "As soon as you can, climb in the back of my SUV and keep your heads down."

"They're waiting for someone called, 'the boss's

toady,'" I told him.

"We'll keep an eye out. At the moment, I want them to think you're being roasted like a trussed hog."

Hobbling behind Bellows, Longworth's slash began to bleed again. When we reached the SUV, I sat soggy and uncomfortable on the cruiser's floor, while putting pressure on Longworth's injury. He lay on the seat, his hand over his head looking as miserable as I had ever seen a man look. What I wouldn't give to see Harry with his macho marine bravado.

Bellows turned his head as we waited at a stop light. "After you called 911, Miss Delilah, we tracked the phone and found where it was tossed. Put two and two together."

"They tried to kill us." Longworth half-sat up he was that mad.

Bellows stepped on the accelerator. "I'll have Fisk take down your statements, but first I've a plan. I want you two to remain hidden. Let them think they got away with murder."

"Arrest them!" shouted Longworth.

"We need to find Savannah. I think those three are tangled up in the kidnappings and can lead us to her."

We slunk into the ER through the side entrance and were ushered into a hallway with a dozen doors. I sat on a chair in one of the little rooms. Longworth was carted to another. Bellows lounged in the doorway between us. He chewed on a cookie he'd confiscated from the doctor's lounge, looking pleased with himself. As he began to eat his second cookie, his pocket played Chopin.

"Got my phone, Sheriff?"

He nodded. The phone emerged, bagged in plastic.

He looked at the caller ID and lifted his eyebrows. "Your phone hasn't been entered into evidence yet, nor dusted for fingerprints. I'll have a chat with your caller on my phone. Excuse me, Miss Delilah." He left the small white-on-white room so I couldn't hear.

The room was cold. I hopped off the chair and

searched for a blanket. Nothing but a thin white sheet. I wrapped it around my shoulders.

Bellows returned munching another cookie. "That was Lyle. Josephine told him you were missing. He wanted to see if he could reach you but eventually found me."

With that, Bellows began to hum. I couldn't get another word out of him as we waited for Longworth to get cleaned up, shot up, and stitched. Longworth had ten stitches—less than my daughter's hand when she'd cut it mowing the lawn—but he sat like a potentate in the transport wheelchair. The man was tiresome.

The sheriff sped us away from the smell of iodine to the Bluegrass Country Inn on the bypass. He announced it was to be our home away from home.

Deputy Sarah McEntire hustled us up a flight of stairs. As she stepped into the hallway her head swiveled left, then right, like you see in the movies. McEntire's boot heels clicked across the hard tile in precise steps—she'd been military trained.

Bellows looked at me. "No phone calls. I want people to believe you are off on a romantic interlude." Bellows opened a room's door.

I looked past him in dismay. "Adjoining rooms?"

"I don't have enough deputies to watch two rooms. You'll have to put up with the inconvenience. If you're worried about our resident judge, he'll have to trust you." Bellows pursed his lips when he gazed at Longworth. "Deputy McEntire will be here for protection. You both will stay until I feel it's appropriate. I must go interview those three murderers and see what they have to say."

Armed for battle, Bellows slammed out of my room.

After the hall door stopped throbbing, I studied the deputy. "Woods were full of poison ivy. I'm going to soap up. See that Longworth does the same." If I could get McEntire out of my room, I'd use the motel's phone to make a quick call. I needed to hear Lyle's calm baritone.

"Longworth knows. Think I'll stay right here and keep an eye on things. Hand me your clothes wrapped in a towel, please. And your boots."

Get wet, soap up, turn off the water, wait five minutes, rinse, had been my mama's mantra when it came to poison ivy oils. I did it twice, even up my nose, which burned, then I added a good cry to the mix. I chalked up my tears to nerves.

McEntire produced blue hospital scrubs for my PJs. After answering the deputy's litany of questions, I sat at a small table and watched my picture and Randall Longworth's appear on the eleven o'clock news broadcast. They called us missing persons, last seen along the 127 heading toward the freeway.

"This will send Josephine over the edge." I muttered as I sampled a hamburger another deputy named Fergus had picked up.

"Bellows has things under control." Fergus nodded as he went through the connecting door to Longworth's room.

"Nothing's under control." I puckered my lips.

The news announcer spoke like he was covering a horse race. "Mrs. Delilah Morgan, widow of famed poet Harry Morgan, and multi-millionaire Randall Longworth are missing tonight." A picture of my truck and his car in Mays parking lot with smoke wafting between them was on the screen. "The mystery deepens with the discovery of a suspected arson-related fire not far from the dealership where Harry Morgan's antique truck was discovered."

The reporter on site thrust her microphone in Melissa Mays' face. "Mrs. Mays, you called the fire department a few hours ago. What alerted you to the fire?"

"I was bringing my son home from soccer practice when we spotted two men with gas cans circling the barn." Petite Melissa Mays was dwarfed by the high-heeled reporter.

"The sheriff's report states they took three men into custody an hour ago." The reporter smiled toothily into the camera.

"Yes. The two strangers and my husband Buck. He owns the used car lot here." Melissa flapped her hand toward the neon sign where Buck's name glowed red.

"Did you notice anything else, Mrs. Mays?"

"We heard gun shots off in the woods." Melissa pointed beyond the smoldering barn.

The reporter stepped back, surprised. "We, meaning?"

"My son and I, the fire chief, and the firemen." A tall youth came to stand with Melissa. "I have to go. The police have some questions for me."

"There you have it, Drake," said the on-site reporter. "Several questions come to mind. Is this related to the recent shooting of the former fiancé of Mrs. Morgan, or the disappearance of Mrs. Morgan's housekeeper's daughter? There is also a court case pending, involving a professor in Professor Morgan's English department. All these incidents have one thing in common—Mrs. Delilah Morgan."

"Good reporting, Kelsey." The anchorman faced the camera. "We will keep you informed on the latest news concerning that break-in at Boone College, the disappearance of Professor Morgan's wife, and this deliberately set fire."

Sarah McEntire turned off the TV. "The sheriff has a lot to puzzle out, Mrs. Morgan."

"Well, my reputation is in tatters, that's for sure." I rolled the paper that had surrounded my burger into a ball and tossed it in the trash can. "I'm going to sleep. Things are bound to look brighter in the morning." That was a quote from Mee-maw when a fox got into the hen house and killed half her layers.

I tried to sleep on the lumpy pillow and crisp hotel sheets, while Deputy McEntire read a book by the table lamp. When the clock read 3:13 a.m., I crawled out of bed. All I'd gotten with my bed wrestling was the story of Elijah and Jezebel. What that had to do with Buck aiming to eliminate me was a mystery. I grabbed the hotel's stationery to scribble notes. They'd tried to eliminate me because I had gotten too close to someone. Who? Had Longworth stumbled into the situation or was he a target too? Questions, no answers. Only thing I'd heard from the Lord was about Jezebel, a willful, over-sexed, lethal woman. Should we be looking for a woman? Was Buck Mays linked up with trafficking? That was the only thing that made sense. Puzzled, I got on my knees to pray that God stuck it to Buck and his pyromaniac cohorts. I began to yawn about six and fell asleep with my head epoxied to the pillow.

I woke to find a change of clothes on the other double bed. They were mine. A makeup bag perched beside them. If Josephine packed them, she wasn't worried about me. I opened my familiar suitcase. In it was Savannah's furry pillow. Josephine trusted me to find Savannah. I blinked back tears.

Deputy Fergus, McEntire, and I were sitting at a small table, nibbling on a fast food egg-on-muffin thing when Longworth limped into my room, inching along using a metal cane with a three-legged bottom. Moving must have hurt some, but his expression suggested agony.

"They say I'm concussed." Longworth flopped into the chair beside me with a dramatic lift of his chin. He stared, then sniffed long and judgmentally, at the food offering. "Plastic cup for coffee," he whined before adding two packages of sugar and one container of cream. "Three-day-old eggs." He held up the paper-wrapped egg concoction, examining the wrapper.

Man wants a personal chef.

"If you don't want your food, hand it over. My mama taught me to not be picky." Deputy Fergus held out his hand.

I nibbled at the English muffin edge that

surrounded my egg.

"Humph." Longworth took a tentative bite, then finished one of the multi-calorie sandwiches and reached for another. "You couldn't find a Bloody Mary?" He put a blue-colored pill in his mouth and lifted a cup of orange juice.

Fergus shrugged.

"Are we going to eat plastic food like we're prisoners?"

Fergus raised his glance to the ceiling and still didn't speak. Longworth had a pinched nose expression. I lifted my eyebrows. "Have another cup of coffee, Longworth, or go back to bed and get up on the other side of it."

Longworth gave me what novelists call a baleful stare—eyes glinting, mouth in a tight line, brow furrowed with displeasure. "Lyle," he articulated slowly, "is in for a rough ride."

"And you, sir, aren't grateful to the police for saving your hide. There's more at stake here than your dissatisfied palate."

Longworth poured himself a refill of coffee, grabbed the unopened newspaper, and eased back as if he planned to loiter.

My hands itched to do something. Anything. Bellows would keep me out of sight, that I knew, so no more adventures.

A knock on Longworth's door sounded in my room.

"Change of shifts." Fergus rose.

"Bored?" Longworth's slow drawl was getting annoying. "This ought to change that." He handed me the front section of the paper.

Stephen Hamilton' picture was front and center on page one. Clutched in his left hand was a sheaf of papers. The headline read, "Harry Morgan's Legacy." The article began, "This is the second of two articles regarding Professor Stephen Hamilton. Hamilton insists he is innocent of any wrong-doing in the former office of Pulitzer-winning poet Harry Morgan. His proof, states Hamilton, lies in the collection of poems he holds in his hand. Hamilton claims Morgan requested that he remove the work hidden behind a picture before Morgan's wife could destroy the writings. "These are," Hamilton states, "masterpieces of literary poetry known as erotica.'"

I gasped. I knew what the word meant. Graphic poems, similar to sections of Shakespeare. I skimmed down to the, "continued on page 6" note and flipped the newspaper until I saw a poem purported to be in Harry's hand titled, "Concupiscence."

"Burying my face
In the warmth
Of her perfect..."

That was as far as I got before I crumpled up the paper.

"Oh, dear. Why would our paper print such trash?" My voice dropped to a whisper. "What will the children think?"

Randall Longworth rose unsteadily to his feet. "I didn't mean to distress you, Delilah. It's a fine poem. The world being what it is will probably give him a Pulitzer postmortem." Longworth, clearly pleased with his pronouncement, reached out and tried to draw me close.

"Erg!" I pushed him away. "Harry couldn't have written this. He used words sparingly. This is a schoolboy's attempt at pornography."

Harry did say I had a perfect body, but I wasn't going down that track or I'd blubber for a week.

"What did you say to Delilah, Rand?" Lyle stood in our adjoining doorways like a Greek statue, legs apart, head up, eyes on fire.

My knees got so weak I grabbed the edge of the table for support.

"Just showed her a news article." Longworth dismissed his previous remarks with a wave of his hand.

I made two stuttering steps toward Lyle then broke

into a sprint.

"The lies about Harry?" Lyle managed to ask as I collided with him. Lyle's voice throbbed with tension.

Randall Longworth shrugged. "Hey. I didn't know the man. Might be lies, might be the truth." I nestled my face against Lyle's broad chest, right where the bullet had penetrated.

Lyle's hand swept over my curls, which were a tangled mess, and rested on my head.

"Did he write some off-color poems? Maybe." Longworth sounded cocky. "The one that was printed is pretty good."

"Fortunately, the sheriff confiscated the rest as evidence, or they'd be printed in the paper too. It'd shock all the locals," Sarah McEntire added.

"It's nonsense, dear. Even Harry's earliest poems were head and shoulders above this drivel." Lyle tilted my head back with a finger and planted one of his earth-shattering kisses on my lips. Breathing became difficult.

"Well, *excuse* us." Longworth's sarcasm was tiring. "I do deserve a thank you for saving the neck of your whatever she is. Fiancée, dearest love, you get the drift."

"I heard it was the other way around, Rand. The sheriff said Delilah's report and your confirmation show that she saved your butt from an inferno, hauled you out of gunshot range, dressed your wound, and hid you in the forest. Seems you owe the lady an apology."

"Okay, okay. I exaggerate. She even gave me a knife so I could cut us free, if you must know all."

Longworth's attitude of being the crowing rooster amid the hens might be changing. He took one look at the pair of us smooshed together and announced, "We were just leaving." Longworth picked up the rumpled paper and escorted the two police deputies into his room.

"How did you, why did you...?"

"Josephine called to say you were missing." He kissed my hair. "Had a conversation with Bellows and George arranged a flight out of Asheville. Couldn't tell George why I needed to head back, though."

"You are the dearest man." I spoke into his chest because my face was again mashed against his clavicle. I backed my head away and studied the bottom of his chin. "Oh, Lyle, we aren't any closer to getting Savannah back and that's the important thing."

"You're safe." He took my hand and we sat on the bed. "We're getting close, or they wouldn't have tried to eliminate you. That means we've made progress."

My head automatically sank onto his shoulder.

"Ah," Lyle said. "A perfect fit." Lyle wrapped his arm around my shoulders. "Di, I have a press conference I must attend. Madison wants to break the news of your disappearance from there. I'm to appear the distraught lover."

"Should be interesting."

Sarah McEntire stuck her head in the doorway. "Excuse me. Sheriff Bellows called. The fire marshal's dogs unearthed a body in the tobacco barn. He wonders if you saw anything before you escaped."

"No!" I leapt to my feet. "There was someone else tied up in there?"

"A buried body. It could have been put there yesterday or some time ago." McEntire shifted her feet and leaned against the doorjamb. She looked tired. "Bellows says Buck Mays and company are up to their necks in murder. He and Madison put the screws on. One of the jail birds is singing."

McEntire put her hands on her hips. "According to Bellows, his tale is as convoluted as a mockingbird's song. The perp also told Bellows that Buck received a phone call mid-afternoon saying you called him a liar."

"I mentioned it at George's. Who would have called Mays from the group at George's?"

McEntire tugged at the cuffs on her shirt. "Turns

out it was Mays' second cousin, Sergeant Mays. Bellows has Sergeant Mays up on charges for obstructing an investigation."

Lyle looked at his cell phone and gave a low whistle. "I've got to run. Now, Delilah, I'm going to need to stretch the truth a little. Not enough to get me disbarred, but enough to ease the mind of whoever is involved in the trafficking ring." Risking his career for Savannah made the worry lines deepen on my forehead. Lyle's fingers reached up and rubbed one of them. "Oh, sweetheart," he said, "I'll use wisdom."

All I could do was nod and stand on my tiptoes to kiss him.

Chapter Twenty-Two

B REAKING NEWS INTERRUPTED THE L EXINGTON STATION at nine forty-three. "The FBI and local sheriff Tom Bellows have called a press conference in McKeansville, Kentucky. This news is regarding the disappearance last night of Delilah Belle Morgan, widow of famed poet Harry Morgan, and shipping millionaire, Randall Longworth."

"Well, here we are again, Mrs. Morgan. Top of the news." Leaning against the doorjamb, Longworth seemed pleased.

"We bring you live to our reporter, Kelsey Adams."

Kelsey, a tall brunette, had been Miss Kentucky two years prior. The camera panned the foyer of the local museum then focused on Kelsey's perfect figure. The museum, formerly the post office, was the only building where the press and cameras could be set up.

Longworth skulked about my room with an empty coffee cup. When he stopped beside me, I wiggled the carafe I held and poured coffee into his cup.

On the news, the sheriff stood to introduce Lyle. Josephine sat off to Lyle's right side. The sheriff had said only three words before Josephine lifted her chin and rose. Josephine with her chin up meant "watch out." I smiled.

"Before Judge Henderson comes to quell any rumors about Miss Delilah and that rogue Randall Longworth," Josephine was using her lady-of-the-manor diction, "I want to clarify a few things."

Longworth made a low whistle. "I love it when a woman is all fired up."

My mouth dropped open I was so flabbergasted at Longworth.

Josephine leaned toward the microphone as if she were a jazz singer. "Mrs. Morgan is a *lady*. She would no more go off with a man than she'd use inappropriate language."

I sucked in mucus, sputtering and tearing when it hit my vocal cords. McEntire whacked me on the back.

"The tales that have been circulating about her and Mr. Longworth are slanderous and typical of those whose minds dwell on unseemly things." Josephine sounded like a proper BBC character. "Mrs. Morgan is investigating the kidnapping of my daughter. I suggest the police look at the three scoundrels recently locked up in the jail. They were the last to see Mrs. Morgan. Perhaps she stumbled upon some information that implicated them in my daughter's kidnapping."

Josephine gave the sheriff her don't-mess-with-me look. Bellows almost blew the whole thing by laughing. Then, he grabbed hold of his holstered gun and gripped it tightly.

"Judge Henderson, here," she pointed toward Lyle, "is doing the best he can, since the love of his life is in harm's way." With that comment, Josephine stepped aside so Lyle could speak.

Lyle wore his somber judge face. There were actual tears in his eyes. "We are gravely concerned for Mrs. Morgan. She would not abandon Harry's truck, which was promised to her sons." His voice broke. He tried again. "The newspaper report on Harry Morgan's so-called poems are a burden that dear lady should not have to bear." Lyle gazed around the room, not a nice, friendly gaze either, but one that stopped hearts. "Anyone who has read Professor Morgan's richly phrased poems and stories is aware these fall short of his literary skills." He paused for dramatic effect. "The drivel that has been purported to be in his hand doesn't compare with his sixth-grade poem on his father's World War II parachute. These are written by an incompetent hack." Lyle's voice rose until it thundered. "When the scoundrel is found there will be a lawsuit that will strip him or her of their reputation, assets, and future assets."

Bellows gently removed Lyle from center stage. He handed Lyle his handkerchief. Lyle turned his back and blew noisily into it then turning to face the reporters, he tapped his teary eyes as a period. Wonder if Lyle had ever thought of becoming an actor?

"Mrs. Morgan is a kidnapping victim," Bellows stated in a flat voice. "Her purse was found in her car. Before she disappeared, Mrs. Morgan called 911 to report that she was being chased. Her cell phone led us to Mays' Used Car Lot. We found her phone nearby." Bellows cleared his throat and glanced around. "Two of the three men I arrested could only be held for trespassing, discharging a gun without a hunting permit, and arson. Because of our confounded laws in this state they are free on bail."

A man shouted, "Our reporter at the fire scene said a body was brought out of the burned barn this morning." That news brought Longworth to my side so he could listen.

"Well." Bellows lifted his chin, while Lyle and Josephine feigned surprise. "The fire marshal found a body in the barn. They're looking for more. Also found cut ropes. At least two people had been tied up in there. Can't say more until the coroner gives us her report. That's all I'm going to say for now. Madison?" Bellows moved aside while Madison stepped to the microphone. Josephine turned to face Bellows, then patted his arm as if she were consoling Bartles.

Madison cast a somber stare on the gathered reporters. "I'll be happy to answer any questions." *Who is the body in the barn? Could it be Carley?* I teared up thinking of fragile Melissa Mays. How does a mother recover when her child has been murdered?

Madison's Q and A didn't hold my attention. I wandered into Longworth's room to get away from the bombardment.

Fergus put on his rain jacket. "Just got a call. Reinforcements are delayed due to the evidence hunt at Mays' barn. I'm heading out for some grub, then I'll relieve Sarah. How's Mexican sound?"

"Perfect. Slather on the guacamole."

"Right." He shot his boyish grin my direction.

Deputy Fergus opened the door part-way to look down the hall. Before he could exit, I heard a woman's voice say, "Of course Harry Morgan wrote them. Can't you see Morgan and his little wife practicing? Why that stuff comes natural from a hillbilly. All they do is make babies. Why else would a Morgan get trapped into marriage unless they were doing the nasty?"

"Really, Charlene. You heard what Olive said. Harry couldn't have written them. Not his style."

I jumped so fast behind the king-size bed, I made a thumping noise as I hit the floor. Fergus was rooted in the doorway.

"Well, well, well, Deputy Fergus. What brings you to this den of iniquity?" teased Charlene Higgenbottom.

"Mornin', Mrs. Higgenbottom, Mrs. Hamilton."

"You got a girlfriend tucked away in there?" Charlene's voice drew closer.

"No, ma'am. Had a report of a disturbance and was checking it out. If you will excuse me."

I skootched halfway under the bed and pulled the coverlet down so I was nearly under it.

"Why, deputy, I've a few questions I need answered. I heard that Delilah Morgan disappeared in the arms of a very good friend of Judge Henderson." Her voice sounded as smug as a political commentator. "You wouldn't know anything about that, would you?"

"Ma'am, I'm going to ask you to stay out of this room until I can get my fingerprint kit."

"Oh, dear, can't you see my friend Lydia here, is feeling faint? She needs to sit down for a moment." Charlene could lie with the best of them. Feet scuffled into the room.

"Now, ladies," Fergus began, clearly outflanked. "You mustn't touch a thing. Keep your hands above your heads. Mrs. Hamilton, sit here on the bed. Don't want you to contaminate the scene."

The large bed went down and stirred the dust along the floor. I pinched my nose.

I heard footsteps behind me. "Hey, Davey. I'm famished. Make it two burritos." McEntire nearly tripped over me before she glanced down and righted herself. Her head swiveled left, then right, then back again. I couldn't tell what she saw. I wasn't poking my head up for anything. "Ah, lovely to see you, Mrs. Mayor, er . . . Mrs. Higgenbottom. Why are your hands above your heads?"

"I told them not to touch anything since this was a crime scene." Fergus sputtered as he talked.

"Right. Why are you ladies in this room?"

"My friend is unwell." Charlene's drawl made unwell last about half-a-minute.

"She'll have to be unwell somewhere else. We need to secure the room." McEntire wasn't putting up with Charlene's nonsense from the way I saw her foot tapping.

"Highly unlikely that you are securing rooms. You two know the rules—no hanky-panky. I'll have to report this."

"You do that, Mrs. Higgenbottom." McEntire's words were sharp. "Why were you ladies in this hotel? Did you create the disturbance that was reported?"

"Us?" Lydia sounded shocked. "Certainly not. We're avoiding the press who've been assaulting us since my husband was unjustly arrested on the word of that *Morgan* woman."

My nose began to itch. I tapped McEntire on her ankle. She looked down. I pointed to my nose before three robust sneezes burst out. She mimicked them a second too late.

"Sorry. Allergies." McEntire wiped her nose with a finger. "You were accusing Mrs. Morgan of a false report, I believe. Have you said that to the sheriff? I'm certain he would be interested."

"Well . . . no." Lydia Hamilton voice got all huffy. "I don't need to. Everyone knows how unreliable Delilah Morgan is."

McEntire moved toward the middle of the room. "Really? Since the chair of the English department at UK was interviewed and stated she was a brilliant student with exceptional morals, I doubt anyone would believe your report."

"Don't be ridiculous. Delilah Morgan is a slut from Appalachia." Charlene Higgenbottom laid out prejudice like a fancy buffet, all doilies and side dishes, no meat.

Deputy McEntire's fists balled.

"I believe you ladies are leaving *now*." Fergus's voice barely concealed his anger. "And don't touch the doorjamb as you exit."

I heard the door click shut and Deputy Fergus release a sigh. "Who knew opening that dern door would usher in the devil with a dye job." He opened the door again, stared down the hall, then nodded. "They're gone."

I slowly rose from my scrunched-up position.

"Could be worse." McEntire shook her head.

"How so?"

"They could have stayed." Laughter filled the room, easing the tension.

Fergus lowered his gaze to me. "I apologize, Miss Delilah. You've enough worries without ducking their vile remarks."

"I only wish I hadn't crouched like a coward. I should have faced them and said nuts to the sheriff's wishes."

Fergus shook his head. "I've been working with Bellows for ten years. I'd be a fool to go against Bellows. Man's wise, clever, and methodical. Now about that lunch. What was it that Mr. Longworth wanted?" Fergus's eyebrows met when he glanced over his food list. The deputy shook his head and strode into the adjoining room. "Hey, Mr. Longworth," he said. "What did . . ." his voice trailed off. "Holy smokes, he's gone. The chief's going to have our badges."

"What do you mean, gone?" McEntire raced into the room, with me a step behind her.

"I mean, the room is empty, and he's evaporated, vamoosed, on the lam."

McEntire sprinted to the window and flung back the thin white curtain. "No, he's not. He's in the parking lot."

Fergus lunged toward the door. "You won't make it." McEntire's voice was tense. "A small foreign car has pulled up beside him." She spoke like an announcer at a ball game. "Longworth's flung himself in." I dashed to her side as she said, "They're racing toward the stoplight on Riva Ridge Boulevard."

Over McEntire's shoulder I watched a blue sports car run a red light and squeal its tires swinging onto Foolish Pleasure Drive.

"Get the plate?" Fergus asked.

McEntire crossed her arms. "It's Travis Jackson's car. He lives down the block from me. His daddy works for Longworth."

When told the news, Bellows shouted so loudly I heard him through Fergus's speaker. "That idiot is dealing with murderers and is going to get his head blown off!" The deputy was beet red when he hung up, but he hadn't made any excuses.

Harry once said, "'It's a weak person who doesn't accept responsibility for what happens on their watch.'"

"We have to move you." Fergus was brusque. "Bellows is sending over an escort."

All I had for shoes were flip flops and my hot pink running shoes. I pulled socks over my toes and tied the long shoelaces into double knots.

As I straightened the pillow on the hotel's bed my mind snapped back to a girl Savannah had brought to church. She was a pretty thing, soft blonde hair, saucy blue eyes, but she'd fidgeted with her hands, twisting them one way then the other. It was her unease and her heart-shaped face that was jostling my mind. I'd seen the girl since that September Sunday. Recently, in fact. I squinted my eyes until the room grew as foggy as Miss Vickie's memory. Bingo! Change her hair color to red and she was the girl in the picture the Weldons had given me.

"Hey, McEntire, could someone enlarge the picture I posted at George's? The one from the Weldons with the four girls? I think one of the girls was a friend of Savannah's. The red-haired girl to Elise Weldon's right."

McEntire set down her cup of water. "Anyone else see the girl with Savannah and can recognize her?"

"Savannah introduced her to George and Mamie. And Reverend Daniel never forgets a face or name."

She related the news to someone at the police department and asked if Mamie would check the photos. A knock made McEntire scurry to the door. Madison entered.

Madison shook the rain from his hair and smiled. "Miss Delilah, a pleasure to see you again." There wasn't a hint of sarcasm in his words. "There's a car waiting for us by the side door. Please put on this hooded sweatshirt and cover up." The soft grey hoodie was two sizes too big.

We slunk down the back stairs, raced in the rain across the parking lot, and I leaped into the backseat of a large, beige sedan almost colliding with a hunched over man who was swathed in a prison-gray sweatshirt and whose face was encased in a hood. I rolled my shoulders to ease their tension. Bellows must want to dispose of a couple of dull sweatshirts.

Madison flung my suitcase into the trunk and plopped into the driver's seat. My backseat companion turned to look out the window and loosened the tie of his sweatshirt hood. As soon as his hair was exposed, I scooted over and kissed Lyle's ear. Between his TV debut and his chauffeur duties he'd sprouted a mustache. Lyle drew a finger slowly over the well-manicured hair. "Disguise. Bellows insisted." Lyle reached over to pat my hand, the sort of pat you'd give to a feeble old lady.

"Hey, what happened to the Lyle in the hotel room?"

"Really, Delilah," he said in a stuffy, upper class voice. "A man has his scruples."

I would have laughed, but his lips fused to mine as quick as super glue adheres fingers together. His facial hair tickled, but within a millisecond it didn't matter a whit. Must have been a few minutes that we stayed that way because I tingled from lack of oxygen.

"Uh, er, that was nice." I gasped out the words when I finally came up for air.

"You're a writer, Di. Think of another adjective."

"Mind boggling."

Madison put the car in gear but watched from the driver's mirror. "Thought this was a good way to kill two birds with one stone, so to speak." A smile drifted over Madison's face then was gone. "I can keep an eye on you two as we head toward North Carolina."

Odd that we aren't going to hole up in some local place.

Sailing past Buck Mays' used cars, Madison again spoke. "Well, Miss Delilah, we're meeting a pair of loose cannons wandering about the countryside. I've convinced them to show up for reassignment." Madison chuckled again as he smoothly passed a semi on a two-lane road with cars aiming our way.

"Where are we headed?" I squeaked out before I closed my eyes.

Lyle squeezed my hand. "Meeting Daniel and George in Asheville. They'll be sharing our tent accommodations at the cabin. I have to hide in the woods because news of my presence will not flush our quarry."

I opened my eyes as Madison swept back into the right lane. "Your place must be pretty this time of year."

"It is."

"You're answering me in truncated sentences. What are you thinking?"

"That Rand must be heading home. I find it hard to believe he's involved with trafficking but it's looking that way."

Within minutes my head lolled on Lyle's shoulder and I fell asleep to the steady rhythm of the tires. I woke as Madison took the sharp turn leaving the 65 and headed east.

I stretched. "Sorry."

"Don't be. You must be exhausted."

When we stepped into a coffee shop, the hug George gave me made my ribs throb. "We thought, well, that you were dead, you see." His voice was husky.

I nodded.

"The reverend here was very worried. Mamie is distraught." George blew his nose. "And I can't tell her a blame thing."

Reverend Daniel's face creased with his enigmatic smile, the one he had when he saw Josephine.

George settled into a booth. "No news isn't good news. We've been investigating in Asheville for two days and gotten nowhere."

At that, Madison raised an eyebrow. George held up his hand. "I know, I know. But you don't have enough feet on the ground and I've credentials." George cocked his eyebrow at Madison and stared. I wanted to ask if they were going to arm wrestle next but sipped my coffee instead.

Reverend Daniel lifted his coffee cup toward Lyle. "Interesting disguise." He grinned at his undercover compatriot.

Lyle waggled his mustache like a villain in a melodrama.

George's phone interrupted Lyle's comedy routine. "Yes? Really! How'd you figure it out? Well now, that's heading us in the right direction. Send the photo to my phone."

George disconnected. "Ten minutes ago, Miss Vickie took one gander at one of the girls in the Weldon's picture and said, 'That's Savannah's friend, Lacey.' Our neighbor, Hank Abernathy, began connecting the dots via computers. The girl is in the FBI's fingerprint data. "Now, there's an APB out on this girl, Lacey. She's tangled up in this trafficking. I just don't know how."

"Wow!" I clapped my hands.

Madison reached for his phone. He got up from the table and went outside.

"They're tracking her down. Should know her address soon. I thought roping Abernathy into our search for Savannah would be his ticket out of purgatory. Living with Candance must be trying." George sucked on his lower lip, then said, "I underestimated the man."

Lifting my gaze heavenward I said, 'Thank you,' to the One who directs our thoughts.

"Relieved?" Lyle squeezed my hand.

I puffed out a breath. "Not till Savannah is in her mother's arms."

Reverend Daniel snapped his fingers. "A shill. A friend that spends time with the victims and gets them to trust her."

"Makes sense." George rose. The pair took off while Lyle refilled his coffee. Standing by the door and waving, I recognized Lyle's four by four truck they climbed into. They would be easy to follow.

We took off in Madison's beige sedan. A silvery rain shower swallowed the landscape. George and Daniel were soon lost in the traffic.

I shivered as rain washed the windscreen. "How long before we're sitting in front of a cozy fire?" As soon as the words exited my mouth, I was embarrassed. I wanted comfort while Savannah was in harm's way.

"One hour, max. But no fire. Just a campsite with a small heater." Lyle squeezed my hand. "Can't build a fire until we've caught my squatters."

Madison flew past semis and RVs heading to Florida. He had a lead foot like Lyle. "I'm having trouble with my cell reception," Madison muttered. "Must be the mountains." The rain cleared as we descended a hill. As I studied the small farms that dotted the landscape, Lyle's phone made its no nonsense ring. At least *his* phone worked.

Madison turned on the blinker to pass a Cadillac going about seventy-five.

Lyle pulled his cell phone from his pocket and punched speaker. Before Lyle could say hello, Reverend Daniel spoke.

"We're being followed by a semi. He was on the shoulder of the freeway until we passed. Then, he pulled onto the road." Daniel's voice was clipped. "We've been watching him in our mirror for several miles. Randall Longworth's logo is on the front of the cab."

I glanced at Lyle.

Lyle drew his thumb along the top of his phone. "What makes you suspicious?"

"They tried to ram us when there wasn't any traffic. George slammed on the accelerator so hard we plowed a furrow in the asphalt."

Lyle held the phone away from his face. "Robert! Someone is after George and Pastor Daniel."

Madison stomped on the accelerator and whizzed past a gray Audi as if it were standing still.

"Daniel, where are you?" Lyle spoke loudly so Madison could hear.

"Passing a sign that says, 'West Haven two miles.'"

"Take the exit! Wait at the Shell station on the right corner." Lyle whacked his hand on the back of

Madison's seat. "Rand must have a hit out on you, Di." Lyle frowned at me, "and thinks I've got you in my truck."

Randall Longworth didn't strike me as the call-in-a-hit-man type, though I wasn't going to argue. Longworth would lacerate someone with his tongue, but not with a sword—too messy. After our fiasco all he'd wanted to do was get a shower, like an OCD hand-washing ritual.

"He's too close." Daniel's voice over the speaker made my hair stand up.

"Help, Lord. Oh help, Lord, help," I begged as I grabbed the hand hold above my head. Not exactly an eloquent prayer, but the good Lord doesn't care a whit about protocol. "No weapon formed against you shall prosper," I reminded the Lord. "Like David prayed, 'Let them fall into their own trap, Lord.'"

"Delilah, call the police. Step on it, Robert." Lyle tightened his lips.

I dialed my phone and prayed while Madison drove like he was possessed.

"Give the police this car's description so they don't pull us over for speeding. Also tell them the description of the truck George is driving and its location. Tell them we need back up," Madison ordered. "This is no time for my cell to act up." Madison leaned forward as if to make the car go faster.

Lyle grabbed the metal pipe that held Madison's headrest in place. We whizzed by cars. With a slow travel-trailer in the fast lane, and a lineup of cars behind it, Madison passed on the right. George had a three-minute start on us. It seemed a forever stretch of time. The emergency dispatcher kept me anchored to the phone as we chased a phantom truck through the mountains.

"They're right on our tail, Daniel." George spoke

above a screech of brakes.

"You all right?" I heard Daniel ask.

"Fine. Hang on."

Another metallic sound coupled with a gasp sent my eyes scanning the road in front of us.

"Can't say as I've ever seen that maneuver." Pastor Daniel's voice was an octave above his normal range.

"Can't say as I've ever had to use that particular training." George's voice was tense. "Breathe, Daniel."

"I'm trying, but you left my stomach in the middle of the freeway when you stomped on your brakes."

"They hit our front side, but we're still on the road. Lyle, I apologize. The front bumper's lying on the pavement behind me, and there's a crease the length of the driver's side. Your truck has seen better days." George sounded amused.

"The semi is ramming their truck," I told Madison and the dispatcher.

"There's our exit." Reverend Daniel's voice was back to normal. The squeal of tires reverberated through our car. "They're still with us."

"Can you pull into the gas station?" Lyle gripped his phone until his fingers were white.

"Going too fast," George replied.

Lyle licked his lips. "I'll aim you in the direction of my uncle's farm. You'll be facing a road that divides. Take the right branch. In a mile there is a road on the left, an old farm road. Pull on to it. In a quarter mile a narrow logging road will be on the left. Ease onto it. Di, see the semi pulling off? It's at the top of the off ramp."

The truck was there and gone. We exited not a minute behind. The semi careened past the Shell station, laying a black line of rubber on the asphalt as it braked to slow, then sped through a red light.

"I see the truck," Madison shouted.

Lyle peered around the headrest. "From the speed he's going, the semi won't be able to make the logging road bend."

Flashes of colored houses and neon-lights were all I saw as Madison floored the accelerator. We left the small town and entered a narrower country road.

We lost the truck on a curve. It reappeared again in a small straight section of tarmac. Madison laid on his horn. Behind us were sirens. "Hang on," Madison ordered as we swung onto the right side of the fork in the road. I couldn't hang on any tighter. We couldn't see the road for the dust.

"Made it to..." Daniel's voice was cut off by the scream of metal.

Chapter Twenty-Three

ONE MINUTE I COULD HEAR THE air whistle in and out of Lyle's nose, the next his face was grayish with his lips pressed tight.

Daniel's voice came over the speaker. "Semi didn't make the turn, Lyle. It's tipped over and the cab scrunched against some beech trees."

"Tell the dispatcher we'll likely need medical attention." Madison's voice was strained.

I nodded. "Righto."

As we pulled up to the crash site Daniel emerged from a dust cloud and sprinted toward the semi. George yelled something at him and Daniel stopped and turned around.

Madison hit the brakes and pulled beside Lyle's Ford truck.

The semi was on its right side, still running. It hovered above a steep ravine as if poised, waiting to descend.

Daniel and George stood toe to toe, faces red, mouths both engaged. Were they having an argument? "I'll go first." George's voice carried our direction as we stepped out of the car. "The driver is probably armed." The pair headed toward the truck. Gun drawn, George lifted himself onto the truck driver's step, cautiously inched his face around the edge of the window and peered in, face black as thunder. Madison and Lyle ran to the oil-belching truck.

Fighting the fear that crawled up my throat and dried my lips, I sprinted after them.

The ground was littered with shards of window glass and slippery oil.

Madison held up a warning hand. "Stand back. Let us take the lead."

George stepped onto the ground. His eyes

narrowed as he looked at Lyle. He shook his head in a motion that was slow and thoughtful. Daniel took his place by the window.

"The driver's unconscious and his passenger moaning," Daniel reported from his position on the step. The truck made a visceral sound as if in labor. "Help me ease him out." Daniel opened the door.

Perched on the edge of a steep incline the truck shifted with the movement. I held my breath.

Daniel glanced at us over his shoulder. "I think his leg is broken. I'll need someone to keep his leg straight."

I stepped forward. "Mrs. Morgan!" Lyle used his judicial voice. "Step aside."

Madison shook his head and climbed beside Daniel.

I didn't move. "Lyle, you are a still recovering from a gunshot wound. And mighty heavy to boot. So is Madison."

As if to underline my point the truck began to move downhill. Not with an easy slide but with metal screeching like a banshee. It stabilized against a copse of beeches.

Reverend Daniel waved his arm. "Get down, Robert. I pick Delilah." Daniel eased the driver's door open. "Shimmy up here, Delilah, and climb around me. His right leg is bent back, and I can't get his upper body out with his leg caught under the seat. The girl beside him is tied up."

Madison peered around Daniel, shot a few pictures of the truck's occupants with his phone camera then jumped to the ground. He walked toward George while punching numbers on his phone.

"Secure the door," Madison ordered as he passed George. George sprinted to the truck, grabbed a length of rope from the back and had Daniel wrap it around the open door. George hung onto the rope like a cowhand secured a steer, keeping the door open so it couldn't slam shut and injure Daniel.

The cab was angled almost forty-five degrees, which made climbing tricky. I put my foot on the semi's tire to get up the cab's side. Lyle grabbed me around the waist and hoisted me up like a new born heifer. I sidled beside Daniel and looked through the doorway. The man's body was canted downhill.

The unconscious driver was Vic from my hide and seek in the woods. Vic with his Elvis sideburns looked ghastly, a place on his forehead was mushed in, with lots of blood running down to the seat from a cut around his eye. I removed Vic's baseball cap and swept the glass off of the seat with it. A girl was beside him, her hands tied in front of her, and the seatbelt by the passenger side window was around her and still connected to its metal hook.

"Oh, dear." I locked eyes with the slight brunette. She moaned softly.

"What!" demanded Lyle.

"It's Savannah's friend, Lacey. She's tied up and bleeding." I whipped my cell phone out of my pocket and snapped a picture of her. She was tucked into herself and hardly moving.

"Get them out first, then we'll secure the . . ." he would have finished, but the cab creaked loudly and shifted with a jolt.

"Well, *really*, behave yourself," came out of my mouth, making Daniel laugh.

What Lyle said was a four-letter word best not repeated.

I crawled over Vic, his blood coloring my pants red. His foot was twisted and wedged under the seat. There was a splash of blood beside him and a pool under his leg. I got onto the floor beside the gearshifts and inched his foot around to dislodge it. Even unconscious, the sounds Vic uttered made my skin crawl.

Sirens closed in as Daniel removed Vic from his contorted position. He passed Vic's unwieldy body down to Lyle and George. I eased his calf into Lyle's arms. Vic's leg must have weighed twenty pounds, maybe more, since he had a beer belly and thick ankles. With Vic's body removed, the weight shifted, and the cab rotated then slipped two more feet down the incline.

"Get out of there, Delilah!" Lyle shouted.

"Can't. This little girl is all torn up." I clawed my way onto the seat. "Lacey." The girl tilted her face toward mine, eyes glazed with pain. Pulling my knife from its holder, I cut the rope that tethered her. A whiff of diesel wandered through the cab. "Can you move, dear?" The right side of her shirt was stiff with blood. I touched her cheek with my forefinger. "Lacey, we need to get you out of here. EMTs have arrived."

"My name isn't Lacey," she whispered. "It's Elizabeth. Elizabeth Forsyth."

"Elizabeth, I'm going to put my arms around your chest and ease you across the seat." The driver's side groaned, and the truck moved another foot downward.

She moaned. "No. I can't move my arm and my chest is on fire."

I moved her anyway. As I inched her along the seat she shuddered. "*Please*. I just want to lie still."

"I know." I made my voice smooth as a kitten's fur. Lyle's head emerged above the door frame. "But Judge Henderson is here to help get you out and I don't like to keep a man waiting." Lyle touched my calf with something cold and hard. I whipped my head around to see him tightening a belt to my leg and holding onto the excess. If Lyle Henderson thought he could jerk me out of here with a hurt child for me to care for, he didn't know who he was dealing with.

The girl began to move. She made it to the steering wheel before collapsing on the seat. Her white tee-top dripped with blood. I put a hand on the cloth and pressed. Elizabeth blinked back tears.

"Mrs. Morgan, you've got to help Savannah and the others."

I nodded, then called down to Lyle, "She's got a

nasty wound on her right side and can't move her right arm. When I get her to you, keep pressure on it."

"Fine."

I lugged her past the steering wheel. My left foot brushed Lyle's shoulder below me, then I searched for purchase. He reached up and grabbed my ankle, placing my foot firmly on the step welded above the gas tank. Elizabeth shuddered. I flattened myself against the truck's metal side, allowing Madison to finish the extraction job. When I turned to look, a swarm of figures dotted the road with ambulance, fire truck, and two police cars crowding Lyle's truck and Madison's car.

"Bio-hazard," an EMT announced as Elizabeth was eased to the ground.

Under me the vehicle shook and began sliding into the thin trunked beeches. Lyle wrapped his arms around my waist and fell backwards. The roots of the trees turned toes up and flung their stabilizing dirt high into the air, dusting us as we flew away from the truck and onto the hard-packed road. A deep thunder of rocks and trees bellowed as the semi rocketed down the hillside.

I landed with a thump on top of Lyle.

"Oof," Lyle said as air escaped his lungs.

"Where are you hurt?" I squirmed in Lyle's arms to take a good look at him. He didn't speak. "Your gunshot wound might be opened up!" I searched his chest for blood, then palpated to the middle of his back.

Lyle offered a soft smile. "I'm fine, Delilah."

George helped him to his feet.

"Di, don't you ever put me through that kind of agony again." Lyle's lips closed in a firm line.

I trembled from my head to my toes. Lyle wrapped me in his arms. "I think I'm going to be sick," I said to his chest.

"This way." Lyle pulled me to the embankment where the semi had been. I knelt in the crabgrass and lost my cup of coffee and scone. It wasn't pretty. Lyle held my long hair in his right hand keeping it away from my vomit. This time his handkerchief wasn't used for tears, but for wiping my mouth. I shakily got up and dusted off my pants.

"Sorry."

"Don't be. Common response."

Madison handed me a bottle of water. "Your Elizabeth has spilled the beans. I need to make a phone call or two." He took off toward his car.

An EMT made an appearance. "Ma'am, the injured girl wants you to know she's responsible for Savannah's kidnapping. She's made a statement to the government officials over there." The EMT pointed at Madison and George. "They were going to kill Elizabeth because she called 911 and tried to tell the police about a murder."

"What murder?" Lyle swung his head around to stare at the uniformed woman.

"Two men. A truck driver called Buddy and someone named Longworth."

Lyle sucked in air.

The EMT returned to the ambulance and sped away with siren blaring and light flashing.

Lyle lifted his gaze to the sky. I took his right hand in both of mine.

One of the policemen came to our side. "Judge Henderson? We need a statement from you and Mrs. Morgan."

Lyle's summary of Daniel's phone call and the semi's demise was succinct. When Lyle was done, he turned toward me. "I need to get you home, Delilah."

"George knows more about Savannah. I need to ask him some things."

"He'll update us at home." Lyle's voice was firm.

"Is anyone going to the hospital with Elizabeth? She shouldn't be alone."

Lyle opened the sedan's door. "Madison will talk with her when she is out of surgery. She's a felon, dear. Part of a trafficking ring. Elizabeth is not some mixed-up kid swiping a candy bar from the local grocery." He handed me a plastic bag. "In case you have a need." He walked to the passenger's side as Madison slid into the driver's seat. Madison signaled George to follow us, and the dented truck, missing its front bumper, sped down the road, sounding like a dissonant calliope.

What was chasing around in my mind was why had Elizabeth called 911. Did she quail at murder, when she'd executed a death sentence on any number of girls by kidnapping them? Something didn't add up.

As we turned onto a county road where farms hugged the grass, Lyle spoke. "How are you?"

"Confused. I'm churned up with worry about the girl and still trying to not lose my cookies."

"Okay."

"I smell like a meat processing plant." I wrinkled my nose with disgust at the sweet odor of drying blood.

"Then the first thing on the agenda, is a shower. Is that all right, Robert?" Lyle pointed at Madison. "Delilah needs to clean up and because I'm flying under the radar the best place is my cabin, not a windblown tent and a spit bath."

"I give up. Next thing you'll want me to cater your dinner from a five-star restaurant." Madison turned to nod to us. "Shower it is. Then we vamoose. You, Lyle, must remain in the tent. As a Federal Officer, George can escort Miss Delilah."

We took an unfamiliar, isolated two track through the woods toward Lyle's 'cabin', passing cars with camouflage tarps over them. Lyle's temporary stakeout domicile. Madison stopped to hide the beige sedan. George and I hiked a dozen yards past the FBI's electronics tent before coming in the back door of the cabin.

Assigned the guest room where the Ohio Star quilt resided, I headed to the shower, suitcase in hand. The mirror revealed hair tendrils reddened by blood and a shirt plastered to my skin. I swished the vomit taste out of my mouth with water and was about to lift my shirt above my waist when George barged in through the bathroom door.

"Close your eyes, George Salas." I struggled to rebutton my three neck buttons.

"It's not what you think, Delilah. We've visitors." He grabbed a washcloth and cleaned the sink, drying all the water droplets, then took my suitcase. We headed for the walk-in closet. He closed the louvered door silently. Before we could duck behind a row of clothes, we heard high heels, loud as thunder, tap on the wood floors. Muffled voices echoed down the hallway and past the room where we hid.

George and I scrunched behind a floor length garment bag.

George leaned close and whispered. "Are you comfortable?"

"I'm a little cold."

George turned on his cell phone's flashlight. Unearthing a fleece blanket from a shelf, he pushed it toward me. "I'm going to find out who's here. Stay put." He crawled away and opened the closet door. A shaft of dull afternoon light made a triangle on the closet floor. He was gone in an eye blink.

Even under the blanket I shivered. The lingering scent of blood brought a twinge of nausea. Wrinkling my nose, I closed my eyes and prayed for the frightened girl who had been Savannah's friend. As my thoughts leaped to Josephine, a woman and man's laughter sounded from the bedroom. A noise like a Fourth of July fireworks penetrated the door.

If they were going to burn down Lyle's cabin with fireworks, I'd better be ready to run. I flung off the blanket.

Where was George? I inched the closet door open. Mayor Higgenbottom stood at the foot of the bed dressed for Halloween in tight leather pants. He didn't have a shirt on. His bare chest and paunch hung out into the breeze blowing through the open bedroom door. It was not his best look. There was a woman with the mayor. She stood by the bed, a riding whip in her left hand. A mask covered her face. I closed the door as quietly as I'd opened it and sat on my heels. The whole encounter was odd. The mayor using Lyle's cabin didn't make sense unless he didn't know it was the judge's.

The doorbell rang. "I'll be a minute," the woman said. Her heeled shoes dashed down the hall. Women's angry shouts echoed down the hall. I squatted and leaned my head against the closet door. Waiting, I listened to Higgenbottom bounce on the bed like a little kid.

The tapping heels came down the hallway. "Now, I think you'll get a kick out of this. It is the kind of thing you enjoy. Come with me, Higgie."

I shivered.

Afraid that if I moved the FBI wouldn't have enough on the trespassers for an arrest, I waited for a long time in the dark. Finally, Higgenbottom and the woman in black returned.

"That was some show," laughed Higgenbottom. "Was she a local actress? You make things better and better every time I come. And that thug with the gun. Very believable. The actress needs to improve on her dialogue, though. Begging me to save her got a bit old."

"Glad you approve of my little drama, Higgie. Where were we? Ah, yes. I believe I placed my whip on the bed."

I could see a small sliver of the pair through the door louvers. She grabbed a little whip and swung it above her head. She might have hit the mayor with it if George and Madison hadn't appeared in the bedroom doorway. Madison pointed a gun at the invaders.

I rose from my snooping position and opened the door, then stood with my mouth opened like a bass catching a fly. George took one look at me and beat a path to my side. I only caught a glimpse of Madison waving his gun at Mayor Higgenbottom when George stepped in front of me.

"What are you doing here, Madison?" demanded our mayor. "This is my time."

I craned my head around George's shoulder and looked closely at Higgenbottom. He had welts across his chest. My nausea returned. George moved to block my view, crossed his arms, and did an impression of a refrigerator.

"You're both trespassing." Madison's angry voice was sharp.

I could put two and two together.

This looked like something on a TV crime show, and I didn't like it. Not one little bit. There were some sort of initials for what the mayor was up to, but I couldn't recall what they were. I shook my head at George as he cleared his throat. "I think I know what this is, but maybe you better clarify."

"Not without Lyle." George put his thumbs in his belt loops and rocked back on his heels. He began to whistle an off-key version of "Zip A Dee Do Da,' trying to drown out the screeching that was emanating from the room. The woman's vocabulary was an embarrassment. Higgenbottom at least kept his swearing to familiar terms.

I put my hand on George's arm to get his attention. "Does Higgenbottom know this is Lyle's house?"

"The mayor has more to worry about than breaking and entering. The FBI has all his shenanigans on video as well as the assault. Why don't you get changed while Madison and I see to Lyle's uninvited guests?"

With an old-world flourish, George presented my suitcase. I hustled to the bathroom, with only one glance at the half-naked politician. I shivered, but not from cold.

In my suitcase was Savannah's purple pillow. It smelled of the spicy hair conditioner she used. Putting my makeup bag on the counter I looked in the mirror. My curly mat of hair was flattened on one side. I formed a ponytail with a scrunchy, scrubbed off the blood, and threw on some clothes. When I opened the door, the bedroom was empty.

I followed the sounds of voices. In the foyer, gun in hand, George lounged against the wall, whistling. Men in FBI labeled jackets stood beside him. They were dripping wet. They also held weapons aimed at our illustrious mayor.

With his back to the wall of black and white prints, Higgenbottom stood handcuffed and red faced. In matching police jewelry was a woman with a wealth of blonde hair. She slowly turned. Staring into my eyes was Lynette, Randall Longworth's girlfriend/office manager. She gave me a sideways smirk.

I staggered backwards. *Why in the world is Longworth's office manager at Lyle's?*

Madison stood in front of Higgenbottom, with his forehead rumpled tight. "Attempted murder and trespassing will get you a free pass to jail."

"You can't do that!" Higgenbottom was sweating. "That woman barging in here looking for her husband was all an act."

"Watch me." Madison was so angry his nostrils flared. "We have you on video threatening her then shoving her into the arms of a man who tried to kill her."

"What woman?" I mouthed to George.

George held up a finger, signaling me to wait.

Higgenbottom's mouth stopped spewing four-letter words as he stared at the gun-in-hand agents. The agents led Lynette and the mayor outside. George closed the door as their language escalated in volume and color.

"Whew," Pastor Daniel said as he walked up the basement stairs. "Haven't heard that kind of language since I was in boot camp." The reverend was soaking wet and his face bruised along his right cheek.

George's phone vibrated on his hip. He stopped his irritating whistling to answer. "You don't say. Sounds good to me." He hung up.

A siren wailed. "Ah, that would be the ambulance for Cissy." Daniel looked at George.

"What?" I grabbed hold of George's arm.

George lifted his eyebrows up and down like a comedian. "Let me explain. Cissy arrived after Longworth's office manager and her muscle. Lynette, I believe her name is, set up the house for a little rendezvous with our circumspect mayor." At the crunch of tires on gravel George swiveled his head toward the door. "On second thought, I'll let Lyle explain after he gets back from the hospital."

Madison flung open the door like Zorro entering a robber's lair. Lyle entered right behind him without the drama.

"We need to get back to Asheville," Madison barked. "George, you're with me. Delilah, you'd better come too, in case we find Savannah. There's a plane going to take off at 8 p.m. with some unwilling passengers on board, possibly Savannah. Lyle will come back here to his cabin after he visits Cissy in the hospital." The special agent pivoted on his heels and strode out the door.

I ran after Madison. His car was parked in the drive. Questions emerged with each step. Before I could utter them, I stopped flat and sprinted back to the house. I raced past Lyle as he was exiting the house.

He grabbed my arm. "Where are you going?"

"I need something."

I found Savannah's pillow in the bathroom and dashed back to the car in time to hear Madison announce to George, "Lynette is cutting a deal."

I plopped in the backseat, hugging the pillow to my chest. If Lynette was the ring leader of a trafficking gang, I wanted her in jail, for years, maybe a lifetime.

Madison sped out of the driveway, spewing rocks every direction. "You have a permit for your weapon, I'm sure."

George chuckled. "Of course."

I leaned forward. "What sort of deal?"

"A lighter sentence for our rescuing three girls about to leave the country. She figured her goon was going to talk and she'd better cooperate."

George put his gun onto the console between us. "Aside for attempted murder of Cissy and trespassing, what is Lynette being charged with?"

"Try heading up a trafficking ring, attempted murder of Randall Longworth, and murder of an associate, named Woodrow Thompson. I think we can also charge her with the young woman found murdered here last spring."

Madison drove fast, sliding around the curves like a roller coaster before launching us onto the tarmac.

I gripped the seat in front of me. "Longworth's alive?"

"Alive and kicking. She locked them into a refrigerator truck and set it for frozen foods." Madison shook his head. "Not such a bad way to go. Everything slows down, including your brain. Thompson had been in there three hours. He didn't make it. Longworth, who didn't trust his office manager, brought a young man with him and had him stay in the car when he went into his office. When Longworth didn't come out, the kid alerted the police."

"George, Lyle's not here so you have a tale to share about Cissy."

"My lips are sealed except for the police and in court." George, sounding sanctimonious, made me smile.

George winked. I scrunched up my nose. "Okay, okay. I'll tell." George laughed. "It was quite the to-do. I was hiding in Lyle's office when Cissy marched into the house and demanded to see Conrad. 'I know he's here with you, Lynette.' Cissy yelled so loudly that when I backed into a picture on the wall and accidently jiggled it, no one heard." George's tongue pushed out his left cheek and he shook his head. "At that point I opened the door a crack and peered out. Cissy had plopped herself onto the sofa and was not to be moved."

I could picture Cissy, arms crossed, eyes narrowed.

"Lynette's henchman drew a gun. At that point, Lynette went to invite the mayor for 'a little drama,' as she put it. Thinking it was part of the act, our mayor said, 'You know I prefer them younger.'" George cleared his throat and looked beyond my head toward the landscape flashing past.

I drummed my fingers on my pant leg. "Get on with it, George. I wasn't born yesterday."

"Well, I followed the group down the stairs. There was a spot under the stairs and behind a small chest where I hid and got ready to act. Lynette gave orders to eliminate Cissy. The man and Higgenbottom both nodded, then while Cissy pleaded for her life, Lynette and our mayor went up the staircase laughing.

"'Move,' the gunman ordered Cissy, shoving her in the back. They went out the French doors. I followed. Caught a glimpse of Conrad casting his line by a copse of trees, and the FBI coming around the side of the house. Because Cissy kept whacking him around his eyes, the man didn't see me crouching behind a lounge chair or the FBI as the gunman grabbed her flailing arms. He picked Cissy up and hauled her to the river. As the goon flipped Cissy into the water Conrad tackled him. There was quite a fight. Then, the man's head bounced off a rock. At present he's unconscious."

Madison tilted his head and smiled. "Con's bleeding like thunder and can't get Cissy off him, even though she's also cut and bruised and hunched over complaining of pain in her ribs."

"Her hovering isn't a problem as far as I can see.

Conrad seems pleasantly dazed but happy." George settled back into his seat.

My forehead tightened. "Madison, are you going to let Lynette skate?"

"I didn't tell her we'd found Longworth. We cut a deal about the trafficking." Madison made a smile like the grim reaper. I wouldn't want to be on the other end of his manipulations.

George shook his head. "Who is taking the girls out of the country?"

"A European. Seems he likes American girls. The younger the better."

My nausea returned.

The clock on the dash read 7:55 when we reached the Asheville airport. It was navy-blue dark with only the hanger lights and plane lights for illumination. The police had opened the gates leading to a private runway. A red plane was taxiing, another, a sleek luxury jet, the color of lead, had a stairway pushed to its side. The jet's door was open, lights twinkled inside the cabin and along a stairway handrail and steps.

Madison drove to an unlit hanger and backed the car in. "You two, stay here." Madison handed George the car keys. Beside us, next to the car, were seven uniformed cops. Two of them lounged by a stack of boxes while the others paced in the shadows. As Madison exited, the two loungers strode up to him and spoke. With a nod, the trio headed onto the darkening asphalt.

I put my hand on the door handle. "Those kids will be scared when they get out of the plane. They'll need a motherly figure to comfort them."

"All in good time, Delilah." George's voice was as tight as a sixth octave piano string.

My face wrinkled with tension. "What aren't you telling me?"

George's laugh rumbled through Madison's car. It wasn't his easy laugh. It was a worried one. "I'm nervous because I don't know how this will play out and can't *do* anything. We have to pretend we're at a movie and going to watch from the front row seats. I'm a man of action and Madison has me twiddling my thumbs."

On the left side of the immobile plane the two cops and Madison disappeared behind a motorized luggage carrier. The silver jet's engines engaged. From the shelter of our hanger four policemen exploded into action. They raced toward the silver jet—guns drawn. The scene seemed more a slow-motion black-and-white film than reality. With pools of light amid swaths of black asphalt, the police seemed swallowed by the dark before bursting into the light. One moment they were near us, the next dashing up the lighted stairs and disappearing through the open door.

Cloaked in stripes of dark and light, we waited impatiently. George wiggled to get a good view around the headrest, while I planted my head between the seats and stared.

The engine of the red taxiing plane thrummed as it turned toward the runway. My eyes refocused on the plane that had been in motion when we'd arrived. *Had we missed them?* When George leaned forward my eyes cut to where he was staring.

A Mercedes limousine rolled to a stop by the silver jet's stairway. A man in a black uniform left the driver's seat and opened the back door. He stood at attention, but his head swiveled left then right, as if scanning the area. From the front passenger side another man slid out of the car. He came around the front and also stood by the backseat door. A portly man struggled to get out of the limo. When he stood, he waited, hanging onto the roof of the car with his hand. The second man reached into the backseat and retrieved a cane. Almost bowing, he offered his arm to the older man. The white-haired man pushed his arm away, then shuffled along with a cane, his left foot dragging.

I blinked and licked my dry lips. My breathing

began to accelerate.

The trio glanced toward our car. We were well hidden by the gray-black shadows extending across the tarmac and into the hanger. The uniformed driver shook his head and stepped back to his duty of flanking the older man as they escorted him toward the stairway. *Move, Madison,* I ordered in my head.

A white food service truck sped through the gates and jerked to a stop alongside the plane. I squinted at the truck. Nothing on it but a red blaze of letters stating it was a food service vehicle. You'd think they would have already loaded the plane with its cokes and Kleenex before now.

George tossed the keys into the front passenger seat, then moved. The hair on the back of my neck stood at alert. I wanted to shout, "Don't," to George, but no words escaped my trembling lips. He grabbed his gun, then slid out of the door. What had George seen that I hadn't? Everything seemed normal.

Slipping to the front of the hanger, George raised his weapon. I blinked rapidly, brain on overdrive. What else could be inside the truck? I rubbed my hands together wanting to do something, anything. Maybe that was why George moved—he couldn't sit still any longer.

The truck driver stepped out of the vehicle and headed toward its back. As the squat little man reached the doors, the pilot emerged from the plane and raised his hands high in the air, like a desperado caught by a posse.

The van driver looked above him and froze, then his hands moved to the side of the truck. He tapped on it and waited a moment. What *was* inside?

Madison and an airport policeman stepped out of the shadows to the left of the plane. The truck driver swiveled his head their direction. He plucked a handgun from his pocket and pointed toward Madison. I sucked in a breath.

The men from the limo turned toward the pair.

Madison and the airport cop kept walking as the bodyguards' hands moved toward their jacket fronts, then stopped. The guards' heads aimed left then right, while their upper bodies thrust forward as if ready to bolt.

Crouching, George eased from his shelter and headed toward the plane. Two more people exited the plane, the first, a woman, dressed in a short tight skirt and white shirt, then a man in a chef's jacket. They too lifted their hands skyward. The four policemen who had entered the plane were right behind them. *Where was Savannah?*

The limo trio separated, the old man heading back to his vehicle. His feet scraped along the ground as if unsure of his footing. He took his time for a few steps, then he turned to look over his shoulder. His cane went before him as he continued his walk toward the car, but now his slow walk had become an undignified scramble.

The truck driver jumped into his seat.

The two bodyguards unbuttoned their jackets, drew weapons, and moved toward Madison and the cops.

I held my breath and rubbed my sweaty palms on my pants. Stupid of them to draw their weapons. It would escalate the encounter.

I glanced at George, who was in full motion, gun in both hands and pointed at the pair.

Lights flickered on, illumining parts of the taxiway as airport security disgorged from their hiding places and sprinted toward the truck and limousine. It seemed like a Keystone Cops flick as they surrounded the truck. I counted six shots, whether fired by the truck driver or the security force I couldn't tell, but someone collapsed onto the tarmac.

The truck reversed, scattering the contingent of security people aiming toward it. One uniformed policewoman grabbed the driver's door handle and hung on as the white truck emblazoned with

"PROVISIONS" spun in a half circle and targeted the hangars.

I jumped out of the car then flung myself into the driver's seat. I pressed the keyless ignition switch. I swallowed hard, letting saliva cover my arid vocal cords. The engine rumbled to life. I clicked on my seatbelt and stomped on the accelerator. Between fear and exhilaration my heart sped to warp speed while the car flew across the tarmac.

The food truck changed directions and raced toward the exit. With guns drawn, three airport policemen ran toward the escaping vehicle. I must have been going twenty when I smashed the van with the front of Madison's car. The jolt sent my head into the neck rest. I blinked. I'd barely missed the policewoman dangling from the door handle. The side of the "PROVISIONS" truck was crumpled inward, below the navy-blue P of the logo. As the van stopped shuddering, the clinging cop wrenched the van's door open, grabbed the truck driver, and tossed him out of the vehicle.

With a squeal of offended metal, I backed Madison's car away from the truck and screeched to a halt. Throwing the door open, I stumbled out of the car, flung open the back seat and retrieved the purple pillow that now was on the floor. The driver—a pint-sized man—lay quivering on the asphalt at my feet. In seconds he was surrounded by irate cops.

The policewoman holstered her gun and headed to the back of the truck. She pried open the back door and hoisted herself into its recesses.

After a minute, a thin man appeared from the truck's confines and slid out of the back like a snake uncoiling. He shrugged like a schoolboy caught in a prank as he handed the policeman his revolver. He was cuffed before the policeman pointed him to a waiting car.

Then, a young girl's face appeared.

A pre-teen girl, waiting to blossom.

Blood trickled down her left cheek and into her dark hair. Her eyes, wide and frightened, moved from our faces to the uniformed figures gathering around the vehicle.

A man in camouflage stepped toward her as if closing in on a frightened puppy. He lifted her from the vehicle. With a sob, she collapsed onto his chest. He enveloped the child in his arms.

Hugging the pillow to my chest, I moved to help her.

An ambulance charged through the open gate with another behind. Without altering his hold on the girl, the policeman leaned against the side of the van, and waited as the ambulance halted by the driver lying on the tarmac.

The policewoman inside eased the next girl from the truck into the arms of a lanky police officer. I stared at her upturned face. Her eyes were closed as if in deep sleep. The child, a slight blonde, was perhaps twelve or younger. Nestling her in his long arms, the man strode to the ambulance, his face taut with anger.

I took one look at the leg of the next girl lifted into a policeman's arms and began to breathe a pray of gratitude. In a low-cut red dress barely covering her was our Savannah. Her breaths were slow, her eyes closed.

"Thank God," I whispered. At the sound of my voice, Savannah stirred and opened her eyes.

"Miss Delilah?" she murmured.

I kissed her cheek. "Yes, sweetheart. I'm here." My tears splashed down my cheeks and onto her face. I kept my cheek next to hers letting my tears bathe her with love. Words congealed in my throat. What could I say to allay her fear?

Savannah reached up and touched my face. A tiny smile curved her lips as she felt the wetness of my tears. After a heartbeat, I placed the purple pillow on her chest, letting her arms embrace the silky, familiar gift from home.

Chapter Twenty-Four

I DIDN'T FIND OUT WHO HAD been shot until a second ambulance roared out and George came to our side. "Madison took one in the abdomen. Doesn't look good." George had an expression on his face that made me wince.

I chewed on my lip before asking. "Did he lose much blood?"

"Looks like it. There was a pool of it under him when he was moved." George glanced past my head, his thoughts somewhere else, judging from his expression.

Lyle and Daniel arrived at the Asheville hospital close to the same time we did. Lyle's tense expression and the longing in his eyes made me wink at him to ease his worry, but my fingers held on to Savannah's until Lyle wrapped an arm around my shoulders.

"Oh," Lyle breathed when he drew near to Savannah. He rubbed a finger across her forehead. Tears leaked from her eyes. He brushed them away and took her hand in his. With his other hand he grabbed mine. As they wheeled Savannah toward a small room where a doctor waited, we walked together, both of us holding onto her as if she might vaporize.

Lyle and George spent the night pacing the corridors while Daniel and I stayed with Savannah, listening to her trembling voice as she choked out her story. At midnight, Madison was wheeled into ICU with five new units of blood coursing through his veins. The bullet caught a bleeder and he'd nearly bled out. The EMTs kept pumping fluids in as quick as he pumped blood out, the doctor said when he spoke to George.

"Madison is as white as the sheets and not a whit thankful," George told me over a cup of coffee. "In too much pain, I'd guess from his sour expression."

George seemed too cheerful. He patted my hand. "He's going to pull through, Miss Delilah. And it will be an interesting recovery knowing his wife is a nurse on a psychiatric ward." George wandered away whistling off key.

Driven by Officer McEntire, Josephine arrived at three. She took one look at Reverend Daniel and melted into his arms like a heroine in a movie. As the sun was rising, Savannah slowly opened her eyes. Kneeling on the cold tile floor, Josephine began to sob when Savannah croaked out, "Mom?"

Josephine lifted her tear-stained face and climbed into the hospital bed beside her daughter. She wrapped her arms around Savannah in an embrace that was so tight you couldn't put a hand between them. The bed shook with their sobs. I backed up to the wall and sunk down to the floor. It was too much. My cries melded with theirs. Pastor Daniel swept his hand across my head as he passed by and went to the bed. Surrounding the hunched body of Josephine with his arms, he began to pray. The words, "heal and help us, Lord to see You turn this to good," bathed me in peace.

I rose with shaking knees and stepped out into the hall. Lyle found me resting my head against the hard hospital wall. He put his warm arms around me, and we walked down the hall, past the nurses' station toward the cafeteria and another cup of coffee.

It took us two days to regroup and set our sights on home. Sitting beside Lyle in his rental car, I marveled at God's kindness. Josephine and her daughter snuggled in the backseat. Beside them was Reverend Daniel, his face purpling nicely.

When we rolled into Lyle's driveway, Miss Vickie and Mamie opened the back door. They had been waiting with hot chocolate on the burner and snickerdoodles on a plate.

"Well, girl," Miss Vickie said when she spied Savannah, "you been in my prayers."

Lyle looked at me over a mug of cocoa. "Ladies, returning to your home isn't going to happen. Having you occupy my guest room seems to keep Bartles at peace." He dug a spoon into his drink and fished out a marshmallow.

I challenged him. "According to the sheriff I've got water."

Lyle pointed to my lips.

I wiped a chocolate mustache off with a paper napkin.

"Water! All you think about is getting a bath. I'll have you know, Mrs. Morgan, that according to Meadows your water heater isn't fully functioning."

"It was new three years ago," I muttered, wondering what else could go wrong.

"Well, someone forgot to turn it on."

Suspicion rising, I lifted an eyebrow. "And who might that be?"

"Don't look at me." He shrugged. "I was far away in North Carolina."

After a restless night, I headed to the cemetery. The early morning sky held wispy clouds edged with dawn's pink. Harry's grave was stark, no plastic figures or balloons wafting in the breeze. "Well, Harry. Our girl is home. I couldn't sleep for worrying about Savannah awake upstairs, shaking with terror." I patted his headstone. "I wish you were here. Savannah can barely string two words together. And the others. Oh, Harry." I buried my face in my hands. "They are twelve and eleven. Children, Harry." My voice trailed off as I remembered the tormented faces of the girls. The mist twisted up my hair as I stood fingering a curl. "Dr. McLeod says, 'they need some time.' And the drugs. Heavens to Betsy, Harry. I thought Lyle was going to drive over to the jail and give Randall's sassy blonde girlfriend the what for."

I couldn't tell Harry all the details. It would offend him. It offended me. The mist thickened to a light drizzle as I paced along the side of Harry's grave. "Now I can set my mind to clearing your name."

I wanted to sit down. "Time for your bench to be put in place. I need to sit and think about what to do next." I typed into my cell phone a note to check on the bench. "I've wanted to talk privately with Lyle, but it's been impossible. I'm getting discouraged, Harry." I left it at that. Harry always knew what was on my heart.

My water heater should be fine by mid-afternoon. With bags packed, all I had to do was traipse across the street to my empty house. Moving Miss Vickie would be problematic. The judge said at breakfast that the Hudson ladies could stay, "as long as they liked."

That settled things for Miss Vickie. She had risen to her feet, lifted her coffee cup above her head, and declared, "Well said, Mr. Judge. Our little girl needs a man around the house. All she does is cry and shake. I don't think much of her going off on a camping trip with those friends of hers, neither. What was she thinking? Too cold this time of year, that's what I say."

The sheriff held a press conference at ten. Lyle and I sat in the front row of a room full of reporters perched on uncomfortable metal chairs. Josephine stayed home by Savannah's side.

Bellows stood tall behind the podium at the museum. He studied the room filled with reporters and cleared his throat. "We've several people in custody. They are part of a human-trafficking operation. One is a local man, Buck Mays. He is charged with the kidnapping and attempted murder of Mr. Randall Longworth and Mrs. Delilah Morgan. When we get the forensic tests back on the body found in his barn, he may be charged with murder. You'll be delighted to know that Savannah Hudson is out of the hospital and home with her family. Neither she, nor her family, are up to answering questions. Judge Lyle Henderson will speak on their behalf in a moment."

Bellows picked up his notes, put on his glasses, and looked out over the waiting reporters. "The rest of the villains are in jail in North Carolina. The news is full of the European shipping magnate's arraignment and his demand for bail, which the Asheville judge has refused, claiming he is a flight risk. Diplomatic immunity is being claimed. I will let television pundits dwell on that aspect of the case."

"Isn't there a murder charge pending?" someone shouted at Bellows.

"Yes. In North Carolina. A girl's body was fished out of a river last spring and a man found in a refrigeration truck." Bellows looked over his glasses and cleared his throat. "Also attempted murder of businessman Randall Longworth. Apparently, Mr. Longworth has any number of people gunning for him." Bellows got a chuckle from his audience. "Longworth's on his way to McKeansville to continue investigating embezzlement by his office manager. That's the reason he snuck off to North Carolina. He'd put all the puzzle pieces together about Lynette Rawlings, the office manager at Longworth Trucking Company and her fraud. I'm certain he will be available to answer your questions at some point."

Longworth wasn't someone I wanted to deal with. In fact, I hoped I'd never see him again.

"Judge." Bellows nodded Lyle's direction, then stepped away from the podium, avoiding further questions.

Lyle walked to the microphone. "I would like to thank you for your interest in the kidnapping of Miss Hudson. Her family is grateful for the prayers of so many in our nation. I regret to inform you that the FBI discovered Mayor Higgenbottom trespassing on my property in North Carolina." From Lyle's expression there was no regret on his part, nor glee, he just stated the facts. "He is being held as an accessory to murder and human trafficking." That caused such an uproar Lyle had to wait five minutes before going on. "Consequently, we will need an interim mayor to facilitate the functioning of our local government. I advise the press to keep an ear on the city council meeting this afternoon." Lyle made a move to sit down. A sputter of questions turned into a deluge. He answered them calmly. It was lunchtime before we escaped the inquisition.

The judge offered me his arm. A fine mist oozed through the air. I stepped beside him.

"I've a plan for lunch." My companion's blue eyes glinted like tinsel at Christmas.

I shrugged. "Whatever you have in mind is fine with me."

Lyle walked me down the street, past the courthouse, the line of shops with picture windows housing china, prom dresses, antiques, and menswear. I knew where we were heading. I was more than happy to eat at The Coop. A familiar booth at Carter's was what I needed. I would sit in Harry's spot, indented by his derriere, and eat the works— mouthwatering fried chicken, mashed potatoes, gravy, and Carter's cheesy corn casserole. The calories wouldn't hurt me. I'd missed a few meals, what with one thing and another.

The Chicken Coop was packed, every stool, all the tables and chairs, and the booths lining the left side of the restaurant were filled. I glanced at the booth where Harry and Lyle used to sit. Two unfamiliar faces sat on the cushioned vinyl.

The perfect place and time to talk with evaporated in the over-crowded diner. When we finally got a seat, I'd have to whisper my proposal, or we'd have an audience rubber necking. We stood at the front desk queuing for a table. Heads rotated our direction. One by one Carter's patrons rose to their feet and began to applaud. Loudly. Carter and Shorty stuck their heads out of the kitchen, then retracted them. I looked behind me to see what celebrity had entered. Pans in the kitchen began to resound like kettle drums.

Lyle nodded his head to their rhythm and presented his lop-sided smile. "On behalf of Mrs. Morgan, thank you. I'm speaking for her because Delilah thinks Dolly Parton walked in and your applause is for her." Laughter erupted.

"Glad you're alive, ma'am." A man doffed his Carhartt cap my direction.

Mouth dropping, I put my hands to my burning cheeks.

"Here, here!" agreed Jim Bouchard from the *McKeansville Gazette,* who had followed us in. Bouchard dropped his eyes when I looked his way. Embarrassed, I guessed about his unfounded exposé regarding the poetry Harry supposedly wrote.

My neighbor, Sophie Brixton, sat with her retired teacher friends in the last booth in the corner. The painting above her, a rooster greeting the dawn, framed her as if she were part of the still life. "Well, Delilah," she shouted, "about time you showed your face and let us know you're still breathing. You had us in a tizz, girl."

When everyone sat down, Lyle waltzed around The Coop greeting two lawyers manning the counter stools, shaking hands with the postmaster, and leaning over the back of an empty chair to chat with three employees of the local bakery.

I clung to the counter by the cash register. Onion and garlic with Carter's special combination of spices wafted across the diner, tickled my nose, and made my stomach grumble. The door opened, letting in the cool October wind.

"Carter!" A shrill voice shouted behind me. "I don't have all day to stand here and wait for my *table.*"

Carter MacDougal emerged from his kitchen sanctuary with a towel over his left shoulder and a scowl on his face. "I suggest, Mrs. Higgenbottom, that you either wait your turn or find another establishment in which to dine." Carter's words had edges clipped to points.

"Mrs. Hamilton and I prefer to dine here."

Had Charlene not seen the twelve o'clock news broadcast from Lexington?

Miss Brixton and her table of friends rose and tottered on aged legs our direction. Sophie searched in her purse for something, ignoring the contentious atmosphere.

"Here you be, Carter." Sophie put the bill and her money in his hand.

"I'll have BethAnn clear the table in the back room." Carter spoke in a whisper. "The quilting bee ladies from the Episcopal church just left."

"I *never* eat in the back room. It's too drafty." Charlene pulled up the collar of her coat as if chilled.

Sophie Brixton gave me a wink that said, "things are getting interesting."

"Then you will have to wait until Judge Henderson and his guest are seated. I'm sure you and Mrs. Hamilton won't mind while I seat McKeansville's newest celebrity?" Carter MacDougal gave me an eighteenth-century bow.

"Wait! Don't tell me it's the star of the Broadway musical that's performing tonight at the college." Charlene jumped around me to see my face. Her expression changed from open delight to pinch-nosed disgust. "I thought you were dead."

"Not quite. In fact, I'm very much alive, Charlene." I stood toe-to-toe with her the way boxers do when advertising a bout. Her derision had pushed me over the edge. I was afraid of what might pop out of my mouth, because what had popped into my mind wasn't charitable. The poor woman was about to be broad axed with her husband's arrest. I didn't want to add more trouble to her domestic stew, but the time had come.

"The civil war was over more than a century ago, Charlene." I reached out my hand to shake hers. Charlene's right hand tightened into a fist.

A lawyer from the counter crew swiveled his seat and waved. "Hey, Miss Brixton. You going to the city council meeting this afternoon?"

Sophie turned and faced the line-up of stools. "Hadn't entered my mind."

"You should. I can't think of anyone better suited to be our interim mayor."

Charlene put her hand on her broad bosom as if she had been shot.

Jim Bouchard strolled over to us and whipped out a pen and pad. "Can you give us a statement, Mrs. Higgenbottom, regarding your husband's arrest?"

"What arrest? Don't be ridiculous, Jimmy." Charlene tone was condescending. "Cyril is at a mayor's meeting in Atlanta."

Bouchard lifted an eloquent eyebrow. "Cyril was arraigned last night on charges of human trafficking and attempted murder."

On their counter stools Carter's patrons turned toward us all at the same time—a sort of Radio City Rockettes move.

Charlene's eyes went black like the death stare of a basilisk. She opened her mouth to speak, but nothing came out but a quacking duck noise.

Lydia Hamilton waggled a finger in Bouchard's face. "You are being rude, James Bouchard. I don't know what you are thinking. First my sweet Stephen is attacked by your paper, and now you are telling lies about our fine mayor."

"Simply reporting what was on CNN at the top of the hour." Bouchard lifted his phone and pointed to it. "Good day, ladies."

With a flurry of motion Charlene and Lydia slammed out of the Coop and marched toward Charlene's Lexus.

Miss Sophie gazed up at Bouchard. "I've been

thinking that an investigative reporter like you, Jim, needs to re-examine that story on Harry Morgan. If I recall, Harry wrote a date at the top of his poems. Had been since grade school. When he reached my class, he even noted the time he'd completed it. Had a habit of it."

Bouchard's face cracked a smile. "Miss Brixton, would you come to my office?" With a sweep of his arm, Jim invited her toward an empty booth. "Please give a statement to that regard."

"Not only that, but I've examples of his poems in my files. Stephen Hamilton's works as well. They both showed promise you see, so I kept copies of their writings." Sophie waved goodbye to her friends and took up residence in Bouchard's makeshift office. From a briefcase he produced note cards and a recorder.

Carter went to a small table and picked up a vase of fresh flowers, then stood in front of the farmers sitting in Harry's usual spot. They had a conversation. The farmers nodded and grinned. BethAnn scooped up their plates and plunked them down on a small table near the back. Carter set the vase on Harry's table. The Coop had a chicken motif, no flowers. It was curious.

"This way, Miss Delilah." Carter offered me his arm. He led us to the table where Lyle had first talked about our dating.

Carter studied the centerpiece of roses and mums in a white cream pitcher, then nodded as if satisfied with the arrangement and aimed toward the kitchen.

Lyle sat across from me. "I believe you had a question?"

"Maybe this isn't the ideal time."

"Will there ever be?" Lyle's eyes were the soft blue of oxford shirts, not like the blazing sapphire when he was angry.

Now or never, Delilah. I opened my mouth.

"What would you like?" BethAnn asked over my

shoulder. We ordered chicken dinner. Lyle included cooked beans. I chose corn casserole.

I rose from my seat and took one step. My knees were shaking.

I was about to get down on both knees when the familiar voice of Randall Longworth shouted from the doorway. "Thought I'd find you two here. Hey, Lyle, surprised to see me resurrected?"

In a millisecond Lyle was rocketing to the door.

"Rand! Join us." He flashed me an apologetic look because he knew I'd mind sharing my table with the scoundrel.

I did mind but sat down and waited. Randall Longworth's hands were encased in bandages. His face was red, and the tip of his nose was gray.

He leaned over me. "Glad to see me, Mrs. Morgan?"

"Happy that you are alive, Mr. Longworth."

He turned to the other patrons and waved his hands in the air like a circus barker. "This lady saved my skin when that bunch of outlaws tried to fricassee us in the barn. I sliced up my calf, see?" He raised his pant leg for the audience that had gathered. "And this tiny little thing half carried me down a corn field, into the woods, and through a stream before the sheriff arrived."

Bouchard galloped over. The reporter breathed down Longworth's neck, his fingers flying over his notepad. Miss Sophie stood behind him, her eyes alive with interest.

"Why didn't Sheriff Bellows make an announcement when the two of you were found?" Bouchard asked.

In a grandiose gesture Longworth crossed his bandaged arms and puffed out his chest. "We were in an FBI sting operation. Had to stay hidden until we caught the trafficking ring." He sat opposite me, letting BethAnn put a water glass in front of him and inquire about his lunch order. "Same as Lyle."

"Can you describe your kidnapping?" Bouchard poised his pencil above his notebook.

"Actually, I'd love to relate all, but I've a contract with a news outlet for an exclusive interview. I was hoping this lovely vision," he pointed to me, "would accompany me to New York."

"Not on your life, Longworth," I mouthed.

"Because Mrs. Morgan, the noted author, not only saved my life but, according to the Asheville EMTs, crawled into the cab of a smoking semi to haul out a young woman."

I buried my face in my hands. The buzz in the room rose to a crescendo. I moved a forefinger to peek at Lyle. He eased back into his seat and smiled, apparently enjoying the tale.

Bouchard lifted his eyebrows. "I think you have things mixed up. Mr. Harry Morgan is the town's Pulitzer Prize winning author."

"She may not have won any grand awards, but I made a phone call to her publisher, who told me her newest novel will be out this spring. Don't you folks around here read D.B. Burns? I saw a stack of her newest books in her office."

Miss Sophie wagged her head back and forth. "Well, well, well. I should have known. Every time I'm at the library there you are, in the history section with a pile of books at hand. Get your fingers off your face, Delilah, and take a bow. You've been under the radar for years."

I removed my finger mask. "Oh, Miss Sophie. This is the last thing I wanted." My voice trailed off.

"We know that, girl. You want to hide in your house and mourn Harry. What this town needs is a kick in its fatuous rear end and a breath of fresh hope."

"All I do is scribble stories. Hope comes from above."

Bouchard put his phone's voice memo on the table and turned it on.

"How laudable, Mrs. Morgan." Randall Longworth spoke in his insincere voice.

Lyle put his hand on Longworth's shoulder. "Delilah is serious, Rand."

I looked at the white ceiling fan, gathered courage, and rose to my feet.

Miss Sophie put her rear end on my former seat and slid across from Longworth. He didn't look pleased. However, Bouchard did. His face broke into a smile as he settled beside Miss Sophie, his phone still capturing the conversation.

I stood next to Lyle. His eyes crinkled up as he looked at me.

I smiled back. Reaching out for his hand I said, "There's a question Harry wants me to ask you."

"You don't want to?"

"It's so high on my agenda it's got nosebleed. Lyle, being with you has changed my life and my heart. I'm in love with you. Not falling, but deeply, everlastingly in love."

Lyle's mouth opened. I'd been certain he knew what I was up to, however, his eyes were big as platters. The question I'd been practicing for days popped out of my mouth. "Will you marry me?"Lyle tilted his head to one side and gazed at me.

"Say yes, Judge," said a chorus of voices.

I waited a full minute, staring at his tanned face. "You didn't answer my question."

Lyle grinned. "When?"

"I don't know. After Christmas?"

"Our license is good for another thirty-six hours." Lyle tapped his breast pocket.

Lillie Mae Pratt, the bakery owner, jumped to her feet. "You design the cake, Mrs. Morgan, and we'll have it ready by noon tomorrow."

Carter emerged from behind the cash register. "And the Coop will provide catering." A whoop of delight greeted his announcement.

"Better kiss the lady, judge," Miss Sophie

observed.

Lyle's kiss was the kind Prince Charming laid on Snow White. He even ended with a dip. Everyone cheered.

Miss Sophie waved Bouchard to his feet, then slowly rose. "You'll have to be married in the church. Let me make a few phone calls to set things in motion."

"Aside from a cake, I think we should have cupcakes for the children," mused one of the ladies from the bakery.

"And candy from that cute new shop by Inman's furniture store," someone added.

Carter arrived at my elbow. "I've a brunch menu in mind, Miss Delilah. Leave it to me."

BethAnn tapped her foot. "Who's going to get out the invites?"

Bouchard lifted a forefinger. "I'll stop the presses and add a front-page headline. My editor will love the story." Bouchard waved over his head as he aimed to hike out of the Coop.

One of the counter lawyers swiveled around. "Word of mouth should do fine. I'll have my secretary contact the legal society." He pointed to Bouchard. "You can call the college. Miss Sophie calls the church ladies. The place will be packed. Better make enough food for an army, Carter!"

"Time something good happened around here. We've been mighty lean on expectations with the Higgenbottom dynasty," muttered BethAnn.

"A toast to better times." A patron at the counter lifted his coffee cup.

The town had settled it for us. We'd be good and married tomorrow. Locked in each other's arms, we accepted the good will of friends, acquaintances, and total strangers.

Book Club Discussion Questions

1. Delilah goes from a sweet visit with her daughter to a major car accident. How does she handle it? Have you ever had your day turn from joy to shock? When things turn from positive to negative where do you focus? What helps you keep your footing and help with decision making in the middle of crisis?

2. Initially Delilah rejects Lyle's offer to rescue her. Why does she change her mind? Do you also like to do things yourself? When is it wise to ask for help? What happens inside of you, when you give up doing things yourself and allow other to help you? Do you feel helpless and dependent, or does it give you the opportunity to be part of a team in solving a problem?

3. The sewer line is a not so subtle analogy of what has happened in our culture. Pornography, using people to give us pleasure as well as seeking self-satisfaction and our own happiness is a stumbling block for many. Has pornography affected your life? How have you dealt with it? Many have been ministered to with counseling and small groups for accountability. Is there an organization in your area that has succeeded in bring healing to the broken lives and relationships haunted by pornography?

4. Delilah wanted to honor Harry by hiring a sculptor to create a statue for Harry. Have you ever wanted to bestow laurels on someone you love in a public way? If you did, how would you go about it? In a non-public way, how can we make those we love, feel honored and appreciated by our words and deeds?

5. Where has joy erupted in the midst of sorrow in the story? Do you search for joy when the journey is filled with pain and suffering? When do you see Josephine turn from her pain and begin to focus on others even though her circumstances do not change? Have you seen people with great loss or physical injury focus on others? How does that honor the Lord? Encourage others? Does it affect your life when the hurting reach out to bless those around them?

6. Several people in the novel, *The Courtship of Harry's Wife*, changed their attitude toward Delilah. How is that change manifested in *The Last Roses*? What do you look for in your own life to reveal that your heart has changed toward a situation or person?

7. Delilah risks her life to find Savannah. Her bravery also puts others in danger. If someone is in danger, what would you do to help? How far would you go to rescue them? We have many examples in the military from Sergeant York in World War I to the Medal of Honor winners from each of our conflicts and wars. But sometimes the danger isn't so obvious. It can be our reputation that is wounded when we take in an unwed mother and give her shelter, open our hearts and homes to foster children, or choose to forgive those who live far from Godly virtues. Have you had your reputation tarnished for doing the right thing?

8. Randall Longworth is not a man who alters his arrogant behavior, but Delilah is able to forgive him when he apologizes and to begin their relationship again. Have you ever encountered someone who doesn't care who they hurt and continues to behave in ways that cause harm? What did you do?   Are you

willing to begin again in that relationship? Do you put boundaries up, waiting to see fruit in their repentance but still let them be part of your life? Is that challenging? If so, in what way?

9. Miss Vickie proves to be a blessing and a challenge. How does Josephine handle her mother's Alzheimer's disease? Do you have someone in your life who suffers with this same condition? How do you respond when things come out sideways, either from their actions or words? Have you asked for advice from Hospice or dementia professionals on how to handle awkward situations? What have they said? Did it help?

Chapter One

SHAKESPEARE HAD IT RIGHT. TRUE LOVE never does run smooth. In fact, it has bumps that make the Alps look like molehills. We couldn't have a normal proposal like most folks. Oh, no—it had to have drama, tears, and a trip to the courthouse. One expects to make certain the license is in order, maybe even a blood test so the legalities are taken care of.

So, after I asked Judge Lyle Henderson to marry me in the dining room of the Chicken Coop restaurant, in front of God, four local lawyers, half the bakery staff from down the street, friends, neighbors, and Carter MacDougal the owner, we ended up heading to the courthouse.

A chill autumn wind attacked my neck. I pulled up my coat collar. Lyle wrapped his warm right arm around my shoulder and drew me close to his side. One does not snuggle in the middle of town for everyone to see but I almost did. Call it relief.

The banners resplendent with fall colors beat in the breeze like they were clapping. I smiled up at Lyle. He winked back. It was a long two blocks to the courthouse square because we kept getting stopped. While shaking hands and receiving hugs, we ambled along as if we were leading a parade. Across the street, even the women in Maylene's Beauty Parlor got up from their chairs and peered out the window at us.

I could have done without the stares. Especially since the gossip about the judge's and my relationship had out sizzled the curling irons. When a widow of a nationally acclaimed poet is courted, everyone thinks it's their business. And, when the man doing the courting is debonair, handsome, and town heartthrob, well, we'd set on fire many a tongue from the college offices to Washington street.

We made it to the scarred wooden counter of the county office without a mishap. The paperwork wasn't a problem. The county clerk hustled it up in record time.

The sheriff was the one who put a kibosh on my exuberance. He found us leaning over the oak counter of the clerk like two star-struck kids. Lyle hadn't let go of my hand until we needed to sign papers. He'd grabbed it again when I laid the pen down and wrapped his warm hand around my right one.

"Congratulations, you two." Bellows clapped Lyle on his shoulder and winked at me. "Word travels fast when the entire town is invited to your shotgun wedding."

The office staff and the line-up of locals getting licenses renewed, laughed because every person in town knew I'd turned down Lyle's proposal the month before.

"I've a need to speak with you both in private." Bellows dark eyebrow met in the middle above his nose. A serious matter from his expression. We followed him down a long hallway and into a cramped room that was more like a closet than office. "We'll chat here rather than make this look official down at the station. Lyle, we're getting some pressure about keeping Clarisse in jail. Her lawyer is filing papers to get her out on bond. She's tried it before but been refused. I don't want her roaming the streets but looks like that's about to happen."

Lyle frowned. "Who is her lawyer?"

"Some three-piece-suit from Chicago."

I looked from one to the other and wondered what was going on. They both seemed worried. Maybe I should be too, but I'd a wedding to plan—well, mostly participate in and that was enough on my plate.

"Delilah and I are about to depart these environs for a few weeks. Don't see Clarisse being a problem."

"Your ex-wife is a problem with a capital P." Sheriff Bellows pursed his lips. "Not only is she a flight risk but where in tarnation is she supposed to stay?

I smiled at them. "The Salvation Army has extra beds."

When we stopped laughing Lyle shook his head and said, "Tom," Lyle clapped the sheriff on the back, "this is one problem I can't solve."

As we mounted the back steps to Lyle's house, my best friend Josephine flung the back door open and put her hands on her hips. "About time you got Miss Reluctant here to accept your offer." She stared at the judge. "Rumor is circulating, though, that Miss Dee Dee did the proposing. But I reckon that can't be true, as she's too shy."

Josephine waited for us to explain.

We didn't.

She raised her eyebrows. "As soon as the news reached my ears, I trotted over to your house and got your dress ready, the one from the kids' wedding. Your mama, daddy, and Meemaw are on their way too." Her face broke into a smile. "Come on, Miss Dee Dee, I'm in need of a hug to get me motivated to tackle Mama and her yellow hat." Josephine's hug nearly smothered me.

Lyle didn't avoid Josephine's scrutiny for long. "Reverend Daniel is in your office to give you both a talking to. Seems he thinks you need some marriage counseling because it's all so sudden." That said, she marched in front of us toward the foyer.

When we got to Lyle's home office, he shook Reverend Daniel's hand, then opened a locked drawer in his desk and produced his divorce decree. He presented it to me without a word. It seemed legitimate, but I'd only studied eighteenth-century deeds and legal papers for my historical novels.

I handed it back with a shrug. "I trust you, even though the legal jargon is Greek to me."

He smiled. "Mostly Latin."

Reverend Daniel cleared his throat. "I've been appointed by the wedding committee to have a chat with you."

I lifted my eyebrows. I didn't recall the church having a wedding committee.

My pastor shrugged, "Well, Josephine twisted my arm. Seems to me you're in your right minds. I have no objections. And when do you think I should propose to Josephine?"

Lyle stared at his friend. "Strike while the iron is hot." Without another word, the reverend deserted the room.

I walked to the chair by the fireplace and sank into it. "Think I've been on a carnival ride. We've Savannah back." I raised one finger. "The mayor's being replaced." I lifted another finger. "I have water, alleluia!" Another finger went up. "And my Harry's name is besmirched from McKeansville to Saint Petersburg." A sigh escaped my lips.

Lyle reached for my hand. "We both know he didn't write the poems. It is beneath him to write such drivel. My money is on Professor Hamilton. A man with little imagination or wit."

"But how do we prove it?"

"I'm working on it."

"I need to get to work on this wedding. I'm in such a tizz, I don't know if I can get everything sorted out."

"Letting everyone put in their two cents about the wedding could be useful," Lyle said, before kissing my forehead. "It doesn't really matter what goes on, because at the end of the day we'll be married, and that is enough."

I grabbed his jacket front and planted a kiss straight on his lips. He'd put things in perspective because weddings seem to take on a life of their own. This one I only had to show up for.

Author's Note

The genesis for this novel was a book by Teresa Flores titled, *The Slave Across the Street*. Her story arrested me—a young girl, trafficked in the midst of prosperity. The book was recommended to us as preparation for a trip with the Christian Medical/Dental Society.

In 2012, Dr. Jeff Barrows, who has worked with the U.S. State Department in researching the consequences of Human Trafficking, facilitated a team of medical and dental professionals to travel to tropical Nicaragua to learn about the subject.

In the steamy city of Managua, a team of physicians and their spouses listened to the stories of women and young girls caught in the web of sexual exploitation. The team also served them with Jesus's love by giving medical and dental care. The clinics for women in the brothels as well as their children extended for a nearly a week. Prayers with each person were offered and accepted.

Non-medical spouses had the privilege of praying for patients, assisting in surgery or in the dental clinic. Even though I'd been on many medical trips, I usually cooked, did laundry, and cared for our family for the months we were on the field, but I had never held a retractor before that venture. A follow-up visit with the patient, a nine-year-old girl, gave me the opportunity to pray with her again. And to pray with her mother.

Surrounded by her four children, through a translator, her mother told her story of being the prostitute in the city dump. Love had rescued her. Her job at Casa Esperanza, a place for rebuilding the hearts of the wounded, provided her with food for her children and housing. The love of Christ changed her life and her children's lives. Her smile said it all. As she gazed at us her eyes softened, her lips curved and face lit with peace as she held her daughter's hand

and thanked us for coming.

He left heaven to come to us. I wonder how far I'm willing to go to touch a life in His name.

That particular mission trip changed our hearts and focus. Thank you, Jeff Barrows DO, Dave Stevens MD, Gene Rudd MD, Gloria Halverson MD, and Clydette Powell MD for your heart toward the hurting. I have learned so many lessons simply watching you.

Ways to connect with me:
Find my blog at: www.jeanettemariemirich.com
Follow me on Twitter: Jeanette-Marie Mirich
Follow me on Instagram: Jeanette-Marie Mirich
Follow me on Facebook:
ww.facebook.com/jeanettemariemirich/author
Follow me on Pinterest:
www.pinterest.com/jeaniemirich
Follow me on Goodreads: author Jeanette-Marie Mirich

Enjoy my newsletter: Jeanette-Marie Mirich author newsletter @mailchi.mp.com

And of course, if you enjoyed this book, I'd love if you'd care to post a review or mention it to a friend!

www.ingramcontent.com/pod-product-compliance
Lightning Source LLC
Chambersburg PA
CBHW071727190726
48292CB00003B/644